Pra

"The tension in this romance is elegantly poised around knowing when to hold on and when to let go—and the Gothic plot in the tropical setting makes this a standout paranormal."

—*The New York Times*

"Jen DeLuca does it again! Like your favorite iced latte from the hot barista who totally hates you (but not really), *Haunted Ever After* is the most delicious mix of chilling haunts and sweetened kisses to perk you right up. It's the perfect read for all the October girls who have to suffer through summer at the beach. A spirited, sexy read!"

—Ashley Poston, *New York Times* bestselling author of
Sounds Like Love

"I, too, want a ghost roommate (and Nick's banana bread and hazelnut lattes) in a charming beach town where the dead linger and the living locals know all the best secret spots. *Haunted Ever After* is so much fun, with characters that feel real, spooky vibes mixed with small-town sweetness, and an intriguing dash of mystery. Just like its invisible residents, I never want to leave Boneyard Key."

—Sarah Hogle, author of *The Folklore of Forever*

"Jen DeLuca brings her signature wit and warmth to a town where even ghosts can believe in true love. Featuring a charming, swoonworthy romance, *Haunted Ever After* is a sheer pleasure to read and has established Boneyard Key as my new favorite spooky vacation spot."

—Gwenda Bond, *New York Times* bestselling author of *The Frame-Up*

"*Haunted Ever After* is Jen DeLuca's best yet, and that's saying something. A deeply satisfying brew of longing, feels, and ghostly hijinks, this is a love story that delivers the goods. Plus, DeLuca's thoughtful commentary on the expectations we place on women—past and present—is cinnamon on the banana bread. Oh, my romantic, feminist heart!"

—Megan Bannen, author of *The Undermining of Twyla and Frank*

"Clever, funny, and a bit spooky, *Haunted Ever After* will appeal to cozy mystery and paranormal romance readers alike. . . . DeLuca creates a charming town full of entertainingly quirky characters sure to leave readers wanting more stories set in Boneyard Key."

—Shelf Awareness

Praise for *Well Matched*

"A great comfort read. Warm, sweet, and hopeful, *Well Matched* is about daring to come out of your shell and building the life you always wanted."

—Helen Hoang, *New York Times* bestselling author of *The Heart Principle*

"This series is one of my ultimate comfort reads. I knew I'd adore April and Mitch together, but I didn't realize how deeply obsessed with them I'd be. *Well Matched* is for anyone whose life hasn't gone according to plan, and about all the joys that come with veering off course. Warm and witty, sweet and sexy—this tender hug of a book is Jen DeLuca at her best."

—Rachel Lynn Solomon, *New York Times* bestselling author of *Weather Girl*

"Jen DeLuca writes with exceptional warmth. *Well Matched* is cozy, sweet, and brimming with charm. It's such a joy to go back to the Faire with Mitch and April!"

—Rosie Danan, national bestselling author of *The Intimacy Experiment*

"*Well Matched* is completely charming and delightfully touching. DeLuca delivers a love story that leaves you feeling as warm and fuzzy as you are hot and bothered. April's vulnerability and humor are endearing, and Mitch is book-boyfriend goals in a kilt—I couldn't put it down."

—Denise Williams, author of *Do You Take This Man*

"With well-drawn characters and laugh-out-loud scenes, *Well Matched* is a perfect opposites-attract romance." —Shelf Awareness

"This sexy, witty, fast-paced romantic comedy has surprising emotional depth." —*Library Journal*

"DeLuca's enchanting tale of unsought love developing over home improvement tasks and making family members happy, cheerfully set against the charming backdrop of a Renaissance Faire, is a joy to read." —*Booklist*

Praise for *Well Played*

"Stacey finds her greatest joy at the Faire, looking forward to its return each year. In DeLuca's hands, we'd have to agree—there are endless tales and excitement to be found in this world, still one of the freshest, most engaging concepts in romance a year after she introduced us to it. A hearty huzzah for *Well Played*."

—*Entertainment Weekly*

Praise for *Well Met*

"What a delight! This is enemies-to-lovers at its absolute finest, folks. DeLuca proves to be a master of creating characters you believe in and a storyline to keep you totally engrossed. *Well Met* is a hilarious, swoony, and captivating romance—hands down our new favorite feel-good novel of the year."

—*New York Times* bestselling author Christina Lauren

"*Well Met* will especially appeal to readers who like bookstores, Renaissance Faire shenanigans, and nerdy English teachers wearing vests. DeLuca will have readers laughing all the way to the turkey leg vendor." —Shelf Awareness

"Full of wit, hilarious banter, and swoon-worthy moments."

—*Woman's World*

"Jen DeLuca's *Well Met* is a way-cute small-town romance."

—NPR

"Jen DeLuca had me laughing out loud from the opening line. *Well Met* is fresh, fun, and the story I never knew I needed. I so wish I could grab a corset and live the wench life with Emily!"

—Alexa Martin, author of *Fumbled*

"The descriptions of [Simon] in his pirate gear . . . are likely to induce a thirst so wide and so deep you could sail a ship across it."

—*Entertainment Weekly*

"Filled with originality, humor, charm, [and] emotional depth."

—*New York Times* bestselling author Samantha Young

"I dare you not to want to travel to your nearest Renaissance Faire after reading the sweet, sexy, and smart *Well Met* . . . the kind of book that you want to live inside. Jen DeLuca is poised to become one of the freshest voices writing contemporary romance today."

—Kate Clayborn, author of *Best of Luck*

"DeLuca turns in an intelligent, sexy, and charming debut romance sure to resonate with Renaissance Faire enthusiasts and those looking for an upbeat, lighter read."

—*Library Journal*

Ghost Business

JEN DeLUCA

BERKLEY ROMANCE

NEW YORK

BERKLEY ROMANCE
Published by Berkley
An imprint of Penguin Random House LLC
1745 Broadway, New York, NY 10019
penguinrandomhouse.com

Title page illustration by solam/Adobe Stock

Library of Congress Cataloging-in-Publication Data

Names: DeLuca, Jen, author.
Title: Ghost business / Jen DeLuca.
Description: First edition. | New York: Berkley Romance, 2025.
Identifiers: LCCN 2025007792 (print) | LCCN 2025007793 (ebook) |
ISBN 9780593641231 (trade paperback) | ISBN 9780593641248 (ebook)
Subjects: LCGFT: Romance fiction. | Novels.
Classification: LCC PS3604.E44757 G48 2025 (print) | LCC PS3604.E44757 (ebook) |
DDC 813/.6—dc23/eng/20250304
LC record available at https://lccn.loc.gov/2025007792
LC ebook record available at https://lccn.loc.gov/2025007793

First Edition: September 2025

Printed in the United States of America
1st Printing

The authorized representative in the EU for product safety and compliance is Penguin Random
House Ireland, Morrison Chambers, 32 Nassau Street, Dublin D02 YH68, Ireland,
https://eu-contact.penguin.ie.

This book is, sadly, for all of you who read *Haunted Ever After* and were excited for Sophie and Theo's book to be next. Whoops. Hope you like this one anyway!

Ghost
Business

One

This guy was way overdressed for an oyster bar.

Sophie squinted in his direction as she hoisted herself onto one of the barstools at The Haunt. The bar made a big L on the left-hand side of the restaurant. Sophie sat at one end, and while she pretended to study the menu she could recite like the Pledge of Allegiance, she kept stealing glances at the guy sitting at the hinge of the L. His blond hair was rumpled, but his light blue dress shirt was immaculate, though the sleeves were rolled up to his elbows. He was most of the way through a platter of oysters on the half shell, and midway through the pint of beer next to it. While she watched, Tony approached the stranger from his place behind the bar.

"All good, man?"

The stranger nodded emphatically. "Incredible. You just catch these oysters today or what?" He had the kind of smile that made his eyes practically disappear, wide and sincere.

Tony snorted but was obviously pleased by the attention. "Yeah, I'm totally a fisherman." His words were dismissive, but he lingered, keeping his attention on the new guy while he put away a load of beer mugs. "How's your stay so far? See any ghosts yet?"

Now it was the blond stranger's turn to snort. "Yeah, right. Loads."

Was that sarcasm? Sophie raised her eyebrows as Tony froze. "Really?"

The stranger barked out a laugh, turning his attention back to the food in front of him. "Wouldn't that be something. Like, if ghosts were actually real."

"Yeah . . ." Tony drew out the word as he put the last of the mugs away. "That sure would be something." He tossed a glance Sophie's way as he went to return the dish rack to the kitchen, and she eyed the new guy again. She'd never seen him before, and he was obviously new around here, even though he carried himself with the ease of a local. But tourists visiting Boneyard Key were usually here for the ghosts. Most haunted small town in Florida and all that. If he wasn't here for that, what was he doing here?

"How about you, Soph?" Sophie jerked her eyes away from the blond stranger and looked instead at Tony, who stood in front of her with one eyebrow raised. "You ordering anything tonight, or do you just want to flirt with the cute guy over there?"

Heat rushed into her cheeks as she shushed him. "I'm not flirting!" She chastised him in a loud whisper, trying to speak softer than the satellite radio station playing yacht rock through the speakers over their heads. She'd heard their whole conversation, so surely the guy down the bar could hear them too.

"Not yet, you're not." Laughter danced in his dark eyes as he nodded toward the menu. "You want your usual?"

She should order something new tonight, just to spite Tony. But he knew her better than that. She'd seen him put glue in Courtney Royer's hair in the second grade, and he hadn't ratted her out when she'd taken a bite out of a green crayon to see what it tasted like. So instead she sighed and set down the menu that she'd barely bothered to look at. "Chef salad, no tomatoes. Diet Coke."

A smile played around Tony's mouth as he set her glass down, Diet

Coke already poured and fizzing around its ice, onto a coaster in front of her. "Coming right up. Go say hi to him. He's from out of town."

Sophie shushed him again. She wasn't the kind of girl who stared at strangers in bars. And she sure as hell didn't flirt with them. But she couldn't help it; as soon as Tony was gone, her gaze wandered back toward the blond stranger.

Who was looking right back at her.

Their gazes colliding was practically tangible, and Sophie wasn't ready for it. She ducked her head immediately, wide eyes dropping down to the bar. Suddenly very interested in the weathered wood-grain in front of her, she took a long pull off her Diet Coke. The cold drink did nothing to quell the fire blazing in her cheeks.

When she looked up, he was gone. No, not gone. Worse. He'd moved closer, sliding his platter of oysters down the bar with him.

"Did I hear you order a salad?" Mr. Blond Business Casual shook his head in mock censure. "A salad? When you can get oysters?" He shook a few drops of Tabasco onto one in illustration and tilted his head back to slurp it down. Sophie tried to not watch the way his throat worked when he swallowed. Slurping down an oyster shouldn't be sexy.

She gave a small shake of her head. "I'm not one for oysters, sadly." And it was sad. She used to love them. Especially lightly steamed and on the half shell, the way this guy took them. But it had only taken one bad oyster, followed by an even worse night sleeping on the cold bathroom floor, for her to swear them off entirely.

"You're missing out." He slurped down another one, laying the empty shell on his plate and giving a happy sigh. "Damn, Florida seafood's the best, isn't it?"

Now, that Sophie could agree with. "They do it right here." She could put away a basket of fried shrimp like nobody's business. But Friday nights were tour nights, and she liked to eat light. A platter of fried shrimp would make her want to go home and crawl into bed, not lead a walking tour of Boneyard Key.

"You live around here?" He took a sip from his glass of beer as he gave her his full attention. His eyes were startlingly light, but it was too dark in here to tell if they were blue or green. The pupils stood out in stark contrast, dark bullet points of attention aimed right at Sophie.

"I do." Another sip of Diet Coke, wetting down her suddenly very dry mouth. "How could you tell?" She wasn't good at this. At being the center of attention. In front of a crowd, answering questions about Boneyard Key and the ghosts that lived there? She could handle that, no problem. But one-on-one, being asked personal questions? People didn't usually want to know much about her.

He nodded toward the bar, at the menu that she'd stashed between the napkin holder and ketchup bottle. "You barely looked at the menu. And he asked if you wanted your usual."

"Ah." The flames in Sophie's cheeks traveled to the back of her neck, setting up prickles there. If he'd heard that, he'd heard Tony make fun of her for staring . . . God, what a mess.

"I'm pretty good at sussing out these kinds of things." He shot her a conspiratorial smile as he wiped his hands carefully on a napkin before extending one of them. "I'm Tristan."

"Sophie." His hand was warm, his nails neatly manicured. Her heart gave a little flip at the way his smile widened, eyes crinkling at the edges. She'd put that smile on his face. Suddenly she wanted to keep it there.

"Are you here on vacation?" she asked. "Because if you are, I have to say you're a little overdressed." Despite his sleeves being rolled up—probably to avoid any errant oyster juice on his cuffs—he looked like he was just coming from a board meeting, not settling in to watch the steel drum band's first set.

His laugh was easy, not too loud, and not at all self-conscious.

This was a guy who laughed a lot. "You got me," he said. "I'm new to Florida. Back home, khakis are as casual as I get." He gestured down to his pants with a rueful smile. "But I see I have to seriously up my leisure game here. Any recommendations?"

"Well . . ." Sophie smiled a thanks to Tony as he set her chef salad in front of her, then unwrapped her utensils and put her napkin in her lap. "Unless you're into Hawaiian shirts, something without a collar is a good place to start. We have several fine T-shirt establishments for all your casual-wear needs."

"That's an excellent start." He reached for another oyster as she started on her salad. "Is there a particular one you'd recommend?"

She shook her head. "You want to know a secret?"

"Of course I do." His eyes sparked as he leaned toward her, and she leaned in right back.

"Okay, you didn't hear it from me. This is a locals-only thing." His eyebrows went up in amused anticipation, and she couldn't help but smile back. "They all sell the same crap."

"What?" He leaned back in feigned shocked surprise. "Are you telling me that souvenir shops in Florida do not offer uniquely crafted, fine artisanal goods?"

"It's true." Sophie forked up a bite of lettuce and hard-boiled egg.

"And where can I find said shops?"

She nodded toward the door. "Go outside, stand in the street, and throw a rock. You're guaranteed to hit one."

He snorted. "You haven't seen me throw. I'd probably break a window and spend the night in the clink."

"The clink?" Sophie blinked. "Are you my great-aunt Alice? Who uses that term?"

Tristan laughed again, and wow. He had a laugh that Sophie could really get used to. "Sorry," he said. "I've got an old-fashioned soul."

"Hmm." She rested her cheek in her hand, studying him. "I can relate to that." With as much time as she spent with her head in the past? She could absolutely relate to that.

Tristan mirrored her pose: elbow on the bar, leaning his cheek on his hand, studying her right back. This kind of thing didn't happen to Sophie. Guys never flirted with her. They flirted with her best friend, Libby, with her blond ponytail, long legs, and sunny smile. Their eyes usually skidded right over short, bespectacled Sophie, who was a tiny, dark-haired nerd in contrast.

But Libby wasn't here, not tonight. And Tristan was still smiling at her.

"You want another round, kids?" Tony showed up at the worst time, and as much as Sophie appreciated his dedication to service, she wished he'd be a little more of a slacker. As a personal favor.

"Sure. Not the oysters, though." Tristan laid a hand on his ridiculously flat stomach. "Not sure I could do another round of those. But I'll take another beer. That lager that you have on draft, that's fantastic. How about you, Sophie? Can I buy you another drink?" He looked pointedly at her Diet Coke, which was down to watery ice. "Or maybe your first drink?"

She would love that. Telling him no had just become the worst part of her night. "I can't." It was flattering, right? The way Tristan's face fell a little at her rejection? That was the only consolation she had here. "Believe me, I wish I could. But I have to get to work." She was running late, by the looks of the band. They'd just finished setting up, and their first set went on at seven fifteen sharp. Her tour started at seven thirty; she'd lingered longer than usual.

"Work?" His eyebrows crawled up his forehead. "You've got to be kidding. On a Friday night? Here?"

Okay, that made her bristle. "Not all of us are on vacation, you know." She slid her debit card to Tony, who took it with only a slight roll of his eyes. Yeah. He was bristling too.

"Point taken, sorry." Tristan at least had the grace to look shame-faced, and Sophie's ire cooled as quickly as it had come on. "What do you do? Let me guess. You sing with the band?" He nodded toward the steel drums.

Only in her worst nightmares. "I'm not nearly that talented," she said with a laugh. "No, I give ghost tours."

He blinked. "You do what?"

"Ghost tours," she repeated. "Every Friday night. Saturday nights too, this time of year when there's more tourist traffic. I don't know how familiar you are with Boneyard Key, but we're the most haunted small town in Florida."

"I'd heard something about that."

There was tension in his nod, an unease in his voice, but Sophie brushed it aside as she warmed up to her favorite topic. She was used to skeptics. Sometimes she could even win them over. "It sounds like a gimmick, I know. Have you ever been on a ghost tour before?"

"I . . ." He shifted on his barstool and took a sip of the beer that Tony had just delivered. "Yeah," he finally said. "A few, here and there."

"Oh, good!" Relief swept through her. That saved time, for sure. "Then you know what they're about. Mine's a little walking tour of mostly the downtown area. You get a history lesson, well, a couple of history lessons. The regular and the haunted kind, you know?"

"Yeah." But something weird had happened to Tristan's face while she'd been talking. His smile was gone, and those eyes that crinkled so enticingly now looked glazed over. Now he drummed his fingers lightly on the bar, fidgeted with his balled-up napkin.

That hadn't taken long. She'd bored the crap out of him in record time. Maybe she should have led with her day job. *I work from home, doing medical transcriptions. It's repetitive and sucks out my will to live most of the time, but it pays the bills.* It was a solid job, though. A career. Guys respected things like that. Running a ghost tour was frivolous in comparison. A silly way to make a living. Part of a living.

Sophie could take a hint. "Anyway." She signed the slip Tony had left by her elbow and tucked her card away. "I have a group waiting, so I need to get going." She hopped off the barstool as gracefully as she could, but from that height it was really more of a controlled fall. "It was nice to meet you, Tristan." Her words hung in the air between them, fading away to the sounds of Crosby, Stills & Nash from the speakers above. Sophie fought back a sigh of defeat. "I hope you have a nice stay here." She didn't wait for him to respond. She just tossed him a wave and turned to go.

The steel drum band started up their set, the beginning of another Friday night party at The Haunt. But it was time for Sophie to go to work. She couldn't dwell on the cute tourist she left at the bar and her failed attempt at flirting. She had a full group tonight, which was why she'd splurged on dinner out before the tour.

But it was still all she could do to not smack herself in the forehead on the way out the door. She was a disaster. No wonder she was single.

Two

Where in the hell had she come from?

Tristan turned his head to watch Sophie leave. He couldn't help it; he'd been drawn into her orbit from the moment she'd sat down, and now his head turned, the movement involuntary. Her dark red turtleneck was formfitting without being aggressively tight, clinging to the dip of her waist where the sweater met the waistband of her jeans. His fingers itched to explore that bottom edge of fabric, that dip. But he made himself stay seated while she bumped the outer door with her hip as she shrugged into her coat. The thud of the thick wooden door swinging shut behind her was like waking up from a dream.

Tristan liked flirting. He traveled a lot, and he'd gotten really good at it. He liked pretty girls. He liked cute guys too. But there had been something about Sophie. The way her laugh felt like a reward, the way her smile was a place he wanted to sink into, get lost in. It had been a long time since he'd seen a smile like hers.

He wished she'd stuck around longer, let him buy her that drink. He wanted to talk to her some more.

Because it had really sounded like she'd said she ran a ghost tour. And that couldn't be right.

Tristan took a long sip from his second lager before setting it down carefully on the square coaster in front of him. The coaster seemed superfluous; the bar he'd bellied up to earlier this evening had obviously seen some stuff. The wood was weathered, pock-marked in places, with initials carved into it at one edge. He really hoped that those crazy kids J.G. and M.L. had managed to make it work.

Across the bar, the house band, composed of what looked like retirees playing steel drums, had swung into the most bizarre cover of "Friends in Low Places" he'd ever heard. It was . . . loud.

That explained it. It was loud in here. Obviously, he'd misheard Sophie when she said she ran a ghost tour. Because Tristan knew better; there wasn't a ghost tour in Boneyard Key, Florida.

He should know, because he was here to start one.

He'd done his due diligence. He always did his due diligence; it had been drilled into him, not only in business school but at his father's knee. Most kids had nursery rhymes; Tristan Martin grew up with phrases like "angel investors" and "balance sheet." Before he'd even booked the flight to Florida, he'd researched the town of Bone-yard Key. He had one rule: never start up a ghost tour in a town that already had market saturation. He'd learned that the hard way, and he still wasn't welcome back in Savannah. (Tristan hadn't even real-ized that being run out of town on a rail was still a *thing*.)

His research on this place had turned up nothing. Which made no sense—a ghost tour in the "most haunted small town in Florida" was a no-brainer. But there'd been no website, no social media pres-ence. A couple mentions on Yelp or Tripadvisor, but in the context of another review: "got a cup of coffee here after the ghost tour," that kind of thing. And besides, those mentions had all been pre-pandemic, and how many small, tourist-centric businesses had gone under during those times?

But now here she was. All dark eyes behind big glasses and curling brown hair, not to mention the sweetest smile Tristan had ever seen. Picking her way through a chef salad, making sure she got all the egg pieces, smiling at him in a way that made him think he had a chance. Then she'd dropped that bomb on the way out the door.

There was only one thing to do now. Go after her.

Tristan signed his credit card slip but left the tip in cash—forty percent. Those were some damn good oysters; he was going to be back. Then he nodded his thanks to the bartender—a tall, dark, and handsome man with a chiseled jaw that reminded Tristan of a theatre major he'd dated briefly in college (yeah, he'd *definitely* be back)—and headed for the door. As it closed behind him, the steel drum band faded to a background thrumming, just loud enough to beckon him to go back inside. Join the party.

But Tristan wasn't in a party mood. Not anymore.

The humidity of the warm Florida evening hit him like a wet towel to the face. Night had fallen in earnest while he'd been inside eating oysters and flirting with a pretty ghost tour guide. Tristan looked up and down the street. How was he going to find her? She'd said her tour was mostly downtown, so that was a good enough place to start.

He'd already walked Beachside Drive—the main drag in town— earlier today when he'd first arrived in Boneyard Key. It hadn't taken him long to fall in love with the place. He'd felt his blood pressure lower the more he walked around the charming downtown teeming with souvenir shops, boutiques, coffee shops, restaurants, and an alarming number of places to get ice cream. The sidewalks were wide, the vintage-looking buildings were painted in soft pastel shades, and the window displays invited slow, meandering strolls. Heading north took you to a bend in the road to the right, past even more charming historic beach cottages to a fishing pier, complete with a bait shack that looked like something out of a postcard.

This wasn't a downtown like a city. He certainly wasn't in Chicago or New York. Here, the streetlights that lined the main drag each boasted a white flag shaped like a cartoon ghost, fluttering gently if not at all spookily in the dark. The glow of the faux gas-lamp streetlights recalled an earlier century. A horse and buggy clattering down the street wouldn't have surprised Tristan in the least.

He loved the look of this town. He'd been so excited when his father had mentioned the latest acquisition to his real estate portfolio: a beachside condo in a small Florida tourist town. It was a modest investment, but guaranteed to turn a steady profit year-round. The name of the town, of course, had sparked Tristan's interest more than anything. A tourist town, by the beach, that had a macabre-themed name? Boneyard Key seemed like the kind of place that screamed for a ghost tour, and Tristan was more than happy to fill that void.

But apparently that void had already been filled. So where was she? Tristan stopped on the corner, where a coffee shop named Spooky Brew was closed up for the night. This was a downtown that rolled up its sidewalks after dark, even on a Friday. Most of the souvenir shops were closed, but a couple of open restaurants dotted the landscape with glowing windows. Up the street, another coffee shop had its lights on, but the Closed sign was flipped over.

Tristan hurried up the street, his own footsteps echoing back in his ears. How hard was it to find a walking tour in this town?

Just then, he heard a voice across the street.

"This was the mayor's house for decades. But about thirty years ago or so, when a new mayor was elected, he moved in—and then moved out the very next day. Resigned his post too. They had to have a special election and everything."

A thrill went up Tristan's spine. He knew that voice. *Sophie.* He also knew that kind of cadence. He knew the sound of being followed by five to ten pairs of feet. He'd found her.

Of course, now that he'd found her, he didn't know how to proceed. Crashing the tour felt stalkery and unprofessional, but that was exactly what he needed to do. There was no way he could hide among a group of six people, so he fell back a step or two, blending into the shadows between streetlights.

Sophie continued her story. "No one knows what exactly happened that night, but no mayor of Boneyard Key ever lived here again. The city moved the Chamber of Commerce here in the late nineties, and whatever spooked the mayor so badly seems to be okay with the new resident."

She led the tour away from the house, and Tristan squinted at it as he followed along a few beats behind. It didn't look like a haunted house—not that he would know, because haunted houses weren't real. Neither were ghosts.

The tour paused at a vacant lot, not too far from The Haunt, where coffee and ice cream carts were closed up tight, side by side. The tour gathered under the streetlight, and Tristan took the opportunity to duck behind the closed-up ice cream cart to stay out of sight. "Now, there's a little path here, between the dunes . . ." She gestured just past the carts, to a sanded-over path that Tristan couldn't see from his vantage point. "If you go down that way, it takes you straight to the beach. A word of warning, though. If you decide to take a walk down there at this time of night, well, you may have company."

He frowned. Sophie didn't do things the way he did. She wasn't playing a character, adding a dramatic flair to her storytelling. She wasn't even in costume—just wearing the same jeans and sneakers she'd been in at The Haunt, same red sweater and blue peacoat that had been hanging on the back of her chair. What was she thinking? She could be doing so much more with this. Give the people a real *experience*, the way he did.

"I don't know the full story of the Beach Bum—that's what I call him. My theory is that he's someone who was wandering home after a night out and went the wrong direction. Like into the ocean wrong direction. If you're out here at night—especially after a night out at The Haunt and you've had a drink or two—chances are you'll have company. Footsteps in the sand, following you all the way home. Some people like to leave him a beer, opened on one of the picnic tables. That's how you win him over, according to my friend Nick."

A couple of tourists made intrigued noises, and Tristan had to hold himself back from doing the same. Well, damn. Maybe she didn't need dramatic flair. He wanted to know more about the Beach Bum, which was of course a sign of a good storyteller. Where had Sophie's stories come from? While he encouraged his employees to riff on the script according to their location, his stories were all based off that first ghost tour script he'd written back in college. Had Sophie been inspired by the beachside location and made up something ocean related? He wanted to ask her.

No, he didn't. He was pissed at her. All that talk at the bar about being a local, but there was no way. She had to be new in town, just like he was. Sure, maybe she'd beaten him here by a few weeks, and gotten her tour up and running faster. But Boneyard Key was still up for grabs.

And he was going to grab it. He needed to.

"We're coming up on the end of the tour now." Her voice was bright, cheerful and happy, and it lit something up in Tristan's chest, almost against his will. The lamplight bounced off her glasses and made her dark hair shine as it tumbled down her back. "We'll head over to where we started, at Hallowed Grounds. I can see from here that the light is on. Nick has very generously offered to keep the place open, in case anyone wants any coffee to go. And as a thank-you for spending some of your evening with me, I have two-for-one drink coupons for The Haunt, right down the street that way. If you'll follow me, I can give those out and we can say good night."

Tristan knew he should stay in the shadows. Once the group had crossed the street and gone safely into Hallowed Grounds, he was home free. But he found himself coming out from behind the ice cream cart and taking a step toward them, wanting to follow them inside. Wanting to see Sophie again. Get some answers. And maybe another shot at that smile.

But then his phone vibrated in his hip pocket, ruining everything. Tristan's heart sank when he checked it. So much for talking to Sophie.

"Hey, Dad." He kept his voice light as he turned his back on Hallowed Grounds, walking quickly toward The Haunt before his voice could carry.

"How's my investment?" Sebastian Martin wasn't one for pleasantries.

Tristan took a stab at answering the vague question. "The condo's great. I got in around noon, and everything was smooth sailing. The management company left the key at the office, and the utilities are turned on. Thanks again for letting me use it while I'm in town." He paused outside The Haunt. Once he wrapped up this phone call maybe he'd stop for another beer. He had a feeling he'd need one. "The wraparound balcony's to die for, and the living room has these huge picture windows. Incredible view of the Gulf of Mexico. You'd love it." Okay, he was babbling now. Talking about the virtues of Sebastian Martin's latest real estate holding as though the man was ever going to set foot in this town.

"Good to know," his father said, but his tone said *wrong answer*. "But I'm talking about my investment in your company."

"Ah." Yeah, that made more sense. And what terrible timing, since Tristan's mind was still spinning about that. "Well, I've hit a little snag." He looked over his shoulder, where the light in the window at Hallowed Grounds was a bright dot in the darkened street.

"What kind of snag?" His father's voice sharpened, and Tristan's spine straightened in an automatic response. He reminded himself that he was twenty-seven and far too old to be grounded, but try telling that to his lizard brain.

"Not sure yet. I'm still trying to figure that out." Tristan pressed a thumb to the space between his eyebrows, staving off the headache that threatened. Maybe that second beer had been a bad idea, though the more likely cause was this conversation with his dad.

"You better figure it out fast, son. You have until October first, remember."

"Dad." A sigh gusted out of him, but sadly the tension in his shoulders remained—also caused by this conversation. "It's February."

"I'm well aware. I'm also well aware that I invested in Ghouls Night Out—ridiculous name—after you graduated with your business degree. I gave you five years to turn a profit, and those five years are up on October first."

"Yes, and—"

But he continued as though Tristan hadn't spoken. Typical. "That's when you turn your books over to me, and I judge whether or not you created a viable, profitable business geared toward long-term success, or if you wasted your time on a vanity project that's gone nowhere."

"The books are fine, Dad—" That was mostly the truth, so he didn't feel too bad saying it.

"If it's the latter, which I strongly suspect it is, I pull my investment. And you come work for me. That was our agreement."

"Dad." His voice was approaching a whine, making Tristan sound like a teenager on the verge of being grounded, but dammit, that was how he felt. "You can't just pull your investment. We'd—"

"You'd never recover." His father finished the sentence for him. "That's the point. You shouldn't need my money anymore. After five years? You should be able to stand on your own."

"Dad," he said again, sharply enough that a couple passersby glanced in his direction and his father finally stopped talking. "You know we had a pandemic, right? Remember when the country all but shut down? That kind of killed the momentum. We're regaining it now, but it's still . . ."

"Still rocky. I knew it." There was a pause. "You have a good brain, son." His voice had softened. It was still terrifying, but softer.

"Thanks." That may have been the biggest compliment he'd ever gotten from his father, yet Tristan's response dripped with sarcasm.

"I hate to see you waste it on this. It's too much like that theatre crap you did while you were in school."

"It's not crap. And neither is Ghouls Night Out. We're turning a profit in almost every location, so expanding here in Boneyard Key makes perfect sense. You should see this place, Dad. This town is made for stuff like this. Once I get this one established, it's going to be a real moneymaker. The books are going to look great by October first. I guarantee it."

"Hmph." His father didn't sound convinced, but apparently Tristan had pled enough of his case to satisfy him for the night. "Just make sure you take care of the condo. Don't trash it."

Tristan rolled his eyes. "I'm twenty-seven, Dad. My frat boy days are long behind me." Okay, maybe not that long, but he was old enough to understand property values. The last thing he was going to do was destroy his father's investment. Either in the real estate market or the ghost tour business.

He needed to make this location work. If his father pulled his investment, then everything he'd been working so hard to build for the past five years would disintegrate like a sandcastle at high tide. Worse, he'd have to go work for his dad. And while Sebastian Martin was considered one of the country's foremost investment bankers, Tristan would make a terrible finance bro.

As much as he hated to admit it, his dad's call came at a good time. Because as much as Sophie intrigued him back at the bar and he wanted to get another look at her smile, his mind needed to be on work. And if she was running a competing ghost tour, well. She'd just become the enemy. And in business, you don't flirt with the enemy.

You crush them.

Three

Sophie couldn't stop thinking about Tristan. Obviously. He'd stayed on her mind during the whole ghost tour; she even thought she'd spotted him in the back of the crowd on Beachside after the Chamber of Commerce stop. Ridiculous. So at the end of the evening she made a deal with herself—she had the entire walk home to get him out of her mind. No more, no less.

It was a short walk: through the historic district, past The Haunt, around the corner past some more souvenir shops, and finally to the newer section of town. Sophie's condo building had been built in the 1980s, targeting tourists, retirees, and snowbirds looking for a second home in Florida. These days the units were mostly vacation rentals, registering as little more than a blip in the ledger for real estate moguls. But here and there an actual year-round resident could be spotted—people who had invested early, back when an almost-beachfront unit in Florida was affordable. That's what Sophie's great-aunt Alice had done, and as inheritances went, it couldn't be beat.

Inside, the place looked much like it had when Aunt Alice had been alive. Sophie had moved her books from her bedroom to the bookcase in the living room, and she'd updated the appliances one expensive year, but those were the only real changes she'd made.

Candles of all sizes were still grouped in the no-longer-working fire-place, and Aunt Alice's record collection still nestled, along with its turntable, in a corner of the living room. Books lay scattered across the coffee table, and the dining table in its nook was more of a home office where Sophie occasionally ate. The place was cluttered, but it was cozy. And it was all Sophie's, as long as she could keep paying the property taxes.

Sophie locked the door behind her and froze. She took a deep breath, all thoughts of Tristan and his smile instantly forgotten. Then she took out her phone and called her best friend, Libby.

"I can smell it again." She barely gave Libby time to say hello. "Jasmine, the second I walk in the door."

Libby didn't answer at first, and Sophie could tell she was biting back a sigh. "Sophie." Her voice was kind, but with a tinge of exas-peration. Sophie was ready for that. They'd had this conversation too many times by now.

"I'm just saying. What if your grandmother was wrong? What if . . . ?" Her throat threatened to close up at the thought.

"Nan wasn't wrong," Libby said gently. "She's never wrong. She did a really thorough scan of the condo after Alice died. She even went back a second time, remember?"

"I remember." Libby's grandmother had given her a dressing-down, telling her that this second visit was a waste of time. There was nothing that a ghost hunter could get on a second sweep of a home that she couldn't get the first time.

"If your great-aunt had stuck around, Nan would have made contact. Simple as that."

"Yeah." She knew it was the truth, but sometimes—more than sometimes—Sophie wished it weren't quite that simple. That this jasmine scent that sometimes greeted her when she came home really was Aunt Alice, sticking around to check on her. There was probably a more down-to-earth explanation: stray molecules of Aunt Alice's favorite perfume living in the air vents, left over from the thirty-something years she'd lived in this condo. "You're right," she finally said, swallowing hard against her sadness. "Sorry."

"No, it's okay." The exasperation was gone from Libby's voice, and now only kindness remained. "Comes with the territory. If there's one thing I've learned in these years as Nan's assistant, it's that grief can do weird things to the brain."

"It can't still be grief, though. Alice has been gone a while."

"Only a few years. That's not long in the grand scheme of things. Grief isn't linear, you know; it comes in waves. Apparently even years later it can hit you in the back of the knees."

"Yeah." Well, that part made sense. Sophie had been hit in the back of the knees herself a few times since Aunt Alice had gone.

"Hey, not to change the subject," Libby said, absolutely changing the subject, "but I heard you met a hottie at The Haunt tonight."

"How?" A startled laugh escaped her chest as Sophie plopped down on the sofa. "How did you hear that?"

But of course she knew the answer before Libby said a word. "Tony." The two women spoke at the same time. Sophie sighed, while Libby chuckled.

"Okay, well, technically it was Cassie. She and Nick were at The Haunt—"

"They were? I didn't see them."

"You know them. They were probably tucked back in some corner, being all lovey-dovey and disgusting. Anyway, Cassie said she saw right as you were leaving, and when Nick went up to the bar to settle the bill, Tony told him—"

"Word gets around here fast, doesn't it?"

Libby kept going like Sophie hadn't interrupted. "He said that you'd been making eyes at some tourist."

Embarrassment covered Sophie in a full-body flush. "I wasn't *making eyes . . .*" But she had been, hadn't she? How had she looked to Tony? Had he been laughing at her? Wouldn't be the first time. "Okay, maybe I was making eyes. A little."

Libby's chuckle became a full-on laugh. "Did he make eyes back? Tell me everything."

Sophie didn't want to tell her everything. Because "everything" included her boring the crap out of Tristan, talking his ear off about ghost tours when he couldn't care less. "Not a lot to tell." That was a lie. There was plenty to tell. He had great eyes, a compelling smile. The way this man—someone she'd known all of five minutes—had looked at her made her feel more seen than she ever had in her life. But Sophie dismissed all that; what was the point? "He's a tourist," she said instead, because she obviously needed the reminder. "Probably just here for the weekend. He was cute, we talked a little, then I left to do my Friday night tour. The end."

"Hmph." Libby sounded disappointed. "That could have gone better."

"You're telling me." Sophie's laugh sounded hollow even to her own ears.

"Eh, don't worry about it." On the other end of the line, Libby was probably waving a dismissive hand. "He's a tourist, like you said. It's not like he's sticking around."

"Yeah." *He's not sticking around.* The words hit like a small dart, all the more painful because Sophie knew that Libby didn't mean it like that. She wasn't trying to hurt her feelings. But that didn't stop Sophie from making a few more polite noises and hanging up as fast as she could. Sophie tossed her phone to the coffee table and closed her eyes, chasing that jasmine scent that had all but faded while she'd talked to Libby. Every time she caught it, she felt like a kid again: held against her great-aunt's soft bosom, surrounded by her powdery jasmine perfume, feeling safe, like the world couldn't touch her.

Sometimes that memory expanded to include her father. Always by the front door, one hand on the doorknob, saying he'd be back soon to visit. And he did come back, at first. But the visits became less and less frequent as it became apparent that he'd moved on. Remarried. Who needed your old life when you had a new one? Better to leave behind the daughter who reminded him of his first wife, the one who'd cheated and left him with a toddler to raise.

Leaving ran in her family, apparently. Her mom did it. Her dad did it. But Aunt Alice had been a constant from the time she was five years old. That was when Boneyard Key had become her home. When Aunt Alice had become her home.

Now Aunt Alice was gone too. Though when you lived in the most haunted small town in Florida it was normal to hope that she'd lingered. Normal to hope that Alice would understand how lonely Sophie felt, now that she was on her own. Maybe she would have wanted to stick around.

But she hadn't.

This home was all Sophie had left. Well, that and the forty-odd years of crap that had accumulated in this two-bedroom condo. When Aunt Alice had first passed, Sophie had held on to every scrap, not able to part with a single thing she'd touched. As time went on, her grip had relaxed, and she'd been able to clear things out. Clothes were donated first, followed by most of her jewelry, then a few furniture pieces. Now the space was a cozy mismatch that was very much Sophie, but with enough reminders to keep Aunt Alice's memory alive. She could feel her aunt's love in the handmade quilt slung across the back of the sofa, the vinyl collection, and the plants that Sophie did her best to keep alive.

The final frontier remained the master bedroom. Aunt Alice's room. Sophie hadn't been able to bring herself to take it over. Easier to just keep the door closed and stay in her smaller bedroom with its purple flower wallpaper.

It was a good life. Really. But every once in a while, Sophie wished she could be enough to make someone stay.

Four

Tristan wasn't the kind of guy who stuck around in one place very long. But Boneyard Key might just change his mind.

"Please tell me you're not eating oysters for dinner every night." Eric, his long-suffering business partner and even longer-suffering friend, smirked at him through Tristan's laptop screen.

Tristan made a *pffft* sound. "Of course not." He lifted the take-out box from its spot next to his laptop on the coffee table. "Tuesday is fried chicken night. Apparently, people start putting their orders in at three in the afternoon, so you know it's going to be good."

Eric shook his head in mock censure. "I wish I had your physique, man. I'd be at the gym three extra days after a dinner like that."

"Come go for a run with me. I think it counts double down here; it's like running in a sauna."

That garnered a full-on laugh, which brought a grin to Tristan's face. Eric was too serious; he liked when he could make him laugh. The years fell away while he was talking to Eric. They'd met at freshman orientation in college, ended up living on the same hall in the same dorm, and had even rushed the same fraternity. They'd tried dating their sophomore year but quickly realized that while they were a disaster as a couple, they absolutely worked as best friends.

Together, they'd spent countless late nights in the living room of
their fraternity house, planning out their fall fundraiser: a walking
tour of campus that was part pub crawl, part ghost tour. Lots of
nights of cheap pizza and even cheaper beer, spitballing ideas, re-
calling every cheesy ghost story they'd heard as a kid. The guy with
a hook for a hand. Hitchhiking ghosts of various backgrounds and
ethnicities. Even that old 1950s song, "Teen Angel"—why had a
song about a girl being hit by a train been a big hit back then?—that
was easy to spin into a story about a ghost lingering near some rail-
road tracks just off campus.

That fundraiser had been so much fun—and so lucrative—that
they'd put it on every semester after that. That meant more late
nights, more brainstorming as they made it bigger and better each
time. Senior year they even gave the endeavor a name: Ghouls Night
Out. Then Tristan took it one step further by fleshing out a business
plan and turning it into his senior thesis project. As a graduation
gift, Tristan's father had agreed to be the first investor, and suddenly
Tristan was a businessman, running a ghost tour operation. They'd
expanded to twelve cities around the country by now, Boneyard Key
being location number thirteen. All this work hadn't been easy, and
a lot of the time it hadn't been the least bit fun.

But Eric, with his knack for spreadsheets and unwavering optimism, had been with him every step of the way. While Tristan was
the face of the organization, scouting out new locations and getting
them up and running, telling the marginally spooky stories with
aplomb and charm, Eric was the true businessman of the outfit. He
was the one who made sure the numbers added up. Even when they
didn't, really.

Tristan knew the business was in trouble. Okay, maybe not
trouble—they weren't on the verge of closing down imminently or
anything. But that graduation gift from his father had come with

strings. Very long strings—they'd stretched for almost five years. Except now Tristan was running out of string, and time was almost up. If Sebastian Martin wasn't happy with the state of things come October, it was the end for Ghouls Night Out.

But when Tristan talked to Eric, he wasn't thinking about any of that. Talking to Eric, he remembered why he did this. He remembered that above all, leading a tour, telling cheesy ghost stories was *fun*.

"Seriously, though." Eric was ready to talk business, and Tristan snapped to attention. "How's the new location shaping up?"

"Fantastic." Tristan popped a french fry into his mouth. "This place couldn't be any more perfect if I'd made it all up. Everything is ghost themed, and I do mean everything. Try and find something in one of these gift shops that *doesn't* have a ghost slapped on it." His collection was already embarrassing: three T-shirts (including one with an intricately tie-dyed ghost on the front), two ball caps (one of which he was about to put in the mail to Eric), and a shot glass so far. Every time he was downtown, he saw something new in a shop window, and before he knew it, he was inside getting yet another souvenir of Boneyard Key. He was going to have no trouble remembering the place once he left.

"Sounds like we'll fit right in, then," Eric said, as though he was ever going to set foot in Boneyard Key. The man practically lived behind his screens; it drove his boyfriend crazy. "Now, if you'll just give me a second, I was working on compiling the reports for the rest of the locations . . ." His attention switched off camera as he clicked and frowned. "Okay. I've got the monthly reports from Richmond and Montgomery. Nothing from Omaha yet, but you know they're always a little late turning in their numbers. For the most part everything is trending upward, but . . ."

"But not fast enough, right?" Tristan sighed. He knew it.

"Well, now, hang on. Just because certain tourist attractions aren't doing well in *February*, when they have half a foot of snow on the ground, doesn't mean that it's time to declare bankruptcy."

"Good point." It was easy to forget things like that when you were in Florida, where winter meant putting on a sweatshirt. He thought about Sophie and her blue peacoat; she had to have been sweltering in that thing. But maybe people's blood was thinner down here. Maybe temperatures below seventy made her shiver.

Nope. Not thinking about what might make Sophie shiver.

Thankfully, Eric pulled his attention back with a compliment. "I think the new Florida location is going to help out a lot. Your timing is good, so there's no worries there."

"All part of the research, my friend." Tristan indulged in a little self-congratulation. "This whole state gets invaded soon for spring break, and I imagine a sleepy little town like this is no exception. I'm just about done mapping out the route, and then I'll match the stories in our script to the locations. We can start taking reservations online, and then open at the beginning of March or so. That gives us a couple weeks to work out the kinks before spring breakers really hit."

"Perfect. That revenue should boost up the lower-performing locations, and then things should be heating up in the more northern locations when you hit the dead time in the summer there in Florida. No pun intended." Eric cleared his throat while Tristan rolled his eyes. "Speaking of which . . ." Eric leaned in closer to the screen. "Seen any ghosts yet?"

Tristan scoffed. "Yeah, right. It's all a gimmick. You should see this place, seriously. Your pun's got nothing on it. Ghost schtick everywhere."

"They claim it's for real, though." Eric's eyes strayed to his phone as he tapped and scrolled. "I found a couple articles online.

Says it's been haunted since the turn of the century. Twentieth century," he clarified.

"Oh, I know. I've even had a couple of the locals try and tell me that. But come on. Ghosts aren't real. We should know, right? We're in the ghost business." And as far as Tristan was concerned, the stories he told on his ghost tour were just that: stories. Snatches of urban legends and Americana that he'd cobbled together to make for a fun night out. Nothing more.

"That we are." Eric put his phone aside with a firm nod. "And we're in good shape."

Tristan felt a warm glow of satisfaction. They'd planned this out meticulously, and if they just stuck to it, this extra location should generate enough revenue to put them far enough in the black to make his father happy. Maybe not *happy*—the thought of Sebastian Martin looking gleeful was too unsettling to contemplate—but at least satisfied enough to not pull his funding and make Tristan shutter their entire business.

"Something's up, though." Eric tilted his head and stared a hole at him, right through the video call. "I can tell. Spill."

Tristan sighed. "There's this girl . . ."

"Hey-o." A wide smile broke across his best friend's face. Not only at the prospect of talking about something other than business, but at dissecting Tristan's love life. It had been a long time since Tristan had had a love life to dissect.

Not that he had one now. Sophie wasn't going to give him the time of day once she found out what he was doing there. Around bites of the best fried chicken leg he'd ever eaten, he filled Eric in on the night he'd met Sophie, from their flirtation at the bar to him lightly stalking her ghost tour afterward.

"But we looked it up." Eric shook his head in amazement. "There's no ghost tour in Boneyard Key."

"I know!" Tristan was glad Eric confirmed it; honestly Sophie's presence made him feel gaslit. "She's gotta be new around here too. That's the only explanation. She got the jump on us by a few weeks or something." It was a theory he'd been working on since that first night. There were flaws in it, of course. Her familiarity with The Haunt, for example, and with Tony behind the bar. Sure, Tristan could make friends easily, but Sophie's demeanor was almost too familiar, like a long-term resident.

"Well, if that's the case, running her out of town should be easy." Eric sounded far too cheerful at the prospect. "I mean, the script's been honed to a T. And let's face it, Tristan. You're good at this. I see how you come alive when you put that hat on. It's like you're back in college all over again."

"Yeah." The memory was like taking a good deep breath, the kind that let his shoulders relax. He'd gone to college for a business degree, sure, but he'd also snuck in a theatre minor as a secret *fuck you* to his dad. Those times that he'd spent onstage had been the happiest of his life. And the top hat he wore when he led the ghost tours was the perfect souvenir of those better days.

"So what's she like? This other ghost tour."

"Sophie?" She appeared instantly in his mind's eye, dark hair gleaming under the streetlight. "She's cute." Understatement. "Tiny little thing. Glasses, so she has that brainy hot librarian look. Dark, dark eyes, shiny like liquid? Her hair's dark too, and curly. And long, right about here . . ." He twisted in an inelegant motion, trying to show with his hand, drawing a line just under his shoulder blades.

As he straightened up again a long silence fell, broken when Eric coughed a smile into his fist. "I, uh. I was asking about her tour, dumbass. What's *her tour* like?"

"Oh." Now it was Tristan's turn for some awkward throat clearing. Good thing he'd stopped talking before describing her smile:

coy and inviting, the kind that made you want to know what her mouth tasted like. "I didn't see too much of it, honestly." His attention had been on that hair, that smile.

"That's your next assignment, then. Check out her tour and report back. See if her stories are any good; if there's anything we can, you know, borrow."

"Borrow?" Tristan pressed a dramatic hand to his chest. "You just said our script is perfect."

"Nothing wrong with improving on perfection, you know. Do a little sneaky recon and let me know."

"I can do that." Tristan cast longing eyes toward his takeout box. He really wanted to finish that chicken before it got cold. "Anything else?"

"No . . ." But Eric's unsure tone made Tristan cut his eyes back to his laptop screen, faint alarm bells going off in his head. Eric opened his mouth, closed it, then finally spoke all in a rush. "It's just . . . how long do you really think you'll want to do this?"

"What do you mean?" Tristan frowned. "I thought we had a good thing going here."

"We have a great thing going here. You know I'm never happier than when I'm elbow-deep in spreadsheets." On anyone else that would have sounded like sarcasm, but Eric really was that kind of nerd. "It's you I'm worried about. All this traveling you do. Never in one place longer than a couple months. And if you win this bet with your dad, you're signing up for more of the same. Indefinitely. You sure you don't want a home and a life?"

"Homes are overrated," Tristan said, "and I like this life just fine." But he looked around as he spoke, at the stark white walls of this condo. He'd seen the listing: *Fully furnished.* Technically, that was true; there was furniture, and the kitchen was stocked with top-of-the-line appliances and cookware. But the place felt cold. Clinical. The hardwood floors made his footsteps echo. He sat on an enormous white sofa that gleamed from its spot between the glass-and-chrome coffee table and matching end tables. The only ornamentation was a giant conch shell—white, of course—sitting in the middle of the coffee table like a remnant of the ocean visible from the big, floor-to-ceiling windows. This place screamed *accommodation*. Nothing about it felt like a home.

"Do you, though?" Eric tilted his head, and even through the questionable quality of the video call, Tristan felt studied. "I just . . ." He sighed. "You've been locked in this . . . contest or whatever with your dad for what, your entire adult life? Those first couple years were exciting, but do you really want to be in it for the long haul?"

Defensiveness rose like hackles on the back of Tristan's neck. "What makes you think I don't?"

"Nothing," Eric said quickly. "Nothing. I just want to make sure this is something you actually want to do, and not something you're doing to prove your dad wrong. Don't get me wrong, that's a great incentive on its own, but we've built something real here. Something that employs a fair amount of people, and—"

"And you're worried you're going to lose your job if I lose my deal with Dad." That defensiveness made his words snappier than he'd intended.

"No. Well, yes. I mean, of course I don't want to lose my job. But I'm not talking about me. I'm talking about every location we've opened over the last five years. Four or five employees in each one. If you lose this bet and the business folds, that's a lot of people out of a job. Not just me."

Tristan's snappishness drained out of him in a rush, as the pressure of keeping those people employed settled on his shoulders. "Yeah." He pinched the bridge of his nose. "I know."

"Look." Eric's voice softened, and Tristan peeked up at him

through his fingers. "I want you happy. That's all. And you're not going to be happy if you spend your whole life trying to outrun your father."

"I'm not trying to outrun him. I'm trying to . . ." What was he trying to do? Sometimes Tristan wasn't sure.

Eric's words echoed off the white walls of the condo, long after they'd disconnected the call. Tristan grabbed his takeout box and a beer from the fridge, settling himself on the glass-and-chrome (this place was nothing if not consistent) patio set on the balcony. The chicken was still warm although the fries were questionable, and the beer was cold. With the lights of the balcony off, he watched the palm trees rustle in the moonlight and, further out, the undulation of the Gulf.

Maybe Eric was right. Since getting Ghouls Night Out up and running as an actual business, he'd settled into a life and a routine that was unchanging in the way it always changed. Sure, he had his own place—a Manhattan apartment that was more of a glorified storage unit with a bed in it. It was where he crashed while he was in New York, taking in Broadway shows and catching up with friends. Most of his things were there, but it was as much a home to him as this condo in Boneyard Key.

Most people his age had settled into their adult lives by now. A place to call home, friends to hang out with on a regular basis. Maybe even a spouse, or kids. Hell, even Eric had moved in with his boyfriend a year or so back. Tristan never had a problem making friends, but they were always temporary, since *he* was always temporary. A relationship was out of the question, since he never stopped moving. Who'd want to sign on for that?

Enough. He had a tour to plan. Time to get started. Pull up the script template he used at all the Ghouls Night Out locations, and start plugging in specific spots for Boneyard Key. That bait shack by the pier looked like it could be haunted; that might be a good place to start. And maybe one or two of those cottages that lined the beach . . . perfect for his favorite story, about a shipwrecked pirate and his lost lady love. Probably should steer clear of Hallowed Grounds, though, since Sophie ran her tour out of there. It would take some careful planning to make sure their tours didn't cross in the night.

Hmm. Maybe Eric was right about the sneaky recon. Knowing the complete route Sophie's tour took would help him plan his, right? It was all for the good of the tour. Nothing to do with potentially seeing Sophie again. Spending an hour or two in her company.

Definitely not.

Five

Sophie was halfway up Beachside, her ghost tour group in sight in front of Hallowed Grounds, when she saw him.

Tristan.

That couldn't be right. There was no way he was still in town. Tourists stuck around for the weekend: three or four days at best. He'd been here for a good time, not a long time, as her friend Cassie would say. And from the way he'd checked out when she'd started talking about her ghost tour, Sophie was pretty sure she was neither of those things.

She dug her list out of her pocket—she'd barely glanced at it when Nick had handed it across the counter to her earlier that afternoon. Thirteen people—nice and lucky—and now her eyes skidded on name number nine. *Tristan Martin.*

She looked up again, and like he'd been conjured from her wild delusions, there he was: artfully messy blond hair and sage-green T-shirt, leaning against a streetlight with his hands shoved in the front pockets of his jeans. No jacket, even though the sun had long since set and it was easily in the low seventies. He was definitely from up north; his blood was a lot thicker than hers. Sophie shoved the list back in her pocket and tugged the sleeves of her hoodie down over her hands.

Tristan chatted with a middle-aged couple, laughing at something one of them said. Sophie had forgotten about the power of that easy laugh of his. She wanted it directed at her. She wanted his attention.

And she got it. His gaze snapped to her when she was still a couple doors down from Hallowed Grounds, and his smile changed, widened, from generically polite to more pointed. He was smiling *at her*, not just smiling in general. She already knew him well enough to tell the difference.

She usually greeted her guests all at once, gave them the rundown of how long the tour was going to be, and collected their cash. But this time her feet took her right up to Tristan, who straightened at her approach.

"Well, hello again." Her voice came out not at all shaky. Good for her.

"Hey." There was that lazy smile again, the one she remembered from The Haunt: open and friendly, yet somehow intimate.

"You're still in town." Sophie was always great at stating the obvious.

"It's the oysters," he replied. "Can't get enough of them." He shook his hair off his forehead while Sophie laughed. "I thought I'd see what your whole ghost tour thing is about."

Sophie's cheeks warmed. He'd remembered her too. And he didn't think what she did was stupid. Amazing.

She clapped her hands together to get everyone's attention. "Thank you so much for coming, everyone! My name is Sophie Horvath, and I'm going to be your tour guide this evening as we take a little walk through the town of Boneyard Key. First things first: I'm going to collect the fee, fifteen dollars each, please. If you need an ATM there's one right there on the corner. Once that's out of the way, we'll get started." She'd been doing this for years now, and this part never got less awkward—demanding money for her services. Which was ridiculous, right? Fifteen dollars a person for a personal walking tour? A bargain!

She was immediately surrounded as everyone handed her their money. Tristan was last, and she tried to wave him off when he handed her a twenty.

"Don't be silly." He pressed the bill into her hand. It crinkled as he closed her fingers over it. "I'm a paying customer, so I expect the whole experience." He shot her a wink that was so fleeting she might have imagined it.

"You got it." Her cheeks were starting to hurt from smiling. She turned to the rest of the group to start the tour. "The tour takes about an hour, give or take, and covers about a mile and a half in total. There's plenty of benches and places to take a break if anyone needs it, and I have lots of stories to tell to pass the time if need be."

Thank goodness for muscle memory. Thank goodness her six years of leading this tour meant she knew exactly where to stop and what story to tell. She barely remembered stopping outside of I Scream Ice Cream for the story of the spirit that kept the ice cream cold in the back. She vaguely registered that they'd made it all the way down to the fishing pier, where the moon on the water made Cemetery Island just barely visible off the coast. All she was aware of was Tristan. He hung at the fringe of the crowd, somewhere in the middle, his attention hyperfocused on her. Which made sense; she was the tour guide. If she wasn't commanding attention, something was wrong. But his gaze was like a laser, and she could feel it on her even when she wasn't looking in his direction.

Sophie was looking in his direction a lot.

"Boneyard Key was founded in the 1840s, but not in this exact location." She tore her attention away from Tristan to gesture across the water, to where Cemetery Island was a dark blur. "The original settlement was on that barrier island, a small fishing and clamming community called Fisherton. Everything changed when a hurricane hit in 1897." She nodded solemnly in reaction to murmurs from her audience. "It was one of the biggest ones on record, and it wiped out most of the town. The families that opted to stay moved inland, establishing a new settlement here."

She moved then, turning to lead the group off the pier and toward the street. "The island is worth a visit, if you have time. Jimmy has kayaks for rent right over there, and it's a pretty easy trip if you're into that kind of thing." Sophie was not into that kind of thing, but she didn't judge those who were. "You can still see some of the foundations of houses, and tucked way in the back is the old cemetery that's still standing today."

There was a group of college-aged women in the tour, phones out, probably filming the whole thing for social media or something. One of them spoke up now. "Was the old town haunted too?"

Sophie could see Tristan's eyebrows crawling up his forehead, as though he considered the question a dare. She fought the urge to make an *oh, please* face back at him, focusing instead on the tourist with her cell phone. "It wasn't. Not that we can tell, anyway. There are a lot of theories about Boneyard Key and how the hauntings started, but the one that makes the most sense to me is that it was caused by the Great Storm of 1897. Big storms, especially in those days, meant big casualties. The families that stayed behind—we call them the Founding Fifteen—found themselves suddenly able to communicate with loved ones that they'd lost. And as time went on, more and more people were able to communicate as more and more spirits stuck around."

They continued down the street and back to Beachside Drive, where she paused at the Starter Home—an old stilt house that had been slowly but surely disintegrating into the ocean over the years.

There wasn't really a story to the place—not that Sophie had ever been able to find, anyway. When she was a kid it had been recognizable as a house, with most of a roof and three of its four walls. Now two of the walls were gone, and only a tiny corner of the roof clung to the top. One day a good storm was going to come along and the whole thing was going to fall into the Gulf, disappearing forever. Sophie didn't want to think about that day.

Now they were at her favorite part of the tour, moving further down the street and around the bend to a beach cottage that was painted a cheerful yellow, its picket fence lined with cabbage roses. It always had a haunted history, but it wasn't until Cassie had moved in last summer that Sophie had learned that the story behind the house, which the whole town had accepted as fact, was wrong. There was nothing like learning the truth from the ghost herself.

"The Sarah Hawkins House was built in 1899 by William Donnelly, shortly after Boneyard Key was established here. Soon after Donnelly left for points north, deciding he'd had enough of Florida. And after that storm, who could blame him?" She paused as a couple of the tourists chuckled, the way they always did at that little joke. Because hurricanes were hilarious.

"His niece, Sarah Blankenship, had been looking forward to living here—just her and her cabbage roses—but then she met C.S. Hawkins. *Mean Mr. Hawkins*, we like to call him these days." She pitched her voice low, as though she were telling a spooky campfire story. Tourists loved that kind of thing. She chanced a glance at Tristan; he was nodding along, his eyes all but invisible from the force of his smile.

Not that the Hawkins story was funny. It was essentially a tale of emotional abuse: a husband who held on to control of his wife, even after his death. Even after *her* death. But everything was all right now; they'd evicted Mr. Hawkins, and now Cassie and Sarah

Hawkins shared the home together. Cassie may not have counted on having a ghost for a roommate when she'd bought the place, but she seemed fine with it these days.

Sophie kept the story light, focusing on the happy ending with the ghostly roommate. That was the kind of thing tourists wanted to hear. They were in the homestretch now, back down Beachside Drive, past the Chamber of Commerce and to the spot where she told the story of the Beach Bum near the break in the seawall, and finally to Hallowed Grounds, where they'd started.

By the time they got to the sidewalk outside the café, Sophie felt wrung out. Leading groups on a walking tour of the Boneyard Key historic district was tricky all on its own; the phrase really should be "herding tourists" instead of "herding cats." Sophie's job was historian and storyteller at the same time, sharing stories of the spirits who lingered here in her hometown, doing her best to keep the stories compelling enough so no one was reaching for their phone . . . it was a lot. Her brain felt like mushy, overcooked pasta at the end of nights like this. But she always kept a smile on her face, always answered every question as though it had never been asked before. (It usually had.)

Once back at Hallowed Grounds, it never took long for the group to filter out, tempted by the drink coupons to The Haunt that Sophie handed out at the end of every tour. Tourists went nuts over a good BOGO. A few people lingered, going inside for a last cup of coffee. Nick could probably handle them on his own, but they were Sophie's customers, and she felt responsible for them. It seemed only right to wait till they were gone and Nick could close up. Sometimes he slipped her the leftover banana bread that hadn't sold that day.

Behind the counter, Nick caught Sophie's eye where she lingered in the doorway, raising a hand in acknowledgment. She nodded back and turned to wait out on the sidewalk.

And almost smacked right into Tristan, who was directly behind her.

"Oh!" She put up defensive hands that accidentally landed right on his chest.

"Sorry!" His hands came up to catch around her upper arms, as though helping her collide against him. For an extended, awkward moment, they froze together in the doorway, neither one giving ground or attempting to gain it.

Those light-colored eyes of his? They were green. Pale, icy green, just a shade lighter than the sage-colored T-shirt he wore. Though calling a garment this soft a T-shirt was probably a crime. The fabric was velvety against her palm but sturdy. Nothing like what they sold down the street; no one was screen printing rude slogans and ghosts on fabric like this.

Tristan cleared his throat, and it was like regaining consciousness. How long had Sophie been standing there, petting Tristan's soft green shirt (and the solid chest underneath it, oh, no) and staring up into his clear green eyes? Way too long to be socially acceptable, that was for sure.

"Sorry." She stepped back, dropping her traitorous hands to brush them against her jeans, trying to scrub away the soft yet firm feel of the man in front of her.

"No problem." His voice was low, gravelly, and that smile he gave out so freely now seemed just for her. He didn't step back; in fact he stepped forward, gaining that little bit of ground Sophie had given up. She caught her breath. She'd been talking all evening, and her voice probably had some gravel in it too, but if Tristan wanted to chat further she'd suck it up.

"So . . ." He cleared his throat and glanced up and down the street, as though worried they'd be overheard. Sophie's heart sped up; she wasn't imagining things after all. This whole time, this whole tour, he'd been watching her, and not just because she was the tour guide. There was a spark here. He felt it too.

He cleared his throat again. "So, you do this tour every Friday night?"

Sophie's heart plummeted. Ah. Small talk. She nodded and tried to keep the disappointment out of her voice. "Every Friday night," she confirmed. "Saturday nights too, this time of year. There's more people here from out of town, which means more demand."

He nodded thoughtfully. "Makes sense. Yeah, I can see that. And those stories? How did you come up with them?"

"Come up with them?" Sophie felt her brow furrow. "You think I'm making them up?" The idea of it made her feel defensive, considering the work she did to keep her stories accurate.

Tristan's laugh was breathy, uncertain. "I mean, they're *ghost stories*," he said. "Stories that have ghosts in them. Obviously they're made-up."

Annoyance prickled the back of Sophie's neck as she reminded herself that it was natural for newcomers to Boneyard Key to be skeptical. Cassie had once been doubtful about the existence of ghosts, and now she lived with one. Tristan wasn't being a jerk. He was just new around here.

Speaking of which . . . "I thought you were only here for the weekend. I didn't realize you were sticking around." Did she sound too obvious? She probably sounded too obvious.

"Oh." He looked uncomfortable, his eyes shifting to the side. "No. Yeah. I mean, I'm definitely sticking around. For a little bit, at least."

Well, that was great news. *Try not to act too eager,* Sophie told herself, and then she immediately didn't listen to her own advice. "Good! It's a great little town, you'll love it here. I mean, if you love small towns. Do you? Like small towns?" Oh God, she was babbling like a dork. The post-tour tiredness had finally caught up to her, fogging up her brain.

But maybe Tristan liked dorks, because his smile, his attention, focused solely on her again. Whatever tension he was holding in his shoulders eased a fraction. "I do." His voice was softer, as though their conversation was private and not right at the front door of a public establishment. "I think small towns are pretty great. And I agree. This one is something special." There was a gentle smile in his eyes, and maybe that last sentence was directed at her, and not Boneyard Key in general.

"Good." She hoped her eyes were smiling back, because she really liked this guy.

The door behind Sophie opened, the bell chiming loud enough to break whatever spell had been forming around the two of them. Sophie fell back a step out of instinct, and so did Tristan, opening a path for the middle-aged couple walking out of Hallowed Grounds, to-go cups in hand. They all nodded good night in a bobbing syncopation, and an awkward silence settled between Sophie and Tristan. Ugh. No. She wanted to keep talking, explore the smile that had been in his eyes. Stupid tourists, spoiling the mood.

She took a deep breath. Took a chance. "Would you like to—"

But he started speaking at the same time. "I should probably get—" Both trailed off, and Tristan made an *after you* gesture.

"I was just going to say . . ." Sophie spoke quickly before her courage failed her completely. "I didn't get a chance to eat before the tour tonight, and I'm starving. We could maybe go to The Haunt?

Get some more of those oysters you like?" Her hopes soared. She didn't ask guys out very often, but there was something about Tristan that made her confident. Made her sure he wouldn't say no.

He huffed out a laugh, but this time the smile didn't reach his eyes. Instead he fell back another step. "I'd love to, but . . . another time, maybe. I have some . . . stuff I have to do tonight."

"Stuff," she repeated back. The word landed between them with a thud as her hopes crashed back down to earth.

"Yeah." He didn't meet her eyes, glancing up and down the street instead. He was doing that a lot. "In fact, I really should go, so if you'll excuse me."

"Right. Yeah. Of course."

"Sorry." The word was said gently, but it still stung like a paper cut. "Maybe I'll see you . . ." But he didn't finish the sentence. He glanced over her head, toward the door to Hallowed Grounds, before shooting her a tight smile as he set off down the sidewalk.

Well. That had been a little bit of a catastrophe. Sophie watched him go before turning and pushing open the door to the café. Inside, Nick was counting out the cash drawer, clearly closing up now that all the tourists had finally left.

"I thought that last couple was never gonna leave." Nick was as customer service oriented as ever. "All they wanted to do was chat. Did you know they're here on their honeymoon?"

"No, I didn't." Sophie bit on the inside of her cheek.

"Speaking of romance, I was wondering how long you two were gonna make eyes at each other in front of my door. I'm trying to run a business here, you know."

"What?" Sophie whirled from the bulletin board. "I wasn't . . . We weren't . . . There were no eyes being made." But her cheeks flamed; there were plenty of eyes being made, and she knew it. Too bad that was as far as it went.

Nick waved a dismissive hand. "You want some banana bread to take home? I've got a little extra."

"I'd love that, thanks." As Nick disappeared into the kitchen area, Sophie's attention fell on the bulletin board near the door. Boneyard Key didn't have a local paper, and the board here at Hallowed Grounds was the closest they got. All job postings, lost dog pleas, and boats for sale went up on Nick's corkboard.

It stood out, like the neon coffee cup in Nick's front window. Like Tristan leaning against a lamppost on Beachside Drive. A bright, shiny white business card pinned smack-dab in the middle of the board.

GHOULS NIGHT OUT
GHOST TOURS

There was a website listed, along with a phone number. It wasn't a local area code.

And a name.

Tristan.

Martin.

Sophie pushed her glasses up her nose and stared at the card, trying to bore a hole in it with her mind. She barely heard Nick's footsteps coming back into the dining area from the kitchen.

"Here you go." A paper bag rustled behind her, but Sophie didn't turn around. She reached for the card, carefully unpinning it, while he headed back behind the counter. "You want a coffee or anything before I close down?"

"No." She walked to the counter where Nick was cleaning up and slapped it down. "What the hell is this?"

Nick's gaze sharpened in surprise. Sophie wasn't a four-letter-word kind of girl, but sometimes the occasion called for it. "What is what?"

"This." She stabbed a finger at the card, as though she could spear it to the table. "A ghost tour? Are you kidding?"

"What's that?" Nick put down the rag and picked up the card, his eyebrows furrowing as he studied it. "Oh, this is Tristan, right? Your new boyfriend? He runs ghost tours too?" Nick was oblivious to her fury.

"He is *not* my boyfriend." She snatched the card back. It was a complicated process, involving her stretching to the very tops of her toes and practically lunging across the counter, but she managed. "How long has this card been there?"

"Today. He came in during lunch. I was doing fourteen things at the same time, and he was waving that card at me, asking if he could put it up. I thought, okay, why not. I didn't even get a chance to look at it, see what it was." Nick looked sheepish, spots of color appearing in his cheeks above his russet-colored beard. "Sorry, Soph. I wouldn't have said yes if I'd known he was infringing on your turf."

She sighed, trying to summon her patience. "You've been busy." She could relate. February was still snowbird season. Lots of people spending long weekends in Boneyard Key. Local businesses were all working long hours these days, but the money was worth it. It kept them going through the lean times, when it was too hot for tourists and there weren't any holidays.

"Hey. Cheer up." The words were hilarious coming from Nick. He was the least cheerful guy on the planet. "He's not local, right? Maybe you can give him some tips for his own tour, wherever that is."

"Yeah." Sophie's voice felt dark coming out of her mouth. "Maybe."

The card burned a hole in her pocket all the way home. Her stomach growled as she pulled off her hoodie and shook out her dark curls. She was starving, and banana bread wasn't going to cut it tonight.

Sophie reached into her pocket and drew out a handful of cash. Tips had been good tonight. She deserved a pizza. Of course, while she'd taken the money out of her pocket, she'd also taken out that damn business card. She frowned at it while pulling up the number for Poltergeist Pizza on her phone.

"Hey, Soph!" Terry sounded as bright and cheerful as he had in high school biology class. Tips must be good for him tonight too. "Tour over already? I saw you herding those ducklings past our place."

"Yep." She tucked her phone against her cheek as she hung up her hoodie. "It was a good crowd tonight."

"I bet. We've been nonstop here. You want the usual? I got some garlic knots coming out of the oven; I can throw those in too."

Her stomach growled again at the thought. "Yes, please." Ever since she was a kid, Sophie only took her pizza one way. Medium with sausage and pepperoni, extra sauce and extra cheese. Obviously, she'd tried pizza other places when she'd been out of town. But nowhere came close to Poltergeist Pizza. Her taste buds loved Boneyard Key just as much as she did.

It would be a while before dinner arrived—Terry had always been a bit of a slacker, but he was meticulous about his pizza—so while she waited, Sophie opened the bottle of Merlot on her counter and booted up her laptop. She needed a glass of wine to steel herself before pulling up Ghouls Night Out's website.

It was a good website, she had to admit. Slick, just like the business card in her hand. *Ghost Tours for the Discerning Traveler* scrolled across the top in a Dickensian-style script. This wasn't a single-location thing, she quickly realized. No, Ghouls Night Out had multiple locations, scattered all over the country like it was the second coming of Cracker Barrel.

The photo on the home page showed happy tourists being led down cobblestone streets by a guide in a top hat and frock coat, carrying a lantern. Ridiculous. Sophie wore jeans and sneakers most of the time, and she'd never heard a complaint. Was this the kind of thing she was supposed to be doing? Cheesy Victorian cosplay?

She clicked the About page and there he was: Tristan Martin. As magnetic in this photo as he was in real life, his blond hair was just as artfully messy, with a haircut that probably cost as much as a car payment. His smile was broad, with perfect, straight teeth, and his eyes were bright and inviting. He really had no business being on the internet looking like that.

She clicked back to the home page and took a long sip of wine. Wait. She zoomed in on the cobblestone street picture. The tour guide, the one in the stupid Victorian outfit . . .

It was Tristan.

Sophie groaned and covered her face with her hand. He'd let her go on and on the night they'd met, telling him about ghost tours, all the while probably laughing on the inside about what an idiot she was. And then tonight. That intense attention while she led him on her tour. Listening to her stories. His questions about scheduling. Turning down a dinner invite because he had "stuff" to do. All the while knowing he'd left that business card there like a time bomb waiting to go off.

Asshole.

And seriously, what was with this costume? Ridiculous. He had a face that knew what a cell phone was. He looked dumb in a top hat.

All of this was bad enough, but then Sophie clicked on the Locations tab, and the bright yellow banner scrolling across the top opened a pit in the bottom of her stomach.

COMING THIS SPRING: BONEYARD KEY, FLORIDA.

"Shit." That was two swears in one night, but Sophie was in that kind of mood.

She wasn't getting rich doing ghost tours. At best, Tristan was going to take half of her audience, with half her income along with it. At worst . . .

Well, at worst, this ridiculously photogenic guy with his stupid hat and his lantern and his fancy website was going to put her out of business.

Six

Tristan's favorite part of establishing a new location of Ghouls Night Out was engaging with the locals. Chatting up business owners and finding out what made a community tick while he passed out business cards, scattering them around town like a modern-day Johnny Appleseed. He wanted to get the word out that he was adding value to their community, bringing in tourism and hopefully additional income for everyone. The goal was to become a familiar, friendly face, smoothing the way for his tour to set up shop. It was a tried-and-true tactic that worked almost every time.

It wasn't working in Boneyard Key.

It had at first. Shop owners had accepted his card, even looked at it with some interest. Nick had let him put one on the bulletin board at Hallowed Grounds, which felt like a particular score. He'd stuck it to the center of the board like a promise. Staking his claim. The folks at the Chamber of Commerce had been friendly and welcoming, letting him leave a stack of cards with them.

But then things changed. Slowly. Painfully. Over the next couple of weeks goodwill drained from the people around him, like a balloon with a pinhole losing air. On his next visit to Hallowed Grounds, he noticed that his card had disappeared from the bulle-

tin board. Nick shook his head, his face stony, when Tristan asked
if he could leave another one.

"I think you've done enough," he said, in a voice that would
brook not an ounce of an argument. He folded his arms across his
chest. "You know we already have a ghost tour here, right?"

"Surely there's nothing wrong with some friendly competition?"
But Nick was immune to Tristan's easy charm and friendly smile.

"You don't compete with Sophie," was all he said. Nick didn't
seem like the most gregarious guy on a good day, but this was next-
level. Today, the way that Nick had squinted at him when handing
him his coffee made Tristan feel wary. Like there was a nonzero
chance that the drink had come with a little extra spit, as a treat.

Oh, well. Spooky Brew was closer to his condo anyway.

On a Tuesday night Tristan found himself at The Haunt, ready
for another round of fried chicken. As he settled himself at the bar,
it didn't take long to notice the chill. Not from the air conditioning—
it was a warm evening in early March—but from the fellow patrons.
More than one squinty-eyed look was shot his way.

There was an old woman at a table by the door. Her hair was
white and curled in that Queen Elizabeth style. She spooned up a
bite of clam chowder with a hand that shook a little, enough to send
the soup swaying but not enough to spill. Across from her was a
blond woman, about Tristan's age if he had to guess. Her ponytail
hung over her left shoulder as she stabbed gently at a giant salad.
They were related—it was evident in the shape of their faces and the
curves of their smiles.

But then the younger woman raised her head, and their gazes
collided. Tristan took a sip of his beer and offered a polite smile—
nothing flirty, just friendly—but the narrowing of her eyes said he'd
offended her personally. She spoke to her elderly companion, who

raised her head, gave Tristan a measured look, then turned back to the younger woman with a dismissive shake of her head.

Something about that shake of her head reminded Tristan of Nick's stony expression, and it clicked. His business card, instead of paving the way for him, had been a line in the sand. With him on one side, and Sophie on the other. And Boneyard Key had chosen Sophie.

On the one hand, he could understand. She was cute—the skip his heart made just now thinking about how cute she was confirmed that. But she'd made inroads in this town with a speed that Tristan had never seen in his life. How had she fostered such loyalty so fast?

Then Tony dropped off his order. Tristan had learned that fried chicken at The Haunt was a religious experience. But the plastic basket in front of him was a sacrilege. A shriveled chicken breast and a leg that looked like it came off a Cornish game hen. The usually crispy-hot fries were limp and soggy, as though they'd been shown the deep fryer as a vague threat on the way to Tristan's table. Tristan looked from his food to a table across the way, where a woman was working her way through a massive leg that looked like something out of a Renaissance festival.

Enough was enough. "Tony." The word came out a defeated sigh, and the bartender paused. "Level with me here. Please. I thought we were good."

"We were." Tony emphasized the second word, and the shake of his head belied his words.

"Then what the hell?" He picked up the chicken leg as though it were Exhibit A. "I'm a nice guy, I tip well. Why am I getting the scrawny pieces of chicken?"

"Sophie."

Realization dawned quickly. "Oh, man. She got to you too, huh?" He shook his head. "Seems like the whole town is on her side."

"Of course we are." Tony crossed his arms across his chest, his face as stony as Nick's had been. Damn, this was bad. "We look after our own around here."

"Seriously?" Tristan was incredulous. "I get that she must have gotten here a few weeks before I did, but that doesn't make her a local."

Tony looked at him as though he'd grown a second head. "A few weeks? Dude, she's lived here her whole life."

"Her . . ." All he could do was blink. "Her what?"

"At least since . . ." Tony cast his gaze toward the ceiling, thinking. "The earliest I remember her from was second grade. She used to swap me her Cheetos for my apple juice at lunchtime."

"Second grade . . . ?" None of these words were computing. "But she just started doing this ghost tour thing, right?" He had a bad feeling, even as he asked the question, and it only got worse when Tony shook his head again.

"A while now," he said. "Five, maybe six years? And she's real good at it too."

Tristan nudged his plastic basket of technically edible dinner away from him. Even if the food had looked good, he wasn't hungry anymore.

"Five or six *years*?" Eric sounded as incredulous as Tristan felt, which was a comfort. Thank God, it wasn't just him.

"I know!" He turned his oven on before rooting in his freezer. There had to be a frozen pizza in here somewhere.

"How did we miss it?" From his phone on the counter came the sounds of Eric typing furiously, probably googling ghost tours in Boneyard Key for the millionth time, as though Sophie's big brown eyes and glasses and dark curls would suddenly show up on an internet search. *Been doing this for years now!*, her cheerful expression would say.

"Nothing!" Eric confirmed, as though he needed to. "Has she never heard of a website? Social media? How does she stay in business?"

"This isn't a social media kind of town." Tristan tore open the frozen pizza wrapper with a little more force than was strictly necessary. The pizza bounced onto the cookie sheet, shedding plasticky cheese and pepperoni in its wake. "There's a bulletin board at the coffee shop and a couple grandmas at the Chamber of Commerce." He reassembled the toppings on his pizza and slid it into the oven. Then he dropped onto one of the stools at the breakfast bar and picked up his phone. "Bottom line is we screwed up." He took a deep breath and scrubbed a hand through his hair. Eric wasn't going to like this next idea. "Maybe we should pull out. Cut our losses."

"No." The word was emphatic, and Eric's eyes went wide. "Admit defeat? Are you kidding me?"

"It's not about admitting defeat. It's about stepping on toes. Come on, if we'd known about Sophie and her tour, would I even be here right now?"

"Well, no. But . . ."

"But what?" Tristan was already mentally packing his things. It wouldn't take long; he always traveled light.

Eric sighed. "But it's too late. You've been there what, almost a month now? The Boneyard Key script is done. The first tour is in two days, and online tickets are selling at a steady clip. We're ready to go. If we pulled out now we'd have to refund all those tickets. Finding a new location and starting over again would set us back a couple months. At the very least. And we—"

He got it now. "We don't have that kind of time." Tristan blew out a long breath and closed his eyes.

"Not if you want to get out from under your dad by October. It'll take too long to get established somewhere else." Eric looked sympathetic. "I'm sorry, but if you want to make this work, it has to be full steam ahead there in Boneyard Key."

"Yeah." If there was another option, Tristan couldn't see it.

"Don't worry." As always, Eric was the voice of optimism. "You have this down. You're going to crush it, as usual."

He was obviously aiming for a pep talk, but all Tristan could hear was *crush it*. Crush Sophie. He didn't feel good about that.

After hanging up, and while he let his almost-burned pizza cool on the stove, he wandered into his bedroom. Eric was right—Tristan didn't have much of a choice at this point. What did he really owe Sophie anyway? What did he owe anyone in this town? This wasn't personal. It was business. Just business. And if he wanted to keep his own business going, he had to do this tour on Thursday, then Friday, then Saturday. And then do it all again next week, and the week after that, all the way through the summer.

In the bedroom closet, Tristan reached for the black leather hatbox that he'd stashed on a high shelf. Setting the round box on his bed, he threw the latches and opened the lid. It gave a slight creak as he raised it. Inside was a charcoal top hat, nestled against the silk lining of the box.

For a long moment Tristan looked at the hat, remembering the day he'd first put it on. *My Fair Lady,* junior year. The costume designer had found it in some kind of rummage sale, astonishingly pristine considering its age. It was as though the hat had been waiting patiently for Tristan to be born, to attend Princeton, to minor in theatre, and to be cast as Freddy Eynsford-Hill. It had taken some work to sweet-talk the costume shop manager into letting him keep the hat. (Well, buy the hat. If there was one thing he had learned from his father, it was that money talked.)

The hat had become a mainstay in his ghost tour costume, first on campus and then out in the real world. Tristan couldn't explain it, but there was something special about that top hat and how it fit on his head. It was his power. It gave him confidence; it gave him a voice.

He put it on now and looked at himself in the mirror, that twinge of guilt fading away. This might be Sophie's town, but that didn't mean there wasn't room for more than one ghost tour. Tristan Martin was here now, and Ghouls Night Out was about to take over Boneyard Key.

He aimed a crooked grin in the mirror. "May the best ghost tour win."

Seven

Even though she wasn't descended from the Founding Fifteen, everyone seemed to assume that Sophie was psychic or something. That just because Tristan was running a ghost tour and *she* was running a ghost tour, that she was privy to all his information.

"What do you think of that new ghost tour in town?" Theo Berington turned a page in the file he was going through, keeping his eyes on his work instead of looking over at Sophie. Smart man, that Theo. He sounded innocent enough, but the question alone made Sophie want to punch a wall. She'd probably only hurt her hand if she tried.

"It's started?" She blinked her attention away from her laptop. Not this again. She'd really thought that here, in the back room of Boneyard Books, she'd be able to get away from Tristan and his Instagram-ready ghost tour. Because hiding her head in the proverbial sand would make it all go away.

Theo froze, a deer caught by a hunter, as he looked up slowly. "I don't know, actually. Soon, though, I think. He came by last week sometime."

"Great. Did he leave you his business card too?" Another business card, announcing his presence all over town. God forbid he have an actual conversation with her. *You do ghost tours, huh? Me too. How about I leave town entirely, get right out of your hair?* No, that would be too easy.

"Oh, he did that a while back. But don't worry." Theo turned back to his file, a smile curving his lips. "I threw it in the trash after he left."

Sophie pressed her lips together to hide a smile of her own, but she couldn't keep it out of her voice. "Good."

"I sold him a copy of *Boneyard Key: A Haunted History,* though."

"What?" Now, that was a surprise. She glanced down at her own copy on the table in front of her. It was studded with little red flags, one for each inaccuracy. Sophie had grown up believing this book was a true history of the town. It was also the reason that she and Theo were here in the Boneyard Key Cultural Center and Museum, which was a fancy way of saying they were in the oversize storeroom in the back of Boneyard Books. Theo ran both businesses, though the former was less a business and more of a vanity project for him. History was his jam, and as it turned out, it was Sophie's too.

For the past few months they'd been going through the book together, chapter by chapter, noting inaccuracies and outright fabrications in the stories chronicled there. Along the way, they'd both noticed stories that were conspicuous in their absence and made note of them too.

Sophie didn't know what they were going to do with all this information once they were finished compiling it. There was a part of her that loved the idea of publishing it—a book with her name on it (well, both of their names on it) existing in silent, smug correction next to the one that was filled with lies. She may not be part of the Founding Fifteen, but she could still leave her mark on this town that she loved so much.

Every time she thought about the hundreds of people over the years that she'd led through the streets of Boneyard Key who had then gone home with their heads full of stories that she now knew were inaccurate, she was a little sick to her stomach.

She'd lied to so many people. Sophie hated lies.

"Anyway," Theo added. "He mentioned he was planning to do a soft opening in the next week or so. Which seems quick to me, if he was just picking up research books."

"Bold of you to assume he was actually doing research."

Theo snorted. "Bet he's got a hitchhiking ghost story planned."

A giggle burst out of Sophie, and she clapped a hand over her mouth. "Maybe a guy with a hook for a hand?"

"Oh, for sure." Now Theo's smile was a grin. "Probably lurks under the fishing pier, or some crap like that." Her giggle became a full-throated laugh, and Sophie found herself regretting those years she'd thought that Theo Berington was an aloof asshole. He was just quiet. And particular.

Theo turned back to his work, but Sophie's gaze wandered around the room at the displays and framed photographs that composed the museum. There was a grouping of pictures of the old graveyard out on Cemetery Island, showing its condition over the years. Her gaze snagged on a painting on the wall right over their heads. Well, right over Theo's head. He always chose the chair underneath this painting. It was a portrait of a woman wearing a high-necked dress, a cameo at her throat. Her blond hair cascaded in a long swoop over her right shoulder, and her deep blue eyes stared at something in the distance.

"Who's that?" She indicated the painting.

"I don't know." Theo's face softened as he studied it, his eyes tracing the lines of the woman's face. "I wish I did, though." The words were soft, and Sophie blinked in confusion. She'd never heard him talk about something—or someone—with so much yearning before. Was it the unsolved mystery? Or the woman in the painting herself?

He shook his head once, hard, then turned back to Sophie. "It was a donation to the museum. The Monahans found it in the attic when they sold the house and weren't able to tie it to any of their ancestors, so they thought I might want it for the museum."

"It fits in here really well." Sophie moved to his side of the table, peering up at the painting. "What's that signature there?"

Theo followed her gaze. "Oh, that's the artist. Niilo James Lewis. I did some research on him. Finnish-American painter in the late nineteenth and early twentieth century. Mostly portraits. So that all tracks, but doesn't get me any closer to finding out who she was."

"Hmmm." The woman was beautiful, and something in her blue eyes sparkled with amusement. They reminded Sophie a little of Tristan, but she banished that thought as soon as it formed. "She must have lived here in Boneyard Key at some point, right?"

"I'm sure she did," Theo said. "Maybe back when it was Fisherton. On the original island."

"Could be." Sophie's voice was small. Something about that made her sad. It made her acutely aware of her aunt Alice, and how Sophie was the only descendant she had. Once Sophie was gone, who would remember Aunt Alice? Who would remember Sophie?

"Anyway." Theo cleared his throat as he turned back to his file. "I talked to Mrs. Erikson over at Eternal Rest. She has some documentation of the family's history, dating back to when they bought the motel in the 1930s. Once I get it I'll cross-check it with what we have here. If you remember, Mr. Lindsay said in *Haunted History* that there wasn't any activity at all there. So we've got lots of new ground to cover."

Sophie nodded. "Something else I've noticed? Mystic Crystals."

"The crystal shop? On the corner there across from Spooky Brew?" He pushed his glasses up his nose, eyes narrowing as he thought. "I don't think they're in the book."

"Exactly." She flipped through the pages of *Haunted History* quickly, like an answer would jump out at her. "A member of that family's been doing psychic readings in the front parlor there for generations, and it doesn't get a mention? Doesn't that seem suspicious?" She didn't wait for confirmation; she knew she was right. "I'm going to talk to Aura about it."

But Sophie wasn't right. There was nothing suspicious at all.

"Sorry, Soph." Aura shook her head, her dark purple-brown hair swinging down her back, her eyes sympathetic. "There's not a lot to tell. My great-great-great-grandma"—she counted off the *great*s on her fingers—"died in the Great Storm, and she's stuck around ever since. I mean, yeah, we monetized it. So there's always a Keefe doing readings up front. Right now it's my mom and my aunt Susie, trading off."

"And eventually, it'll be you." Sophie knew how that went. The Keefes were one of the Founding Fifteen—descendants of the families that stayed behind after the Great Storm destroyed the original settlement. Those families by and large had psychic abilities that Sophie couldn't even imagine.

Aura's smile slipped a fraction. "Yep," she said. "Eventually."

"And they're just . . . talking to great-great-great-Grandma."

"Something like that. She's good at delivering the other-side gossip."

A loud squawk came from behind Aura, and they both turned their attention to the bright blue-and-gold macaw sitting behind Aura on a high perch.

"Einstein," Aura said in a chiding voice. "Can't you see I'm talking?" The bird ducked her head, looking almost shamefaced. "Sorry," Aura said to Sophie. "She craves attention."

"I remember." Einstein had practically been the mascot of their high school class, spending much of the day on Aura's shoulder, headbutting in a bid for snuggles or attention.

Now the bird climbed from her perch to Aura's shoulder, and Sophie stretched up on her tiptoes to lean across the counter, stroking the macaw's beak with a fingertip as she thought of her next question.

"But if that's been going on for all this time, why isn't it in the book?"

Aura shrugged. "No idea. That book was written way before our generation. But I know the family was glad to be left out of it. Who knows what kind of relationship my folks had with the Lindsays. My theory . . ." Aura raised her eyebrows. "Do you want to know my theory?"

"Of course I do." Sophie straightened up. There was nothing like Boneyard Key gossip; there was always at least one haunting involved. Would this be something she could use? Einstein, missing the attention, shifted his weight from one foot to another, making Aura wince slightly.

"Einstein, knock it off. Anyway, I think that Triple G had some dirt on the Lindsay family. You know how they all moved away after he retired from teaching?" She touched her forefinger to her nose as though passing along a secret. "Running from something, I think."

"So I shouldn't make the house a stop on my tour?"

Aura laughed. "God, please no. And if you're really revising the book, you can leave us out of that too."

"Deal." Sophie's phone dinged in her pocket, and she knew without looking it was going to be Libby. It was Thursday night, and

Sophie was running late. She fired off a quick text (Next door at the crystal shop, be right there) before turning back to Aura. "Hey, you don't happen to like bad reality television, do you? Libby and I are heading over to Cassie's place to watch *Romance Resort*. We've got pizza and wine."

Aura laughed and shook her head. "Another time maybe. I'm heading out for sunset yoga down at the beach. I was just about to close up when you came in." She walked Sophie out, Einstein the macaw along for the ride on Aura's shoulder. "Hey," she said as she was locking up behind them. "What do you know about this new ghost tour in town?"

Not her too. "Nothing." Sophie's voice was sharper than she wanted it to be. "I know nothing."

"Hmmm." Aura's tone echoed Sophie's. "I'll tell you this. If he brings his tour down this way? I'm gonna mess with him."

"Oh," Sophie said. "No." There was no sense of urgency behind her words. She tried again. "Don't mess with him." Nope. That wasn't much better.

"Mess with who?" Libby was down on the sidewalk, a bottle of red wine in her hand.

"Tristan," Sophie said as though she were announcing the Grim Reaper.

"That new ghost tour," Aura said. "I'm gonna mess with him."

Libby did what Sophie could not. She grinned. "Good."

Aura left them with a cheerful wave, yoga mat under her arm and bird on her shoulder, while Sophie and Libby started up Beachside.

"What was that all about?" Libby asked. "I didn't know you hung out with Aura." She sounded incredulous, and Sophie could understand. When they'd all been in high school together, Aura had been cooler than everyone else put together. Aloof too. She was friendly and all, she just . . . did her own thing.

"Just doing some fact-checking," Sophie said. "Did you know Mystic Crystals isn't mentioned in *Haunted History* anywhere?"

"It isn't, is it?" Libby tilted her head while she thought. "You'd think he would have mentioned Triple G, at least. Nan went over there a few weeks ago to check up on her, and she still doesn't want to move on. Apparently, she likes being the TMZ of the afterlife."

"Is it okay to be telling me that?" It felt perilously close to a HIPAA violation.

But Libby was unconcerned. "Eh, it's just ghost gossip. I bet Triple G wouldn't mind."

The sun was low in the sky as they got to Cassie's place, and Sophie still felt an aftershock of a shiver when she walked up the porch stairs. Her whole life, this had been the house in town to avoid, reportedly haunted by a malevolent spirit. Now that had been all cleared up (Sophie had even been there for the exorcism), and it seemed like Sarah Hawkins had forgiven Sophie for telling the story wrong all this time. Thank goodness. She was pretty sure Hallmark didn't make a card to say, *Sorry I told every tourist who forked over fifteen bucks that you were a murderer and terrible person.*

Cassie had ordered in pizza, and Libby brought the wine, so all Sophie had to do was show up. Time to stop worrying about Tristan and his ghost tour and enjoy a night of bad television with her best friends.

"Are we ready for the new season?" Cassie ushered them inside. "I read that they're going to make the sexy singles actually work at the resort this time."

"Are you serious?" Libby said. She opened a kitchen drawer, rummaging for the corkscrew. "That makes no sense. Why would you cover up eight-pack abs with a bellhop outfit?"

"Maybe they just have to wear the little hat." Sophie flipped open the pizza box and started laying out slices on paper plates. They made themselves at home on *Romance Resort* nights.

A spoon on the counter clattered to the floor, and on cue all three of them looked to the refrigerator. The door of Cassie's fridge was covered in little magnetic poetry words, most of which were scattered in random patterns, but a few were lined up in the middle. Those words were how Sarah Hawkins had been able to make herself known, back when Cassie had first moved in.

stupid idea

boys should be naked

"Sarah!" Cassie squealed through a scandalized laugh as she accepted a glass of wine from Libby.

"Someone's horny tonight." Libby tossed her blond ponytail over her shoulder.

"No comment." But Cassie looked smug, which was a comment all on its own.

"Did Nick already flee to The Cold Spot?" Because the last thing Sophie wanted was Nick strolling downstairs during their girls' night.

Cassie nodded. "He was gone before the pizza got here." They each picked up a loaded paper plate and made their way into the living room.

"Still can't get him into *Romance Resort*, huh?" Libby settled into one of the armchairs that flanked the sofa, tucking her feet under her and balancing her plate of pizza on her knee.

"Nope," Cassie said cheerfully as she aimed the remote at the television. "And that's fine. It'd be boring if we liked all the same stuff." The familiar, cheesy synth-pop that was the opening theme of *Romance Resort* blared out into the living room, and Sophie took a bite of pizza with a happy sigh. There was nothing better than a night with her girls.

There was one slice of pizza and less than a glass of wine left when the episode was over. Libby leaned forward on the sofa, reaching for that last slice of pizza, when her phone buzzed on the coffee table. She picked it up and frowned.

"Ah, crap. I gotta go." The words were said lightly, but there was a pinch between her eyebrows that Sophie didn't like.

"Everything okay?"

"Yeah . . ." But her voice wavered. "It's Nan," she finally said with a sigh. "She hasn't been feeling great lately, and I told her to let me know if she needs me." She glanced at the screen again before clicking it off and stowing it away. "And apparently she needs me."

"Let me know if we can do anything," Cassie said with a concerned frown.

Sophie nodded in solidarity as she got to her feet. "I'll walk you home."

"I'll be okay." Libby waved her off. "Who gets mugged on Beachside?" She was obviously aiming for a joke, but her smile was watery, and Sophie let her go with a quick, tight hug.

After Libby left, Sophie stayed to help clean up. Not that there were many dishes—three wineglasses and some paper plates that went in the trash.

"I hope Nan's okay." Cassie frowned as she rinsed out the wine bottle to put into the recycling. "She's the toughest old lady I've ever met."

"She's one of a kind." Sophie's mind was filled with memories of her years growing up with Libby. Aunt Alice and Nan were close friends, so Libby and Sophie stuck together a lot. First by necessity, and soon out of genuine friendship. She didn't want to think about anything happening to Nan. That would be too much. She blinked hard at the wineglass in her hand and scrubbed at it with the dish towel a little harder than necessary.

"So tell me . . ." Cassie took the last freshly dried wineglass from Sophie and stretched on her toes to put it on the upper shelf in the cabinet. "What's up with that new ghost tour in town?"

Sophie groaned. What a terrible subject change. But at least this time she could be honest with her feelings. "I'm mostly trying to pretend it's not happening." She folded up the pizza box more aggressively than was necessary before shoving it into the trash. "That's the mature and professional way to handle it, right?"

Cassie snorted. "Absolutely. How's it all going to work, though? Nick and I were talking about it the other night, and he said the next couple weeks will be crazy busy, with spring break, but then it dries up, right? Until the summer season? How are there going to be enough tourists to fill up two ghost tours?"

"That's the part I'm trying not to think about." Sophie sighed. It had been really nice there; for an hour or so she hadn't been thinking about Tristan and the hit her business was about to take. "Because honestly? There definitely won't be enough people. I'm not sure what—"

Her words were cut off by the spoon, the one that lived on the countertop for Sarah to knock off when she had something to say. Sure enough, there were new words in the middle of the fridge.

wrong

again

outside

"Wrong again outside?" Sophie said the words out loud as though she could make them make sense that way.

"Wait." Cassie froze, kitchen towel tangled in her hands. "Do you hear that? Outside. It sounds like . . ." She looked at Sophie. "Well, if you weren't standing right here I'd think it's your ghost tour going by." Her eyes widened. "Oh my god. Is it *him*?"

"On a *Thursday*?" For some reason, that was the thing Sophie's brain snagged on. Who the hell would do a ghost tour on a Thursday?

"Come on." Cassie ditched the towel and grasped Sophie's wrist. They went up the stairs and into the front bedroom, leaving the light off so they wouldn't be seen. "We can watch from up here."

"Do you do this when my tour goes by?" Sophie didn't love the idea of being spied on.

"Sometimes." A smile played around her mouth. "Usually I just leave the downstairs window open so Sarah can hear." Cassie held a finger to her lips as she eased open the door and they crept silently onto the balcony, keeping to the shadows to watch the show below.

And there was quite a show. Tristan's period costume was just like the one on the website, down to the top hat. He led a group of six, more than Sophie would expect on a weeknight; during the slow season she'd done tours as small as two or three. (There'd been that one time that a singular guy had shown up. He gave her an up-and-down look and suggested he buy her a drink. Sophie instead went home to another sausage-and-pepperoni pizza.) They were stopped on the sidewalk in front of Cassie's house, and he was midway through whatever story he was telling.

"You see that balcony up there?" He raised his lantern—he actually had a freaking lantern, just like on his website—up in their direction, making Cassie and Sophie shrink backwards, pressing their backs to the clapboard siding to avoid detection. "There's one just like it on the other side of the house, looking out into the sea. That's where, on summer nights when the moon is full, they say you can see the apparition of poor Arabella, pacing the balcony and gazing out into the water. Hoping that someday her pirate love will return to her."

"What?" Sophie kept her voice as low as possible, the word little more than an exhale.

Cassie's snort was loud in Sophie's ear. "Who the fuck is Arabella?"

Their exchange didn't seem to carry down to the street, because no one reacted. Or maybe they were all too caught up in that ridiculous story Tristan was telling. Sophie noticed more than one happy sigh as a middle-aged woman pressed her hand to her heart, wearing a dreamy smile. Her husband put his arm around her, and they strolled slowly after the group, bringing up the reluctant rear as Tristan led them north, toward the Starter Home and the fishing pier.

Sophie could barely contain her outrage. He was going the wrong way—the opposite route that she took. And what was with these stories? There had never been a single report of a pirate in Boneyard Key. No one named Arabella had ever lived in Hawkins House; that Sophie knew for sure.

That was confirmed when they went back downstairs. Sarah Hawkins had left new words on the fridge. And she was pissed.

lies

wrong name

stupid

"I agree," Cassie said with a sympathetic nod. "It's all stupid."

"Incredibly stupid. He's getting it all wrong." Sophie was incensed. Which was ironic, since she herself had spent years telling the wrong story about the Hawkins House. But it felt wrong to let someone else get away with the same crime she'd once committed.

She knew this much: Boneyard Key wasn't big enough for two ghost tours. And Sophie was here first. Tristan was going to have to pack his stupid top hat and go.

Eight

Tristan knew this much: Boneyard Key wasn't big enough for two ghost tours.

He did his best. He'd never planned a route more meticulously, doing everything he could to not run into Sophie and her tour. But it was like two people trying to brush their teeth at the same time in an airplane bathroom: constantly bumping shoulders and never enough room.

The first couple weeks were awkward, the way they always were. But Eric did a little fine-tuning of the online advertising. A few ads boosted in the right places had resulted in decent-size groups, and the audience only built from there. Now he was leading sold-out crowds through Boneyard Key on Saturday nights. Friday was slightly less crowded, and Thursdays had been a joke—they'd cut those pretty quick.

Tristan's heart always beat a little bit faster on Friday nights as he adjusted his cravat in the mirror by the door. No matter how many tours he'd led at this point in however many cities, every Friday felt like opening night. He ran an anxious hand through his hair, making sure it lay just right even though it was going to spend most of the night underneath his top hat. Then he shrugged into his tailcoat. How long was he going to be able to wear this costume in the

Florida heat? Actual pants were bad enough, but the dress shirt / waistcoat / cravat / coat combo was an insane amount of layers. He was going to sweat himself to death in July.

On the walk to the pier, he calmed his racing heart by reminding himself that he knew the script inside and out. He could do this. It was easy to pretend that the trickle of sweat on his lower back, creeping toward his waistband, had everything to do with Florida's humidity and nothing to do with this new beginning. So much was riding on this Boneyard Key location becoming a success, but he couldn't afford to think about that right now. The seventeen people waiting for him at the pier wanted a fun Friday-night outing, and he was here to provide that.

He adjusted his top hat, settling it firmly onto his head, and turned on his LED lantern. Showtime.

He led the group down Beachside Drive, his nervousness falling away as he slipped into his character as a nineteenth-century gentleman—or maybe he was a ghost? He liked to keep it ambiguous—tipping his hat to the ladies, walking backwards while facing the crowd, glancing over his shoulder occasionally so that he didn't run into anything.

"Now, right here—" He stopped at random in front of a closed-up storefront, barely glancing in the window. It didn't matter what kind of shop it was. This was a Florida tourist town; odds were good that it was one of the many T-shirt shops Sophie had joked about his first night in town. The night they'd met.

Sophie. The fleeting thought of her brought with it the usual twinge of guilt, along with the usual quickening of his heartbeat. Tristan willed them both away. Plenty of time to think on her later.

"Right here," he said again as he refocused, "we have one of the friendlier spirits in town. You ever hear the phrase 'work yourself to death'? Well, the entity here took it quite literally. A few decades ago, this very shop was the local pharmacy . . ." His voice trailed off as he took in the shop window he'd chosen tonight. Mostly T-shirts, some flags, a fine selection of trucker hats. The most prominent T-shirt read I Went to Boneyard Key and All I Got Was Ghosted. He hadn't seen that shirt yet, and now that he had he couldn't wait to add it to his collection.

Regroup, Martin. Regroup. "You know the kind," he said smoothly. "Kindly old pharmacist, soda fountain in the corner? Even a jukebox. The pharmacist loved his job. So much that one day, he just keeled over at work, right there behind the counter. His death was, of course, mourned by the whole town, but as time marched on, the pharmacy went away, replaced by the shop you see here. No one told the pharmacist that, though. They say on certain nights you can see him inside, behind what used to be his counter. Employees come in the next morning to find a bottle of aspirin next to the register. But the thing is"—he paused for dramatic effect—"this place doesn't sell aspirin. That's old Mr. Middleton, still trying to help out."

He gave a grin and a tip of his hat, leading the group down the street. A couple people lingered behind, cupping their hands around their eyes, peering inside the window, trying to get a glimpse. There was nothing to see, of course. Tristan had made that story up, back in college after a late-night viewing of *It's a Wonderful Life*. It was just specifically old-fashioned enough to be a good story, but generic enough to tell in every town. In fact, he'd probably stopped in front of a different shop when he'd told the story the weekend before. It didn't matter; it was all about entertainment.

And entertain he did, all the way down Beachside Drive, past The Haunt, pausing in front of a shop on the corner that sold crystals and other New Age trinkets. The sign out front said MYSTIC CRYSTALS. It was a great building—one of those Sears kit houses that were so common in the early twentieth century. Tristan had spotted a few of those here in town: solid, square buildings with covered front porches and squared-off columns.

But the tourists weren't here for a lesson in architecture. "This may look like an unassuming shop, but it houses a terrible secret." He gestured with his lantern, pitching his voice low as though telling a campfire story. "As you can see, it used to be a private residence. In fact, it was home to Boneyard Key's most prominent doctor. A genial old sawbones, but his wife was the jealous type. Every time he headed out on a house call, she was sure he was cheating. One night it got to be too much for her. You know the phrase, 'physician, heal thyself'? Turns out, there's no healing thyself from poison.

"In fact, when he—" Tristan turned back to the house and his voice simply stopped working. When he'd started his story, the house had been dark, the shop obviously closed up for the night. But now there was a light in an upper window. A greenish glow, surrounding a shadowy figure that had suddenly appeared in the window. While his jaw went slack and his group gasped behind him, the figure slowly raised an arm. In greeting? In censure? Tristan didn't want to stick around to find out. In fact, he wanted to pack his stuff and get the hell out of town.

"Now if you'll follow me . . ." Tristan mentally shoved down his fight-or-flight response. "We'll cross the street here and head back up Beachside Drive." His voice sounded too loud, too tinny in his ears, and his heart beat so fast, so loud, that it made his breath shudder.

"Did you see that?" A man Tristan's father's age turned around, keeping his eyes on the house and its green, glowing occupant. The two teenage boys with him scoffed.

"It's a trick, Dad." The kid sounded bored, but the apparition had at least gotten him off his phone. "This guy probably set it up. Ghosts aren't real."

That's right, Tristan reminded himself and his spiking blood pressure. *Ghosts aren't real.* He surreptitiously took some deep breaths as they headed up the street, and once they reached the vacant lot next to the Chamber of Commerce, he was feeling back to normal and ready for his next story.

"This particular plot of land is haunted. There have been three separate buildings here over the last hundred years, and each one has burned down." Was that true? Probably not. He didn't care. "The townsfolk here finally got the message, and now they keep the land vacant. These coffee and ice cream carts are open during the day, but as you can see, they're on wheels, so maybe the ghosts don't count them as permanent structures. It seems that we found a loophole, making everyone happy: both the living and the dead!"

A couple of chuckles in response to this story. Okay. Good. Tristan felt back in control. They continued up the street, and mentally Tristan was rubbing his hands together in glee. It was time for his favorite part, which was one of the reasons he saved it for last. The yellow house at the end of the street, before the bend in the road that took them back to the pier. The first time he'd walked past that house he'd fallen in love with the little balconies off the bedrooms, and it had been so easy to spin a story about a pirate and his lady, who watches for him from the balcony that faces the Gulf.

"As I'm sure you know, the Gulf of Mexico isn't too far from Cuba and the Caribbean. And what was the Caribbean full of in the olden days? You Disney fans will know this one."

Silence. Damn. He thought the Disney reference would have been a good giveaway.

"Fish?" someone finally ventured.

"Hurricanes?"

"Pirates!" a young boy in the back finally shouted. Tristan pointed at him.

"Yes! Got it in one!" Well, they got it in three, but Tristan wasn't going to quibble. "This particular one was called Reed Bonney, known far and wide as Reed the Ruthless." Tristan had used parts of this story before, particularly on his tour in the Outer Banks in North Carolina, where memories were full of Blackbeard and a pirate ghost story was expected. But whereas in those places he told a story of a terrifying pirate who met a satisfactory—if gruesome—end, here Tristan wanted to tell a more romantic story. Maybe he was getting more sentimental in his late twenties. Sue him.

"But this pirate had one weakness . . ."

"Rum!" the same boy shouted, even though this wasn't an audience participation portion of the tour.

"Women!" That came from a man in the crowd, who was presumably the boy's father. He looked down at the kid with an indulgent smile. "What do you know about rum?"

"Well, you've got it right," Tristan said to the man. "But not just women in general. There was one particular woman, who he had been madly in love with, though she was married to another. Her name was Arabella, and she lived in this very house. Reed the Ruthless and Arabella would meet in secret, under the light of the full moon, and they would—"

"*Bullshit!*" The word was a shriek, from behind him, and for the second time that night Tristan was startled into silence. His mind whirled to impossible things: Had the green ghost from the crystal shop followed them? Did the yellow house have a ghost too, and now he'd pissed it off? Neither of those things seemed likely, and yet . . .

Slowly he turned around, and . . . oh, no.

Sophie.

Standing right there on the sidewalk, a gaggle of tourists behind her. They'd obviously come from the north side of town, and now the two tour groups had practically collided on the sidewalk in front of this little yellow house.

While Sophie glared at him, her mouth set in a tight, thin line, Tristan grasped for his ghost tour guide character. Hard to do when he'd been scared shitless twice over the course of ten minutes. "Excuse me, milady," he finally managed while Sophie tried to set him on fire with her mind. "I don't think I heard you correctly." He tipped his hat in her direction, and from the way her mouth screwed up and her nostrils flared, that was the exact wrong thing to do.

Sophie's dark eyes practically blazed from behind her glasses. "Bull. Shit." She enunciated the hell out of the word, turning it into two, as though maybe he hadn't heard her the first time she'd screamed it. His ears were still ringing. "What is *wrong* with you? There's no pirate here. There's never been a pirate here."

He laughed, a loud, forced sound, trying desperately to drown out her words and save face in front of his group. "Oh, I know *that*. If you'll let me finish the story, you'll hear that it's not the pirate, but Arabella who—"

"I've heard the story." Her voice was ice, her words little chips flying in his direction.

"You . . . you have?" Confusion made him drop all pretense at character. "When?" He certainly would have remembered if Sophie had been in the audience.

She didn't answer either of his questions. "There's never been a pirate," she said again. "There's never been an Arabella. You're leading these people through the town and you're telling them *lies*. You should be ashamed."

Tristan blinked. He wanted nothing more than to defuse the situation, but the laugh he forced up from the depths of his chest was awkward at best. "We're all just out here for some fun, and you—"

"Bullshit!" she said again, with a vehemence that said she'd just discovered the word, and she wanted to use it as many times as possible. "Your tour is bullshit! Your stupid top hat, that's bullshit too. Everything about you . . ." She waved a hand in a circle, encompassing his costume, his lantern, his entire being. "You. You especially are bullshit."

"I'm bullshit?" Now that the adrenaline had drained from his bloodstream, this was getting funny. The more flustered Sophie appeared, the more times she said the word *bullshit*, the more ridiculous she looked. As long as he stayed calm, he'd have the upper hand in this. "Is that even a sentence?"

"Not really," said the dad behind him, and oh. For a few seconds there Tristan had forgotten that it wasn't just him and Sophie, facing each other on the street like gunslingers about to duel at high noon. But now he looked over Sophie's shoulder at her group. More than half of them had their phones out, trained on the two of them. He glanced over his shoulder; five pinpricks of light showed that some of his group was filming too. This fight, this showdown of the ghost tour groups, was likely to be all over social media by the end of the night.

Sophie yelling at him could go viral.

Tristan couldn't believe this.

It was fucking *fantastic*.

Nine

What a night.

Sophie had never felt so humiliated. It was like she'd blacked out, seeing Tristan with his tour group, ready to tell that stupid story about the pirate in front of the Hawkins House. After unloading on him, she'd expected Tristan to be shamefaced. Maybe even mad at her. But instead he'd looked over her shoulder at her tour group, then over his shoulder at his. When he turned back to her a slow smile spread over his face, taking her in like she was something cute or funny, and not a pissed-off adult woman. Sophie was used to that. "You're cute when you're angry" was a phrase that seemed to be made for her.

It wasn't until the darkest of her rage had cleared that she realized what she'd done: absolutely unloaded on this guy, not only in public but in front of an audience. Two audiences. That had their cell phones out.

Oh, no.

She'd turned back to her group, aghast, while Tristan took advantage of her shift in focus to get his group the hell out of there. She'd tried to cut the tour short and refund everyone's money—even though they were in the homestretch, with more ground behind them than ahead. But the general consensus was that it was the most any of them had been entertained in a while. So she finished the tour, with shaky legs and an even shakier voice, doing her best to keep her composure until they got back to Hallowed Grounds, where Nick could take over.

Even though the tips had been enormous that night, she didn't order pizza when she got home. She didn't deserve pizza. Not after the way she'd behaved. The best thing she could do was try and forget this whole night had ever happened.

But Sophie hadn't counted on the internet.

She'd never been much into social media. Growing up with a great-aunt as a parental figure had admittedly left her with some very old-fashioned ideals. She didn't swear much—that past Friday night notwithstanding—and she didn't spend much of her free time online. Her day job was in front of a computer; the last thing she needed in her life was more screen time. She didn't need Facebook or Instagram to keep up with her high school classmates; most of them either still lived here in town or their families did, so she saw them on holidays or on a random karaoke night at The Haunt.

The first clue that things had gone all wrong came on Monday. Cassie had texted her a little before noon (Lunch?), and that had been all the incentive she'd needed to indulge in a treat from Hallowed Grounds. The weekend had been enough penance; she deserved nice things again, and a very nice thing on a Monday was a lunch she didn't have to make herself. The café was full for a Monday, with lingering three-day weekenders stretching that last day out as long as possible before heading home.

Sophie leaned against the counter, waiting for her turn to order, not paying attention to the low conversation behind her. It didn't concern her. It never concerned her.

Except this time it did.

"Is that her?"

80 JEN DeLUCA

"It is! I was on her tour on Saturday."

The back of Sophie's neck prickled. Oh, no. She froze, while adrenaline coursed through her in a slow-rolling wave. Now that she knew the background conversation was about her, she didn't know how to act. How to stand. Did she look too casual? Not casual enough? Her hands were suddenly heavy at the ends of her arms, and she had no idea what to do with them. These shorts didn't even have pockets.

"Did she lose her shit on Saturday too? Maybe it's a bit or something."

"I thought that too after I saw the video. Like, maybe they stage the fight on purpose, since there are two ghost tours in town? But apparently not. We didn't see the other tour at all."

"Huh. That's too bad."

"Hey." Sophie blinked as she realized that Nick was standing there in front of her, God knows for how long, waiting for her. He looked at her with sympathy, which frankly wasn't like him. "You okay?"

"Yeah, I'm good," she said tightly, her voice betraying that she was not good. She was not good at all.

But Nick, bless him, didn't call her out. Only a raise of his eyebrows gave him away. "You know what you want?" He passed a diet soda across the counter to her.

She had the Hallowed Grounds menu memorized; it wasn't like it was extensive. But her mind was so preoccupied with the conversation behind her and what it might mean that she had no brainspace left. Like she'd never eaten lunch at a café in her life. "Uh . . ." She scanned the blackboard above Nick's head and picked the first thing she saw. "Chicken Caesar wrap, please."

Nick nodded but didn't move. What did he want now? Sophie stared at him blankly until he sighed. "Fries or chips?"

"Oh. Right." This lack of brainspace was becoming alarming. "Fries, please. Extra crispy." It was a trick Libby had taught her. Nothing better than fries burned almost to a crisp.

"I'll bring it right out." Was he smirking when he wrote her order down?

Sophie took her drink with a tight smile and was about to take a sip when she heard her name being called. She turned, shoulders tight, but relaxed almost immediately. Cassie. Right. She was meeting Cassie here. Brainspace was coming back.

Sophie threaded her way through the café, doing her best to ignore the murmurs in her wake, before joining her friend at her back table. Cassie was halfway through a large iced latte, and her plate only held crumbs.

Cassie closed her laptop and set it aside as Sophie settled into the chair across from her. "You doing okay?"

"Why is everyone asking me that today?" Condensation from her glass had made her palm cold and wet, and she pressed her hand to her still-warm cheek. "Friday's tour was a mess, but that happens, right? Doesn't everyone have bad days at work?"

"Well . . ." Nick appeared at her side, sliding her plate in front of her. "Not everyone's bad day at work goes viral."

Cassie nodded emphatically. "Exactly."

"What do you mean?"

Cassie's eyes widened, and she and Nick exchanged a look over Sophie's head. "You don't know?"

"Know what?" She looked from Nick to Cassie and back again while Cassie pulled her phone out of her bag.

"You really should get some actual food for lunch," Nick said while she scrolled through her phone. "You can't live on banana bread alone."

"Then you shouldn't have fed me three slices," Cassie said

absently, still scrolling. She glanced up long enough to wave Nick off with a smile. "I promise I'll eat protein for dinner." She stopped scrolling, making a small, satisfied sound before passing the phone across the table to Sophie.

"I don't need to see this again." Nick fled as Sophie tapped on the video.

Cassie snorted. "Chicken."

But Sophie wasn't listening. She was focused on the video, which had started playing with the sound off. The video was a little dark, but it was easy enough to recognize herself.

Except that she didn't recognize herself. Her eyes were wild, her face screwed up in rage as she stepped closer, getting up in Tristan's face. She watched in growing horror as the Sophie in the video angrily gestured at him and his top hat, before pointing emphatically down the street. She didn't need the sound on; it was easy enough to tell when she said *bullshit* over and over.

"It's everywhere." Cassie's voice was apologetic, and somehow muffled against the dull roar in Sophie's ears. The video ended and then started again, playing in an infinite loop. There she was, angry and yelling. There was Tristan, all amused smile, tipping his top hat in her direction. It was weird, watching the action and remembering how absolutely violent that gesture had made her feel.

Now Sophie looked at the post itself. Over ten thousand likes. A couple hundred comments, and even more shares. Her thumb tapped the comment button, bringing up a white pane full of text, glaring after the relative dark of the video.

"Nope." Cassie leaned across the table, snatching the phone out of Sophie's hand. "We're not reading the comments."

"Why?" Sophie was confused over the sudden loss of the phone. "Are they bad?" What were people saying about her?

"I don't know." She placed the phone face down in the middle of the table. "Because we're not reading the comments."

"She's not wrong," came a voice from behind them.

Oh, no. Not him. The last person Sophie wanted to see. For a fleeting moment, she hoped that she was imagining things, that the stress of seeing that video had caused an auditory hallucination. But Cassie's eyebrows drew together, a line creasing her forehead as she looked just over Sophie's shoulder. And a heartbeat later there he was, pulling out one of the empty chairs at their table and dropping into it like he'd been invited. Like he had every right to be there.

"Hey." He extended his hand across the table to Cassie, a warm smile on his face. "Tristan. Tristan Martin."

Cassie didn't shake his hand. "Hi." She pointedly crossed her arms over her chest, fixing him with an icy look.

He either didn't notice or didn't care. "And she's right." Tristan leaned in toward Sophie with a friendly smile. How had she ever liked that smile? Now she wanted to smack it off his face. "Never read the comments on the internet. It's never worth it. What *is* worth it, though, is that we have gone viral."

"I'm aware," she said, even though she hadn't been aware of the video's existence five minutes ago. Even though she was only vaguely aware of what *going viral* meant.

Tristan nodded emphatically through a sip of his coffee. It was in a to-go cup, which irritated her. Why couldn't he take that to-go coffee and . . . go? "You can't manufacture a viral moment like that." He sounded positively gleeful. "It's organic. And it's raising interest. My website traffic is way up. Isn't yours?" The pointed way he asked the question implied that he knew what her answer would be.

"I don't have a website." She'd never needed one. She'd never even considered it. Not till now. Not till this yahoo came to town.

Tristan squinted at her, as though she was speaking nonsense. "Well, maybe that's not a bad thing. Especially when you hear my offer."

"Your . . . offer?"

Cassie cleared her throat. "This better not be anything dirty."

Tristan's lips quirked in a smile. "All aboveboard, I promise." He focused back on Sophie, and she wished he wouldn't. She really hated the force of his smile. The way it made her want to smile back, even though she hated him. "I don't know about you, but I feel like this town doesn't really need two ghost tours."

Now it was Sophie's turn to cross her arms. "No," she said. She would not smile back at him. "It doesn't."

"I try to time my tour so that we don't run into each other, and we saw how well that went on Friday." He nodded toward Cassie's phone, still in the middle of the table. "Like I said, I'm loving the viral moment, but we can't go on like that."

"We really can't." Something began to prickle on the back of her neck. It felt like . . . relief? Was Tristan here to let her know he was packing up and leaving town? It seemed unlikely, but a girl could dream.

"So . . ." He took another sip of coffee, an action that this time felt deliberate. "I want to offer you a job."

"A . . ." Sophie's mouth went dry. The burgeoning relief drained away, but the prickle at the back of her neck intensified. "A job?" She hated how weak her voice sounded. But this was the opposite of what she was expecting.

Tristan's nod showed that he saw none of her discomfort. "Exactly. You're obviously good at this, so it would make sense for me to bring you on board. Someone's going to have to run this tour for me anyway; I certainly wasn't planning to stick around this backwater forever."

"Hey." Cassie's voice was sharp now. "Some of us like this backwater."

"Of course," he said quickly. "No offense. There's a lot to like about Boneyard Key." Was it her imagination, or did his eyes cut her way during that last sentence?

Nope. Now wasn't the time to think about Tristan's eyes or his smiles. Besides, her fries were getting cold. "What about my tour?" she asked. "My stories?"

He shook his head. "We don't need them. I get that you're going for that whole 'historically accurate' angle"—the air quotes he made were absolutely enraging—"but it's not necessary."

"Why not?" Sophie was puzzled. "It's what happened. Isn't that the point of a tour?"

"Not a *ghost* tour," he said with irritating authority. "Tourists aren't exactly looking for a history lesson while they're on vacation. They're looking for fun, made-up ghost stories."

"Not when you're giving a ghost tour *in a haunted town!*" Sophie was practically shaking with fury, and her voice had gone up an alarming octave. Was he really mansplaining ghost tours to her?

"Listen, I've been honing our scripts for the past five years now. They're almost exactly the same, no matter what city you're in. And audiences love them. Trust me. We sell out everywhere. No, if you come work for me, you'd be using my script."

"So my stories. Everything I've been building for the past six years. It'll all be gone. Like they never existed."

"Well, that's dramatic," he scoffed, but Sophie wasn't listening. The roaring in her ears was back, and it was deafening. Because it was like Theo's painting of a woman that nobody remembered. Like her aunt Alice. Probably, eventually, like Sophie herself. Just another thing that would be lost to history.

Sophie couldn't speak. She couldn't trust herself to. But thankfully Cassie was still there. "I think what she's trying to say here is 'fuck, no.'" She picked up her iced latte and took a pointed sip, raising her eyebrows at Tristan.

Okay, Sophie wouldn't put it like *that*, but the sentiment was there. Her lips quirked up, and that gave her the strength to participate in her own argument. "Thank you very much for the offer," she said as sweetly as she could manage, "but I have no desire to be part of your little endeavor here, which is—"

"Bullshit." His lips curved in a smile. "I remember." He sighed. "Then I guess we're gonna do this the hard way."

Sophie stilled. "What's the hard way?" And why did he make that sound kinda dirty?

"Look, I hate to do this." His tone of voice said he had no problem doing this. "But we can just let the public decide."

"The public." Sophie squinted at him. "Are you wanting to put it to a vote?" Was he insane? Everyone in town knew her. Who was he going to get over to his side?

His chuckle as he shook his head was as irritating as it was condescending. "You run your tour, and I'll run mine. Eventually we'll be able to tell who's selling more tickets. Who's more popular." He leaned back in his chair oh so casually, as though he weren't talking about destroying the thing that was practically Sophie's identity in this town. Who would she be around here if she wasn't the ghost tour girl?

Not time to go there yet, though. Focus on the present. "And what if mine is more popular?"

Tristan's shrug was a slow roll of his shoulders, unconcerned.

"Then I'll close mine down and move on. I have no desire to keep a failing location going. Let's see how things are on . . ." His voice trailed off while he thought. "How about the end of September? We should be able to tell by then."

"Fine." Sophie was ready for this conversation to be over. She didn't want to think about closing down her business. But she had to admit he had a point. If people really did prefer his tour to hers, maybe she should pay attention to that.

Tristan extended his hand like a peace offering. "May the best ghost tour win."

"Excited for you to leave this fall." Sophie did her best to keep her grip firm. As firm as her resolve to send this guy packing by October.

Cassie remained silent until Tristan had left, taking his coffee with him. "Well. He's cute."

"Cute?" Sophie couldn't believe this. "Were you not listening? He's trying to put me out of business!"

"Oh, please." Her dismissive wave reminded Sophie of the way Tristan had dismissed her claim of historical accuracy. "There's no way you're going to lose. You're the hometown hero. Everyone loves you. They're gonna support you in this."

"Yeah." She had a good point. "Plus, I have accuracy on my side. He just makes up stuff. Who wants a tour full of fake information?"

"Exactly." Cassie gave a decisive nod. "I mean, pirates are great and all, but not if they're made-up."

"And he's wearing a *costume*, for God's sake. Turning the whole thing into a . . . I don't know. A *show*."

"Which just makes the crowds rowdier, and no one likes that." Cassie's smile slipped as she chewed on the inside of her cheek. "The groups that passed the house last week were super loud. Laughing a lot . . ." Her voice trailed off and then she visibly shook herself. "But who cares about that, right? Like you said, you have accuracy on your side!"

Cassie was doing her best to sound supportive, but somehow she managed to make *accuracy* sound like *nerdy and boring.*

Oh, God. Sophie was totally screwed, wasn't she?

She crunched down on one of her extra-crispy fries. Cold. Of course.

Ten

Tristan should be feeling good. The tour was off to a great start, and while there was a competitor, he felt confident that he'd be able to run Sophie out of town, so to speak, in no time. He had the power of the internet on his side, and he knew how to turn a viral moment into ticket sales. He'd already remixed some of the video of Sophie yelling at him in the street and turned it into a sponsored ad. *See what all the fuss is about! Have a Ghouls Night Out in Boneyard Key!* The ad ended with a slo-mo clip of him tipping his hat. He was already sold out for the next three weekends.

But despite all this, Tristan felt like the world's biggest shit-heel. Because when Eric had checked in this afternoon with the latest sales numbers and projections, every time he went over the Boneyard Key script to prepare for the next weekend's tours, all Tristan could think of was Sophie's face the night they'd met. Those big brown eyes, that smile. Her bright sunny nature as she led her ghost tour, a disposition that outshone the moon above them. He remembered the way they'd leaned into each other, sitting together at the bar at The Haunt. She'd absolutely captivated him, and he'd wanted to know more. He'd wanted to know everything.

And then he remembered her face the day before, sitting across the table from him at Hallowed Grounds. She looked disgusted, as though he was something unpleasant on the bottom of her shoe. And beneath that, she looked betrayed. Sad. It had taken every single trick he'd learned in every single acting class he'd ever taken to look unconcerned. To look like shutting her down was his primary goal.

Making her look that sad was the hardest thing he'd ever done.

But if he was going to show his father that he could run a successful business, he had to see this through. It didn't mean he had to do it completely on his own, though, he reasoned as he pulled up his father's number on his phone. Asshole or not, Sebastian Martin was a genius when it came to business. Maybe he'd have a solution for navigating this tricky ethical dilemma.

Tristan had forgotten. His dad didn't give a shit about ethics.

"This is great news!" Tristan could count on one hand the number of times that his father had sounded pleased with him, and he would still have enough fingers to flip off said father. But tonight, all he'd had to do was call and let dear old Dad know that he was on the verge of crushing a competing small business.

"Yeah, it really is." He imbued as much enthusiasm into his voice as he could. All he had to do was not think about Sophie's stricken face when he suggested she close up shop. "I'm totally going to crush her." Nope. Impossible. How could he not think about Sophie?

Meanwhile, Sebastian Martin couldn't sound happier. "That's my boy. So what's the plan?" But he kept speaking, even as Tristan took a breath to answer. "Here's what you do. First, make sure you set up a shared spreadsheet, so you can both enter in your numbers each week. That way, you can keep track of how she's doing. Then, it's time to cut prices on your tour. Whatever she charges? Charge five dollars less. Not forever, of course. But you want to undercut her for now. Even that little bit will make people more likely to take your tour than hers. Bump up your advertising too. Florida during spring break is one of the peak tourist seasons, so you opened at just the right time."

"Huh," Tristan said dryly. "Almost like I planned it that way."

The sarcasm flew right over his head. "Then once you've established yourself and run her out of town, you can raise your prices ten dollars. Increase the profit margin."

Yeah, his father had been the exact wrong person to call to discuss ethics. Tristan fought against a sigh. This phone call had been a mistake. He wanted to hang up. Throw his phone into the Gulf of Mexico. Call the whole thing off, see if he could take Sophie to dinner instead.

"And while you're at it, see if you can run into her again."

Tristan started. "What?" Had his dad read his mind through the phone?

But no. He wasn't talking about Tristan taking Sophie out. "I'm not fully on board with all that social media stuff. But it seems to be the way the next generation does business, and I'm not going to sneeze at that. You said that first video went viral? A second one should do the same, right?"

"Sometimes. Not always." Tristan pinched the bridge of his nose; here came the headache again. "You can't force something to go viral. People can smell a staged moment a mile away."

"Hmm. Well, I'll leave that to you. It sounds like you have a good plan. Better than this other person, anyway."

Tristan had to snort at that. "That's not too hard." He hit the speaker button and left the phone on the kitchen counter, crossing to the fridge to get a beer. "She doesn't seem to have a plan. I had no idea she was here."

"I thought you did your research first? You always—"

"I did." He popped the cap, letting it clatter into the sink, and took a swig. "You can't find her on the internet anywhere. The guy at the coffee shop writes down a list of people who want to take her tour. Then she shows up on a Friday night and people just hand her cash. She could be doing so much better if she had some kind of business plan. But operating like this . . . it's like she's self-sabotaging." Something about that frustrated him. Like an itch between his shoulder blades that he couldn't quite reach.

"From the sounds of things, you won't have to deal with her much longer." His father sounded positively gleeful at the prospect. "Once you've run her out of business, I bet she'll change her mind about working for you." His father was still talking. "And you'll be in a position of power at that point. Offer her twenty percent less than you were originally going to. What choice will she have?"

"Right." Tristan felt about as gleeful as if he were at a funeral. After hanging up with his father, the condo was quiet. Way too quiet. He leaned his elbows on the counter and picked at the label on his beer bottle.

He hated to admit it, but his father had a point. The best thing Tristan could do, business-wise, was stage another confrontation. Sophie was super sensitive (oh wow, he didn't like that his brain instantly wondered what else she might be sensitive about, or where else she might be sensitive . . . nope, not going there), so if he could time it so their tours collided again, she would easily take the bait. It would be so easy to goad her into another confrontation. Another viral moment.

But God, the idea was depressing. Depressing, and unnecessary. This whole competition thing was already like shooting fish in a barrel. All he had to do was stick to his business plan, the one that he and Eric had started way back on that living room floor in the fraternity house. That was what worked. He didn't need to cheat.

As the weeks went by, Tristan's early-morning runs happened

earlier and earlier. Once spring break was over and late spring in Florida turned tourist traffic into a trickle, he was setting his alarm clock earlier than he'd ever thought humanly possible. But one of the first things he'd learned was that if he wanted to get a decent run in, he'd have to be winding down by the time the sun was fully up. It was still dark when he laced up his sneakers, the faux gas lamps winking out around him as he jogged up Beachside Drive toward the fishing pier. He let his feet take him up almost to the highway, hooking right at the last possible moment onto a side street and heading back toward the downtown historic district. Another right at the Supernatural Market and down that street, past Simpson Investigations (who needed a private detective in a town this small?) and the crystal shop on his left (good time for a sprint, he thought as he remembered that weird glow in the upper window that one night) and Spooky Brew on his right, and he was back on Beachside again. A couple laps of this section of town added up to a 5K, which was plenty this early in the morning.

He ended his run at the fishing pier, slowing to a jog as he hit the wooden boards, then to a walk when he got to the end. The sun was up by now, watery rays of early-morning sunlight reflecting off the water. He bent at the waist, catching his breath, before mopping his forehead, his face, with the bottom of his shirt. The sun was already prickling his scalp and gently burning his arms. Time to head home.

The walk back to the condo was meant to be a pleasant cooldown from the morning's run, but he hadn't counted on being accosted right there at the edge of the pier.

"Got a bone to pick with you, boy."

Tristan froze at the deep, rumbling voice that seemed to come out of nowhere, and his mind scrambled. What ghost stories had Sophie told at the pier? Was this one of them now, come to life to yell at him? Despite all these years running ghost tours, Tristan had never believed in ghosts. But now, standing on this pier, cold sweat making his shirt stick to his back, he wondered if maybe he should.

A couple frantic heartbeats later, he saw the old guy leaning against the side of the bait shack. JIMMY's was painted not far above his head, apparently sometime in the last century. Not a ghost, then.

Tristan tried on a pleasant smile, though his heart was still hammering against his ribs. "Jimmy, I take it?"

"That's me." He pushed off the wall, taking a swig from the soda can in his hand. Sunlight glinted off metallic gold, and even from this distance the can looked familiar. Miller High Life. Not soda, then. His grandfather used to drink that beer; Tristan didn't even know they still made that shit. "We need to have a talk." He didn't sound drunk, despite the whole having-a-beer-at-sunrise thing.

"Uh-oh," Tristan said through a grin. He was shooting for nonchalant, but he was still tired from his run, and while his heart had slowed, the endorphins draining from his body made him long for a bench nearby he could sag onto. "What can I do for you?"

Jimmy squinted at him. "You're the one doing that new ghost tour, right? All dressed up in a fancy suit and shit?"

"That's me," he said as pleasantly as possible. "Fancy suit and shit."

"I heard you the other night . . ." He took another swig of beer, glancing out toward the water. "You were telling a story about ghost manatees, or some bullshit like that, right? Eating kayakers?"

Tristan was surprised into a laugh. "Yeah, that's the one! It's funny, right? I came up with the idea the day I got here. I saw the kayaks you've got there and wanted to . . ." He trailed off as he caught sight of Jimmy's face. He didn't look amused. Not in the least. Shit. "It isn't funny?" he asked sheepishly.

"No, it isn't funny! You telling tourists crap like that, you think they're gonna come running to rent a kayak from me the next morning?" He threw an arm out, gesturing to the kayaks leaning against the side of the shack.

"But . . ." Tristan looked from Jimmy to the kayaks and back again. He hadn't even thought of that. "But it's not real," he said. "Manatees don't attack people, do they?" The idea was ridiculous. It would be like being attacked by a lava lamp.

Jimmy snorted. "Of course they don't, dumbass. But listen here . . ." Another swig from his can, which had to be close to lukewarm by now, but Tristan swallowed hard anyway, because his water had run out a mile or so ago. And while he really didn't want a beer at this time of the day, just about any kind of liquid looked good right now.

Jimmy belched gently before crumpling the can. "Something you need to know about tourists. They'll believe any old thing you tell 'em. Especially if they're on vacation. *Especially* if it's here in Florida." He leaned in conspiratorially. "I think it's the heat. Does something to the brainpan." He swirled his index finger next to his head.

"Okay." Tristan nodded slowly. "I see where you're going with this." He put his hands on his hips and looked over his shoulder, out toward the water, his brain working. "Let me see what I can do, okay? I never meant to cause any harm to your business."

Jimmy gave him a dismissive wave, even though he'd been about to come for Tristan's throat earlier. "You're fine. The real tourist season hasn't kicked in yet; you haven't cost me nothing yet." He moved back to the fishing shack, where he took another gold can out of a battered blue-plastic cooler by the door. He offered the can to Tristan, and for a second he was tempted. He was really tempted to drink the beer that his granddad had loved with the old guy in the Vietnam Veterans baseball cap, Hawaiian shirt, and no shoes while the sun started its daily climb in the sky.

But cooler, more sober heads prevailed, and Tristan turned the beer down with a smile. "I'm more of a coffee-in-the-morning kind of guy."

"Eh." Jimmy cracked the pop-top on the can. "Everyone's got their thing."

It wasn't hard to change the tour, as it turned out. Tristan spent a few days brainstorming an alternate story that could take place at the pier, but ultimately decided that simplest was best.

"You'll want to be careful kayaking in the Gulf, especially if you're heading toward Cemetery Island." He adjusted the top hat on his head as he led the group from the edge of the fishing pier back toward the street. "You never know when those ghostly manatees are going to hit."

He timed the story just right, waiting till he'd led the group in sight of Jimmy's bait shack before continuing. "There's a work-around, though, that only the locals know. So if you'd like to rent a kayak but you don't want to get eaten by a manatee, I'll share with you something I learned from Jimmy himself." He gestured toward the shack. "Tip your friendly neighborhood kayak rental guy. Tip him really, really well." A few chuckles rumbled through the crowd, and he found himself smiling.

As they started back down the other side of Beachside Drive, he tossed one more comment over his shoulder. "And maybe try and remember that manatees don't attack humans." Now the chuckles became full-blown laughs, and past the crowd of people behind him Tristan saw that the door of the bait shack was open. There was a figure in the doorway that he could barely see, but when he raised one arm, moonlight glinted off a gold aluminum can. Tristan's grin widened as he tipped his hat in answer to the toast, a warm feeling spreading in his chest.

That warm feeling persisted through the end of the tour and all the way home. Intellectually, he shouldn't care. He wasn't sticking around long-term; by the beginning of October he'd be gone.

But there it was. He liked this town. And maybe this town was starting to like him back.

Some of the town, anyway.

On the walk home, his steps slowed in front of Mystic Crystals. Never one to back down from a challenge, he hadn't altered his tour since that first night the green glow had appeared in the upper window. It felt too much like chickening out. Since then, it hadn't happened every time. Some nights the house just looked like a house, closed up tight, windows dark. Then, just as Tristan started to relax, let his guard down, it would happen again. A ghostly figure, a green glow in the upper window. A skeletal hand pointing right at him, which felt like a dart to the heart every time, making his blood run cold.

But it wasn't real. Because ghosts weren't real. The green glow, the skeletal hand, it was all make-believe. Someone messing with him.

Footsteps sounded on the sidewalk behind him, and his heart sped up as he turned. What fresh hell . . . ?

It only took a moment to recognize those brown curls, those big glasses. That same face he saw in his mind's eye more often than he'd like to admit. He knew that he was the last person Sophie wanted to see, and he wished he could do something to change that. Because despite everything, she was the first person around here he wanted to see.

He at least could try and be polite. "Hi." He offered her a smile.

She didn't return it. "What are you doing here?" She glanced up at the crystal shop, then back at him. "Shop's closed. You'll have to come back tomorrow."

"That's okay. I'm already stocked up on crystals." But he had to ask. He just had to. "So tell me, girl with all the accurate stories, what's the deal with this place?"

"Deal?" Her eyebrows went up. "Like what?"

"Like . . ." He couldn't tell her, could he? About the green glow? The shadowy figure? He was going to sound like some kind of conspiracy theorist. "Any hauntings take place here?" He was half joking. Well, maybe less than half. Tristan wasn't sure what he believed anymore.

"Why do you ask?" Sophie's eyes cut to him, and he saw unexpected eagerness in their depths. "Did you see something?"

Tristan narrowed his eyes. "Should I have seen something?"

"Maybe." Her shrug gave nothing away. "It's been my experience that if someone isn't happy with the stories you're telling, they find a way to let you know."

That skeletal hand, pointing right at him. Tristan fought back a shiver at the memory; he wasn't going to show weakness. Not in front of his competition.

"Are you telling me that you've never seen anything here?"

"The ghosts here in town don't have a problem with me." Her tone firmly ended the conversation. If she was playing him, she wasn't going to admit it. Fair enough.

He tried changing the subject. "You want to get a drink?" He nodded in the direction of The Haunt. He'd been planning to go straight home, but he wouldn't mind a beer. "We could . . ."

"No." The word slammed between them like a nail in a coffin. "I'm on my way to see my friend Libby." She pointed down the street in the opposite direction. "Besides," she continued. "I think it's best that we don't . . ." She took a deep breath. "We're not friends."

"We're not?" Tristan kept his tone light, but her words made his chest hurt.

She shook her head, curls bouncing, mouth set in a determined line. "We can't be. Not now."

"Oh." Was it his imagination, or did she sound sad as she said it?

She was right, though, wasn't she? Even though he kept finding himself pulled to her like she was his personal North Star, he was in too deep. All Sophie could be to him now was business competition waiting to be crushed.

His father would be thrilled at the notion. But as Tristan watched Sophie head down the street, her dark hair shining under the streetlight, he realized that right now, winning felt a whole lot like losing.

Eleven

"You're the girl in the video, right?"

Sophie was getting used to the question. The first few times she'd been asked, it had been embarrassing, as though going viral in a video where you're calling a guy *bullshit* was something to be ashamed of. (It was.) But she had to admit, Tristan was right. Her tours were packed, and she'd started to lose count of the number of times she'd been asked about the viral video. Yes, that was her. No, they hadn't staged it. Yes, she really did think Tristan's tour was BS. No, she didn't think Tristan was cute. (Okay, that last one was a lie, but Sophie wasn't going to admit that to anyone.)

The increased income was good, she reminded herself as she pasted a sunny smile on her face and nodded at the middle-aged man in cargo shorts who'd asked the question. "That's me! But I promise there will be a lot less swearing on this tour," she said, now bringing her attention to the entire group congregating outside of Hallowed Grounds. "Unless, of course, we run into that absolute . . . miscreant who thinks he can run a better ghost tour than I can!" It was a speech she'd been working on, even throwing in a fun word like "miscreant" to make the tourists laugh. And she delivered the words with a cheerful bravado that she didn't feel. She wasn't in friendly competition with Tristan.

It was good that she'd established that, on that one Friday night a few weeks ago. They weren't friends, and they could never be friends. Every time she reminded herself of that it hurt a little less. Eventually—like once he finally gave up in October and left town—she'd be able to forget how drawn to him she'd been once.

But tonight, she just had to get through this tour. Hopefully without running into Tristan.

She took comfort in the route. This was her hometown, her turf. She'd been running up and down these streets, and along this beach, since she was a child. She knew this town, and she liked to think it knew her right back. And tonight was a special night; she had a surprise for Boneyard Key. She hoped it was a good surprise.

After the usual stop at the end of the fishing pier, where Sophie told the story of Cemetery Island and the Great Storm of 1897 that had leveled the settlement there, she led them in a slight detour: onto a path that snaked toward a small strip of beach to the left of the pier.

"Now, you'll have to forgive me," she said as she picked her way down the narrow path, her charges following behind her. "This is a brand-new story, so I'll do my best to get it right. As I may have mentioned before, I've been doing some research on the history of Boneyard Key with the help of a friend and local historian. We've uncovered some unique slices of life around here, and I'm sharing one of those new bits with you tonight."

She clicked on her flashlight, shining it around the sandbar she currently stood on. A couple of the more intrepid tourists had followed her to stand on the damp sand, while the rest grouped along the narrow pathway.

"The Great Storm of 1897 had many casualties. People lost mothers, daughters, wives. Sons, brothers, fathers. It took a special kind of person to decide to stay. Decide to make this place their home after it had already taken so much from them. This spot is sacred ground." Her flashlight slipped in her suddenly sweaty hand, the beam of light bobbing, and she switched it from one hand to the other so she could wipe her palms on her jeans. "Before the pier was built here, it was the spot where families mourned their dead. Where makeshift coffins were loaded onto boats and taken across to the original cemetery for the last time. The last remains buried there were victims of the Great Storm."

Sophie's uncertain voice gained strength from the respectful silence around her. "It was also at this spot where the surviving families who chose to stay behind established the town here on the mainland. And I don't have hard evidence for this, but there are writings that say this spot was the first time a member of the Founding Fifteen families talked to their loved ones who had passed beyond. A lot of very important moments in the history of Boneyard Key happened on this small stretch of beach that no one really notices these days."

She shined her beam to the right, to the more modern structure that was the fishing pier. "This pier first went up about ten years later, and knowing what I know now, I don't think the location is a coincidence. I think the Founding Fifteen wanted all of us in the years to come to keep an eye on Cemetery Island, and honor where they came from."

It was breezy down here, this close to the water, and the wind whipped her hair in all directions. Sophie didn't want to think about how she'd look once she got home. But as she guided her charges back up to the main road by the glow of her flashlight, a warmer breeze sifted its way through her hair, settling it, like an otherworldly pat on the head. The breeze felt like a hug. It felt like thanks.

Yeah. Adding this stop to the tour was the right thing to do. Sophie couldn't wait to tell Theo about this. She may not have word magnets on her fridge, or the ability to have conversations with the dead, but she had this. Her tour, her stories. And they mattered.

No matter what that miscreant might say.

Her crowd was hushed, almost reverent, as they hit the main road and she continued on with her tour. She brought some levity back to the evening as they passed the Starter Home, its broken-down silhouette in sharp relief against the night sky. "A cute little fixer-upper, right? Just imagine, your honey-do list would be never-ending!" The men in the crowd groaned and the women chuckled, just like every heterosexual middle-aged couple that took this tour. It was an easy joke, but it helped bring the mood back up.

Then they got to the Hawkins House, and the evening went sideways.

Sophie heard them first. Laughter, loud and raucous. One voice stood out over them all.

"I'm serious!" The laughter in Tristan's voice said that he wasn't serious. What a surprise. "Now, our next stop is this little yellow cottage, right up here. It's got an amazing history. So tell me, how much do you fine people know about pirates?"

Oh, no. The last thing Sophie wanted was to run into Tristan. Not again. Not in front of Cassie's house. But, like something out of a nightmare, it was happening, in slow motion and way too fast all at once. Sophie set her jaw and whirled around, stopping her group's progress just before they reached the house. Out of the corner of her eye, she could see that Tristan had done the same. She and her group were just to the right of the house, and Tristan's tour was just to the left.

"I can tell you the story right here!" She spoke too fast, too loud. She sounded like a cartoon mouse as she all but sped through the story of Sarah Hawkins, her home, and her cabbage roses. All the while, the hair on the back of her neck stood on end, hyperaware that every time she paused for breath, Tristan's voice was right there filling in the silence with his ridiculous pirate story. Sophie really hoped that Cassie and Nick were out of the house, having a date night. The fewer witnesses to this debacle, the better.

In an incredible feat of synchronization, they finished their stories almost at the same time. Sophie clicked on her flashlight and turned to lead her group down the street just as Tristan turned to do the same. She could do this. She could pass him, pass his group, and just give them a friendly nod like he was nobody. Or better yet, she could ignore him completely.

She should have known better. Ignoring Tristan Martin was an impossibility.

His smile widened at her approach, and the two met, face-to-face, under the glow of the Hawkins House porch lights. Sophie narrowed her eyes at him, her mouth set, determined to just walk by like he wasn't there.

But then he had to go and tip his hat. Bow his head. Look up at her under his brow. What was with that smile of his? It was a tractor beam, drawing her in. It was infuriating, because the last thing she wanted was to be drawn in.

"Milady." His voice was low and throaty, with the trace of some kind of accent. His eyes crinkled, a secret smile only she could see. He needed to stop smiling at her. He needed to stop talking to her. He just needed to stop.

"I'm not your lady," she snapped, remembering a moment too late that they were surrounded by tourists, who had fallen into an excited hush. *Here they go*, she could practically hear them thinking. *She's gonna yell at him again!* Sophie threw a surreptitious look over her shoulder, and yep. In that one glance she counted three cell phones, out and aimed in her direction. There were four pinpoints of light over Tristan's shoulder; his tourists had already started filming. Had he planned this? Tipped them off? Was he trying to go viral again, make more money off her image?

Ugh. Screw this guy. She forced a smile that felt more like a snarl. A cheerful tone she didn't feel.

"Have. A. Great. Night." *Go. Right. To. Hell.*

Sophie turned on her heel, back to her group, firmly putting her back to Tristan. "Sorry for the interruption, folks! If you'll follow me, past these fine people here, we're going to head south toward the Chamber of Commerce, where our next story takes place!"

It wasn't easy, leading a group of people past another group of people that you were desperately trying to pretend didn't exist. But Sophie was a professional. She didn't even look in Tristan's direction as she led her group away. She held her breath when his arm brushed against hers on the crowded sidewalk, so close that she could feel the heat of his body, the brushed wool of his coat. It took all the restraint she had, but she pretended like he wasn't even there.

Because soon enough he wouldn't be. If she was lucky.

On the way home she stopped for a couple slices of pizza, as a reward for not letting Tristan bait her (too much). She heard her name the moment the door closed behind her, and Aura was waving from the counter.

"Sophie! Oh my god, I was hoping I would run into you."

"Into me?" Sophie looked around, in case there was another Sophie that Aura was talking to. Since when were they besties?

But Aura nodded enthusiastically, taking a pull off the vat of soda that passed for a large drink around here. "I've been haunting the top hat guy. It's freaking hilarious."

Well, hello bestie. As soon as Sophie placed her order, she leaned on the counter next to Aura. "Tell me everything."

"It's so dumb," she said with a giggle. "I had this green light bulb left over from a photo shoot, so I stuck that in the ceiling light in one of the upstairs bedrooms. At first I just hid under a bedsheet and waved my arms around, right? But then—then! I found a plastic skeleton in a box of old Halloween decorations. So now I poke the arm out from under the sheet, point it right at him." Now the giggle was a cackle. "The first time I did it, I thought he was going to pass out."

"Aura," Sophie said, "I think I love you."

"Right back atcha. You should bring your own group by sometime. I can scare them too."

"Wait, what?" Sophie tilted her head. "I thought you wanted to be left out of the tour."

Aura dimpled. "That's before I knew how much fun it was to be a creepy ghost!"

"I don't know . . ." She thought again about that spectral pat on the head she'd gotten earlier. It made her feel even more protective of this town, those souls who remained here after death. "I'm trying to keep my tour more factual. You know, for contrast."

She considered that. "Good point. I'll keep the bullshit for the bullshit tour."

"Okay, there's no loitering here." Terry shook his shaggy blond hair out of his eyes as he plonked two to-go boxes on the counter in front of the girls. He nodded toward Aura's order. "I threw an extra garlic knot—with no garlic—in there for Einstein."

Aura blew him a kiss on the way to the soda fountain to refill her drink for her walk home. "You spoil me. And my bird."

"Always have." His eyes followed Aura for a beat too long before looking over at Sophie. "Garlic knots in there for you too. I don't know why you didn't add them to the order. We both know they're your favorite."

"You're too good to me, Terry." He was right, of course; she polished one off on the walk home, happily sucking garlic salt off her thumb as she unlocked her door. Tristan notwithstanding, it had been a good night. She loved where she lived, and with any luck she'd managed to not go viral on the internet.

What more could a girl ask for?

Pale eyes looking up at her under blond brows. A gravelly voice speaking low, just to her. A secret smile.

No.

She didn't want to ask for any of those things.

Twelve

All things considered, that had gone pretty great.

It would have gone even better if Sophie had taken the bait. Really gotten mad and lit into him, the way she had the first time, when they went viral. But it was still a perfect organic moment, and plenty of the guests—both from her tour and his—had their phones out. Chances were good that a video should be hitting the internet soon. Damn, his father was right after all.

Not that Tristan was ever going to admit that to him.

His run-in with Sophie had been the best part of the night, which honestly was pretty sad. The green glow had been back tonight at Mystic Crystals, and a shadowy figure had waved to him from an upper window as he was wrapping up his dead doctor story. And while Tristan had been creeped out, it had been great for the tour. A couple patrons had actually screamed, while some others had laughed, certain that Tristan had planted someone up there to scare them. It almost made him wish he'd thought of that. Something to file away for a future tour in another city, maybe?

He'd even debuted a new story tonight. On one of his morning runs he'd spotted a little side path by the fishing pier that led down to a small strip of beach. The wheels had started turning, and before long he'd come up with a story to set there. He hadn't found a spot yet for one of his old standards—the guy-with-a-hook-for-a-hand ghost, preying on innocent teenagers looking for a place to make out. This secluded alcove looked like as good a make-out spot as any, and he was excited to get this story back into rotation.

The path was narrower than he'd expected it to be—he really should have scoped out this little sandbar ahead of time—and it wasn't as neglected as it had seemed. There were even fresh footprints in the sandy soil. Only about half of the tour group followed him all the way down to the water. The rest had chickened out, staying grouped safely up by the pier, so he'd had to speak from his diaphragm to project that far. An easy job for a former theatre kid.

"Just as he was about to steal a kiss—and let's face it, more than a kiss—they were interrupted by a *scraaaaaaaping* noise, coming from the pier. The young man went to investigate, but the girl ran home, terrified." He paused for effect, knowing that holding the lantern just so would make his face light up in the most unnerving way. "The next morning, the authorities found two things hanging from the pier: a hook, and the young man's head!"

Tristan was worried this new story would be a little gruesome for his audience, but they ate it up, reacting with faux terror and mostly laughter. It was all in the delivery, he reminded himself with a mental pat on the back. Ghosts weren't real, so they didn't deserve to be taken seriously.

As they headed back up to the street, Tristan brought up the rear, holding his LED lantern high. He was just about to step off the sand when a shiver wracked his whole body, an involuntary spasm that felt like a bucket of ice-cold water had been dumped over his head. Tristan stumbled, lantern light wavering, but he recovered quickly.

"Tripped over a root, there!" he said a little louder than necessary, then he led the group on before anyone could point out that there weren't any trees nearby. Thank God this night was almost over; too much weird shit was happening.

Once his charges had dispersed, he took off his top hat and shook out his hair. It was just his nerves, he told himself. He'd had to contend with the green glow at Mystic Crystals, the skeletal hand pointing right at his heart, and just when he'd gotten his composure back, he'd run into Sophie. No wonder he was on edge. Now he was imagining things, like a cold breeze down by the water that made him shiver. A beer on the way home should set things right.

The night started looking up once he got to The Haunt. Tony had warmed up to him again, so in no time Tristan had a pint of his favorite lager in front of him, with the promise of that night's cheeseburger special on the way. That first sip was heavenly, and Tristan closed his eyes in bliss. His throat was scratchy from a night of storytelling and a touch of hay fever played hell with his sinuses. The beer helped with both, but after a few sips, weariness settled over him. Something felt off, and he didn't know how to describe it. Sophie's words from a few weeks ago echoed back in his ears. *The ghosts here in town don't have a problem with me . . .*

Implying that they had a problem with him.

It would be something to be concerned about—if ghosts existed and weren't just a marketing schtick employed by an entire town. Tristan knew about marketing schticks, but there was something about this one. He thought bringing his ghost tour here was a no-brainer, but something about his tour, something about *him . . .* didn't quite fit here.

And that didn't make sense. Tristan fit in everywhere.

The Haunt was bustling tonight. The steel drum band had the night off; instead, a ramshackle-looking group of mostly retirees played their way through songs that had been hits before Tristan was born. Around him, tables of tourists talked and laughed, ate and drank their way through another night of vacation. And while Tristan's favorite thing to do was make friends, and his favorite place to be was at the center of attention, tonight he wanted to blend in. He sat at the bar, and between bites of the best burger he'd had in his life and sips of good, cold beer, he let the atmosphere around him, the conversation and music and laughter, fill his ears and settle in his bones. It felt like a night off. It felt good.

Until he heard the words "ghost tour."

All of Tristan's senses sharpened, focused on those two words picked out of the general commotion. His eyes narrowed. He willed his ears to work harder. Where had that come from? There. A couple tables away—four people finishing off a platter of onion rings—a man in a blue T-shirt, his back to Tristan, nodded emphatically.

"Totally!" he proclaimed. "Absolutely worth every penny. I think it's on tomorrow night too. You should go!"

Tristan's spine straightened, a smile spreading across his face. That was the kind of praise that made it all worthwhile. He didn't recognize the man, but Tristan also didn't take mental inventory of what everyone in his tour looked like.

Across from the man in the blue shirt, a blond woman looked skeptical. "Is it a lot of walking, though? We're going kayaking in the morning and kind of want to take it easy afterward."

"Not at all! It's a pretty short loop, mostly downtown. The whole thing was an hour and a half, tops! It was a nice little tour of the area."

It was hard to keep the smile off his face as he handed Tony his credit card to pay for dinner. He had a few business cards in his pocket—he never went anywhere without them. He could drop by the table on his way out, thank them for the kind words, and try and drum up a little more interest from the people at the table who hadn't been on the tour yet. Maybe—

"And you're a history nerd; you'd really like it! The tour guide really seems to know what she's talking about."

She.

Tristan froze halfway through signing his receipt. Ah. They weren't talking about his tour. They were talking about Sophie's. Shit.

Well, he was *definitely* going to drop by their table on the way out. Those four needed his business cards. He couldn't let them think Sophie's tour was the only one in town.

Thirteen

Tonight, Tristan's eyes were ice blue. Not green, but a blue so pale that they looked like they had no color at all. It was unsettling. Almost as unsettling as the sight of him standing knee-deep in the Gulf of Mexico at sunset, the tide undulating in and out, water foaming around his legs. He wore a pair of board shorts in a loud tropical print—neon palm trees and bright pink flamingos—and nothing else.

Wait. No. He was wearing that stupid top hat. Because why wouldn't he be?

"You want to come in?" It was an innocent question, but it came out as almost a growl. Low and throaty, it was an entirely different kind of invitation that made her heart speed up.

Sophie shook her head. "Too many sharks."

"I don't think so." He craned his neck to look up at the sky, squinting against the sun (because it was daytime now). "It's not the right time for them. Come on." Those ice-blue eyes were focused on her, and he held out his hand.

"What if I'm worried about you?" He seemed about as dangerous as a shark. But his gaze was a tractor beam, and she couldn't resist. She didn't want to resist. She slid her hand into his, and the touch of his skin sent a thrill all through her. This close, she could see the slightest sprinkling of blond hair on his tanned chest. She could see the muscles in his tight stomach, tensing even further at her touch as she laid a hand flat on his belly. His skin was as warm as the afternoon sun.

"See?" The brim of his hat threw shade across his face, and then across hers as he bent closer. Sophie swallowed hard. All she could see were his eyes—ice green now—and his mouth, his full lips, curving gently into a smile as he leaned in to whisper in her ear. "I told you you'd want to come in."

That sounded really dirty too. "Yes." The word was little more than breath as desire stole her voice.

"Not so bad, right?" The words were spoken against her skin, his mouth hot. His tongue was hotter, tracing a line down her neck. Her nipples tightened, and she felt a throb inside. Further down.

Sophie wanted to speak, but her mouth had gone dry, even as water lapped at her legs. Tristan's tongue lapped at her too, busy against her throat, his arms closing around her, and she knew. She just *knew* . . .

Seagulls squawked as they circled overhead. Sophie slipped her hand under the waistband of Tristan's board shorts, her palm skidding against his hip bone. Tristan caught his breath, gasping against her neck as he palmed one of her breasts (her shirt had disappeared, but that was fine), and the seagulls squawked even louder. Over and over. Louder and louder.

Sophie gasped awake, fumbling for her phone and turning off her alarm. Then she rolled to her back, clutching her phone in one hand, her chest heaving for breath. Everything was hot, her body wound tight like a stretched rubber band about to snap. She was still half asleep, still half in her erotic dream. She had to be. Why else would she slide her other hand down her belly, under her sleep shorts, to where she was so. Freaking. Wet. Her body knew what was up, and it only took a few strokes to bring the completion that dream had promised. Sophie bucked against her hand, her fingers skidding, mouth open wide in a gasp that became a slow whine.

For a few moments she let her body calm, her breaths eventually coming slower, until her phone went off again in her hand, the snooze alarm chirping merrily until she finally groaned and turned the alarm off completely. Now that she was awake, her brain finally clicking on, she sat up in bed and tossed her phone onto her quilt. The whole dream came tumbling back through her mind. The top hat. The flamingo board shorts. The oh-so-talented mouth.

Had she really just had a dirty dream about Tristan Martin?

"Ugh!" She pushed her sleep-tangled hair from her eyes and kicked the bedclothes aside. She needed coffee and a shower. Shower first—she needed to scrub this dream away.

The shower didn't help. Instead, the hot water against her skin reminded her of Tristan's hands. Tristan's mouth. *No.* She had no idea what his hands really felt like. Or his mouth. Thank God. It had just been a dream. A nightmare even, and the quicker she put it out of her head, the better.

But her head wasn't cooperating. All day her heart beat just a little faster, and her skin felt just a little too tight. Every time she blinked, there was a flash of half-naked Tristan on the backs of her eyelids: all toned abs, golden skin, and inviting smile. Her cheeks were warm against the palms of her hands, flushed in a way that no amount of ice water, either chugged or splashed against her face, could cool down. Part of her wanted to track Tristan down so she could either jump him or push him off the fishing pier. By the time seven rolled around and it was time to head to Hallowed Grounds for the ghost tour, she was an unsettled mess.

It was a small group tonight; they were firmly in the doldrums between tourist seasons, where a large crowd barely took two hands to count. Thank God she'd recruited Libby and Cassie to walk the tour with her. It always helped to have friends make the crowd look bigger. But tonight was a bad night to be perceived by friends; she stumbled over her words, and stories she'd told for years felt shaky in her throat.

Most nights, Sophie loved hanging out at the end of her ghost tour, available to answer any questions about Boneyard Key and its many documented ghost sightings, or to follow up on any of the stories she'd told. But tonight, Sophie's feet hurt, and everything inside of her felt like it was shaking from the remnants of last night's horny dream.

So of course, now they had questions. And it was Sophie's job to paste on a smile and answer them.

"Are there really dead bodies out on that island?"

"It's a cemetery, so yes." Sophie threw a glance toward the coffee counter. Boneyard Key's founding families were buried on Cemetery Island. Nick was a member of one of those founding families, and probably wouldn't like to hear his great-great-grandfather referred to as a "dead body."

She widened her smile and turned her attention back to the middle-aged gentleman in front of her. "As I mentioned in the tour, the cemetery is maintained by members of the local historical society. You can rent a kayak from Jimmy's, over by the pier, if you're interested in taking a look yourself. It's a wonderful piece of local history."

But his attention had wandered, away from the cemetery and to the drink coupon in his hand. "What time does this place close?" He waved the coupon. "Nothing else around here is open. Y'all roll up the sidewalks at five or what?"

"Something like that," chimed in a voice behind her. Sophie

looked over her shoulder to see Nick leaning his elbows on the counter. "The Haunt is about all the nightlife we've got around here."

"Hmm." He looked down at the coupon again, then nodded at Sophie. "Thanks. Tour was . . . well, it was interesting."

She kept her smile bright. There were worse things to be called. "Thanks! That's what I strive for."

Finally, finally, the last of the ghost tour patrons filed out, heading for The Haunt, and Nick followed them to the door, throwing the lock behind the last one as Sophie leaned against the bar.

Libby peered at her. "You've been a little out of it tonight. Everything okay?"

"Of course." Sophie sighed. Libby wouldn't want to hear about her horny dream, and Sophie certainly didn't want to talk about it. "Just an off day, I think."

On the other side of her, Cassie bumped her arm. "I say we get pizza." She glanced over at Nick, busy shutting things down. "I don't know about you, but I'm starving. Nick and I kind of lost track of time this afternoon and forgot to have dinner beforehand."

"Ew." Sophie grimaced. "I don't need to know that much about your sex life."

"I second that." Libby raised a hand, and Cassie rolled her eyes with a smile.

"We were watching a movie. Perverts. Sarah hadn't seen *The Mummy* yet, and it was time to educate her. Anyway, you wanna join us? You look like you could use some food."

"I'm starving," Sophie confessed, and Libby nodded in agreement beside her. "You're not getting it to go?" Poltergeist Pizza wasn't exactly a place where people went for fine dining. It was more of a to-go spot. Delivery, when the scooter was working.

"Nah, we can eat there." Nick flipped off the rest of the lights, plunging the café and its inhabitants into darkness, lit from the streetlights out front. He came up behind Cassie, sliding his arms around her waist. "I promise Cassie and I can keep our hands off each other for a couple hours."

"Lies," Libby said with a grin on her face.

Sophie couldn't help but agree. "I don't know if I believe that." But there was no way she was turning down pizza with friends. Nothing was waiting for her at home but a barren fridge and a shared spreadsheet with Tristan that needed updating. She always imagined him sitting at home, staring at his laptop on tour nights, waiting for her latest numbers.

Screw him. He could wait.

Poltergeist Pizza had six tables set up in the front of the restaurant, their chipped Formica covered with the cheapest of red-checked vinyl tablecloths. Sophie couldn't remember the last time she'd stayed to eat there. While Libby and Sophie pushed together the two tables in front of the window, Nick and Cassie went up to the counter to order, returning with a pitcher of beer and four glasses.

Sophie waved it off; she was a wine girl if she drank at all. So she took her own trip to the counter to get a soda. She wasn't alone at the fountain; Jo Seavey stared intently into her cup, waiting for the fizz to go down in her Diet Coke. Jo glanced over her shoulder and smiled.

"Hey." She shook her dark hair out of her eyes, and Sophie smiled back. She didn't know Jo very well—Sophie had been four years ahead of her in school, so they hadn't run into each other much. Jo helped her parents run the consignment shop down the street, which explained her eclectic style. Her dyed black hair, choppy haircut, and heavy eyeliner screamed nineties goth, but she wore a pink lace cardigan over her dark blue tank dress, and the watch around her wrist was an ornamental bracelet easily from the Edwardian period.

"Ghost tour night?" She stepped aside so Sophie could fill her own cup.

"Every week," Sophie said pleasantly. "What about you? Working late on a Friday?"

Jo nodded and rolled her eyes. "Inventory. Thought I'd just eat here rather than get dishes dirty at home." She glanced into the dining room, which was starting to look packed now that there were five whole customers in there. "I didn't realize this was the place to be on a Friday night."

"We know how to party," Sophie said. "I may need to add this place to my tour."

"Please don't!" Terry called from the counter. "Too many people here already. I'm only letting y'all stay because I like you."

Jo and Sophie shared a grin. "Wanna join us?" Sophie asked.

"You sure?" Jo raised her eyebrows in surprise, and Sophie's heart melted. Something about Jo seemed lonely, and Sophie wanted nothing more than to bring her into the fold.

"Of course." She led Jo back to the group. Nick was nestled into a chair next to Cassie, and Libby sat across from them. Sophie took a seat next to her, and Jo flanked Sophie's other side.

"I already ordered for everyone," Cassie said. "Hope that's okay."

"That's fine." Sophie's heart dipped a little, but she reminded herself that Cassie could be trusted with pizza toppings. Even if it wasn't what Sophie would order for herself.

Not that she needed to worry. When the pizzas arrived, Terry slid Sophie's favorite in front of her with a wink. "I got you, girl."

Cassie blinked. "Did I get it wrong?"

"Not at all. Terry just knows what I like." She pulled a couple slices onto a thick plastic plate. "And I mean, it's pizza. I'm not going to complain about pizza."

"Oh, good." Cassie started sawing at one of her slices with a plastic knife. "Besides, what's that old saying? Pizza's like sex?"

Libby chimed in. "Even when it's bad it's pretty good."

Sophie nodded emphatically. It was way too soon to take a bite, but she did anyway and promptly burned the roof of her mouth. Worth it.

"Except maybe if there's pineapple on it." Nick shook his head. "That shit's not natural."

Sophie tilted her head as she chewed. "On the pizza or the sex?"

Jo snorted, but Cassie's plasticware clattered to the table. "Wait. You don't like pineapple on pizza? How did I not know this till now?"

"You never asked." Nick shrugged while Cassie shook her head.

"I'm rethinking this whole relationship."

The front door opened, drawing everyone's attention to Theo strolling in. Something about him looked weird, but Sophie couldn't put her finger on it. Seeing him outside of Boneyard Books looked unnatural, like catching your teacher at the bar. On certain nights she wondered if he was a ghost himself, doomed to stroll the shelves. But that was ridiculous.

"Hey, Theo!" Libby said cheerfully. "Come join us." She pulled out one of the chairs on her side of the table.

"No, that's okay. I was just on the way home." Now Sophie realized why he looked different: his bow tie was off, and the top button of his shirt was undone. That was as casual as she'd ever seen him.

"So was I," Jo said, much too darkly for someone who was wrestling with a cheese pull. "There's no use resisting. You may as well sit down."

"That's right." Libby's cheer was off the charts. "You can't say no to me."

"Apparently not." He took the proffered chair, and a few moments later Terry appeared with a to-go box.

"Let me guess, you're staying too?" He sighed and put the box on the neighboring table before pulling said table over into an impossibly long configuration. "Y'all are going to need more room if you're making this a party." He did his best to sound long-suffering, yet he returned almost immediately with a pitcher of soda, a second pitcher of beer, and extra cups.

"We're not going to need all these cups," Theo said after taking one.

"We might." Cassie passed him one of the pitchers. "You never know who's going to walk in next."

Almost on cue, the door opened again, and Sophie turned, prepared to cheer the newest member of this impromptu pizza party. But the cheer died in her throat, because of course.

It was Tristan. Cravat loosened and top hat in hand, his blond hair sweaty and plastered to his forehead. Just another Boneyard Key resident at the end of a long Friday night.

He stopped short when faced with the oversize table at the front of the pizza place, and his startled look gave Sophie pause. It was like a mask had slipped from his face, and he looked uncertain. He looked tired. Lonely, even.

Maybe she *wanted* him to look tired and lonely. As tired and lonely as she felt sometimes. But she didn't have long to think about it before the mask was back on, his smile as easygoing as ever. "Hey." His greeting encompassed the whole table. "Don't let me interrupt."

Across the table, Cassie looked at Sophie, telegraphing a question with her eyes. Sophie felt a flare of anger—why was this even an option? Tristan was the guy putting her out of business. He was the *enemy*. But there was something about that glimpse behind the mask that threw everything into question.

Maybe she could be an adult about this. Be polite to him in public.

That dream she'd been trying all day to forget came roaring back, setting her blood thrumming. She didn't feel like an adult. She felt like a horny teenager. Everything was muddled now when it came to Tristan, and Sophie didn't know how to feel anymore.

Ugh. Fine. "Sit." She folded her arms across her chest as she slouched down in her seat. "There's plenty of room."

Fourteen

It was getting too damn hot for this outfit.

Summer hit a lot sooner in Florida than it did in the rest of the country. Taking off the top hat at the end of the night had helped, though Tristan's hair was sweat soaked and plastered to his head. His shirt had started to stick to his back under his coat, and all he wanted to do was strip down naked and run full tilt into the ocean, but he would settle for a long, cold shower once he got home.

In short, he was an unsettled mess, and he just wanted to grab a couple slices of pizza to go. He hadn't intended to walk into what looked like a private party, with Sophie Horvath in the middle of it all. Before he could back away and flee into the night, she'd done the unthinkable by inviting him to sit. Okay, there was a slight glint of murder in her eyes when she'd done so, but the invitation had still been there.

"You sure?" He raised his eyebrows in her direction, wanting to give her an out in case she was just being polite. She didn't take it; instead she slid down further in her seat, which was confusing until the chair in front of him shot backwards, knocking him in the knee. The tiniest of smirks played across her face, and even though his knee throbbed a little, it felt like a friendly gesture.

He'd take it. Besides, his stomach was growling and there were four pizzas scattered across the table. He nestled his top hat and lantern into the empty chair next to him, then peeled off his tailcoat, sighing with relief as he hung it on the back of the chair. His body temperature dropped almost immediately, but that was probably just the sweat cooling on his back. He glanced around the table as he sat, and to his surprise, he knew almost everyone there: Nick and Cassie, and the guy who owned the bookstore—Theo? Sophie, of course. The only stranger was the younger, dark-haired woman.

"Hi." He reached across to her, hand extended. "Tristan Martin."

She narrowed her heavily lined eyes. "I know who you are." She didn't take his hand. "You left a business card at the store a few weeks ago. You talked to my dad."

"Your . . . ?"

She nodded toward the door. "I'm up the street. The consignment shop?"

"Oh!" He remembered now. He'd dropped by on one of his canvassing missions. "You have a kick-ass music section in the back."

Mentioning the music section must have been the way to her heart. Her lips quirked up in an almost-smile while Nick nodded. "That's Jo's project," he said.

"Yeah," she confirmed. "People seem to like shopping for vinyl when they're on vacation. The snowbirds like it too. I dunno. Nostalgia maybe?"

"Impulse buying driven by emotion. I can see that." Tristan nodded as he unbuttoned his cuffs, rolling up his shirtsleeves. Sophie's eyes narrowed at him across the table, and he felt the look like a dart. Did she want him there or not? Flustered but determined to not let it show, he turned his attention back to Jo. "Did I see some musical instruments back there too?"

She nodded around her bite of pizza. "Yep. Vince helps me appraise that stuff. Have you met Vince yet? He runs The Cold Spot, the bar on the edge of town, out by the highway."

"That small gray building, with the gas pump out front? There's a bar in there? I thought it was abandoned." Tristan helped himself to a slice of pizza from the pie in front of him. Sausage and pepperoni. And was that extra sauce? His mouth watered.

Nick refilled his cup from the beer pitcher before offering it across the table to Tristan. "Vince likes to keep it on the down-low."

"But wouldn't he get more business if he advertised? There isn't even a sign out front." He filled a plastic cup and handed the pitcher back. The beer was crisp and so, so cold. He took a slow sip when what he really wanted was to chug. God, he must have sweat out half of the water in his body tonight.

"He doesn't need one." Sophie's voice was short, each word sounding like it had been sliced out with a sharp knife. "The locals know where it is."

"But what about the tourist traffic? How do they find out about the place?" What was with this town and its lack of advertising? Tristan wanted to tear his hair out. Did they want tourists to spend their money or what?

"They don't," Nick replied. "He likes it that way." His tone of voice ended the argument, and Tristan raised defensive hands.

Across the table, Libby groaned. "I don't see any red pepper flakes, do you?" She addressed the question to the table at large. Not waiting for an answer, she raised her voice. "Hey, Terry! Can you send some red pepper out?"

"Cheese too?" came a voice from the kitchen.

"If he doesn't mind. Thanks!"

"If who doesn't mind?" Tristan turned in his chair to look toward the back of the place. The only employee he'd seen was the guy working the counter and the kitchen. Was there a waiter hiding around here somewhere?

A sound from the table made him turn back around again. A glass shaker of Parmesan cheese slid in a steady motion down the center of the table, coming to rest in front of Libby. Before Tristan's mind could make sense of what he was seeing, a matching shaker of red pepper flakes, like you'd see at any pizza joint anywhere in the country, floated in the air—in the freaking *air!*—to the table, touching down and sliding across in the same path as the Parmesan.

"Thank you!" Libby addressed her words to the air, picking up the red pepper flakes and shaking some on her slice, as though it hadn't just appeared out of fucking *nowhere*.

"Um . . ." Tristan didn't even know where to start. What question to ask first.

"Do you want some?" Cassie offered him the red pepper flakes, but Tristan just stared at it. When had this dinner become a fever dream?

"You okay?" Jo smirked as she picked up the Parmesan cheese and passed it to Nick after using it herself.

"What's the matter there, Tristan?" Nick asked. "You look like you've seen a ghost."

That was met with snorts and laughter from around the table, but Theo shook his head. "Technically it's a poltergeist." He neatly cut off another bite of his pizza with the plastic cutlery.

"True." Sophie nodded at Theo, but her eyes were on Tristan. She seemed to be waiting for something. Maybe for him to cop a clue of some kind.

Slowly, much too slowly, his brain came back online. He looked around the tiny restaurant, searching for any sign of . . . anything. Hidden pulleys, fishing wire. Any rational explanation. Finally his gaze lit on the neon sign in the window. Poltergeist Pizza. In that moment a switch finally flipped in his mind.

Maybe it wasn't all bullshit.

Maybe it was time to believe.

"So . . ." His voice felt thick in his throat, like he hadn't used it in days. He took a sip of beer and started again. "It's not just a cute name then." He was pleased to see that his hand barely shook at all as he reached for the Parmesan. "And I thought the owner was into alliteration."

"More than one thing can be true." Jo must have come around to him, since she now threw him a smile.

"It's okay." Cassie's voice was sympathetic. "It freaked me out at first too."

"You'll get used to it." Sophie's voice was understanding until she seemed to realize who she was talking to and caught herself. "Not that you'll be here long enough to." Now her voice was ice, as chilling as the air conditioner in this pizzeria.

"Who says I'm not?" He tried to keep his tone light, teasing even. But Sophie's face darkened and she pushed her plate away.

"You're not." It was a declarative statement. "Because this is my town."

"Wow, you bought it? All on your own?" He made his eyes wide innocence. Sophie narrowed her eyes even further. Nick started to laugh, but it was quickly squashed by Cassie, digging her elbow into his side.

Okay, then. Time for a subject change. He turned to Jo. "So is that what you do at the consignment store?" he asked as he took a bite. Haunted pizza was still good pizza, and this stuff was fantastic. "Run the music section?"

She shook her head. "Mom's the office manager, she does all the business stuff. Dad goes to estate sales all over Florida and brings stuff back. I read them and help him price things."

"What do you mean, read them?"

"Oh." Jo popped a bit of pizza crust into her mouth. "I read objects."

This meant nothing. Less than nothing. Sure, he understood the words individually, but together they were nonsense. All he could do now was repeat them back like a parrot. "Read them how? Like labels on them?"

"It's called psychometry," she said, as though they were discussing the weather. "It's what I do."

"What you . . . do." Nope, he was still stuck on the parrot imitation.

Jo gave an impatient sigh. "You know about the Founding Fifteen, right? The original founders of modern-day Boneyard Key, and how members of these families all have different abilities to communicate. That whole deal."

"Jo, I'll bet you he doesn't know anything about that." Sophie didn't look at him; she talked to Jo, loudly, as though he weren't even in the room. "He's not exactly one for historical accuracy."

"Okay, ouch." He was starting to regret sitting down as much as Sophie was probably regretting inviting him. But he had to defend himself. "I know about the Founding Fifteen. You talked about it in your tour. And it's in that book, right? *Boneyard Key: A Haunted History*." He looked toward Theo for confirmation. He'd sold Tristan the damn book, and Tristan had read it cover to cover. But his brain was just now coming around to the idea that this was all *real*. Like, ghosts handing him condiments real. "Your family is one of the Founding Fifteen?"

Jo nodded. "Nick's too."

Tristan's gaze swung to the café owner. "You talk to ghosts?"

Nick shook his head, which was a relief. Until he said, "Not anymore," and Tristan's head started gently spinning again.

"Okay." Tristan felt like he was holding on to reality with both hands, but he really wanted to understand. "Tell me more about reading objects. What do you learn?"

Jo shrugged. "When I hold things, old things, and I concentrate, I can see images. Of the former owners, their lives, their . . . I dunno. Their general vibe. Like . . ." She gestured across the table. "Let me see your hat?"

"This?" Tristan looked down at his top hat like he'd never seen it before. "I don't know if you'll get much out of it."

"It looks antique, though. Is it?"

"Yeah, but . . ."

Sophie sighed. Loudly. "Just let her read your hat, Tristan."

Jo made a *gimme* gesture with both hands, and what else could he do? He passed it across. She handled the hat carefully, turning it over in her hands, before closing her eyes and letting out a long, low breath. A placid look settled over her face, replaced quickly with a furrowed brow. "That's weird. It's old." Her eyes stayed closed, and her voice had gone dreamy, like she was speaking under a trance. "But it doesn't have a long history."

Damn. She wasn't kidding about her ability. "That's right. It was found in the back room of a department store, when they were selling off some old stock. It had never been worn before."

"Just by you." She was quiet for a few moments longer, then blinked open her eyes. "It misses the lights," she said as she handed it back across the table. "Just as much as you miss the singing."

"The . . ." Tristan blinked hard. Why was it suddenly hard to speak? He looked down at his hat, as though maybe it would speak for him. It had certainly told her *something*.

"What lights?" It sounded like Sophie asked the question against her will. He glanced up and was surprised to see her looking at him; he'd thought she'd posed the question to Jo.

But she'd asked him, so he answered. "Theatre lights. I was a theatre minor in college. When I was in *My Fair Lady* this hat was part of my costume."

"*My Fair Lady*?" Nick snorted. "Colleges don't do shows from this century?"

"I wish. Even a little Sondheim would have been nice." Tristan grinned. "But when the biggest patrons are baby boomers, you're doing the finest shows from the nineteen sixties." He glanced down at the hat as memories began to hit him like a fire hose. All those nights and weekends spent learning lines and blocking, all those extra voice lessons. His nickname around the fraternity that semester had been I Can't, I Have Rehearsal, in honor of all the parties and functions he'd missed. It had been brutal. And he'd loved every moment of it.

These memories must have shown on his face, because Sophie's expression softened. "And did you sing? Like the hat said?"

"I did." He was still lost enough in those memories for the idea of a talking hat to not be weird.

"Do you miss it?"

"I do. Yeah. I really do." Memories combined with emotion became overwhelming, and Tristan practically stabbed himself in the eye with his thumb and forefinger, trying to stave off tears. His life was full of doubts, full of moments where he contemplated the inevitability of his business going under. Of having to start over doing something soulless and boring. Of becoming his father. Those moments, where he feared he'd hit a fork in the road a few years back and taken the wrong path, were when he missed performing the most. Those moments made him incredibly sad.

But he'd never had one of those moments in front of other people. People he barely knew. People whose business he was currently in the process of destroying.

Never let them see you weak, his father loved to say.

But when Tristan looked up, he was caught in Sophie's gaze like a spotlight was shining on him. And for the first time, he didn't want to perform under that spotlight. He just wanted her to see him. Weakness and all.

And from the look on her face, maybe she did.

Fifteen

Eventually Terry kicked them all out. Not because it was closing time, but because, as he said, it was just too weird to have so many people eating at his restaurant. Sophie could relate; at the end of a long day she was usually sick of people too.

For a few minutes the disparate group hung around awkwardly on the sidewalk in front of Poltergeist Pizza, in that weird space of the evening being over but no one really wanting to admit it.

Finally, Theo turned to Jo. "I never knew you could do that," he said. "You know, the thing with the hat. Does it work on anything?"

Sophie let out a gasp. "The painting!" How had she not thought to suggest that? She felt like an idiot.

Theo kept talking like she hadn't interrupted. "I have this painting, in the museum. Of this woman that no one's been able to identify. I'd love to know more about her . . . er, I mean about the painting . . ." His voice trailed off and he swallowed hard.

Jo shrugged. "Worth a try. You want me to stop by sometime, when the store is closed?"

"Yeah." His nod was an awkward bob of the head. "Yeah, that would be great."

Meanwhile, Nick was talking to Tristan, the two men under the glow of the streetlight. "You should come by the house. Next week sometime. Dinner?"

"Really?" Tristan looked surprised. "Yeah, I'd love that."

Sophie and Libby both turned wide eyes to Cassie, betrayed. But Cassie had a small smile on her face as she leaned into them. "It's Sarah," she murmured. "She wants to have a word with him about that pirate story he keeps telling in front of the house. She's, uh. Not happy."

Sophie did her best to hold in a snort. Tristan had looked wary enough in front of Mystic Crystals not too long ago, and that had just been Aura in one of the upper windows with a plastic skeleton, a bedsheet, and a green light bulb. Then he'd almost come out of his skin tonight when the Parmesan cheese had been delivered. Getting an actual dressing-down from a ghost was going to send him screaming off into the night.

If only it were that easy. God, she really couldn't wait till October, when he would be out of her town and out of her life. It was a familiar refrain by this point, but somehow she couldn't drum up the same old vehemence against him.

Part of it was that dream, of course. Earlier tonight he'd rolled up his shirtsleeves and her throat had gone dry. Just seeing his lightly tanned skin, arms sprinkled with blond hair, had brought on the visceral memory of pink-flamingoed board shorts and salt water, his mouth moving on her neck . . .

Which had *never happened*, she reminded herself firmly. Because it had been a *dream*. But it was a hard thing to remember when the subject of that dream was right across from her, shooting her a hesitant smile.

There'd been something else about him tonight, a vulnerability in his expression. Especially when he talked about his top hat. It was still really stupid, but it was obviously more than a silly costume to him. He'd seemed almost human this evening, with his sweat-damp blond hair and rumpled shirtsleeves. She'd even let him steal a slice of her pizza, which was very unlike her, and had felt a warm glow inside when he went back for a second piece, declaring it the best pie on the table.

Eventually everyone split up to go their separate ways. Nick and Cassie left first. They'd each grabbed a drink to go—a bottle of water for her, a longneck beer for him—and they headed toward the break in the seawall by The Haunt. Libby tagged along with them, breaking off to the right at the corner by Mystic Crystals. Theo and Jo left next, still talking about Theo's mysterious painting as they walked up the downtown streets toward their neighboring shops.

Now it was just Tristan and Sophie, standing together under the glow of a streetlight. She turned to him, and he at least looked as awkward as she felt.

"Can I walk you home?"

The question made her bristle. He noticed. "I'm not trying to be friends," he rushed to add. "I promise. No friendly thoughts here. It's just that it's dark and I want to make sure you get home okay."

"Oh," Sophie said. "No. It's not far. Lots of streetlights." She gestured down the street in illustration, which looked too much like something she did during her tours, so she shoved her hands in her pockets. "Besides, this is Boneyard Key. Not a lot of mugging goes on around here."

His laugh was an exuberant puff of breath. "Point taken."

Silence fell between them again, so total that she could hear the buzzing from the streetlight above them. Enough. She was tired and wanted to go home. "Well," she finally said. "Good night."

"Yep." He rocked on his heels. "Good night."

Was he waiting for something? Or maybe he just didn't know

how to end their conversation. So Sophie took charge, throwing a little wave over her shoulder before turning south on Beachside, heading toward The Haunt and eventually her condo. When his footsteps followed after a few moments, she didn't think anything of it. It was still early; he was probably stopping at The Haunt for a drink before heading back to whatever ivory tower he was living in. Not that Boneyard Key boasted a lot of ivory towers, but over in the new section of town there were a lot of expensive homes. Ones that rich people built with a killer view of the Gulf, that they stayed in for a week or two every year, not caring that their fancy-ass houses drove everyone else's property taxes through the roof.

She passed The Haunt, kept heading south, but the footsteps behind her remained. Slow and measured, keeping pace with her. She stopped at the next corner and turned around, fuming.

"Quit following me!" She glared at Tristan, about a half block behind her.

"I'm not following you!" His eyes were wide as he protested.

She motioned at the rapidly dwindling space between them as he kept walking closer. "Then what do you call this?" She put her hands on her hips, waiting while he caught up to her.

"I call it walking home," he shot back. "Am I not allowed to do that?"

"But *I* live this way." She gestured down the street, toward her building. They were nowhere near the rich side of town; where could he possibly be going?

A terrible thought occurred to her. She squinted at him warily. "Where do you live?"

He gestured in the same direction she had. "A couple blocks that way. My dad has a condo there. He's letting me use it for the summer."

"A condo," she repeated faintly. She looked doubtfully down the street, as though there could be another condo building this way, one that she didn't know about. But no. There was only one apartment building that had been turned into condominiums a couple blocks down this way.

Her building. He lived in her building.

Great.

She gusted out a sigh. "Fine." She started walking again, and Tristan took her resignation as an invitation, falling into step beside her.

It was a warm night, and even though the sun had set, the humidity in the air held on to the day's residual heat. It was irritating, and it was Sophie's own fault. No one had told her to wear jeans. At least she wasn't wearing Tristan's whole stupid getup. "It's going to be too hot to wear all that soon." Her voice was snappier than she intended, but the heat made her cranky as she gestured at his costume, half of which he wasn't even wearing anymore. He carried his top hat in one hand and his lantern in the other, his tailcoat draped over one arm.

"Believe me," he said darkly, "it already is."

Her gaze lingered on his hat. "Everything Jo said. About your hat. It was really true?"

"Yeah." He looked down at the hat in his hand. "That was . . . that was wild, to be honest." He glanced over at her. "Has she ever read anything for you?"

Sophie shook her head, but that was only a little bit of a lie. "I asked her to read a couple things after my aunt Alice died. Some of her jewelry. Her favorite book. But she couldn't tell me anything I didn't already know." That was the thing about Jo's ability. She read the energy that was left behind on objects. She couldn't communicate with anyone after they'd gone. Not that Sophie knew of, anyway. No, anything that Sophie had forgotten to ask her aunt Alice before she died was going to be forever unasked. It had taken a long time to accept that, but she was getting there.

"I'm sorry." His voice was low. Sincere. Sophie hated that. She didn't want sincerity from him. It was too much like his voice in that dream she'd been trying to forget while he'd been sitting across from her. She stuffed her hands lower in the front pockets of her jeans before they betrayed her by trying to touch him or something. That would be a disaster.

They walked in relatively companionable silence, both turning into the parking lot of the condo complex. Sophie gestured to the squat stucco building. "You're sure you live here?" The question reeked of desperation.

"I am." A smile played around Tristan's mouth. "Been here a few months now." He switched his jacket to the other arm as they went through the pedestrian gate of the condo complex and through the parking lot. "My question is, how have we never run into each other all this time, if we live in the same building?"

"Just lucky, I guess." Any second now he was going to peel off from her, head to another section of the building. But Tristan kept pace, up the center staircase and then hooking a left to walk down the breezeway.

"Really," she said. "You don't need to walk me home."

"Still not doing that," he said cheerfully.

"Seriously?" Her heart sped up as they walked down the exterior corridor on the second floor. There were only five doors ahead of them. Then four. Three. Then two.

Sophie came to a stop at her door, and Tristan barked out a laugh from behind her. Her heart pounded in her throat, and ridiculous thoughts swirled in her head as she fumbled for her keys to unlock her door. Was he going to attack her? Strangle her, throw her dead body into the Gulf? That was one way to get rid of the competition, right?

"You have got to be kidding me." Instead of whipping out a knife and taking her out, he walked briskly past her to the very last door. The corner unit with the perfect view of the Gulf. Of course. "All this time, you've been my next-door neighbor?" He grinned over his shoulder as he took out his keys. "What are the odds?"

But for a long moment Sophie couldn't breathe. Anger-based adrenaline had been replaced by fear-based adrenaline, and now it was replaced by something else. While she'd been having that erotic dream about him last night, he'd been sleeping a few feet away, on the other side of her bedroom wall? This was messed up.

"You want to come in?"

"What?" She looked up sharply. Tristan had unlocked his front door and ditched his lantern, and now he lounged in the doorway, his jacket still draped over the crook of his elbow. He'd unbuttoned another button of his shirt at some point during the walk home, and now the white line of his undershirt peeked through. He practically glowed under his front light, and a sprinkling of blond hair was visible just below his collarbone. It was too much like the dream, the one that had snaked its way into her blood and hadn't let go. He'd said that before, when Dream Tristan was half naked and shin-deep in the surf. *You want to come in?*

"Too many sharks," she whispered. That response had made a lot more sense in the dream than saying it out loud now.

"Pardon?" He took a step toward her, and her breath caught. Green now, slate-green eyes. They'd been blue in the dream. Hadn't they?

"Nothing." She shook her head hard. He shouldn't be so close. She'd been okay when they had a table separating them at the pizza place. She'd even been fine when they'd been walking home side by side, but now, this close, where she could see the rise and fall of his chest as he breathed, the way his lips parted just a little when he was about to speak . . . it was too close. Too much like the dream.

"You don't want to come in?" He gestured behind him. "We could . . ."

She didn't know what possessed her. What absolute insanity had washed over her, but she couldn't help it. She had to know.

Sophie took a step closer, stretching up onto her toes. She had just enough time to see Tristan's startled expression, see those lips part in a gasp before she pressed her mouth against his.

Kissing him felt just like her dream. And she never wanted to wake up.

Sixteen

Kissing Sophie was like something out of a dream. But Tristan's dreams had never been this good.

If this were a dream, for example, there would probably be a dinosaur somewhere. As the hard press of Sophie's mouth relaxed against his, as both of them realized that yeah, this was really happening, if this were a dream Tristan would open his eyes and see a T. rex peeking over Sophie's shoulder. Or there would be a pterodactyl perched in a nearby palm tree. Kissing in dreams, doing more than kissing in dreams, always had some fantastical element, something that didn't make sense.

But everything about kissing Sophie made sense. Tristan's hat and frock coat tumbled to the ground, and his hands found her waist, the curve of her hip, as though he'd always been touching her and knew just where to do it. Her mouth moved against his, lips parting against the soft stroke of his tongue, as though they'd been kissing like this all of their lives. Her soft moan as he gained access to her open mouth made him want access to all of her.

He'd fallen a step back, his spine pressed to the doorjamb, when she'd all but leapt on him. But now that she'd relaxed into him, he relaxed too. Well, as much as he could relax while his heart pounded in his chest and all the blood in his brain rushed to points south. He let one hand map the curve that went from her hip to her waist and back again, learning the way her body felt against his. With his other hand he cupped her cheek, sliding his fingers through those dark curls he hadn't stopped thinking about since the night they'd met. God, her hair felt as soft as it looked, and Tristan pressed himself closer, craving her warmth even in this humid, hot evening.

One moment everything was perfect, and the next moment she was gone. Tristan blinked his eyes open to see that Sophie had fallen back a step, two steps, her back pressed to her front door and her hands pressed to her mouth. Why did she look so shocked? This had been her idea!

"What . . . ?" He tried to speak, but his command of the English language failed him. He didn't want to talk. Talking was for people who weren't kissing Sophie, and he was no longer interested in being one of those people.

His one consolation was that Sophie seemed to have trouble forming words herself. She shook her head, curls bouncing around her shoulders. "That was . . . I'm not . . ."

Before he could ask what the hell she was talking about, she was gone, fumbling for her doorknob before practically falling backwards into her condo. The door closed firmly in his face like an exclamation, and the sudden silence of Tristan being left alone in the breezeway was total. He was in a daze as he collected his costume pieces from the ground. This was a new experience for him; no one had ever kissed him and then fled the scene.

His condo seemed even quieter than usual. Even more drab and stark white. Kissing Sophie had been like a Technicolor movie, and now the world was in black and white. He was Dorothy, returning to Kansas and wondering if all the good stuff had just been a dream.

The next few minutes passed in a blur, as Tristan somehow put away his hat and coat, unbuttoned and shucked his vest, and shrugged his suspenders down off his shoulders. All the while he paced his living room, pausing at the huge windows to look out into the night, taking in nothing, before doing another lap. His mind was still full of Sophie: her dismissive attitude toward him (which was warranted, to be fair), the way her mouth felt against his (incredible), the warmth of her body under his hands (maddening), and the brand-new knowledge that there was only a single wall separating them. It was too much, and his brain had clicked offline in self-defense. He probably would have paced the living room of this condo all night, wearing a track in the immaculate tile, if Eric hadn't called. He didn't remember answering his phone, but suddenly there he was, phone in hand, Eric's face on the screen.

"Hey! What's up?" Eric barely looked up at the screen as he typed on his laptop. "I wanted to make sure you weren't murdered on the mean streets of—"

"Sophie and I kissed."

Eric stopped typing, and the view wobbled as he picked the phone up from wherever it had been propped. Then Eric's face filled the screen, his eyes as wide as Sophie's had been just a few minutes ago.

"Say that again."

"Sophie and I kissed." Tristan said it slower this time, a smile overtaking his face as he let himself hear the words. It wasn't some crazy fantasy he'd conjured up. It really had happened.

Eric didn't seem to believe him. "You're kidding."

"I'm not." Tristan dropped onto his sofa.

"She's your competition! You're not supposed to be kissing the competition."

"She kissed me!" His lips still tingled from the press of her mouth; that first kiss had been hard. Like she'd been frankly a little pissed off about it. It wasn't until he'd cupped her cheek in his hand, taking over the kiss, steering it, that she'd gentled against him.

"Well?"

Tristan snapped back to the present. "Well, what?"

"Well, how was it?" Eric propped his phone up again, resting his chin in his cupped hands. "Tell me everything."

"No." He pressed his lips together, partially to hide his smile, but mostly to hold on to that tingle. "I'm not telling you anything."

"Oh, come on! This is probably the longest dry spell you've ever had, and—"

"I've been busy! Trying to keep this company afloat. Trying to keep our jobs. Remember? Stuff like that."

"Meh." Eric waved all that aside with a grin. "I've missed hearing about your love life."

Tristan scoffed. "It's not a love life. It was one kiss. And she ran away immediately afterward." He was still disappointed about that.

"Hey, it's better than what you've had lately. Which is nothing."

Tristan shook his head. "Did you call for an actual reason?"

"Probably something business related. Who cares? This is much more interesting."

"Eric . . ." Tristan tried to sound authoritative, like his father would with an employee. But he'd known Eric too long, and his father probably didn't talk to subordinates right after kissing a pretty girl.

Eric sighed in exasperation. "Ugh, fine. You've usually updated the shared spreadsheet with Friday night's numbers by now. Which, honestly, makes you boring. You're still a young, mostly attractive man—"

"Thanks a lot."

"—you should be going out on a Friday night, not updating spreadsheets. But you didn't call tonight. So where were you?"

"I was out on a Friday night." He grinned as Eric cheered. "I stopped for some pizza and was there for a bit with . . . with some friends." The word caught in his throat even as he said it. Maybe it was a bit of a stretch to call them friends, but they were the closest thing he'd had since he'd arrived in Boneyard Key.

"No. Wait. You're making friends? I thought they hated you there. Especially since you're trying to drive their girl out of business."

Tristan snorted. "Well, Nick and Cassie invited me over for dinner next week. So that's something."

"Sure, that's something. But . . ." Eric squinted through the screen at Tristan. "Why do you care so much?"

"Why wouldn't I care? You haven't been here the past few weeks, trying to be friendly while all the locals give you the cold shoulder. Believe me, no one can freeze you out like a small town."

"Right. I get that. But again, why do you care? It's not like you're settling down and building a life there. It's just like every other time you start up a new GNO location. You come, you establish, you get the hell out and go back to New York. In fact, why don't you just get that Sophie girl to run your tour as well? That seems like a no-brainer."

"I tried that. She wants nothing to do with me."

Eric raised an eyebrow. "She just kissed you. Sounds like she's sending you really mixed signals."

Tristan had to laugh. "Sophie's . . . well, Sophie's complicated." That was putting it mildly.

After hanging up with Eric, the silence was back, ballooning to fill the condo. But now he welcomed the quiet. He stretched out on the sofa, propping his head on one end as he let his brain process the entire evening.

So much had happened. He'd met his first ghost—he was still

getting his mind around that. He'd been leading ghost tours for years now, but this was the first time he'd had to consider that ghosts were real. And could hand him Parmesan cheese.

That still wasn't even the biggest news of the night.

He'd kissed Sophie.

Well, Sophie had kissed him.

He pressed his lips together again, bringing back the sense memory of Sophie's mouth on his. Her soft lips, the frame of her glasses bumping lightly against his cheek. He wanted more, and if he'd had his way she'd be in here with him right now.

But she'd fled, and Tristan had to respect that.

He stayed in the living room of his darkened condo for a long time, watching the moonlight bounce off the water, stalling going to bed. It was going to be hard to sleep, knowing she was right on the other side of the wall. Why did she have to live right on the other side of the wall?

And how was it that they lived right next door to each other, and he'd never known? Sophie had looked just as surprised about it as he was, her eyes huge behind her glasses as she stood with her front door at her back. Right before she'd practically lunged at him . . .

. . . And there he was, thinking about the kiss again.

He was never going to get to sleep.

Tristan held his breath every time he opened his front door. Which was ridiculous; he'd been in this condo for months now, and nothing had changed.

But he hadn't known that Sophie was right there, on the other side of the wall. So everything had changed. Every step outside his door was fraught with potential. Would they run into each other? Would she kiss him again if they did? (Okay, that second one was doubtful, based on the whole running-away portion of the evening.) Sophie's door remained closed and silent every time he walked past it, as ordinary as all the other doors on their floor, yet in his mind it was ringed in a warm glow. *Sophie lives here.* Saturday night's tour was packed, but he could barely enjoy it. Every nerve ending was on alert, searching the downtown streets for a sign of Sophie. But just like the empty condo breezeway, he didn't catch sight of her.

Monday morning there were two notifications on his phone. A text from Nick Royer (Dinner on Wednesday?), and a news notification. The Start of Hurricane Season: What You Need to Know.

Hurricanes had a season? Tristan tapped on it, but the linked article was behind a paywall, so he clicked his phone off again—no one had time for that. Then he fired off a response to accept Nick's invitation while his coffee brewed.

But he couldn't stop wondering—what did he need to know about hurricane season? He'd never lived somewhere where that was a thing he needed to know. A little googling helped. Hurricane season ran from June first to November thirtieth, with the peak falling somewhere between August and October. He would be here for most of that, so that news was alarming. Another article showed him a checklist of supplies he was supposed to keep on hand. A gallon of water per person per day. Enough nonperishable food to last for a few days. Flashlights and extra batteries. A radio that somehow powered with a hand crank. The list went on, and Tristan hadn't realized that living in Florida also apparently meant preparing for the apocalypse every summer. Was this what made living in Florida so crazy? Spending so much of your time waiting for the big storm that was going to wipe you out? It sounded exhausting.

He tried to put it out of his mind as he pulled up the spreadsheets that Eric had sent over that morning. Spokane had had a great month and had absolutely cleaned up on Memorial Day weekend. It was enough to make up for the fact that Flagstaff had apparently had no tourist traffic, so all in all they'd come out ahead. Ahead was good. Ahead meant profit. Ahead meant a successful company. But would it be enough to satisfy Sebastian Martin when the time came?

Enough. Tristan closed his laptop with a snap. He was too much in his own head, so he grabbed his keys and headed out, but doom lingered in the corners of his mind as he stepped outside—half about the future of Ghouls Night Out, and half about hurricane season. New things to worry about were always neat. But it wasn't time to panic. About either of those things.

It took half a block to remember why going outside in the early afternoon in June was a bad idea; his T-shirt was already sticking to his back, and every breath felt like a wet towel was wrapped around his head. He'd planned to walk downtown, but once he hit Spooky Brew on the corner of Palmetto and Beachside, he stopped for an iced coffee and a few deep breaths of air-conditioning. Once his damp T-shirt had become good and cold he set out again, taking a right and heading for the corner grocery instead. Sure, downtown was just up the road, but in this heat it was too far.

The Supernatural Market must have gotten the same memo about hurricane season. There was a huge display just inside the entrance. Pallets of gallon-size water jugs shared space with jumbo-size packs of batteries next to another display of artfully arranged canned ravioli and Spam. Oh, shit. Maybe he should be panicking after all.

He grabbed a cart and had loaded three gallons of water and six cans of ravioli into it before he realized he wasn't fighting anyone for anything. A glance around showed three other people in the store, milling around like it was any other Monday, without so much as a single gallon jug of water in their carts. He was the only one grabbing supplies like a frantic doomsday prepper.

The cashier didn't even seem concerned. "That time of year again, huh," was all he said as he waved the scanner gun over each gallon of water. Tristan nodded like he knew exactly what he was doing, but his bravado was long gone once he'd lugged everything home. Grocery bags with water and canned goods counted as a workout, and by the time he'd put everything away, he wondered what the hell he'd been thinking. He didn't even *like* canned ravioli.

Oh, well. The store had a decent wine selection, so he'd grabbed something for Wednesday night. Hopefully Cassie liked red wine.

Seventeen

Sophie was never leaving her home again.

She stood with her back pressed against her front door for what felt like hours on Friday night. She covered her racing heart with one hand, willing her breath to slow so she didn't sound like a marathon runner gasping for air. What had she been thinking, kissing him? She hadn't been thinking, that was the problem. Hence, never leaving the condo again.

Okay, never was a very long time. But it wasn't like she needed to leave anytime soon. Her fridge was basically empty, but there was ramen in one of the cupboards, and she should drink more water anyway. The commute to her day job was the distance from her bed to her laptop, either on the living room couch or kitchen table. She loved her home. It was peaceful. It was a warm hug from Aunt Alice, whose presence she still felt here, despite what Nan might say.

But there was no peace now. Her skin itched and she couldn't settle to any one task. She watched TV without seeing a thing; she read the same page of a book for half an hour. The only thing she was good at all weekend was pacing her living room like a caged tiger. He was right there, her brain screamed. Right *there*, on the other side of this wall. How was she supposed to keep on living here, all comfortable and normal, when Tristan was right next door to her?

Every sound from outside made her want to jump out of her skin. Was someone out there? Was *he* out there? Sophie twitched her blinds for the millionth time that day, peering out her front window into the breezeway. She'd never been so invested in the patch of concrete outside her front door. If she pressed her forehead against the window and turned just enough, she could see the very edge of his door. The motion set her glasses askew every time, but she did it anyway.

It was possible she was losing her mind.

It had been days, after all. An entire weekend where she hadn't left her place once, except to lead her Saturday night tour, and then she'd scurried out, practically sprinting down the center stairs as soon as she'd established that the coast was clear. Then she'd done the same in reverse on the way home. She knew Tristan's schedule; his tour ended before hers, so if she took her time going home afterward there was no chance she'd run into him. No chance she'd humiliate herself again by kissing him a second time.

She couldn't live like this.

By Monday she was more irritated than cautious, and desperately needed to talk to someone. So after sending a group text to Cassie and Libby (SOS! Lunch at HG today?) and attempting to get some actual work done, Sophie pressed her forehead to the front window, dropping to the ground in panic when Tristan's front door opened. She stayed on the floor, heart racing, while his footsteps strolled past her door and down the breezeway. As soon as the coast was clear, she slipped out her door, keeping tabs on Tristan as he headed up the block. Once he hooked a right toward the Supernatural Market, she heaved a sigh of relief, continuing up Beachside and to Hallowed Grounds.

Cassie had saved them a table. Though knowing Cassie, she had probably been there since breakfast. She'd adopted the café as her work-from-home spot, and Nick was so wrapped around her finger he apparently forgot that he hated people who spent all day in his place, using their laptops to mooch off his Wi-Fi. Libby arrived soon after, and over plates of extra-crispy fries Sophie filled them in.

"You and Tristan *kissed*?" Libby's eyes went wide, never looking away from Sophie as she reached for the ketchup.

"I did sense a vibe that night at Poltergeist Pizza." Cassie nodded firmly, and maybe just a little smugly. "Figured it was only a matter of time before he kissed you."

Sophie shook her head hard. "I kissed him." The sentence was low, muttered mostly to the plate of fried potatoes in front of her.

It didn't seem possible for Libby's eyes to go any wider, but she managed it. "You kissed *him*?" The words were a squeal, and the ketchup was forgotten as she leaned in, grabbing on to Sophie's arm. Her nails dug in and it only hurt a little.

"Shhhh!" Sophie threw an anxious glance over her shoulder, but no one around them was paying attention. More importantly, there was no sign of a certain tousled blond haircut anywhere. Relieved, she turned back to her girls. "I know. It was stupid. So, so stupid." Hadn't she been telling herself that all weekend?

"Are you kidding?" Cassie took a last, watery sip from the dregs of her iced latte. "That was the least stupid thing you could have done." She shrugged when Sophie and Libby both turned amazed eyes her way. "What? I said before that he was cute. And that y'all have a vibe."

"Who has a vibe?" Nick chose the exact wrong moment to stop by their table.

Sophie shook her head frantically, but Cassie ignored her. "Sophie and Tristan. You saw it too, Friday night?"

"Oh." Nick slid Libby's BLT in front of her and placed another iced latte at Cassie's elbow. "No comment."

Cassie dimpled up at him as he took away her empty glass. "Wuss."

"One hundred percent." He glanced over his shoulder, obviously trying to find a way out of this conversation. "But hey, I texted him earlier; he's coming over on Wednesday for dinner. You can grill him then about his intentions."

"Excellent." Cassie practically rubbed her hands together like a supervillain. She gave Sophie a speculating look. "You want to come over too? Make it a double date?"

"Absolutely not." Sophie crunched into her fry harder than was strictly necessary as Nick fled the scene. "And we don't have a vibe. We can't have a vibe. He's my mortal enemy, remember?"

"Well, that's a little dramatic." Libby picked up one half of her sandwich and inspected the quality of the bacon.

"Eh, she's not wrong," Cassie said. "He's coming for her job, and there's only two choices here. Either he wins and puts her out of business, or he loses and then he leaves town. Neither option exactly leads to long-term happiness."

Sophie sighed. Cassie had a point. She hated that Cassie had a point. "Please, let's talk about anything else."

Libby's eyes lit up and she straightened in her chair. "Hurricane season's starting! That's exciting."

Sophie groaned. "Okay, let's talk about anything but that."

"Why?" Cassie looked from Libby to Sophie. "What's wrong with hurricane season? Except for, you know, the hurricanes?"

Sometimes Sophie forgot that Cassie was relatively new in town, and hadn't grown up with the two of them. "Libby's a storm chaser."

Libby scoffed as she bit into a fry. "Oh, I am not. I just like to track the storms."

Sophie turned back to Cassie. "From now till November, it will be her entire personality. If a butterfly flaps its wings off the coast of Africa, she will blow up the group chat. Trust me."

Libby tossed her blond ponytail over her shoulder. "Well, they're predicting an active season, so be prepared for lots of texts, then."

"I love lots of texts," Cassie said with a smile. "So keep me posted." Just when Sophie thought she was safe, Cassie turned back to her, chin resting on her hand, a dreamy look in her eyes. "Is he a good kisser?"

"Oh, God." Sophie took off her glasses, laying them on the table while she covered her face with her hands. "I don't want to think about it."

"Why?" Libby dropped her voice to a murmur. "Was it bad?"

"Aw, damn." Cassie clucked her tongue. "Hot guys shouldn't be allowed to be bad kissers."

"It wasn't bad." Sophie's voice was muffled by her hands. Her friends were blurry when she took her hands away, but maybe that was good. She didn't have to look them in the eye. "Once the, you know, surprise wore off." That was the moment she kept replaying in her mind. When his mouth, which had dropped open in surprise when she all but jumped him, gentled against hers. He'd settled into the kiss while she'd settled into him, and it felt like sliding into a warm pool of water. Comfortable. Gentle. Perfect. She'd wanted to stay in that kiss for the rest of her life. It was better than her dream . . .

It was the memory of the dream that had done it, that night. Made her realize that she wasn't dreaming, and she'd really just grabbed Tristan—her rival, her enemy, her next-door neighbor??— and laid one on him. In real life. The realization was a splash of cold water to the head, and she'd pulled away. Jerked away. There was enough time for her to catch a glimpse of his startled eyes—light green, and clear as ice—before she fled.

Sophie reached for her glasses and slid them back on. Cassie and Libby were both staring at her, and she realized she'd been sitting there for a stupid amount of time while her mind replayed their kiss. The silence at the table had stretched past the awkward point, and Cassie was obviously stifling a laugh. The corners of Libby's mouth twitched too. Traitors, the both of them.

"It was a *goooooood* kiss." Libby's voice was singsong.

"Oh, stop it. Let's go back to talking about hurricanes." But she was smiling too now as she reached for her Diet Coke. Enjoying a kiss wasn't a crime. Even if it was with the last guy she should be kissing.

Cassie tried a couple more times to turn her dinner with Tristan into a double date, so Sophie had to take evasive action. Sorry, I can't, she texted on Tuesday afternoon. Theo and I are meeting up to compare research notes. Then she texted Theo to see if he was free Wednesday evening to compare research notes. Thankfully, he didn't make her a liar. Even more thankfully, on Wednesday evening he didn't want to talk about hurricanes. Or kisses.

"We've taken a lot of notes over the last few months," he said by way of greeting when she showed up at Boneyard Books with a massive bag of Chinese takeout.

"You're not wrong." She followed him to the history museum in the back, where his laptop and a pile of notes were already set up on the card table by the filing cabinets.

"After I got your text yesterday I took the liberty of putting everything that we've already compiled into some semblance of order." He moved a few framed photographs off a glass-enclosed display of fishing equipment, making a space for Sophie to unpack the food.

"Oh, really?" She set her messenger bag in the seat across from his, getting out her own laptop.

He nodded, reaching for the orange chicken. "It's set up in a shared document. I sent you a link."

"Perfect." Another shared document? Sophie was getting good at those. She settled in front of her laptop with the container of chicken lo mein—why order anything else, honestly?—and accessed the document. It was longer than she expected it to be; all these weeks chipping away at one story after another, one location after another, had resulted in a substantial document when it was all put together.

"Theo, I don't want to alarm you, but I think we've got a book here."

"I know." His smile was almost, but not quite, hidden by a bite of fried rice. He chewed carefully and swallowed before he continued. "I took a quick stab at organizing it into sections, mostly based geographically. But feel free to move things around. We want to tell a cohesive story, but also make it entertaining."

"And that's what I do, right?" She shot him a smile across the table as she scrolled, speed-reading through notes she'd already read. But an unfamiliar paragraph made her stop and scroll back for a closer read. "You got the stuff from Eternal Rest in here!"

"I did, finally. Mrs. Erikson took her sweet time getting me her documentation, but once she did it was fascinating. Did you see the part yet about the phantom housekeeper, who leaves extra toilet paper outside everyone's doors?"

"I bet that came in handy in the early days of the pandemic." Sophie grinned at Theo's snort of a response. "Oh, I forgot to tell you that Mystic Crystals is a dead end. It's just Aura's triple-great-grandmother serving as a spirit guide for whatever descendant is doing psychic readings."

"Hmm. Could be worth a mention?"

Sophie shook her head. "I think they want to stay out of it."

"Fair enough. But you know . . ." Theo nudged the takeout carton aside and rested his elbows on the table. "It's a closer location than Eternal Rest. You could maybe add it to your tour."

"Probably not the best idea." Sophie fought back a laugh, thinking about Aura and her bedsheet and her green light bulb.

"How's all that going, by the way? I'd heard that you and Tristan made some kind of . . . arrangement?"

"What?" Sophie asked sharply. "What do you mean?" He'd been there last Friday at Poltergeist Pizza. Had he picked up on the vibe that Cassie wouldn't shut up about?

"This whole . . . I don't know. What are you calling it?" He gestured with his chopsticks while Sophie tried not to panic. Because what did you call one kiss that you immediately ran away from? "Contest," Theo finally said, and Sophie almost sagged with relief. He wasn't talking about The Vibe. He was talking about the potential loss of her passion project. Much better.

She huffed out a laugh she didn't feel, trying to cover her racing heart. "I guess you could call it that." She closed her laptop, folding her arms over it. "It's all very 'may the best businessperson win.' I just need to be the best businessperson by October first."

"Ah." Theo waved an unconcerned hand. "You'll be fine, then."

She tilted her head. "You think so?"

"Definitely. Your tour is better."

"Really." Now, that was something she never thought she'd hear Theo say. A slow smile spread on her face. "Tell me more."

He rolled his eyes, but there must have been something in her face that made him soften his expression. "Yours is accurate. It's more informative."

"Wow," Sophie deadpanned. "You make it sound so fun."

Theo scoffed. "You know what I mean. I caught some of Tristan's tour a couple weeks ago. Did you know he really does have a story about a guy with a hook for a hand?" He shook his head in disgust. "He's just recycling every canned story that you ever heard as a kid at scout camp."

"I didn't go to scout camp."

"All the better. You're not just someone from out of town trying to make a buck. You're one of us. You love this town, and it shows when you're telling people stories about it. That love shines through. Believe me, you're going to be okay."

"Thanks." But Sophie wasn't sure. Theo was right; she did love this town. And the idea that her love was palpable in the stories she told and the tour she gave meant a lot. But she was stuck on his descriptors: accurate, informative. A ghost tour was supposed to be a fun tourist experience. Not a college course.

She put it out of her mind temporarily and opened her laptop, turning back to what was becoming a rough draft of a book. Soon she was absorbed, making note of things she wanted to fact-check here, cleaning up language there. Across the table from her, Theo had finished the fried rice and was reading a book while polishing off a second egg roll, occasionally making notes on a yellow pad in front of him.

Her gaze strayed to the portrait above Theo's head. "Did Jo ever come by to take a look at that painting?" She jerked her chin in that direction, and Theo looked up at it.

"Not yet. She had to go on a buying trip with her father over the weekend, and I think she's been busy with the new acquisitions." His gaze, as always, softened when he looked at the portrait, as though he were a man in love. It was all she could do to not sigh dreamily. What would it take for someone to look at her like that?

"I'm sorry," she said. "I bet you were hoping to get some answers."

He gave an unconcerned shrug. "It's all right. I've gone a long time not knowing who she was. I can hold out a few more weeks."

Sophie watched Theo watch the portrait, then her eyes moved to the wall clock above the door. She gave a start. "Is that the time?" It was almost eight, and she was not a girl to stay out late on a weeknight.

"Do you need an escort home?" Theo asked as they cleaned up the takeout detritus and set the museum to rights.

"I'm okay," she said. "Lots of streetlights." A sense of déjà vu swirled in her stomach. She'd just had this conversation, hadn't she? It took a moment for her to place it: last Friday night with Tristan. After the pizza, before the kiss. Ugh. She'd managed to go a few minutes without thinking of him.

She pushed the memory aside. "I'll keep working on the manuscript. Let me know if you find anything else we want to include."

A sad satisfaction swelled within her. Tristan might be able to take away her ghost tour, but no matter what, her stories would live on.

It wasn't much. But maybe it would have to do.

Eighteen

Turned out, Cassie *loved* red wine.

"Oh, yes, please." Her eyes lit up as Tristan handed over the bottle.

"Is it a good one? I admit I'm not much of a red wine guy." He asked the question absently as he stepped over the threshold. He was already in love with her house, just from standing on the porch and ringing the bell. It was genuinely historic, not something that was built in the last five years with a historic aesthetic. The wood slats of the front porch were just the slightest bit slanted, and there was a look to the weathered but tidy siding that only came from time and good craftsmanship.

"No idea." She grinned and waved him inside. "But it's wine, and it's red. That's good enough for me."

He couldn't believe that this was where Cassie lived: the cool little beachside cottage he'd given his pirate story to. One of his favorite stories for one of his favorite houses. Whenever he led the tour past the house, he found himself lingering just a little longer than necessary, taking in the scent of the cabbage roses that bloomed against the picket fence. The lights in the living room were always on, and the front windows were always open, even now that summer had set in. The lace curtains moving in the breeze seemed to wave at him every time he walked by.

Tonight the windows were closed, and inside looked just like he'd imagined: cozy and comfortable. It smelled warm, despite the air conditioning—like basil and garlic. As he followed Cassie into the house, he glanced into the living room, looking for those familiar curtains. There they were: hanging against the closed front windows, a battered leather recliner nearby. Cassie's decor was mostly modern, set against the backdrop of details like crown molding and built-in bookshelves in the living room. The hardwood floor creaked pleasantly under his feet, the melody of a historic home.

If his father had bought this house, he'd have ripped it all out. Updated it to a modern clean look, as soulless as the condo Tristan was staying in. But Tristan loved this house just the way it was.

Nick was at the counter in the kitchen, plating a loaf of garlic bread he'd obviously just taken out of the oven.

"Hey, glad you could make it." He tossed a friendly smile over his shoulder. "You want a beer?" Nick moved to the fridge—an older one that was covered in little words on magnets. Tristan hadn't seen a magnetic poetry set since his college days.

"Tristan brought wine." Cassie held up the bottle.

"Even better." Nick nudged the fridge closed and reached for the corkscrew.

Dinner was simple: baked pasta and garlic bread, and the red wine had gone with it perfectly. The conversation was just as simple: small talk about their lives, where they'd gone to college, careers. It felt like equal parts dinner and job interview—that awkward first time hanging out with new friends, looking for common ground.

Finally, Cassie put down her fork, folding her arms on the table, and Tristan instantly went on alert. She'd had that look before, in the café, when he and Sophie had struck whatever deal they were currently in the middle of. "So," she said. "Sophie."

Dammit. Dread mixed with pasta in Tristan's stomach; he didn't want to think about Sophie. Nothing made sense in his head when it came to her. He was supposed to be focused on ruining her, professionally. But what he really wanted was to ruin her in much more fun ways. When he thought about her now, all he could see were her mussed curls and her kiss-swollen mouth when she'd pulled away from him in front of their doors. He'd messed up that hair. He'd kissed that mouth. He'd wanted to keep doing both of those things, but then she'd fled.

And then she'd avoided him. This was not a town that hid people easily; Tristan knew when he was being avoided. So while his thoughts—and often his dreams—had been on fire with the memory of Sophie in his arms, his waking life had been depressingly Sophie-free.

But he couldn't escape this line of questioning here at Cassie's table, so he might as well dive in. "Sophie," he repeated, fortifying himself with a healthy sip of wine. "I'm familiar."

Amusement played around her mouth. "From what I hear, y'all have been getting quite familiar."

Heat crawled up the back of Tristan's neck. She knew. Of course she knew; she was Sophie's friend, and friends talked. He wanted to know everything Sophie had told her. No, he didn't. He didn't want to know anything. But before he could speak, a spoon resting on the edge of the table clattered to the floor.

Cassie blinked and broke her gaze from Tristan's, as though the spoon had broken some kind of spell. "Oh, right. Sorry, Sarah. I got off track for a minute there." She bent to pick it up, glancing over her shoulder at the fridge. Tristan followed her gaze, an automatic reaction, but froze. Because the random words on the fridge weren't random anymore. Now they formed a kind of starburst pattern, with a few words in the middle, drawing attention.

tell him

story wrong

"When . . ." The word came out a croak, so Tristan cleared his throat and tried again. "When did you move those words around?"

Cassie placed the spoon in a very deliberate action, leaving it on the edge of the table again. "So, I'm afraid we had an ulterior motive, inviting you over." She gestured toward the fridge. "Tristan, I'd like you to meet Sarah Hawkins."

"Your refrigerator is named Sarah Hawkins?" That weird swimmy feeling in his brain was back, like when the Parmesan cheese had appeared out of nowhere at Poltergeist Pizza. Something was happening here that his conscious brain wasn't ready to handle yet, and his lizard brain wanted to flee from.

Nick snorted. "You gotta admit, Cass, that makes about as much sense."

"Point taken. Okay, let me start over." She folded her hands on the table, looking serious. "Sarah Hawkins lived in this house before I did. Like, about a hundred years before I did."

Then it clicked. "Sophie's story," he said. "On her ghost tour. I remember."

Cassie nodded. "Sarah doesn't like you."

"Me?" That brought him up short. He was fine—well, not *fine*, but you know—with Sophie not liking him. And her friends by extension. But an incorporeal spirit, that until this moment he wasn't even aware existed? That was a new one. "What did I do?"

"You're making shit up in front of her house." Nick was obviously also on Sarah Hawkins's side. "Telling people what, that a pirate lived here?"

"No," Tristan said. "Not a pirate. A pirate's *lover* lived here." Did no one listen to the story he was telling?

"Oh, my mistake," Nick drawled, rolling his eyes in Cassie's direction.

"I don't mean *here* specifically. I didn't research this house; I have no idea who used to live here."

"Obviously," Cassie broke in, but Tristan wasn't finished.

"I use it in all my ghost tour locations, and the crowds always love it. It's tragic, but romantic at the same time. It's always been my favorite story."

"Not Sarah." Nick shook his head. "Sarah doesn't like it at all."

"She . . ." He looked uncertainly from the fridge to Cassie and Nick and then back again. The swimmy feeling was still there, but had receded as pieces fell into place. "So you're not saying that Sarah Hawkins used to live here, but that she, uh. She still does?"

Cassie nodded. "She *after*-lives here."

The spoon fell to the floor again, and this time Tristan ducked down to pick it up. "Here. It keeps falling off the table." He tossed the spoon to the center of the table, next to the empty platter of garlic bread. There. It shouldn't roll off the table anymore. It wasn't his place to tell Cassie that her kitchen was obviously on a slope.

But Cassie's attention was back on the fridge, where the words had changed.

story wrong
lies bad

"I know, babe." Cassie sighed kindly in the direction of the fridge before turning back to Tristan. "Look, it's not entirely your fault. She's sensitive to her story being told wrong," she said apologetically. "And she insisted on letting you know, and wanted to tell you herself."

"Tell me herself." Tristan knew he was doing that thing again, where his brain had stopped forming thoughts and all he could do was parrot back what people were saying to him. But he was currently processing a hell of a lot of information. Information that didn't feel real, even though it was literally right in front of his face.

"Yep." Cassie motioned to the fridge. "The words. That's Sarah." She was so matter-of-fact about the whole thing. This had to have freaked her out too at some point, right? The rational part of his mind tried to work out a way that she and Nick were playing an elaborate prank on him. Something that involved distracting him by throwing that spoon on the floor . . .

But as he watched, the spoon in the middle of the table, the one he'd picked up and placed himself, rotated slowly until the handle of it clinked against the platter. He couldn't explain that away with an uneven floor.

"That's Sarah too." He indicated the spoon. "Right?"

Cassie nodded. "That's how she gets my attention. Lets me know she has something to say. Otherwise I'd be staring at the fridge all day."

"Right," Tristan said. "Because that would be weird." He took a deep breath, then he did something he never imagined he'd do. He apologized to a refrigerator.

"I'm sorry," he said. "Please believe me when I say that it's nothing personal. I'm not trying to slander you, or tell stories about you that aren't true. Honestly, Sarah . . ." He turned to Cassie. "Sarah? Mrs. Hawkins? What should I call her?"

"Call her Mean Mrs. Hawkins," Nick said. "She loves that." He jerked then, knee bumping the table, and Tristan nearly came out of his skin before he realized that Nick had been hit the old-fashioned way, by Cassie kicking him under the table.

"Sarah is fine," she said. "She was elderly when she died, but she doesn't really present as an old lady."

Tristan nodded carefully. "I get that. I'm coming up on thirty, but in my mind I sometimes feel like I just got out of college, you know? Maybe it's the same way for ghosts?" The rational part of his brain remained mind-blown, unable to comprehend a serious conversation that involved actual ghosts.

But that was where he was now: in a serious conversation that involved an actual ghost. He turned back to the fridge, as though talking to the words made the most sense. "Anyway, Sarah, all the stories I tell are made-up. I'm not trying to educate the public here. I'm just telling stupid stories to tourists. And I have to tell you, the pirate one's my favorite. Every time I put a tour together, I save it for my favorite location. As soon as I got to Boneyard Key I fell in love with this house. With the roses in the front yard, and the way it backs up to the water . . . it made me think of romance and pirate ships."

The refrigerator didn't respond. It was a marvel that Tristan expected it to.

"Don't look at the fridge," Cassie said.

"Why not?" He brought his gaze back to Cassie.

"We think she doesn't like to be watched while she's moving the words." Across the table Nick was leaned back in his chair, finishing off the wine in his glass.

That was a good idea. Tristan reached for his own glass, but before he could take a sip, the spoon clinked again.

dark hair girl glasses

story real

"She's talking about Sophie," Nick said, as though Tristan couldn't put that together on his own. "Sophie tells the real story. The history of the house and Sarah. She likes that one better."

"I understand why." Tristan nodded slowly. He was becoming a pretty big fan of Sophie himself.

"But I think she gets it," Cassie said. "That you're not trying to tell a real story. You're not slandering her name or anything. It's just fiction. Right?"

"Exactly." He nodded emphatically at the fridge. "Is it okay that I go on telling it, now that you know, and I know, that we're putting something over on the tourists?" It was suddenly very, very important that he get the approval of a long-dead woman.

After a few moments, it appeared that he had it.

i like your hat

He'd take it.

Nineteen

Sophie hated that she didn't want to go home.

Her home was her sanctuary, her safe space. She worked there, she slept there. It was the one place in the world that she knew was hers.

But as she left Boneyard Books and started heading south on Beachside, she realized she didn't want to go home. Because Tristan was there.

Well, not *there*. It wasn't like he was waiting for her in her living room, lurking over by Aunt Alice's vinyl record collection. But he was right next door, and the threat of running into him was constant. Sophie didn't like what it was doing to her blood pressure.

So instead of going straight home, she headed for the break in the seawall, not far from The Haunt. The coffee and ice cream carts were closed up for the night—Wednesday evenings were the absolute low point when it came to tourists—and she followed the sidewalk as it became more and more covered in sand that crunched under her flip-flops before finally giving way to the beach. This secluded little picnic area boasted one streetlight that hadn't winked on yet, two picnic tables, and a killer view of the sunset. Tonight it featured one more thing.

Tristan.

The sky wasn't dark yet, so she could see him just fine. His back was to her as he sat in the middle of one of the picnic tables, his feet resting on the bench seat below. Shirtsleeves pushed up, elbows resting on his knees, he stared off at the water, in the direction of the sunset that it wasn't quite time for. The light breeze ruffled his blond hair, and he was the picture of a pensive thinker. He was the last person in the world she wanted to see.

"Oh." The exclamation fell out of her mouth before she could check it, as sharp and as sudden as her feet skidding to a stop on the sandy path. She wanted to turn on her heel and flee back up the path toward Beachside before he noticed her, but it was too late for that.

Tristan turned, his torso twisting in her direction, and Sophie caught her breath at the look on his face. Usually, his default expression was of amused nonchalance. Like the world was his oyster and he had his shucking knife at the ready. But tonight, something had rattled him, and his usual confidence had drained away.

Before Sophie could say anything, the moment shifted, and a small smile came to his lips.

"You here for the sunset?" He nodded out toward the water. "The show's about to start."

Sophie shook her head. "I was trying to avoid you." The sentence had sounded fine in her head, but when she said it out loud, she wanted to wince.

"Whoops." His face fell, and his shoulders slumped a fraction as he turned back to the water. "Sorry about that."

Sophie shouldn't feel bad. She could hear Cassie's voice in her head: *Fuck this guy's feelings.* She could see Libby nodding along emphatically. Sophie didn't owe Tristan a darn thing. But something propelled her forward to join him at the picnic table. He turned to her in surprise when she climbed onto the table beside him.

"You want me to go?" He made to climb down, but she shook her head.

"May as well stay," she said. "Show's about to start, right?"

And what a show. There was nothing like a sunset on the beach. The water stretched out to the horizon, and beyond into infinity, reflecting all the colors of the setting sun above it: wild oranges and purples.

"I met Sarah Hawkins tonight," Tristan said, his eyes scanning the sky.

Sophie nodded. "I heard you might."

"That was . . . She was . . ." He shook his head hard, and Sophie understood. She'd lived here almost her whole life, and she'd seen a lot of things. But Sarah and her refrigerator magnets were next-level.

Tristan wasn't done. Something big had happened to him tonight, and he was still processing. "On your tour, you talk about the Beach Bum, right?" She nodded out of courtesy, but he was still talking. "Is he here right now? Is he real too?"

"Oh, he's real." Sophie looked around, as though the Beach Bum was someone she could spot in a crowd. "I don't know if he's here, though," she said. "I've never actually seen him. Nick has."

He nodded slowly, taking in this new information. "I told Sarah I was sorry for making shit up about her house." A small laugh escaped him as an exhale. "I'd never apologized to a ghost before."

"Well, there's a first time for everything." She shouldn't be smiling around him, and she sure as hell shouldn't be joking with him. But she couldn't help it; it was as involuntary—and as necessary—as breathing. "I used to tell her story wrong too," she finally said, a small confession in the almost dark. "Then once I found out, it meant a lot to me to get it right. For her. You know that's why Cassie leaves her windows open on ghost tour nights, right? So Sarah can hear her story."

"I didn't know that." He fell silent while they both turned their focus back to the sunset.

"Sarah means a lot to me," Sophie said. "So does the Beach Bum. They all mean a lot to me."

"I get that now." The sky around them grew darker until finally the streetlight blinked on behind them and the water swallowed up what was left of the sun. In the glow of the streetlight she could see Tristan out of the corner of her eye, nodding thoughtfully. "I never thought of ghosts as real people. All the time I've been doing this tour, in all the places I've been doing it, they've always just been stories to me. But they're more than stories around here, aren't they?"

He didn't need confirmation, but Sophie nodded anyway. "My family isn't one of the Founding Fifteen. My parents divorced when I was little. Mom left, and Dad and I moved in with his aunt Alice, here in Boneyard Key, when I was five. Then my dad left too. Last I heard he's somewhere up in Tennessee, with a new family."

Tristan sucked in a breath. "Jesus. That's—"

"Yeah." Sophie cut him off; she wasn't telling him all this for sympathy. "Aunt Alice raised me. But this town did too. I love this place, and I feel connected to it, as much as the Founding Fifteen families do. At the same time, I'm still not one of them, you know?" Her sigh felt like it came from her toes and gusted out into the night, mixing with the sea breeze. "Doing this tour, telling their stories. It's a way to honor this town. Honor the people who were here before us." She glanced over at Tristan, whose head had bowed while she talked. It almost felt like kicking him when he was down, but she finished her thought. "So no, here they're not just stories."

One more slow nod. "I get that now," he said again. He looked up then, almost surprised that night had fallen while they'd been talking. He hopped off the picnic table and extended a hand. "Can I walk you home?"

People were asking her that a lot lately. Sophie's lips quirked up as she shook her head. "I'm okay." But she slid off the edge of the table to the sand to join him, pointedly not taking his hand. She still didn't take his hand as they fell into step together, following the path back up to the street. He wasn't walking her home. They just happened to be walking in the same direction.

Silence fell between them again, but this time it wasn't as easy as when they were watching the sunset. Sophie was aware of the sound of her flip-flops as they slapped the pavement, and the swish of her sundress around her calves. Tristan cleared his throat twice before finally speaking.

"Are you ready for hurricane season?"

"What?" She almost stumbled on an uneven part of the sidewalk as her attention went fully to him. "There's a hurricane?" She hadn't been glued to the internet today, but if there was a storm on the way she should have known, right? Libby would have texted her a time or twenty.

"No," he said, "not right now. Just like . . ." He waved a vague hand. "In general. It's hurricane season now, right? I saw these articles. Checklists. Stuff you're supposed to get."

"Ahhh." Newbies were so cute. "A gallon of water per person per day, a hand-crank radio, that kind of thing?" Once again, she couldn't help the smile that came to her face in response to his earnest nod. "My supplies are more like red wine and chocolate-fudge Pop-Tarts." Her smile widened at his furrowed brow. "Don't have to refrigerate them. Anyway, call me when there's at least a Category 2 storm on the way. Then I'll worry about the rest."

One side of his mouth curved up. "Okay, but don't come asking to share my canned ravioli because you didn't plan ahead."

"Deal." Sophie hated canned ravioli anyway.

Tristan chuckled under his breath. "I think Eric is worried about me. He's convinced that I'm gonna get swept away in a storm. He'll probably be surprised if I survive the summer."

"Maybe you should evacuate now. Make him feel better." Unlike the last time she wished out loud he'd go away, this time her suggestion had no heat behind it. Weird. "Who's Eric?"

He glanced over with a surprised expression. "I haven't mentioned him before?"

Sophie shook her head. "We're not friends, remember?"

"Oh, right." He nodded solemnly, but his eyes danced under the streetlights. Sophie loved putting that expression on his face. No, she hated it. Being around him was getting confusing. "Anyway, Eric's my best friend. Business partner." He paused. "He's also my ex, but we don't focus on that too much."

Now Sophie did stumble, over a nonexistent crack in the sidewalk. His ex? Oh, God. Her brain reordered the past few days of memories. The way she'd jumped on him. Kissed him. Oh, *no*.

"I am so sorry." The words burst from somewhere in the middle of her chest, and Tristan turned to her, a question in his eyes.

"Thanks," he said, "but it was a while back. He and I are both over it by now, and we're much better off as friends. He's got a boyfriend now, though, honestly, I think his true love is spreadsheets."

"No, I mean that I . . ." Sophie gestured between them as her brain began to lose the ability to form coherent sentences. "I didn't realize that you . . . When I kissed you, I didn't know that you're . . ."

Tristan's eyebrows shot up when he understood what she was fumbling to say. "Bisexuals," he said. "They're a thing." His expression was guarded, wary.

"Oh," she said. Then, "*Oh*," again as her memories reordered themselves a second time. Relief flooded through her, but there was something about the set of his shoulders that showed tension. It was a scary thing, being vulnerable. She'd given him a peek at her soft underbelly, back there at the picnic table. And he'd just given her a peek at his in return.

She cleared her throat. "Well," she said, "I'm glad to know that I didn't completely misread the situation."

Tristan's laugh was a surprised bark. "You didn't misread a thing."

Sophie spent the rest of the walk home trying not to think about how comfortable this was. They weren't friends. They certainly couldn't be more than friends. She absolutely should *not* be thinking about kissing him again.

When they got to the outer stairs leading up to their floor, he gestured her to walk ahead, and Sophie hitched up her dress as she started the climb; the last thing she wanted was to trip and face-plant in front of him. He followed at a respectful distance, falling into step with her again as they headed down the breezeway to their units.

"Thanks for not walking me home." Sophie tossed the words over her shoulder as she unlocked the top lock on her front door. Tristan snorted, walking past her toward his own door.

"Hey, it's what not-friends do." She heard the jingle of his keys, the thocky sound of the bolt being thrown back. She was about to unlock her own bottom lock, her mind already on which frozen meal she was going to stick in the microwave, when his hand caught her elbow.

"What . . ." She whirled, tried to fall back a step, but his hand slid up to her upper arm, tugging her closer.

"I'm sorry." He didn't sound sorry. He didn't sound like much at all, his voice little more than a murmur. His other hand caught her cheek, hot against her skin, and despite the residual heat of the evening, she found herself leaning into it. "I know we're not friends. I know you don't want me around. But I haven't been able to stop thinking about this . . ." He stepped closer now, impossibly closer, fitting his body against hers, and Sophie's mouth went dry. "About you."

"Me neither." It was a tiny confession, two little words dropped into the space between them. She tilted her head to look up at him, and his eyes roamed across her face as though trying to memorize every little detail. "We need to, though."

He nodded solemnly. "This is a terrible idea." He bent to her, lips parting, just a breath away from hers. She gusted out the tiniest of sighs and he breathed it in.

"Awful," she agreed, tilting her head up some more, so close that she could feel the heat of him, that perfect anticipation of being close enough to touch but just. Not. Quite.

And then his mouth was there, a tentative brush against her own. The contact made her whimper, and all thoughts of frozen microwave meals were forgotten as his hand slid into her hair, holding her, tilting her head just the way he wanted it. His nose bumped against her glasses, and his jaw against her palms had that faint rasp of five o'clock shadow, and his hair felt as silky as it looked, slipping through her fingers like warm water. He held her like she was something delicate that he was afraid he'd break if he played with it too hard.

She wanted him to play with her too hard.

She pressed closer, mouth opening, and he groaned from deep in his chest as their kiss deepened. His hand slid up to the curve of her shoulder, fingertips flirting with the strap of her sundress, and she wanted more. She wanted him to push those straps off her shoulders, let her dress fall . . . let him . . .

No. No, she didn't. She didn't want that at all. Or she shouldn't want it. Everything had become so confusing. She felt safer than she ever had, there in the arms of the man who was threatening to destroy everything.

She shouldn't want this.

She wanted it more than anything.

She shook her head, pulling back just enough to take a breath, and Tristan let her go immediately, if reluctantly. He blinked, his eyes glassy and color high in his cheeks.

"Sorry." His voice was breathy, his chest heaving for air, and he still didn't sound sorry.

"We can't do this." Tears stung the corners of her eyes even as she spoke, as though her heart knew she was saying the exact wrong thing. But her heart wasn't in charge; her brain was. It had to be.

"I know." He pressed his kiss-swollen lips together—she had done that—and shoved his hands in the pockets of his khakis. "It won't happen again. I promise."

Well, that was terrible news. But Sophie made herself nod firmly, accepting those terms. "Good night, then." She pushed open her front door, retrieving her keys with fumbling fingers. She didn't let herself look back at him, but she could feel his eyes on her, watching her until the very last moment.

"Good night." His parting words were swallowed by the firm close of her door, and she wanted to open it again. Take back everything she'd just said.

Instead she threw her locks. Upper first, then lower. Each thud felt like another bar in the cage around her heart. Keeping him out. Keeping her in. This was for the best.

At some point, it would even feel like it.

Twenty

Tristan's routine changed a lot over the next few weeks, and it all had to do with kissing Sophie. Or the opportunity to kiss Sophie.

When he'd first come to Boneyard Key, he'd tried to be professional. He'd gone out of his way to avoid her ghost tour, and make sure his didn't cross hers. But these days he felt like a stalker, desperate for crumbs of her attention. He'd never realized before how much effort it took to "accidentally" run into someone, but damn if it wasn't worth it. Every Friday and Saturday night, when her ghost tour ended and the guests finally broke off and wandered out into the night, there he'd be, lounging against the streetlight outside of Hallowed Grounds.

The first couple times he'd acted surprised to see her, like he'd just happened to run into her, and offering to walk her home was common courtesy. But it didn't take long to drop the pretense and just be there, every weekend night, so they could walk home together from their ghost tours. And then of course, there'd be a kiss good night in front of their neighboring doors. It was all very 1950s: walking a girl to her door after a date and stealing a kiss under the front porch light. Except they never went on a date; that would make things too real, too official. Which was probably for the best, since they were the last two people in Boneyard Key who should be dating each other.

After that first night, he didn't invite her into his place again, and she never invited him into hers. He'd caught a glimpse of it once, a stolen glance over her shoulder when she'd pushed open her front door. His mind's eye retained a snapshot of walls painted a warm, dark color, with the glow of lamps from within. The exact opposite of his sterile, white-and-glass-and-stainless-steel condo. It looked cozy. It looked like home. Tristan found himself yearning for the other side of Sophie's front door, even though he knew he'd never be allowed in.

Damn if the whole thing didn't make him feel like a horny teenager. Tristan took a lot of cold showers after ghost tour nights, and not just because of the Florida humidity.

During the day, however, nothing between them had changed. Sophie offered him little more than a scowl when he ran into her at Hallowed Grounds, and he understood right away that she wasn't going to publicly acknowledge their after-hours kisses. Tristan had never been someone's dirty little secret before. It was intriguing. It was frustrating.

That wasn't the only thing frustrating him these days.

As early summer had become midsummer, sliding into July, ticket sales soared and lowered like gently rolling hills. He obviously hadn't done the right kind of market research; while common knowledge indicated that Florida was a tourist destination, those tourists weren't constant. He'd assumed that he'd have busy, steady traffic for the entire summer—that was when people took vacations, right? But when the heat of summer set in, the streets were empty and the place became, well, a ghost town. Tristan didn't even want to make that joke out loud. In a place like this it would be low-hanging fruit.

It felt ridiculous, leading a tour of three people through town doing his whole top-hat-and-frock-coat schtick, but he reminded himself that it beat working in New York with his father. Probably saying things like *blue chips* and *amortization* and having no idea what he was talking about.

The other thing frustrating him? Right back to Sophie again.

"She doesn't even have a website!" It had become a familiar refrain, one he raged in Eric's direction at least once a week.

"You want me to build her one?" Eric sounded amused through Tristan's earbuds.

"No!" He paced the living room; that third cup of coffee this morning probably hadn't been the best idea. "I'm just saying, to her, a successful marketing plan is leaving a few flyers at the Chamber of Commerce, on the corkboard at Hallowed Grounds, and maybe at Jimmy's bait shack if she's feeling spicy. Leaving flyers at a bait shack is not a marketing plan!"

It was possible that Eric responded, but Tristan was too wound up to hear anything he said. "She doesn't even have a catchy name! Ghouls Night Out—see, that's a name people remember. I don't even think she's named her business at all! I hear Nick, over at Hallowed Grounds. 'You should check out Sophie's ghost tour on Friday night.' Another prong in her brilliant marketing plan."

"Okay, but what about this? She's been doing pretty well with those flyers. Right? I keep track of the spreadsheets. She's certainly keeping up with you."

Tristan gave a groan of frustration. "Yeah. We're outperforming her, but not by much." It didn't make sense. His tours were packed on Friday and Saturday nights, but so were hers. He had the website, the viral marketing. He should be leaving her in the dust by now, but his margin wasn't nearly as big as it should be. "God, I'd love to get a look at her books. See what her profit margin really is. Get a full picture, you know?"

"I bet you would." Eric was a master of innuendo, and Tristan had to laugh despite his frustration. "Friendly reminder, though?" Eric continued. "You don't want to help her succeed. You're trying to put her out of business, right?"

"Right." He gusted out a sigh. It was hard to remember that sometimes.

After that course correction, they went back to going over projections, trying to estimate the state of the business by October first. It was something they did on a biweekly basis these days, and the closer they got to that dreaded date, the more solid the projections became. And those projections weren't looking good. He'd put way too much faith in this Boneyard Key location, buoyed by those first few weeks when tourist traffic had been at its peak and he'd been playing to sold-out crowds. They'd relied too much on the data from those original crowds, and not counted on the ebb and flow of tourist season in a Florida summer.

Frustrated, he stalked out of his condo and jogged down the stairs. It had been a long morning, and it was only eight thirty. He deserved a treat. A mocha latte at Hallowed Grounds should do it—nothing wrong with a fourth cup of coffee before nine. Maybe he could run into Sophie, try and get her to smile. That was always fun. Maybe he could talk her into setting up a website while he was at it.

Except the neon sign on the front window of the café—a big coffee cup with ghosts wafting from it instead of steam—was switched off for some reason. As Tristan got closer, he noticed the inside of the café looked suspiciously dark. It wasn't until he tugged on the door—locked—that he noticed the sign taped to the front.

CLOSED. GONE FISHING.

Tristan blinked. Then he blinked again as he felt his brain leaking out his ears. Was he losing his mind? "Gone fishing?" The words dropped unbidden, his mouth trying to make sense of what his brain was rejecting. Who in the hell closes their café to go fishing? Did no one in this town know how to run a business?

He tugged on the door again, just to piss himself off a little more, then turned to head back down the street. There was more than one coffee shop in this town.

The line at Spooky Brew was out the door. Tristan's place on the sidewalk was two people behind the person leaning against the door, propping it open. He was just close enough for the cold, blessed air conditioning to whisper past his face. He sighed and took out his phone; may as well check his email while he waited. This was a lot of effort for a midmorning treat, and it wasn't making him feel any better.

He'd moved up to first in line behind the door when there was a sigh from behind him. "Let me guess. Nick went fishing today?"

It took a moment for him to place the blond woman behind him. Blue eyes, ponytail . . . she was one of Sophie's friends. He remembered her now, from the pizza place.

"Libby, right?" The line moved; it was his turn now to prop open the door. He set his back against the glass and put his phone back in his pocket, turning his attention to Libby. "Does he go fishing a lot?"

She shrugged. "Sometimes, in the summer. Especially when things aren't busy."

"Oh, yeah." Tristan pointedly looked at the five people in front of them, then at the growing line behind them. "It's totally dead around here."

Libby ignored the pun, which was probably for the best. "What are you getting?"

"Why?" Was there a reason she needed to know his coffee order? Was she going to slip the barista a bribe to sabotage his drink?

Libby glanced around, then leaned in as though imparting a secret. Tristan couldn't help but lean in too, closing the loop. "Don't get a latte." She continued before he could protest, because that was really what he was in the mood for. "The cold brew is really good here, but Oliver never really learned to work the espresso machine." Her nose wrinkled and her voice dropped even more. "Avoid the lattes," she whispered. "Trust me."

"Oh." He considered that. He'd gotten a hot cup of coffee here once or twice, but all his more elaborate orders had come from Hallowed Grounds. "Thanks."

Libby's eyes twinkled as she shot a secret smile in his direction. "Just a little locals tip for you."

Something inside his chest softened at this, an unexpected gratitude that he was being brought into some inner circle. He didn't really deserve it.

Once inside, he ordered the largest cold brew they had, and while he added far too much cream at the condiments counter, he listened to Libby place her order. Cold brew with chocolate cold foam (damn, that was an option? He'd have to try that next time.), a large black coffee, two scones, a lemon bar, and a blueberry muffin. He sipped at his coffee, and when Libby's order was ready, he took her bakery bag while she juggled both drinks.

"I've got this," he said. "Where are you headed, and what army are you feeding with all this?"

She indicated out the door and to the right. "The office is just over there, next to Mystic Crystals. I never know what Nan is in the mood for, so I get a little bit of everything. It's my job to make sure she eats in the morning."

"Is Nan your boss?"

Libby nodded around a sip of her coffee. "She's that too. But mainly she's my grandmother."

"And what does she do?"

"Paranormal investigation," she said, the way anyone else in the world would say *insurance salesman*. But that was Boneyard Key for you, wasn't it?

Tristan tightened his grip on the bakery bag. "You and your grandmother are ghost hunters?" He tried to sound casual about it, he really did. But this was all still new to him, Parmesan cheese and refrigerator magnets notwithstanding.

"Nan's a ghost hunter," she clarified. "I'm an office manager. And procurer of breakfast."

The crystal shop was closed too, and Tristan clucked his tongue as they walked past it. "Is no one open today?"

Libby shrugged. "Hours get a little wonky in the low season. Especially during the week. Boneyard Key is more of a weekend kind of place."

"I don't get it." Tristan took a frustrated pull from his coffee. Libby was right; the cold brew was excellent. "Even when it's slow, places should stay open, right? Catch the customers that might be around."

"Maybe. But think of it like this." She gestured up Beachside Drive, back the way they had come. "Spectral Souvenirs, down around the corner, is mostly a bunch of kitschy crap. T-shirts, shot glasses, trucker hats. Not a lot of locals in the market for a Boneyard Key souvenir shirt, right?" Tristan had to reluctantly agree, despite his own growing collection. "If they're open on, say, a Wednesday? They might sell one, maybe two T-shirts. A couple candy bars to local kids, maybe, even though those kids can get 'em for cheaper over at the Supernatural Market because Spectral Souvenirs sells them at a bigger markup. So on a day like today, they're gonna bring in fifty, a hundred bucks if they're lucky. Now think about costs . . ."

Tristan gave a firm nod. Now they were in his territory. Profit and loss statements danced in his mind's eye. "Overhead, electricity, water, paying your employees . . . you're going to come out in the red."

"Exactly. Or you cut overhead by manning the store yourself. Seven days a week? When do you take a day off?"

"Okay, I get it." Tristan would hold up a hand in surrender, but his hands were full.

"Not to mention . . ." Libby shot him a grin. "Hard to have a lot of work ethic when it's this hot outside."

"Can't argue with that." He followed her up the sidewalk to the front door of another Sears kit house, similar to Mystic Crystals. The sign out front said SIMPSON INVESTIGATIONS in plain white lettering against a black background—nary a cartoon ghost in sight. He'd thought it was a PI's office all this time, but he supposed it was that too.

Tristan took the bakery bag in his teeth, holding Libby's coffee for her while she unlocked the door. It was hot and stuffy inside; she was obviously just getting there for the day.

"You can set that over there." She indicated the large desk set in a living room turned reception area. He obeyed, placing her coffee and the pastries in front of her computer while she bustled into a back room. A moment later the air conditioning whooshed on, and he tilted his head up toward the vent with an involuntary sigh of relief.

"What about during the pandemic?" He picked up the thread of the conversation. "When things were locked down? How did y'all make it through that? Like, what did Sophie do with no tours?" He tried to sound nonchalant, but Libby squinted at him when she emerged from the back.

"She worked." Libby arched one eyebrow. "She has a day job, you know. I don't know how you're making ghost tours pay the bills, but for her it's a side hustle. A passion project."

Those words hit him: *passion project*. Ghouls Night Out was a passion project for him too. At least it had been, back when they'd started. He genuinely had fun leading these tours. He loved wearing the outfit and making people laugh. It was all the businessy stuff, projections and forecasting and spreadsheets, that gave him a headache. He'd always been happy to let Eric handle that side of things.

Something must have shown on his face, because Libby tilted her head as she regarded him. "Aw, what's the matter?" She batted her eyes at him as she swirled around the ice in her drink. "You upset that Sophie's beating the pants off you?"

"What?" Tristan's brain stumbled. He didn't want to think about Sophie and his pants in the same sentence. "She's not . . . My pants are . . . What?"

Now Libby's grin became a laugh. She settled herself behind her desk and switched on the desktop computer. "Thanks for helping me with my stuff." Her tone was dismissive, but her blue eyes sparkled in his direction. "You're not all bad, I guess."

Tristan saluted her with what was left of his coffee. "It's what I strive for."

Nothing had been resolved, he realized as he went back into the late-morning heat. His business was still on the brink of failure, and he still was locked in a ridiculous battle of wills with a woman he'd much rather be kissing. But he knew what to order at the second-best coffee shop in town, and that wasn't nothing.

Twenty-One

like him." Libby hit a few keys, closing out of a document before leaning back in her chair and grinning up at Sophie.

"What?" Sophie felt like she'd come into a conversation somewhere in the middle, and didn't even know where to begin. "Who?"

"Your guy. You know, Tristan." She clicked a few more keys, bringing up her email screen while talking to Sophie at the same time. "I know I'm just supposed to tolerate him for the sake of being polite, but he's really not that bad. You know, except for the whole 'trying to put you out of business' part."

"What?" Sophie said again, because her thought process had skidded at the words *your guy* and hadn't quite come back online yet. "He's not . . ."

Her words were drowned out by the ringing of the old-school, push-button landline phone on Libby's desk, leaving Sophie's denial about Tristan only half-spoken. Which was probably where it should be. Because he wasn't her guy. But he wasn't *not* her guy, either, right? There were only so many times you could kiss your next-door neighbor good night before you had to think that something might be up here.

Libby held up one finger as she answered the phone. "Simpson Investigations, this is Libby, how can I . . . Oh. Hey." Her professional phone voice dropped at least an octave, her cheerful tone going flat. "Yeah, *Lawrence*"—Libby put a weird emphasis on the name—"she's here, but . . ." She screwed up her mouth, chewing on the inside of her cheek as the voice on the other line spoke. "Okay, but did you take care of . . ." Once again, she couldn't get a sentence out, and her face tightened even more. "Okay. Yeah. *Okay*. Hold on." She pushed a button, and the light that indicated the incoming call started blinking as she pushed a couple more buttons. "Hey, Nan. Yeah, it's him. He took care of the job, but he's still in South Carolina. I guess there's a problem with a haunted house a couple towns over he wanted to fill you in on before . . . ?" This time the trail-off midsentence seemed deliberate, and Libby listened, nodding along. "Yep. Oh, and Sophie's here. You got it." A couple more button presses, and Libby hung up and leaned back in her office chair, making it roll gently back a few inches. A loud sigh gusted out of her mouth.

"Everything okay?" Sophie raised her eyebrows. Nan had exactly two employees: Libby, who served as her office manager, and a guy named Lawrence who, for some reason, never set foot in Boneyard Key. He spent his time on the road, running down leads and dispelling hauntings that Nan deemed too far away from home for her to concern herself with. Sophie didn't know much about him, but the one thing she did know was that he seemed to push Libby's buttons. And not in a good way. Phone calls from him were few and far between, but Libby did a lot of sighing afterward. Sophie had asked once or twice about him, but Libby always changed the subject, and Sophie had gotten the message.

"Yeah." Libby shook her head as though waking up from an annoying dream and reached for her coffee. "Now, where was I?"

Sophie didn't want to remind her, but it would come around eventually. "Tristan." Just saying his name conjured up the muscle memory of kissing him good night in front of their doors, making her heart skip a beat and a flush creep up the back of her neck.

That reminder seemed to chase away any remnants of Libby's bad mood, and she smiled around her sip of coffee. "Right. I just want you to know that I approve."

"Approve?" Sophie gave a start. What did Libby know? What had Tristan told her? Was she going to need to check the breezeway outside her front door for cameras? Be more discreet when kissing Tristan? Or worse, stop kissing him altogether? "Approve of what?" Why couldn't she sound casual, like a normal person? Why did she have to sound all nervous and prickly?

But Libby waved an unconcerned hand. "Just . . . in general. I approve in general." The words were a pronouncement.

"Thanks," Sophie said dryly. She took a slow, deep breath while trying to get her panicking heart under control. "I'll be able to sleep better knowing that. Is that why you wanted me to come by? To tell me you approve of basically nothing?"

"Oh. No." Libby glanced down at the phone, where the line was still lit up. "Nan wants to talk to you. I'll send you in once she's off the phone."

"Okay." Sophie watched Libby take another pull of her coffee. Now that the panic about her and Tristan was wearing off, she took a good look at her best friend for the first time. Libby didn't usually drink coffee this late into the morning; it was practically noon. If she hadn't switched over to her pink Stanley full of ice water, she was cracking open a Diet Coke. But now, as Libby turned back to her computer, Sophie noticed that her face looked drawn and there were circles under her eyes. Her usual sleek blond ponytail was pulled up haphazardly.

"You okay?" Sophie asked. "No offense, but you look like you could use a nap."

"None taken." Libby yawned, as though the mention of a nap had prompted her subconscious, and stifled it with the back of her hand. "Sorry. Nan hasn't been sleeping well the past few nights." She pressed her lips together, her face drawn with worry, and now Sophie was worried too.

"This has been going on for a bit, right?" She remembered back in the spring, when Libby had cut *Romance Resort* night short. She'd had to miss one or two since then as well. "Has she been to the doctor? Is something wrong?" Dread climbed up her throat. Something couldn't be wrong with Nan.

"She's . . ." Libby choked on the word and blinked hard, her eyes shining. Oh, no. "She's okay," she finally said. "Technically. The doctors say she's fine, and you know Nan. She won't hear any different. But . . ." She threw a look over her shoulder, toward Nan's closed office door. "She's definitely slowing down." Libby's voice was hushed. "More bad nights than good right now." Libby heaved a sigh. "It's scary. You know that." The look she gave Sophie was full of meaning.

"Yeah." Sophie had a hard time getting the word out. "Yeah, I know that." She reached for her best friend, covering Libby's hand with hers, and they held on tight to each other for a few pained heartbeats.

Then Libby let go and sat back, dashing a tear away with her fingertips. "Anyway." She turned back to her computer. "Have you seen the latest on the storm?"

Any other time Sophie would have groaned, but today she'd allow it. They both could use a distraction. "What storm?" She tried to keep the *here we go again* out of her voice as she moved to look over Libby's shoulder. One of Libby's favorite hurricane tracking websites was up, showing a map of the Atlantic Ocean. She was in full storm hunter mode today.

"This one." Libby tapped a fingernail against the screen. "I don't like the looks of it."

Sophie squinted at the X somewhere in the middle of the ocean. "You can't be serious. That one's barely off the coast of Africa."

"Conditions are good, though. Everyone on the forums is saying that this could be a big one."

"Oh, well, if everyone on the forums says so . . ." Because people on the internet were notorious for knowing what they're talking about. She'd learned that much from going viral.

"Of course, it depends a lot on the currents, but the water's been warm lately, which makes it more likely to become a bigger storm if it hits it right. And then of course if it makes it to that channel down around Cuba, it could make a run up the Gulf . . ."

"I'm hearing a lot of ifs."

Libby kept going as though Sophie hadn't spoken. "Probably going to be Flynn. I mean, the next name up is Evangeline, but that'll probably be this one." She tapped at another X, way up in the North Atlantic in the middle of nowhere. "The wind speeds are about at the point where it'll get a name, but it's just going to be a fish spinner. Not going to come close to anywhere."

"Evangeline? Who comes up with these names, anyway?" Sophie looked at one X, then the other. Neither one looked particularly threatening, and she had no idea what made Libby declare one dangerous over the other. But Libby's job as an office manager for an elderly ghost hunter meant a lot of long days with only the internet to keep her company. She spent a lot of that time reading up on hurricanes and their patterns. There were probably worse ways to waste time on the internet.

"I'm just saying. Mark my words. This one could come this way."

"You got it," Sophie said. "Your words are marked."

Libby quirked a smile, and that made Sophie feel better. She made a mental note to keep better track of her best friend. She'd been thinking too much about Tristan lately, and not the things—and people—who mattered.

Libby obviously disagreed. "So back to Tristan . . ." She grinned while Sophie groaned. "Have you driven him out of business yet?"

"Not yet." Sophie sighed. She'd rather go back to talking about hurricanes. At least she knew she didn't want a hurricane in Boneyard Key. Tristan she was feeling less confident about.

"How is it all being determined, anyway? I know you said 'most successful,' but what's the metric? Are we talking attendance, profit . . . ?"

"Ticket sales." That was something she knew definitively, at least. The only thing. "He started saying all this stuff about profit margins and net income, and that's all too complicated."

"Hmm." Libby chewed on the inside of her cheek. "I've seen some of his ads online. He charges less than you do, so I'd think he'd have to have much bigger crowds to make up the difference."

"His crowds are pretty big." Sophie hated to admit it. In the months they'd been competing, she'd watched him make adjustments to his tour, showing he was able to pivot in ways that would have overwhelmed her. He'd trimmed down the number of days his tour ran, for instance—she could have told him from the start that doing them on weeknights was an exercise in futility. He had a good head for business. Much better than hers was, that was for sure.

Tristan had charisma on his side too. That easy smile, the crinkling of his eyes under his top hat; the way he tipped it to the ladies on the tour, making them giggle. His stories remained stupid, of course; from what she could tell he hadn't changed any of those. Their tours still crossed sometimes, and Sophie practically bit a hole in her tongue every time, wanting to avoid another viral video.

But she couldn't block out the laughter, the animated conversation, coming from Tristan's side of the street. His tour killed, so to speak.

And that killed Sophie. She wanted Tristan's ghost tour out of her town.

But if Tristan's tour was gone, Tristan would be gone. And Sophie wasn't sure she wanted that.

The phone on Libby's desk rang again, the change in tone indicating an inside line.

"Oh! She must be off the phone." Libby cradled the receiver between her ear and shoulder, still looking at the potential hurricanes on the weather map. "Hey, Nan, did . . . Yep, she's still here, you want me to send her in?" She nodded twice before hanging up. "You can go on in."

"Back there?" Sophie looked down the hallway, toward the closed door at the back. Nan's office, which till now had been uncharted territory. Here there be dragons. Not that Libby's grandmother was scary, per se. But she did not suffer fools lightly, and in Nan's eyes, most people were fools.

The floorboards creaked under her feet as she made her way back to the closed door, rapping on it lightly with her knuckles before pushing it open.

Calling this room an office was a misrepresentation. There was a desk, and it even had a computer on it. But that desk was pushed up against the wall without even a chair next to it, and both the monitor and keyboard had a fine layer of dust on them. Instead, Nan was nestled on a small floral fainting couch, ensconced in a giant cardigan despite it being late July. The rolling table next to her was covered in papers, a notebook and pen lay abandoned next to her hip, and the telephone was on the coffee table in front of her on a long cord that stretched back to the wall next to the unused computer desk.

Sophie expected to be interrupting Nan's very busy workday,

but instead the octogenarian appeared to be about halfway through a battered paperback romance novel. She looked up as Sophie closed the door behind her.

"Ah. Sophie." Nan seemed surprised to see her, even though Sophie had just been summoned. Sophie shifted her weight from one foot to the other while Nan carefully placed her bookmark back in the book and set it on the couch next to her. "I've been meaning to talk to you. Have a seat." She waved around vaguely, and Sophie looked for someplace to sit that wasn't on the chaise next to Nan. After an awkward moment she cleared some books off a nearby wingback chair, dumping them softly to the floor before taking a seat. The chair was ancient and could do with a reupholstering, but it felt like a hug, and Sophie wanted to sigh as she sank into it.

Nan fixed Sophie with a piercing gaze, one that reminded her of Aunt Alice. "Liberty mentioned that you wanted me to go to your place again. That you'd been smelling jasmine?"

"Yes." She answered the question with some confusion. That had been a while back, and Sophie had already dismissed the idea of Aunt Alice sticking around, despite the jasmine perfume. She thought Libby had too, but had she brought it up to Nan anyway?

"You think it's your aunt Alice." It wasn't a question; Nan spoke very pointedly.

"I thought it might be." Sophie clasped her hands together in her lap, trying hard not to fidget under Nan's gaze. "I mean, what else could it be? She wore that jasmine perfume all the time."

"I remember." A small smile flitted across Nan's face. "Your aunt was a hell of a card player."

"That's right," Sophie said as a sudden memory took hold. "Bridge nights on Wednesdays." She'd spent her high school years fending for herself for dinner almost every Wednesday night. Lots of microwave macaroni and cheese.

"Bridge?" Nan snorted. "Is that what she told you? Texas Hold'em was her game. I'll have you know your great-aunt was mopping the floor with half the town, week after week."

"What?" Sophie blinked. She'd had no idea. Aunt Alice had certainly lived comfortably in retirement, and Sophie had just assumed it was due to good investments. Had her great-aunt been a card sharp?

"Bridge," Nan said again under a chuckle. "Your aunt was something else. Her passing was . . . well. I don't have to tell you how sorry I was when she passed." Nan's expression softened, and Sophie blinked hard, swallowing against the emotion that rose up her throat. "I've been thinking about her lately. I miss her very much too. And believe me, I'd love nothing more than to be able to speak to her again." She shook her head not unkindly. "But me going over there and trying to contact her again . . . it's not going to do any good."

"I know." Sophie's voice was a tiny pebble thrown into a deep pond, swallowed up immediately.

"This town is unique, and it can be a real blessing when our loved ones stick around. I've found when that happens, it's usually because they're worried about those still living. But not everyone stays behind. Not everyone needs to."

"I know," Sophie said again, but she was lying. She didn't know. She looked at the door, at that unused computer desk—everywhere but at Libby's grandmother, whose bright blue eyes seemed to be looking right into her soul. She opened her mouth, closed it, and when she blinked a tear landed on her cheek, cold against her hot skin. "But I wasn't ready."

"No one ever is." Nan's voice was kind, but her face was blurry, and Sophie tried to blink her vision clear again. "It may not feel like it to you, or to any of us that are left behind, but it's a good thing that she didn't linger. That means that Alice didn't leave anything unfinished. She was able to move on in peace, and we should all be so lucky to have that."

Sophie hadn't thought of it that way, and it helped. A little. Not enough. "She was all the family I had. And I still had questions." There was so much she didn't know. She'd never asked about those framed black-and-white photos that were obviously family— ancestors that Sophie had never met. She didn't even know how her family had come to this country. Aunt Alice had talked once about the branch of the family left behind in Slovakia, and how she always meant to go there someday. But she never had, and Sophie had never gotten around to asking about their family's history. Because she'd never realized that one day she'd lose the chance to.

And now Aunt Alice was gone, and it was just Sophie. A computer-searched family tree could only do so much. She didn't care about online records. She'd lost stories. She'd lost family. Identity.

"I know, dear. But you still have Libby. Me. That young man in the coffee shop, and his girlfriend who lives with Sarah Hawkins. Every spirit here in town whose story you tell. They're all so thankful for you."

"What?" Sophie was startled out of her sadness.

Nan raised her eyebrows. "You think Sarah Hawkins is the only ghost who hears you telling stories all around town every weekend? They know they're not forgotten." Nan reached out, patting Sophie on the arm. "Believe me. You have plenty of family here in Boneyard Key."

Nan's hand on her arm was so kind, so loving, that more tears fell to join the one on her cheek. Sophie had missed that: simple gestures of comfort. Maybe she'd been living alone too long. "Thank you." Her voice was thick with emotion, and Sophie had to clear her throat. "I think I needed to hear that."

"Yes. Well." Nan sat back on her chaise and picked up her book. The moment was over, and Sophie was dismissed. She had her hand on the doorknob when Nan said one last thing. "They sure like you better than that smug boy with the top hat, anyway."

"He's not so bad," Sophie said softly to the doorknob. She glanced over her shoulder on the way out; Nan remained on her chaise, smirking at her bodice ripper. Sophie had the oddest feeling that Nan was smirking at *her*.

Twenty-Two

I t was Thursday evening, and Tristan hadn't seen Sophie once today. This was unacceptable.

Not that he could do much about it. Although he wanted nothing more than to pound on her door, that would cross the unspoken line that had been drawn between them. Running into each other out on the street, that was fine. Walking her home was also allowed. They lived next door to each other; certainly she couldn't forbid him from going to his own condo. And if she kept letting him kiss her good night . . . well, he wasn't going to complain.

That was it, though. Accidental run-ins were the extent of things. No calling each other, no texting. And certainly no knocking on each other's door. It was no way to have a relationship.

But then again, they didn't *have* a relationship. He really needed to remember that.

If he couldn't have Sophie, he thought on the way to The Haunt, he could have oysters. Replace one favorite thing about this town with another. He already knew it wasn't going to help, but hey. At least he got oysters.

Most bars, in Tristan's experience, had televisions sprinkled all over the place, tuned to different games of different persuasions. The Haunt was typically no different, but tonight the biggest TV—

the one over the bar—was tuned on The Weather Channel. That was new.

Tristan gestured at it as he settled himself at the bar. "Any particular reason?"

Tony glanced over his shoulder, as though he'd forgotten what was on. "Just getting the latest on the storm. I can put the game on if you want. Baltimore's your team, right?" He reached for the remote, but Tristan waved him off.

"Don't worry about it. The Orioles suck this year anyway. The weather's probably more exciting to watch." While Tony had answered one question, he'd sparked another. "What storm?"

"Flynn. Haven't you heard?" He laid a coaster down on the bar between them before moving to the taps. Tristan was officially a regular here; he didn't even have to order. "Became a named storm yesterday, and they're saying it should become a hurricane in the next day or so."

"Is that bad?" It sounded bad. He had tours scheduled for tomorrow night. Did he need to cancel?

But Tony looked unconcerned as he finished filling Tristan's pint. "Maybe. Probably not. This time of year it's just something to keep an eye on. You want oysters? They're good tonight."

"Load me up." Tristan took a long sip and sighed happily. There was really nothing like being a regular in a small town. Soon he had a platter of his favorite oysters in front of him, a side of perfectly cooked fries, and despite his protestations, Tony had changed the channel to the Orioles game. The steel drum band started setting up in the far corner. Conditions were perfect for a night off. No thinking about his business that may or may not survive to the end of the year. No thinking about the girl who lived next door that he really wanted to kiss again, if he could only figure out how. None of that. Tonight was about oysters, beer, and baseball.

"Hey, Tony! Can I get a . . . Oh."

All of Tristan's senses went on alert at the sound of Sophie's voice. He turned his head and there she was, bellied up to the bar next to him. Her eyes went wide when she saw him, and she froze.

"Sorry," she said. "I . . . I didn't realize you were here. I can . . ." She took a step back, and Tristan hated this. Hated that seeing her was the best part of his day, while seeing him was obviously the worst part of hers. He wasn't going to do this. Business rivals was bad enough, but he couldn't take her neighborhood bar away. That was just mean.

"Hey, no problem. I'll get this to go, okay?" He pushed himself to his feet, leaning over the bar to peer toward the kitchen. Where the hell had Tony gotten to?

"No," Sophie said. "But I appreciate the gesture." Her gaze went from him to sweep across the room. This early in the evening, they were the only two at the bar, while some sunburned tourists took up a few tables near the far window that looked out over the Gulf. "Look," she finally said. "It's a big place. We can be adults here."

"I'm always an adult here." Tristan offered her a raised eyebrow and one of his best crooked smiles, and Sophie's lips twitched in response. He fully expected her to take a seat at the other side of the restaurant and ignore him for the rest of the evening, like she usually did when they were in public, but she surprised him by hoisting herself up onto the stool next to him.

She didn't even need a menu. "Fried shrimp platter and hard pineapple cider, please," she said when Tony reemerged, and he nodded immediately.

"You got it." Tristan thought he had become a regular, but Sophie got a grin and a finger gun from Tony, so obviously he had a ways to go.

Silence fell between them, but it didn't last long. The steel drum band started their set, which was mostly Jimmy Buffett covers, fronted by a long-haired middle-aged man with an acoustic guitar. The frontman sang with a lot of enthusiasm and a fair bit of talent to back it up.

"They're pretty good." He spoke despite himself, knowing he should probably leave Sophie alone.

Sophie nodded. "That's Vince. You know that old band, Veiled Threat? He played bass for them back in the day."

"Wait, really? My mom was really into them. She had all their CDs when I was a kid." He tried to remember those CD covers, but all that came to mind was a lot of hair and leather outfits. He looked at the frontman again. The hair was basically the same, though the black had faded to salt-and-pepper. Thankfully the leather outfit had not transcended the times; he didn't need to see that while he was trying to enjoy a platter of oysters.

Tristan took a sip of his beer and watched the band for a bit before focusing on the game in front of him. He tried to look anywhere but to his left, but it was impossible. Sophie was right there in his periphery; he couldn't not look at her. She was a magnet, she was gravity. And he was an apple with a nail through it. Or whatever. When he finally let himself glance over at her, she looked away immediately, turning her attention to the television.

"How's the game?"

"Good, if you're not an Orioles fan. So terrible for me. You like baseball?"

She shook her head. "I tried watching it a couple times, but it moves too slow. I like basketball. The Magic had a good season this year."

"Those games move so fast, though; they're over before you've finished a hot dog." This was nice. They were doing small talk. Pleasant small talk, even. He could handle this. "Hey, did you see the news about the hurricane?"

"You mean Flynn, right?" She waved an unconcerned hand. "It's barely a tropical storm."

"Nothing to worry about, then?"

"Nah. I'll let you know when to worry."

He raised his eyebrows. "You sure about that?"

"Hmm." She put down her cider. "Good point. Maybe I'll wait till it's a Cat 5 and then tell you to go for a little stroll along the beach."

"Thanks a lot."

"You're welcome." Her smile lit up her whole face, and maybe it was the second beer talking, but Tristan was getting a little lost in those dark eyes of hers. He forced his gaze away and over to the steel drum band. The frontman had gone, replaced by a guy with a brutal sunburn holding a half-filled pint glass. He held the mic in a loose grip, swaying to the beat so violently he came dangerously close to spilling his beer. He shouted vaguely in the direction of the mic in his hand, the melody only a drunken suggestion.

Tristan shuddered. "Why are they letting this guy sing? He's terrible."

"Don't worry, it'll be over soon. It's just one song."

"It's one song too many. It's criminal."

"It's karaoke," she corrected.

"What? No. Karaoke is with a machine and a bad backing track. Not a steel drum band."

Sophie shrugged. "The karaoke machine broke sometime around the holidays, and they haven't gotten around to fixing it. So now instead of the machine, the steel drum band just plays anything you want so you can sing along."

"That explains a lot." Tristan hadn't even known that old Def Leppard songs could be played on the steel drums. They probably shouldn't be. He dragged a couple fries through the small puddle of cocktail sauce on his plate before munching down on them while the guy with the microphone absolutely fought for his life through the second verse of "Photograph."

Tristan shook his head in sympathy. "He's never going to hit that high note."

Sophie tsked at him. "You think you can do better?"

"Than this guy?" He had to scoff. "On my worst day."

"Okay, then." She gestured toward the band with a fried shrimp. "Let's see."

"What, now?" Panic gripped him, which was ridiculous. He could sing better than this guy in his sleep. What did he have to panic about? "I don't really do hair metal."

Sophie scoffed. "I told you. They play anything you want. You can do one of your musicals or something." She gave him a pointed look. "So, prove it."

Onstage, that drunk guy absolutely did not hit that high note, and that decided it. Tristan tossed his napkin down on the bar. "Fine." As the sunburned singer struggled through the final notes, he took one last swig of beer for courage before threading his way through the tables between him and the band. While he and Sophie had been sitting there, the place had filled up; there weren't many empty tables left. If Tristan was the kind of guy who got stage fright, this could be very bad.

But Tristan did not get stage fright. The more stage the better, that was his philosophy. He'd sung in front of plenty of crowds in his lifetime. Some drunk, most not. This was nothing new to him.

"You next?" The long-haired musician—Vince—addressed

Tristan from the small table next to the band. He seemed to be the one in charge.

"I guess so. Don't suppose you guys know any show tunes, huh? A little *My Fair Lady*?" Tristan had meant it as a joke, but they nodded along, as though this wasn't even close to the weirdest request they'd gotten.

"What're you looking for? 'Get Me to the Church on Time'? 'On the Street Where You Live'?"

Well, he'd be damned. "The second one."

"Good call," Vince said. "It's not our usual thing, but why the hell not. That's what steel-drum karaoke is for, right?" He handed the microphone to Tristan. "You ready?"

He was. The mic was warm and a little sweaty, but it felt familiar in his hand, as though he were returning home after a long time away. He squinted under the hot lights, trying to find his beacon in the crowd. There she was, right where he'd left her at the bar.

Tristan had sung this song plenty of times over the years. In front of an orchestra when he'd played Freddy in the musical back in college. Occasionally after that to a CD backing track, and once even accompanied by a local rock band the fraternity had hired for a party. (Tristan had had a few, and at that point so had the band.) But it had been years since he'd paid attention to the lyrics; that had been his biggest failing as an actor, something that had driven directors nuts. Tristan was always more concerned with hitting the notes and making whatever song he was singing a showpiece. The lyrics were just the vehicle to show off his range.

But as the steel drums picked out the melody, and the song came pouring out, he really listened to the words, and it felt like he was singing the song for the first time. It felt like he was simply a man, confessing that life was just that much better when he was near the person he loved. That all of his life was now nothing but the anticipation of seeing her again, and getting to be by her side.

Yes, he'd performed this song countless times over the years, but this time was different. Because he was singing for Sophie.

And when it came down to it, all he wanted was to be on the street where she lived.

Twenty-Three

S he could have listened to him all night.

Sophie hadn't meant it when she'd dared him to sing. She'd just been irritated. Tristan was complaining about the music, making fun of that drunk who was, admittedly, absolutely slaughtering an old eighties song. More than once she'd glanced over and caught the horrified look on Vince's face. But she was impressed; he'd stayed in his seat instead of beating the tourist with a chair and wrestling the mic away. Vince must be in a good mood tonight.

When she'd dared Tristan to do better, she'd been kidding. It wasn't until he was up there, microphone in hand, taking a first breath, that she remembered that night at Poltergeist Pizza, when Jo had read Tristan's top hat. Saying he missed singing. Sophie wanted to groan; she'd played right into his hand. Daring him to do something he excelled at.

She wanted to leave. Abandon the rest of her fried shrimp and get the heck out of there. She didn't want to witness this showing-off session he was about to do. Giving him the satisfaction was against her religion.

But then, right as he started to sing, his eyes met hers and locked on, as though he was gripping her hand from across the room. Ah. Maybe he was a little nervous after all. So instead of hopping down from her stool, instead of bolting out into the night, she sent him a small smile, mentally giving his hand a squeeze of support.

Not that he needed it. His voice was pure, like smooth running water. A clear tenor that soared up to the notes it needed—he would have nailed that note in "Photograph"—his voice filled the room, and conversation stilled as more and more patrons turned in his direction.

Sophie wasn't a musical theatre fan. She didn't know *My Fair Lady* from a hole in the ground. But that had to be what he was singing. She could tell from the way he carried himself, the set of his shoulders, even the curve of his hand around the mic, that this was a song that was in his DNA. Something that he hadn't accessed in a long time. He somehow looked younger, up there while he was singing a song about how everything he saw looked different, looked more magical, because he was walking down the street where his lover lived.

After what felt like a few moments but also eternity, the song was over. Tristan handed the mic back to Vince and threaded his way through the tables to scattered applause.

Back at the bar, Tony gave a low whistle. "Damn, dude." He offered a fist bump, and Tristan reached across the bar to accommodate.

"Thanks, man." Tristan's blond hair was darker at the roots, damp with sweat, and he raked it back with one hand. Likewise his face was flushed, his grin a little manic. Wow, Jo had been right. This was a man who loved performing. Even now that he was back at the bar, he stood a little straighter. His smile that was always so easy was now effortless. He was electric, he was magnetic. She wanted nothing more than to be in his orbit.

What a terrible turn of events. She couldn't let herself think like that. Because they were still enemies. Her entire identity, the only thing that brought her joy, was staked on beating this effortlessly charming man at something they were both very, very good at.

She raised her glass moodily, but it was empty. Cider was gone. Ugh.

She put her glass down as he turned to her, aiming that effortless, blinding smile in her direction. "Well?" The word was practically a laugh. "What'd you think?"

"Nice song." She raised her empty glass in Tony's direction. What the heck; she wasn't driving anywhere. "A little creepy, though."

"What?" He plopped onto his stool next to her, the wattage fading a little from his grin. "It's not creepy. It's romantic."

"This guy just wants to hang around outside her door, hoping to catch a glimpse of her?" Sophie shook her head and reached for her second pineapple cider. "It sounds like stalking to me."

Tristan gave a good-natured shrug. "It was a different time." She snorted.

Their spot at the bar was near the door, and it seemed like every group that left had to stop by their corner to compliment Tristan on his singing. Sophie kept a pleasant smile on her face, but she felt it dimming more and more as he racked up the praise. People weren't supposed to like him around here.

The last straw was when Vince dropped by during a break in the band's set. "Great pipes, man!" He clapped Tristan on the shoulder.

"Thanks, I really appreciate that. Listen, I can't wait to tell my mom that I met you. She'll absolutely lose it. Veiled Threat was her favorite band in college."

"No shit, really?" Vince lit up, the way he always lit up when people mentioned his past with Veiled Threat. "Hey, you know The Cold Spot, out past the fishing pier? That's my place. Come by sometime for a beer. I know I've got some old CDs or something I can sign for her."

"Oh, man, that would be great."

Sophie wanted to groan out loud. Tristan had no idea. He couldn't, of course. Vince didn't invite just anyone to The Cold Spot. In fact, he usually went out of his way to make sure it was a locals-only place. Inviting Tristan there only meant one thing. He was becoming a local too.

This was the worst.

Twenty-Four

The hardest part of going for a run in Florida in late July, Tristan found, was pulling himself out of bed at oh dark thirty. The second hardest was putting on pants at that hour. But once his shoes were laced up and he was out the door, it was like magic. Lingering stars winked out as the deepest blue sky gave way to indigo before the earliest touches of dawn crept on the horizon. By the time he'd pounded out five miles, the sun was fully up, bringing her best friend, humidity, with her. Normally he went straight home, but this morning he deserved an iced coffee, and Hallowed Grounds was right there. The rush of cold air as he pushed open the door made him gasp in relief.

The weekday morning rush was mostly locals—folks stopping by to support this local business on the way to open up their own local businesses. Most of them gave Tristan a smile or a small wave, and he was surprised that hardly any of them scowled at him anymore. It may have taken a few months, but he was no longer the new asshole in town.

From behind the counter, Nick inclined his head in Tristan's direction. "Coffee?"

Tristan gave a grateful nod. "Iced, please. With one pump of vanilla. Unless . . . I don't suppose you have a protein shake back there?"

Nick gave an amused snort, which was the response Tristan had expected. "Not that kind of place."

"Didn't think so." Tristan's smirk matched Nick's. "That's okay, milk's got protein."

"The amount you put in, that should be plenty." Nick handed Tristan's drink across the counter. "There's a rumor about a smoothie place opening up in the fall, out by the pier. Cassie's about to pee herself with joy."

"Wow, what a delightful way to put it," came Cassie's voice from the back corner. Tristan glanced over his shoulder, and she rolled her eyes in Tristan's direction from where she sat at a back table, laptop open in front of her.

"I'll have to check that out," he said, but the end of the sentence trailed off as his brain caught up with his mouth. He wasn't going to be here in the fall, was he? Even if Ghouls Night Out was a success here, he wasn't sticking around. He'd establish a manager here—maybe Sophie if he could get another attempt at talking her into it—ensure everything was running the way it should, and he'd be off. Scouting a new location and doing it all over again.

Tristan was usually excited at this stage of things. Adding a new location to the stable and thinking about where to go next. But right now, he was more intrigued by the idea of the smoothie shop down by the pier.

He took a sip of his iced coffee, smooth and creamy with just a hint of vanilla, as the bell over the door chimed. There was Sophie, frozen in the doorway. He froze as well, like a kid caught in the cookie jar. When he'd first come to town, Hallowed Grounds had been Sophie's territory, so he'd backed off. But things seemed to have turned a corner since the night he apologized to Cassie Rutherford's refrigerator. Nick hardly ever glowered at him anymore, and Cassie was even outright friendly. Which, thank God, because while the pastries were good at Spooky Brew, Nick's coffee was vastly superior. But the fact remained: he was on Sophie's turf. Could they share this place, the way they'd been able to share The Haunt the other night?

Sophie's smile was minuscule, hesitant. It was an olive branch. "Hey."

"Hey." Relief flooded through him. Maybe more than one corner had been turned here recently. Thank God; his heart rate was still coming down from his run. He was too tired to do battle. He didn't *want* to do battle with Sophie. He wanted to kiss Sophie. Where was her front door when you needed it?

He'd leaned forward, starting to take a step in her direction, when Cassie's voice came from her back corner like the voice of doom. "Ah, shit."

Tristan startled, and so did Sophie, and they shared a wide-eyed look before they both turned in Cassie's direction.

"Everything okay?" Nick frowned in concern.

Cassie nodded absently. "It's the storm. Hurricane Flynn? He's coming."

"You serious?" Nick put down his kitchen towel and came out from behind the counter.

Sophie groaned. "Not you too. I've been getting text after text from Libby, ever since they named the storm. It's barely a thunderstorm."

"I don't know . . ." Nick had moved to stand behind Cassie, and he bent to look over her shoulder at her laptop screen. "This looks like more than a thunderstorm now. Shit."

Cassie groaned. "And what a stupid name. Flynn? Are we naming storms after cartoon princes now?"

Sophie's nod was solemn, but her eyes danced in amusement. "Disney's probably gonna sue the weather people."

Tristan tried to get them back on topic. "Wasn't that storm always coming, though?" He felt like the kid in the room, clueless while the grown-ups were talking. "It's been in the news for days now."

"Yeah, as a hypothetical. It might go this way, it might go that way. News stations love to fearmonger." Nick's eyes stayed on the screen while he talked. "But as a storm gets closer, they're able to track it more accurately."

"And it's looking a lot more accurate now." Cassie turned her laptop around to show Tristan. He bit hard on his bottom lip to not laugh, because what on earth was he looking at?

"This looks like someone let their toddler loose on MS Paint. It's just a bunch of random squiggly lines all over the state."

"That's the spaghetti model," Sophie said, as though he should know what the hell that was. "All the possible outcomes, according to projections."

"He's not wrong, though," Nick said. "Those things are always a mess."

"But if you look at all the lines . . ." Sophie stepped forward, and her fingertip grazed Cassie's screen. "See how most of them are clumped together here? That's the likely track the storm will take."

The map showed ten different lines, and now Tristan could see the pattern. While two spun off into the Gulf and one cut through Key West and Miami, seven of them went straight through the Gulf of Mexico. Right toward Boneyard Key.

Now he understood. Shit.

Cassie looked up at Nick. "We good on supplies?"

Supplies. Right. Tristan's mind whirled. He remembered this. An article on the internet a couple months back. His frantic shopping trip. In the weeks since, he'd drunk most of the water and tried one of the cans of ravioli (terrible). He had a meeting this afternoon, but there was enough time for him to double back to the grocery, do a restock . . .

Meanwhile, Nick was nodding at Cassie. "I think so. There's three, no, four bottles of red in the cabinet at home. Could probably use another bottle or two of rum, and some mixers. Just let me know what you're thinking in terms of snacks, and I can pick that up when I go into town tomorrow for a supply run."

"Oooh, are you going by a Publix?" Her eyes lit up, and Nick sighed with good-natured amusement.

"For you? I can make the trip. One chicken tender sub coming up."

"Yes, please! And see if they're doing any hurricane cakes this time. I know they stopped officially doing them, but there's got to be someone going rogue in the bakery department."

"You got it." He bent to kiss her, and she curled a hand around his head. The kiss lasted a good long while, and Tristan started feeling awkward. He cleared his throat loudly, which didn't do much to hurry things along.

He turned to Sophie, desperate for a subject change, and judging by the redness of her cheeks, she was all for it. "Snacks?" he asked. "Rum? I thought hurricane supplies were things like bottled water and canned goods."

Sophie nodded. "You're right. Those are hurricane supplies."

"The *basic* hurricane supplies," Nick corrected, who had apparently come up for air. "Believe me, if you're stuck in your home with no power for a few days, you're going to be glad for the alcohol. And the snacks."

"Red wine and chocolate-fudge Pop-Tarts," Sophie said. "Remember?"

He did now. Stuff that didn't need refrigeration. "Of course."

"Anyway, we're not talking about those hurricane supplies,"

Cassie continued. "Not yet. The storm's still way too far off; we don't know what it's going to do."

"But . . ." Tristan gestured with his almost-empty coffee toward her laptop. "The spaghetti model . . . ?"

"Oh, it's heading this way for sure. Or at least, it's coming up the Gulf instead of hitting the east coast of Florida. No matter what, we're getting some weather." She sighed. "Between you and me, I could go for a nice Category 1 right about now. A little wind, a little rain, maybe a day or two off work . . ." Cassie's face turned dreamy.

"A nice hurricane party," Sophie chimed in.

"Hurricane party." He was doing that thing again, repeating what was said to him, but he was so far out of his element that he didn't feel capable of doing much else.

But no one seemed to notice. "Hurricane party," Nick repeated with glee. "Don't worry, you're invited. It'll be at our place. Drinks, food, a little running around outside in the rain while the storm comes through." He clapped Tristan on the shoulder on his way back to the counter. "You'll love it."

Tristan tried to not rotate his shoulder in an effort to work out the slap. "I'm sure I will." He took another sip of coffee and tried to calm his racing thoughts. If Nick and Cassie weren't overly worried about the storm, then he wouldn't be, either. They were the experts.

"Then again . . ." Sophie looked doubtful. "It could be a big storm. And you've never ridden out a hurricane. Might not be a bad idea to evacuate."

"Evacuate?" The urgency of the word shot adrenaline through Tristan's blood. "How soon would I have to evacuate?"

"Oh, probably really soon. You know, beat the rush." There was that amusement again, dancing in Sophie's eyes. Now that it was trained on him, it made his heart go all fizzy.

"You'd like that, wouldn't you?" He leaned in closer, and the gleam in her eyes spread to a full-fledged smile on her face. "Nice try, Horvath. It's going to take more than a natural disaster to get rid of me."

But he was smiling, and so was she, and she was right there, so close. Closer than she should probably be, considering they were in public, and as far as anyone knew, they were barely tolerating each other. Tristan wasn't thinking about that, though. He was thinking about the way the tip of her tongue looked, peeking out between her teeth as her smile turned wicked . . .

Nick cleared his throat loudly, making the both of them jump. "Cassie," he said, "what the hell is a hurricane cake?"

Oh, thank God. Both for the subject change and the question. Because Tristan couldn't even begin to picture what a hurricane cake might be. Did it have special storm-repelling powers?

But Cassie just smiled as she started typing on her laptop. "Not that deep, y'all. It's a cake. Decorated with hurricane symbols. Usually something nice like 'leave Florida alone' . . ." She turned her laptop around, and there was a page of image results. Outlines of the state of Florida done in green with blue for the ocean, with a big red blob in the middle representing the impending hurricane. Names on the cakes like Dorian, Ian, Irma. They were beautiful. They were a little disturbing. A weird thing to celebrate.

But Tristan could understand. He'd whistled in the dark more than once in his life. And an imminent hurricane seemed very, very dark.

Twenty-Five

The thing about hurricanes is that they can change on a dime.

Sophie went to bed knowing that Hurricane Flynn had barely earned his name. He was a Category 1, and a slow one at that—not much stronger than a tropical storm. She'd attended cookouts in worse weather. While most of Libby's text messages contained multiple exclamation points and emojis now that the storm had a name, Sophie and Cassie exchanged more level-headed texts about the upcoming hurricane party. Sophie promised to bring some mixers since she was vehemently against shots. Especially after the last hurricane party.

The next morning, she woke up to the news that Flynn had strengthened overnight and had just graduated to a Category 3. Libby was beside herself, which was to be expected.

"It went through an entire eyewall replacement cycle overnight. See that eye?" She handed her phone to Sophie while they waited for Nick to finish making their coffees. "It's ridiculously well-defined now."

Sophie watched the video on a loop on Libby's phone. The hurricane was massive, creeping its way closer and closer, before abruptly stopping and dropping back as the loop started over. Dread swirled in Sophie's stomach as the hurricane swirled its way through the ocean over and over.

They were in Libby's element now; she knew exactly when the weather updates would be posted and could spout jargon like a full-fledged meteorologist. Sophie, on the other hand, lived in the same cone of uncertainty that was currently covering most of the state of Florida. But no matter what terms she knew or didn't know, it was impossible to miss the eye of that hurricane: a sharply defined dot in the middle of the spreading circle of clouds on the satellite image. And she knew enough to know that a sharply defined eye was bad news.

"It's due to hit Cuba tonight," Libby said. "Some people on the forums say it'll weaken, but there's so much warm water on the Gulf. This could be bad."

From behind the counter, Nick clucked his tongue in their direction. "You always think it could be bad. Do you want banana bread or a blueberry muffin?"

"Muffin, please." Libby stowed her phone in her bag as she took the iced coffee and the bakery bag he handed her. "And I'm telling you, watch out for this one."

Turned out, this time Libby was right.

On the news that night they used the phrase "rapid intensification" an awful lot, and suddenly Flynn had left Cuba in his wake and was heading for the Gulf Coast of Florida as a Category 4 storm.

"One hundred thirty-seven miles an hour!" The meteorologist on television sounded positively gleeful, his jacket off and his shirt-sleeves rolled up to his elbows as he gestured at the green screen behind him. Sophie didn't see anything to be happy about. Some-how in the space of a handful of days, a wave off the coast of Africa was now a storm that was larger than the state of Florida itself. The spaghetti models remained a joke, covering the entire state in brightly colored lines, showing the possible paths it could take.

Not that it mattered. With a storm this size, the only way it could avoid hitting Florida would be if it suddenly reversed course and died. One model showed it doing just that—the moving-away part, at least—but there was always an outlier in situations like these. Nobody took it seriously. No, this storm was going to hit. It was just a matter of where and how hard.

Nick and Cassie's hurricane party was quickly canceled as landfall somewhere between Sarasota and Suwannee in the next twenty-four hours became inevitable. The day before the storm was set to hit, Nick came over to Sophie's place to hang her hurricane shutters.

"You know, you could get something a little more high-tech." He grunted as he wrestled the steel panels out of the storage closet in the breezeway. They'd already hung plywood over her east-facing windows and her sliding-glass door. All that was left were these big ones for outside. "They make retractable ones these days, so you don't have to keep putting them on and taking them off."

"Oh sure," Sophie said. "Let me just go get some cash off my money tree and make that happen."

Nick snorted. "Point taken. Grab that end, at least. These things are kind of heavy, and awkward as hell."

That she could do. Sophie moved to hoist one end of the shutter.

"Hold it steady!" Nick said. "It needs to be straight so I can line it up with the screw holes."

"I'm trying!" But she had zero upper-body strength, struggling to hold the shutter up while Nick worked to screw the panel in place.

"Sophie!" His voice held a warning tone as her grip on the panel slipped.

"Sorry, sorry!" The sharp steel panel bit into her palm, but she held it as steady as she could, when suddenly—

"Here. I got it." A hand appeared below hers, grasping on to the side of the shutter, and Sophie was surrounded by the scent of clean soap and an undertone of pine that she'd come to associate with Tristan. He was just *there*, his chest at her back, his arms around her, but it wasn't an embrace; instead, he grasped her end of the hurricane shutter. She should protest, she should tell him to go away, but instead she slipped under his arm, leaving the shutter installation to the two men who were stronger than she was. Feminism was all well and good, but dropping the stupid thing on her foot wasn't going to do anything for women's rights.

"Thanks, man. I appreciate it," Nick said when it was finally screwed into place. He set his screw gun on the ground and wiped his forehead with the sleeve of his T-shirt. "Do you know where your shutters are? We could go ahead and . . ." His voice trailed off as he took a step toward Tristan's place, frowning at the window. While Sophie's front window was edged with bolts that were now holding up the shutters, Tristan's front window had no such line of bolts around the edges.

"Or not," Nick finished. "I guess you've got the fancy retractable shutters?"

"Do I?" Tristan's eyes were wide and guileless as he followed Nick over to the front window. Both men examined it the way they'd examine an overheated car engine, hands on their hips with no idea of what they were really looking at. Sophie leaned against the railing; she'd be no help at all, so sitting this one out was the best call.

"Huh." Nick's forehead was practically plastered against the window, looking up into the frame. "I don't see a track. You do have hurricane shutters, right?"

"I . . . I have no idea." Tristan took out his phone. "I can ask the property manager."

"You can, but I don't think you do."

Tristan looked up from his phone. "And that's bad, right?"

"Pretty sure the hardware store's out of plywood by now . . ." Nick chewed on his bottom lip, squinting at the big picture windows of Tristan's condo. Then he shook his head decisively. "I'm sure those windows are hurricane rated. You'll probably be fine."

"Yeah?" Tristan looked pointedly at Sophie's front window, which was totally concealed by corrugated steel.

"Yeah." Nick only sounded a little doubtful as he picked up his screw gun. "You good, Sophie?"

She nodded. "Thanks again." Nick waved off her thanks, and she watched as he headed down the hallway and toward the steps. She didn't want to look at the shutters. Sure, they were necessary, especially when a storm like this was imminent. But they blocked out all the light, turning her home into a dungeon for the foreseeable future. It was gonna take a lot of candles for this place to feel like a home. Of course, hurricanes and power outages went hand in hand, so candles were as inevitable as the oncoming storm.

But as much as she didn't want to look at her shutters, she didn't want to look at Tristan, either. He had become the most conflicting part of her life, and she didn't like conflict. Maybe if she just stared down the hallway where Nick had gone, Tristan would get the hint and go back inside his own place and leave her alone.

No such luck. He cleared his throat behind her, and when she didn't turn around, he just started talking. "I don't know if you've canceled your tours yet this weekend, but . . ."

"Trying to get one up on me?" She spit the words out before she could check them, but was he serious? The last thing she was thinking about was her ghost tour. She'd already emailed her day job, letting them know she'd likely be unavailable for a few days, assuming they lost power. The loss of that income wasn't great, and of course there wouldn't be tours for a couple weekends, either. Cassie might appreciate a few days off work, but to Sophie, hurricanes were a money pit. The last thing she needed was Mr. Businessman over here telling her they should plan for tourists to be in town, clamoring for a ghost tour during a hurricane. Idiot.

And then of course, Tristan had to keep talking and prove her wrong. "I went ahead and canceled all of mine. I figured trying to lead a walking tour in a hurricane wasn't the way to go."

All of Sophie's ire escaped in a long sigh. "Your top hat could fly off." Sophie tried to be solemn as she nodded, but her lips twitched in a smile that she couldn't quite hide.

That earned her a snort, and her smile widened despite herself as she turned to face him. Ugh. How dare he lean against his front door like that. How dare he smile at her like that, his eyes catching hers. He was just rude.

She nodded toward his phone. "You find out about your hurricane shutters yet?"

"I texted the property manager. Hopefully she knows something. But . . ." He glanced down at his phone as if expecting a response. "I dunno. Nick didn't see anything, and he seems to know what he's talking about." He slipped his phone into his back pocket and glanced toward his front window, doubt clouding his expression. "Maybe you were right before. Maybe I should get out of here. Get a little further inland, or up north."

"You can't do that now," Sophie said before she could check herself. "It's too late."

"Too late?" His brow furrowed. "Didn't they say the storm isn't hitting till tomorrow?"

"Right. That's way too late. There's one road out of town, and by the time you get to I-75, it'll be a parking lot. Not to mention, every hotel from here to halfway through Georgia is probably already full. If you got in your car now, I can guarantee that you'll still be sitting in gridlock traffic when Flynn makes landfall. And trust me, you don't want to be in your car when Flynn makes landfall."

"Damn." He sighed. "I guess I should have taken your advice and gotten out of town at the beginning of the week."

"I wasn't really . . ." She didn't want to finish that sentence. Because she'd never actually wanted him to evacuate. But shouldn't she? Life would certainly be easier if he were gone. A little less colorful, maybe. A lot fewer clandestine kisses, certainly. But easier.

She tried changing the subject. "Did you stock up?"

"On what?" He looked at her blankly. "Red wine and Pop-Tarts?"

"No!" Was he serious? "Water, batteries, all that stuff."

His expression became incredulous. "I started to, back in June. Then you told me not to bother!" He threw up his hands and paced away from her in frustration. "Earlier this week you were all throwing a hurricane party!"

"Well, plans changed!" she shot back, but deep inside she felt a twinge of guilt. When Flynn intensified overnight, she'd run down to the Supernatural Market and grabbed the last two gallons of water and some nonperishables to get her through a few days without power. She'd stocked up on batteries, and called Nick to ask him to come help her with the hurricane shutters.

But she hadn't checked on Tristan. And she probably should have. Instead she'd left him to spend the week in his fancy condo, doing whatever fancy things he did in there, his mind still on rum and hurricane cakes.

So maybe she'd messed up a little here. But she wasn't his mother. It wasn't like she owed him anything.

"It's okay. I can tough it out." Tristan looked out toward the water. The Gulf looked the same as it did any other day, with the rays of the afternoon sun sparkling on the water as it lapped lazily at the shore.

A silence fell between them, and Sophie's heart quickened. Most of the time, when they were together like this, it was at night. They'd linger in front of her door, both of them tired from an evening of running their respective ghost tours. Tristan would have his top hat in one hand, his cravat hanging limply around his neck as the glow of their porch lights around them was almost otherworldly. Tristan would step closer, Sophie would lay a hand on his chest. His mouth would cover hers . . .

But it wasn't night. It was the middle of the afternoon, and they didn't do things like that when the summer sun was high in the sky. Still, Sophie lingered, and so did he, the awkwardness growing. Was she supposed to invite him into her condo turned dungeon to ride out the storm with her? It was probably the nice thing to do: provide sanctuary to the unprepared.

Sophie didn't know if she could cross that line. All these weeks, all these kisses. They'd been on neutral ground. Inviting him into her space was an unprecedented step she wasn't ready to take.

She took a shaking breath. "Listen . . ."

"Yeah?" Hope lit up his eyes, and a smile lifted his lips.

"If you have any Ziploc bags, fill them with water and put them in the freezer. The ice will keep your frozen food cold longer when the power goes out. And when it does, don't open your fridge, either. And . . ." She took a deep breath. "If the storm gets really bad . . ."

"Yeah?" That hope was still there, and he even took a step toward her. She fell a step back. He was so, so close to that line now, and she just couldn't let him step over it.

"That's when you should hunker down in the bathroom or your

bedroom closet. Any room without any windows. Good luck!" Before she could watch his face fall, she turned on her heel and headed inside, closing her front door behind her with a snap. Then she threw the bolt for good measure.

She was riding out this storm alone. It only seemed right. Sophie knew how to do alone.

Twenty-Six

The day of a hurricane was like Christmas, if the idea of Christmas filled you with dread.

Sophie woke up in her darkened apartment, already feeling cooped up even though the storm wasn't hitting until later in the day. She'd be hunkering down soon enough; may as well get some time outside while she could.

Tristan's front door was closed, and she only let her gaze linger on it for a moment before turning to the stairs. He was going to be fine. He didn't need her.

The Supernatural Market was already boarded up—so much for picking up more snacks. Red spray-paint graffiti scrawled across the plywood: FUCK OFF FLYNN.

Nice. Alliterative. Who said people weren't classy in this town?

There was an additional sign taped to the inside of the front door: CLOSED TILL AFTER THE STORM. STAY SAFE OUT THERE! The store was ready to ride out the storm, just like the rest of the town.

She didn't need any more hurricane snacks, anyway. She just needed to ration. There was nothing worse than eating all the hurricane snacks before the hurricane actually hit.

For a day that promised landfall of a major hurricane, it had no business being so beautiful. The morning was sunny and warm, with barely a hint of a breeze off the Gulf. If Sophie didn't know any better, there was no reason for all this hurricane-prep nonsense.

She thought, as she often did in times like these, about the people who'd lived here before her. Back in the days when Boneyard Key was a newly settled city, in the days before meteorology and twenty-four-hour news coverage. What had that day been like, when the Great Storm of 1897 had hit? Had there been any kind of warning? Did they think they were getting just another summer Florida thunderstorm until the winds picked up, and then suddenly everything they knew was gone? Destroyed in a hurricane that they hadn't even seen coming.

It was a sobering thought, one that didn't match the gorgeous morning outside.

Everything downtown was closed and in some stage of being boarded up. The Chamber of Commerce had their hurricane shutters rolled down over every window, protecting the old house as much as possible. Across the street, Hallowed Grounds was boarded up too, but without the profanity of the corner grocery. Nick was just locking the front door of the café, and he threw Sophie a wave.

"What are you doing out here?" he called out with a frown. "The news said to be inside by noon."

"And it's ten thirty," she shot back. "I'll be fine." She looked up and down the street, where even on a Thursday in the hottest part of the summer there should be some signs of life. Shoppers, locals, somebody. But it was a literal ghost town. She all but expected a tumbleweed to blow down Beachside.

"Suit yourself. Nothing to do down here, though. I was the only one stupid enough to open. I think I've had four customers all morning."

"But that's good, right?" she said. "That means the tourists got out." The next couple days were likely to be challenging enough without people wandering around demanding coffee and expecting pizza delivery.

Nick checked his phone before stowing it in his back pocket. "It's about that time," he said. "We'll start getting some of the outer bands any minute, and you know it's gonna get bad fast. Stay safe, okay?"

A common refrain on hurricane days. "You too." She watched as Nick headed north up the street, past the closed shops toward home. She was officially the only person downtown. It was unsettling.

The wind had picked up now. Not a lot, but enough to feel ominous. Whitecaps had started popping up out on the water, and dark clouds gathered on the horizon, like evil witches with sinister intent. *Something wicked this way comes.* Nick was right. It was time to go home. Her dungeon might be dark and depressing, but the storm was coming, and it was safe behind those shutters.

A drop of rain hit her shoulder as she walked past The Haunt, which was boarded up tight. More rain bounced off the hot sidewalk, leaving dark dots in their wake. By the time Sophie made it back to her place, it was a steady drizzle. Not quite a downpour yet, but it was coming. Not long now.

Inside, Sophie turned on all the lights—smoke 'em while you've got 'em—and clicked the television on, tuning into the cable news coverage. Libby's text this morning had been all about landfall happening somewhere around Key West. The TV had said the same, showing lots of footage of the Southernmost Point monument being pounded by rain and angry ocean waves. But things were different now. The weatherman looked a little more manic this time. Tie off, sleeves rolled up, he looked like Casual Friday as he gesticulated to the weather map behind him.

"Looks like Flynn has some surprises for us! We expected landfall down in the Florida Keys, followed by an inland turn, but he's still riding the coastline right now. We're now expecting him to make landfall somewhere around here . . ." He moved his arm in a wide arc, somewhere around the Tampa Bay area. That was a lot closer to Boneyard Key than Key West was. Sophie didn't like the look of that at all.

As Tristan took his second cup of coffee out onto his balcony, he watched as the sunrise threw pink streaks across the sky. He didn't know what he expected on the morning of his first hurricane, but he thought it shouldn't be this peaceful. This quiet.

It was too quiet, he realized almost right away. Usually this time of morning things were happening. The grounds maintenance crew should be outside, doing its thing with lawn mowers and leaf blowers and weed whackers, keeping the green spaces in the common areas manicured. Like Tristan with his early-morning runs, those crews got the work done before the sun was too high in the sky. But they weren't there today. Today it was just Tristan and his coffee and the early-morning sun sparkling off the water.

The air of anticipation was unavoidable. Once it hit nine, his phone started lighting up with texts. The property manager first, to confirm that no, this unit didn't have hurricane shutters. It had been recommended when the place had been renovated, but had ultimately been cut as a cost-saving measure. *Thanks, Dad.* Eric had texted three times in an hour, each time with links to national news stories about Hurricane Flynn and its potential danger. Are you sure you shouldn't get out of there?, he asked each time, only stopping when Tristan threatened to block his number.

His father didn't text at all.

It was fascinating, how subtly the weather deteriorated outside. He spotted the dark clouds out over the water first, then noticed that the palm trees outside his building started swaying as the wind picked up. Then the rain came, a trickle that intensified until it was coming down in sheets, and the world became dark and gray and nothing but water pounding down from the sky and wind sending that water crashing into his windows and the sliding-glass door leading out to the balcony.

He felt helpless. He couldn't do anything about the storm outside. All he could do was sit on his couch and watch it happen. Wait for it to be over. He got a beer out of the fridge—he was turning into a real Florida Man, beer before noon and all—and settled himself on the sofa with the news coverage. Somewhere in southwest Florida a roof was getting torn off a trailer, like the lid coming off one of the cans of ravioli in Tristan's pantry. Waves crashed against a faraway seawall, angry and violent.

"We're looking at storm surges of at least ten feet," the weatherman said, as though that was something Tristan was familiar with. "So you're going to want to—"

The power went out before he finished his sentence. Tristan had no idea what he was going to want to do.

Sophie's phone chimed with a text from Libby.

Landfall due to hit north of Tampa!! I knew I should have gotten Nan out of here.

I'm all shuttered up if y'all need to come hunker down here.

We're boarded up too. Should be ok.

Stay safe!

Sophie blew out a long breath. This could be bad. If they'd known a day or two ago that landfall would be this close to Boneyard Key, the town would most likely have been evacuated. But with a few hours' notice? It was too late now. She thought of her friends, everyone she knew here in town, hunkered down and waiting for the storm to pass. It helped to know that most everyone was safe behind their storm-protected homes. This wasn't any of their first rodeo.

Tristan. Her stomach plunged. This *was* his first rodeo. And he was about to ride out the meanest bucking bronco ever, in a condo that was practically nothing but windows. She shouldn't have left him alone.

Outside, the storm had intensified. Rain pounded on the roof and slapped against her hurricane shutters. The television showed a trailer park getting decimated by driving winds.

"We're looking at storm surges of at least ten feet!" Sophie didn't like the tone of worry in the meteorologist's voice. She relied on those guys to be calm when the storms hit. Not pacing the studio, running a hand through his hair as he turned back to the weather map. "So you're going to want to   "

Everything went black. The room, the television, everything. The last couple words from the meteorologist echoed in the sudden silence of the living room. The end of that sentence was for people further away from the storm.

Twenty-Seven

Tristan sat frozen on his couch. When he blinked, the afterimage of the weatherman on television burned against the backs of his eyelids. The condo was utterly silent: no ambient noise from the fridge or the air-conditioning, making the storm outside seem even louder.

Shit had just gotten real. For the first time, Tristan felt a real sliver of apprehension slide down his spine. Everything he'd heard over the past few days played in his head in an almost simultaneous jumble: *Category 4 . . . 130 miles an hour . . . hunker down . . . you don't have shutters? . . . storm surge . . .*

Any room without windows. His living room was nothing *but* windows. From the big picture window that framed his excellent view of the Gulf—a gray-and-white blur now, thanks to the wind and driving rain—to the sliding-glass doors that led to the balcony, he was surrounded on three sides by glass. Glass that could shatter and kill him at any moment.

As if proving his point, a palm frond slapped against the sliding-glass door with a loud, wet *thwap* before falling to the floor of his balcony. The sound sent Tristan to his feet in alarm.

Maybe it was time to hunker down in the bathroom.

He'd just finished his beer while sitting on the bathroom floor, his back pressed against the cool ceramic of the bathtub, when he remembered his phone, stashed in his back pocket. It still had bars and a relatively full charge. It didn't take long to pull up a weather map. Flynn was still offshore but coming closer; outer bands reached like long skinny arms toward the state of Florida. One of the thicker bands was firmly over Boneyard Key, which explained all the wind and rain, but the bulk of the storm was still to the south.

So things were about to get worse. Great. He was going to need another beer.

The act of opening the fridge reminded him that he should be keeping it closed. The power was out; wasn't he supposed to keep the cold air in as long as possible? He grabbed two beers before slamming the door shut. Now he saw the value in the red wine and Pop-Tarts that Sophie and Cassie had been talking about.

Sophie. His head automatically swiveled in her direction, toward the bedroom wall that abutted hers. She was okay, right? She had to be, inside that fortress that her place had become behind all those metal shutters.

He should have left. He had no business riding out a hurricane like this. Those thoughts swirled around and around in his head, the way the wind and rain swirled around outside. Dammit. He really should have left.

Outside, things were only getting worse. He'd never realized just how loud rain could be when it pounded against the walls, the roof, the windows, like a living thing trying to get in. Water started to puddle at the base of the sliding-glass door, and Tristan stashed the beers on the bathroom counter and grabbed a towel. It felt like trying to bail out the *Titanic* with a bucket, rolling up that towel and shoving it against the door, but at least he was doing something?

It was probably time to head back to the bathroom. He wasn't going to be able to do anything about the water coming in, and with everyone else he knew barricaded behind steel and wood, hiding in a windowless room was probably the smartest thing he could do right now.

Despite the power outage, visibility wasn't a problem in Tristan's place, until he got to the bathroom. He flipped on the light switch, only remembering the power was out when the room stayed dark. The wind howled from the living room and he closed the bathroom door behind him. The total darkness was almost more terrifying than all the windows out in the living room. He felt for the beers on the counter as he sank back to his place next to the bathtub. His phone was blindingly bright as he refreshed the weather page between swigs of beer. Oh, shit. Flynn was right here. Tristan watched, almost numb, as the storm on its little radar loop came closer to Boneyard Key, finally obscuring it completely.

No wonder it felt like the end of the world out there. Because it really might be.

The storm outside got louder and louder, until suddenly it wasn't. The noise lessened, and fast, like someone had turned the volume down on the outside. Tristan hesitated before reaching for the doorknob. Was that it? Was it over?

Sophie had expected the power outage, so the sudden darkness didn't frighten her. She leaned forward on the sofa, groping for the lighter on the coffee table. Within a couple minutes, she'd lit the grouping of candles in front of her, then the ones in the fireplace that were ornamental every other time of year. Next, she moved to the kitchen, where she popped on one of her LED lanterns. Her living space glowed now, warm and friendly despite the howling storm outside. Nothing left to do now but wait it out.

But Sophie couldn't sit still. Not with the storm getting worse out there. Not that she could see it, with all her windows blocked, and that somehow made it worse. She paced to the kitchen and uncorked one of the bottles of red wine on the counter, but it was what, barely noon? Hurricane or not, it seemed a little early to be hitting the bottle. Still, who was here to see her?

She splashed a little into a glass and carried it back into the living room along with a bag of pretzels, settling herself onto the couch with a book. It wouldn't get stuffy for another couple hours or so; for now, the remnants of the air conditioning lingered. But after that it would get a little unpleasant. She wouldn't be able to open a window until after the storm had passed and Nick came over with his screw gun to help her take the shutters down.

Sophie took a long sip of her wine and opened her book. She needed to distract herself from the storm outside and the impending claustrophobia. Not being able to see out was maddening, making every little sound even more sinister and her nerves on edge. But she gritted her teeth, sipped some more wine, and concentrated on her book.

Something slammed into her shutters a couple pages later, causing her to almost drop her book as her gaze snapped to the covered-up window. That had been some force. If not for the shutters, she'd probably have a palm tree in her living room right now.

Her phone chirped on the coffee table; cell towers were still up at least.

> Landfall at Tarpon Springs any minute now! Then coming up this way. You lose power?

Sophie shook her head with a small smile. Trust Libby to bring the latest.

> Power's out here. Something hit the window, thank God for shutters.

Knowing her phone still had reception gave her an idea. She opened up a weather app to watch the radar. Flynn looked wicked, buzz-sawing his way along the coast of Tampa Bay. The loop cut off right as the storm started to slide east, on a direct course with landfall at Tarpon Springs, like Libby said.

Not far from Boneyard Key now.

She was safe here. But it was hard to remember that when the storm got louder and the rain lashed harder, like a live thing trying to get inside. Phone in hand and feeling like the final girl in a horror movie, she fled to the bathroom, shoving the shower curtain aside to climb into the bathtub. It felt ridiculous. It *was* ridiculous. But being surrounded by smooth ceramic felt like an added layer of protection between her and the storm.

She huddled in the tub and refreshed the radar on her phone. The storm dipped inland—landfall at Tarpon Springs, indeed—and the movement over land started to break up the storm. But not a lot, not enough; the wind picked up outside, in time with the radar loop showing the storm getting closer and closer, until the world was nothing but wind and rain and howling outside like banshees trying to get inside, trying to get to Sophie, to grind her bones to make their bread—

—and then it was over. The silence echoed in Sophie's ears as she crept out of the tub. It wasn't really over, of course; this was the eye of the storm, a half hour or so of stillness before the back half of the hurricane showed up for a grand finale.

Back in the living room, which glowed with candles and the LED lantern, she took out her phone again. She should check on Libby. She should make sure Nick and Cassie were doing okay. But the contact she pulled up was much closer by. Right next door, in fact.

You okay?

The answer came back right away. She pictured Tristan huddled in his bathroom, phone in hand. He had better be in his bathroom, anyway, and not in that death trap he called a living room.

Look ma, I made it through my first hurricane!

Sophie bit back a groan. He thought it was over. When it was actually about to get worse.

"Ugh," she said out loud to no one. She shoved her feet into a pair of shoes by the door and grabbed her umbrella from the stand nearby. "Fine."

With a sigh she wrenched open her front door. It was still raining, the wind pushing it practically sideways into the breezeway. It took almost the entire fifteen feet between her door and Tristan's to wrestle her umbrella open.

Because the storm wasn't over. More was coming, and soon. And Tristan, that big dummy, was still riding it out in a plate-glass box. She couldn't let him do that.

Time to cross a line.

Tristan eased the bathroom door open, blinking against the sudden brightness of the rest of the condo. Everything looked intact, except for the puddle on the hardwood floor by the sliding-glass door. The towel he'd put down was soaked—what a ridiculous, futile gesture that had been. It was still raining outside, but it looked like a normal rain, like any given summer afternoon in Florida. Fronds from the nearby palm trees littered his balcony, but that would be easy to clean up.

Tristan let out a surprised little laugh. He'd done it. He'd ridden out his first hurricane. He felt invincible, like nothing in the world could touch him. Take that, nature!

The knock at the door nearly sent him out of his skin. For an insane moment he thought Flynn was there; the hurricane itself coming to finish the job personally. Longneck still dangling from one hand, he eased open the front door.

Sophie stood there under a ridiculously large umbrella—the kind they gave out at charity golf tournaments—her eyes enormous behind her glasses.

"Come on."

"What?" He blinked.

"Come *on*," she said again, as though that would clarify things. "You don't have a single window boarded up. Come on over."

"Now?" He looked toward the windows, out at the storm that wasn't really a storm anymore. "But the storm's over."

She shook her head solemnly. "This is just the eye. It'll be calm for a few more minutes, then it's coming back with a vengeance. It'll be the dirty side of the hurricane too," she added, as though that meant anything to him.

But Tristan wasn't going to argue with her tone of voice. He slid his feet into a pair of flip-flops by the door before pulling it closed behind him, throwing the bolt and stowing his keys in his pocket. A sudden wind gust had Sophie wrestling with her umbrella, and Tristan grabbed for it, holding it steady. Their hands overlapped, and her hand was cold under his, fingers holding on tightly. Sophie reacted visibly to his touch, her lips parting and a startled look coming into her eyes, but after a beat her grip softened, fingers loosening under his as she relinquished control of the umbrella. He held it over them both, angling it to keep away the rain that blew in sideways as she led him into her place.

His heart quickened as she pushed open the door, and he caught his breath. He'd never crossed this threshold; she'd never invited him to. Something about this moment felt significant, and he wanted to mark it. Savor it. He took his time folding her umbrella before handing it to her.

"Well?" She stuck the umbrella in a stand next to the door, then she turned to face him again, crossing her arms across her chest. "Are you a vampire or something? Need an invitation?"

"No." *Yes.* He let out a long breath as he stepped over the threshold and into her home.

Her place . . . glowed. That was the word that popped into his brain, and no other word could replace it. It was dark, obviously, since the power was out and all the windows were sealed off from the outside world. But there was a grouping of candles on the coffee table, and another in the fireplace. An LED lantern sat on the edge of the kitchen counter to his right, throwing light down the hallway. Her place smelled warm and soft. Like vanilla and comfort.

The square footage was smaller, but he could see traces of his condo here in hers. The layout of the living room was the same but mirrored; in his place the kitchen was to the left. His living room was more expansive, or maybe it just looked that way because his place had less furniture. Sophie's living room was filled with bookcases along one wall, and an old record player in a far corner with stacks of vinyl records. An enormous floral sofa took up much of the real estate in this main room, and there were two neatly folded quilts across the back of it. A fringed shawl was similarly draped over a recliner nestled into a corner near the record player. The walls that weren't filled with bookcases were filled with framed photographs and paintings. Tristan immediately spied among the jumble a framed photo of a young girl with huge glasses, big curls, and a bigger smile. Sophie. He couldn't keep the grin from his face.

Next to him, the adult Sophie shifted her weight as she toed off her shoes. Tristan took the hint and followed suit, leaving his flip-flops next to hers by the door.

"I love your place." The words were an understatement but they would have to do. He'd lived in a lot of apartments in a lot of cities during his life, so "home" was a nebulous term for him. But right now, in the dark of Sophie's living room as the storm outside started picking up again—he could hear the wind intensify, throwing raindrops to rattle against the shutters—for the first time in his life, it felt like he was home.

It felt like nothing between them would ever be the same.

Twenty-Eight

Over the past few months, Tristan Martin had invaded every part of Sophie's life. Her town. Her business. Even her friends. Now he was in her home. She shouldn't want him here.

There'd never been many men around here. Growing up here with her aunt Alice, this condo had always been a purely feminine space, full of flowers and music, framed photographs and scented candles. Handmade quilts and an outdated, overstuffed floral sofa. Aunt Alice had spent most of her evenings on one end of that sofa, wrapped in her fringed shawl no matter the temperature, watching *Wheel of Fortune* and *Jeopardy!* and knitting yet another pair of socks. Sophie had enough socks to last the rest of her life, and so did most of the residents of Boneyard Key.

This place was bursting with feminine energy, so Tristan shouldn't belong here.

But he did.

She couldn't explain it, but when he stepped out of his flip-flops and bent to line them up neatly next to her shoes by the front door, it looked . . . normal. Like she'd seen him do it a million times before.

"I love your place."

That was the last thing she'd expected him to say. She'd never been inside his condo, but she'd caught a glimpse just now when she'd knocked on his door. Calling it minimalist was an understatement; despite the dark and gloomy day outside, everything in his place practically gleamed. The living room was a symphony of white and chrome, like the most expensive and least personal hotel room. He lived like that?

Now her eyes narrowed as she turned to him, waiting for the punch line to whatever joke he was making. Waiting for him to make fun of Aunt Alice's quilts, or maybe the record player. But everything in his face was open, honest. He really did like her place.

"Thanks." The word landed flat between them, and she almost cringed. That sounded sarcastic, and she wasn't trying to be.

Outside, the storm started picking up again, reminding Sophie why Tristan was there in her living room. She motioned toward the couch. "Please, sit. I can't offer you a whole lot. You know, power's out and all, and I can't . . ."

"Open the fridge. I know. I remembered that much." Tristan gave a small smile as he took a seat on her sofa. He perched on the edge, either not yet comfortable enough to relax or judging the shabbiness of her sofa. Aunt Alice had bought that sofa, back before Sophie had started college, and it was super dated. But it was comfortable, and there was no reason to replace it.

The image of the white leather couch in Tristan's apartment persisted. Along with that weird sense of déjà vu, of feeling like he belonged there even though this was the first time he'd set foot past her front door. It was unsettling.

She shook off the feeling and turned toward the kitchen. "I've got an open bottle of merlot, and a few bottles of room-temperature water. I've also—"

"Already started breaking into the good hurricane supplies, huh?"

"At least I waited till the rain started." Sophie snagged the bottle of wine and an extra glass, bringing them back into the living room.

"The picture of restraint." He grinned, taking the proffered glass and holding it out while she filled it.

"That's me." His grin was infectious, and she sat beside him, reaching for her own glass on the end table and holding it up in a toast. "To Flynn."

He toasted her back. "To hurricane shutters. I see the point of them now."

"Once this storm is over you should really look into getting them. We get plenty of storms coming through here, and I always feel a lot safer with them up." A voice in the back of her head objected. *He won't be here that long, remember?* She told that voice to hush.

"You're absolutely right." He took a thoughtful sip. "Tell me about the dirty side of a hurricane. How's it any different than a clean side?"

Sophie swallowed carefully before answering. "Okay, first of all, Libby is the local hurricane expert, so I won't explain this nearly as well as she does. That said, you know how Flynn is coming up the coast?"

Tristan nodded, shifting in his seat to take his phone out of his back pocket. "I've been watching the radar." He set his glass down on the end table to pull it up—the same weather app Sophie had been using. Now he sat back on the sofa, getting comfortable as he angled the phone toward her, and she leaned in over his shoulder to watch.

"Every hurricane has a dirty side, with higher wind speeds and more potential for things like tornados. The dirty side causes more damage overall. And when you're talking about storms that hit the Gulf and go north, that's the east side. Look . . ." She pointed at Flynn on the weather map, tracing its path with her fingertip. "See how he made landfall here, near Tarpon Springs, and then it's basically riding up the coast?"

He nodded, a movement she could barely see out of the corner of her eye since she was sitting so close. "And Boneyard Key is here, in the clear section." This close, his voice was a murmur in her ear, his breath stirring a lock of her hair.

"Yep. That's the eye. That's why the rain slowed down for a bit. But as it continues up the coast and past us, we're still on its east side. It's a big storm; it's got a big dirty side."

Tristan's gaze went to her windows, where the rain pattered again, the wind driving the drops like bullets toward her shutters. "And it's picking up again. So the eye's almost past?" He looked down at his phone again to confirm.

"Exactly." She took another sip of wine. "Time for round two."

"Fabulous." Even in the candlelight, she could see the apprehension in his eyes. Her heart swelled; she'd done the right thing, bringing him over. He shouldn't be riding through this alone.

Sophie nodded toward his phone. "You should turn that off for a bit. Save the battery."

"Good call." He clicked it off and laid it on the end table, trading it for his wineglass. "How long does the power usually stay out during these things?"

"Hard to tell. A couple days? Maybe more? It all depends on how much damage there is. Not to mention the flooding. The water has to recede before the linemen can come in to get the power restored. We'll see how things look tomorrow."

"Tomorrow? That long?" Tristan looked stricken. "It's barely afternoon."

Sophie nodded. "And by the time the storm's over it'll be almost sunset. Believe me, no one's going out tonight."

He raised his eyebrows. "Is there a curfew? I saw that on the news. Some cities down toward Key West have curfews in effect."

Sophie shook her head. "Nothing that formal. I mean, the mayor could declare one. It's mostly to keep people home, so everyone can stay safe. But we're a little more casual around here. We just choose to not go out at night after a storm."

"That sounds like Boneyard Key." A small smile came to his face as he sipped at his glass of wine. Sophie wanted to bristle at the way he was so casually familiar with her town, but somehow the bristle didn't come. She could call him a stranger and a newcomer all she wanted, but he'd been here for months now. He'd become part of the scenery, part of the *town*, the way Cassie had when she'd arrived last year. To her consternation, Sophie realized she'd grown comfortable with Tristan, the way he'd grown comfortable here on her couch over the last few minutes.

Outside, the wind had picked up again, and so had the rain, but now the storm had become background noise. The grouping of candles around her living room contributed to the cozy scene, but the lack of air conditioning made things a little too cozy.

Warm.

Stuffy. The word she was looking for was "stuffy." It was getting hard to breathe in here. Sophie drew in a long, slow breath, staving off the panic that always threatened when she was cooped up like this. But it wasn't easy. Her living room felt like a bank vault. The candles on the table were using up precious oxygen, and the man sitting next to her . . .

Well, he was making it hard to breathe too. Everything in her chest was a jumble when it came to Tristan. Looking at him now in the darkness of her living room, candlelight throwing his cheekbones into sharp relief, she remembered the first night that their tours had collided on the street. When she'd heard him telling that stupid pirate story and had absolutely unloaded on him. She'd hated him so much that night.

Tristan felt her gaze and turned his head, blue eyes meeting hers, and now she remembered kissing him for the first time, after he'd joined them at Poltergeist Pizza. That was the night everything had started to change, wasn't it? When she'd stopped seeing him as the enemy.

No, he hadn't been the enemy for a while now. Now he was the guy who kissed her good night on her front step. The guy who never pushed for any more from her than she was willing to give. At least when it came to kissing.

It was so easy to forget that when it came to her business, he was here to take it all.

And he was about to. The sudden thought made tears spring to her eyes, and Tristan noticed right away. His face softened with concern.

"Hey." He reached for her, his fingertips tracing the back of her hand. "What is it?"

She shook her head and tilted her head back, blinking hard and willing the tears to go back into her eyes. "This town . . ." she finally said. "It means everything to me."

"Don't worry." His hand covered hers, sitting in her lap. He gave her a quick squeeze before suddenly withdrawing, as though remembering that familiar touches like this wasn't something the two of them did. (She kind of hated that it wasn't something the two of them did.) "Everyone's going to be fine." His words were a verbal hand squeeze, and if that was all she could get, she'd take it. "Hopefully there won't be too much damage once the storm is over. We'll go out as soon as we can, check and see how everything is."

"Oh." She shook her head. "No, I don't mean that." A smile

came to her face then, a watery one, but still a smile. "Boneyard Key's been through so many hurricanes. Honestly, this place should be wiped off the map, just like the original town was out on Cemetery Island." She waved that thought away, because speaking that kind of thing out loud during an active hurricane felt like tempting fate. "No, I'm talking about the ghost tour." She struggled now to put her heart into words. She'd never talked about this to anyone. And now, here in the dark while a storm raged outside, she was confessing her heart to someone she barely knew, and barely even liked. "It was my contribution to Boneyard Key. My way of being part of things. Aunt Alice was still around when I wrote it, when I first started giving the tour. She was there the first night." Lost in memory, she gave a small laugh. "I was so nervous, stumbling over my words. My throat was all dry, but my hands were all slippery . . ."

"Flop sweat?" Tristan raised his eyebrows as she nodded. "I know it well, believe me." The smile on his face became a smirk, but a self-conscious one, his attention focused inward. "No matter how many times I've rehearsed, there are always nights when a show is an absolute disaster. Every joke lands wrong, I suddenly forget what I'm supposed to say. I'm a wreck afterward. I always need a super long shower after a night like that."

It helped a little, knowing that Tristan wasn't perfect. "But she was so proud. She said I'd made a mark on this town." There was maybe one more mouthful of wine in her glass, and she swirled it around, tilting her glass so the deep red liquid caught the candlelight. "I'm really going to miss doing it."

"You don't have to worry about that." His voice was so soft that she barely heard the words over the storm outside.

She wanted to scoff, but this hurt too much. "Of course I do. I know we're barely into August, but I'm not stupid. I don't just enter my stats on the spreadsheet, you know. I study them too. You're beating me on every single metric." She tossed back the rest of her wine and set the glass down with a thud. This confession was painful. But once she started talking, she couldn't stop. It was like lancing a wound; get all the poison out, and maybe then she could move on with her life. Whatever that life was going to be.

"It doesn't matter."

"Of course it matters!" She was choking on her words now; that poison was strong. "Isn't that the point of all this? Proving which ghost tour is better, makes more money, brings in more people? And it's you. It's all you." God, the words tasted so bitter on her tongue. "I worked for years on this tour. I still work on this tour—I've added new stops this year. It's not just for me; I want to represent the ghosts of Boneyard Key the best way I can. They mean something to me. And then you show up with your top hat and your pirate stories and you blow me out of the water." Wineglass abandoned, she tossed her glasses to the coffee table and buried her face in her hands. "I'm going to lose everything because of this stupid bet."

"No, you're not." His voice was loud now, drowning out hers. "You're not going to lose anything. Because I'm not going to let you. I'm canceling this whole bet."

What?

Twenty-Nine

What?

Tristan hadn't intended to say that, but as soon as he did, he knew he meant it. It was the only real solution.

Sophie raised her head, blinking at him, and she looked so different without her glasses on, so vulnerable, that it stole Tristan's breath and made him forget what they were talking about. Then she groped on the coffee table for her glasses, sliding them onto her face, and the world righted itself again.

"I don't understand," she said, and rightfully so. Tristan barely understood himself. "All these months you've been outdoing me. Now you're just giving up?"

All he could do was nod. At this moment everything was clear, the way it had never been before.

Eric was going to kill him. Guaranteed. But that was Future Tristan's problem. Current Tristan had enough going on, what with a hurricane raging outside while here, inside, he was about to throw away his entire business.

But the woman in front of him was worth it.

He'd never thought of a hurricane as a romantic setting before, but with the rain and the wind whipping around outside, and Sophie's skin glowing in the candlelight, his heart was so full that his chest could barely contain it. He swallowed hard against the lump in this throat, and Sophie blinked, a tear dropping from her lashes onto her cheek, sparkling in the light of the vanilla-scented candles nearby.

That tear clinched it. Sophie was crying. It was his fault. He had a way to fix it. Future Tristan was going to have to suck it up and deal.

"I said I'm conceding." Conviction made his voice louder, his resolve stronger. "This was a stupid contest anyway, and I never should have proposed it. This is your town. I can't take that away from you."

"You weren't going to." The tiniest of smiles played around Sophie's lips. "It's not like I was gonna move away." Her feet were tucked under the skirt of her sundress as she sat curled up on one corner of the sofa. She looked snug—like she was in her safe spot, her retreat from the world. He wanted the whole word to be a safe spot for her, but he'd settle for Boneyard Key. Removing himself as a threat.

"Jesus. Of course you're not." That had been a consideration? Tristan couldn't take this. He surged to his feet, nervous energy propelling him around the room. "Even so, I bet it would be super fun, having me around all the time. Spending your weekends watching me lead ghost tours, knowing that I took that away from you?"

"Okay," she said. "Good point." Her mouth twisted. Not quite a smile, but close.

"Besides," he said. "It was a ridiculous bet. I don't know what I was thinking."

"You were probably thinking that this town isn't big enough for two ghost tours," she said, her tone saying she'd had that same thought once or twice, and he huffed out a laugh in response.

"The point is, I'm not the same guy that I was when I first came to town, and when we made that bet. All that guy could think about was winning. When I made that bet, all I was thinking about was . . ." He faltered. He could finish that sentence. *All I was thinking about was winning against my father*, but that would just bring up more questions. And the last thing he wanted to do right now was hash through his daddy issues with Sophie. Those were his to deal with, and he never should have mixed her up with them.

He still had his October first deadline. But it was far from the most important thing on his mind. Tristan cleared his throat, effectively erasing that half-finished sentence and beginning a new one. "Anyway, it was a ridiculous bet."

"Then why did you do it?" Sophie wasn't aggressive or accusatory. She simply tilted her head to watch him pace around the room. "The whole thing was your idea."

"It was a dumb idea. I have those sometimes."

She made a noise that could have been agreement, could have been disapproval. He would never know. But for the first time, her lips curved up in a smile—a real smile—and Tristan felt like he could fly.

"So now what?" The question came from deep in Sophie's throat, and Tristan felt it in the base of his spine. Now what, indeed.

"Well, I don't know, Sophie." Her question, and the way she was looking at him right now, gave him courage. He moved to sit on the edge of the coffee table, the grouping of candles to his right, directly in front of where Sophie curled up in her nest on the sofa. "Because I know that we're not friends." She caught her breath at their old refrain, and the soft sound sent a thrill across the back of his neck. "I'm sure you'd love for me to get the hell out of town as soon as possible."

"Well . . ." The tip of Sophie's tongue peeked out between her lips, wetting them, and Tristan forgot how to speak. "I mean not right this second. There's a hurricane and all."

"And after the storm's over?" This was it. Now or never. Slowly, as though watching someone else do it, Tristan reached out, laying his hand on top of Sophie's where it lay in her lap. "Because the thing is, I've gotten really attached to . . . this town."

It was all he could do to keep his hand still, to not curve it around and grasp hers. The next move was hers, and he wasn't going to be able to breathe until she made it.

An excruciating few seconds passed, and then Sophie moved her hand under his, tangling their fingers together. His breath caught at her touch, and her gaze snapped up to his. And there was that smile again. Small, wicked. Making him feel like he could run through a wall. "I know what you mean," she said. "This town's . . . come to mean a lot to me."

"Yeah?" Now he let himself tighten his grip on her hand.

"Yeah." She tugged, and it was the easiest thing in the world for him to slide to his knees in front of her. He sat back on his heels, drinking in the sight of Sophie in the candlelight. Her eyes glowed in the subtle flame as they met his, and God, he'd never seen anything more beautiful in his life.

Her free hand came up to cradle his jaw, and Tristan's eyes fell closed. "I mean, I wasn't sure at first," she said. "About this town. If you want to know the truth, I wasn't much of a fan."

"Really." He tried to sound as casual as he could while his heart pounded against his ribs.

"Oh, yeah." She quirked an eyebrow and bit down on her bottom lip, trying to hold in her smile. Tristan couldn't help it; he leaned forward, drawn to her. She was a siren, and he was an ancient sailor. He wanted to bite that bottom lip. He wanted to do so much more than that. *Patience*, he reminded himself. *Patience*. This wasn't about what he wanted. It was about Sophie.

In the silence that followed, she continued. "But then I got to know the town. And there's so much . . ." She drew in a shaking breath, and she tugged at him, pulled with her hand in his until he was kneeling up straighter, his lower belly against the edge of the sofa. He was a supplicant, worshipping a queen on her overstuffed, floral-patterned throne.

Sophie shifted in her seat, leaning closer, bringing her forehead close to his. "Let's just say I like this town a lot."

"Oh, God, so do I." The words burst from his chest, and he couldn't take it anymore. He reached for her, cupping her face in his hands. "I've really, really fallen for this town." Her skin was so smooth, her hair curling around his fingers as he slid one hand back to grip the base of her skull. "Sophie. God." He leaned closer, impossibly closer, his mouth hovering a breath away from hers. "You have no idea . . . the things I want to do to this town."

A laugh burst from her, a giggle that any other time would seem childlike, but right now made him hard as iron. He'd never been that turned on by a laugh before. But now he was laughing too, and her smile felt so, so good against his mouth when he finally kissed her.

He'd kissed Sophie before, of course. Several times, at her front door. They'd been sweet, mostly tentative. But this was different. This was a slow, rolling wave, pulling him under. He would gladly drown in her.

Sophie's arms came up around him, pulling him into her as much as she pulled herself into him. Her mouth opened against his, and her tongue—God, her tongue. He tugged her closer and she went, her legs sliding around his hips as easily as her arms slid around his neck. The coffee table behind them made a loud groan as the force of their bodies sent it backwards across the hardwood, and Sophie came up for air long enough to gasp.

"The candles!"

"Sorry." He sat back and blew out a long breath. This had gotten a little out of control. Setting the place on fire anytime was a bad idea, but during a hurricane? That seemed especially negligent.

Sophie fisted a hand in his shirt, pulling him back. "Where do you think you're going?"

"I just . . ." Those sweet kisses they'd shared in front of her door were long since gone in the rearview. Up until now, Sophie had been so reluctant to let him in—to her home, to her life. And for good reason.

But now . . . everything seemed turned on its head, tossed like the wind outside tossing around palm fronds. He could taste the red wine on her tongue, and it reminded him to proceed with caution. So he leaned back, edge of the coffee table digging into his back, keeping Sophie cradled soft and warm in his lap.

"Are you sure about this? This isn't the hurricane wine talking?" He kept his voice as light as he could, even though this was the opposite of casual. He was about to explode with wanting her, but he had to check.

Sophie huffed a laugh. "I've had more to drink on *Romance Resort* nights with Cassie, Libby, and Sarah."

That got his attention. "Sarah Hawkins? You watch reality television with a ghost?" He had so many more questions, but that conversation would get them very, very far afield of Sophie's thighs around his hips and the many things he wanted to do with her. To her.

So instead he smiled. "God, I love this town." He reached for her, pulling her mouth to his.

Sophie laughed against his mouth, but their laughter dissolved fast as they got more and more caught up in each other. Tristan dropped a hand to Sophie's leg, the skirt of her sundress pooling around his wrist as he glided upward. She shifted in his lap, a slight rocking motion that made the top of his head want to pop off. His senses were filled with her, the warmth of her mouth, the smoothness of her skin, the way her breath hitched when he reached the crease of her thigh . . .

She rocked again, rising up on her knees, helping him move her sundress out of the way. "God." She exhaled a moan into his ear, clutching his shoulders. "Yes, *please*." It was more than just a moan, a beg.

He wanted to go slow with this. It was what Sophie deserved. She deserved a bed strewn with rose petals, slow sips of champagne over declarations of love. She deserved to be undressed slowly while he discovered every inch of her with his hands, his mouth, his tongue. She did not deserve a quick fumble on her living room floor. But he couldn't think; his cock was straining against his shorts, and she was moving against him while he slid one finger, then two, under the elastic of her underwear to find the spot where she burned the hottest. Her nails dug into the back of his neck when his fingertips stroked her clit, and it only took a few strokes to send her trembling. She made a soft, almost surprised noise when she came, a sound that was a dart to his soul. He knew then that he was lost.

No. He was found.

His future had so many question marks, but Sophie . . . Sophie was an exclamation point.

Thirty

The day before Hurricane Flynn, Sophie would have best described her sex life as "self-inflicted." She'd had some fun in college, and had even dated a guy that back then she was sure was "the one." But he hadn't lasted past graduation, and then she was back in Boneyard Key. Living with her great-aunt had severely limited her options, which were already woefully scarce. Unless she wanted to date either Tony or Terry—the food fight she'd witnessed between those two in the seventh grade negated that—or Theo, who she'd hated up until a year or so ago, she was out of luck. It was one of the reasons she and Libby—who knew something about spending her twenties as a caretaker for an octogenarian—had stayed so close as adults.

But now, while the second half of Flynn beat at her shutters and pounded down on her roof, and while her body shimmered from the first orgasm in years she hadn't had to give herself, Sophie's future felt wide open.

That future started with pulling Tristan to his feet and getting him into her bedroom.

"Wait, where are we going?" He tried to look innocent as she led him by the hand, past her kitchen and to the darkened hallway that led to the bedrooms. But there was nothing innocent about the way he pushed her against the wall, his hands holding her shoulders while his mouth found that soft spot where her neck met her shoulder.

Even as he explored her skin with his tongue, he was still talking. Sophie was beginning to suspect that Tristan never stopped talking. "Are you sure you want to show me the rest of your place? We're not friends, you know."

The old Sophie would have huffed at this. She would have probably thrown him out on his ear. But this Sophie, the just-had-an-orgasm Sophie, grinned into the darkness of the hallway. "I don't do this kind of thing with friends." She'd felt him, hard against her, soft moans in her ear as she'd rocked against him in his lap. He was still hard against her now, pushing slowly against the thin layers of cotton that separated them. She knew his protest was toothless; he was hanging on by a thread. And despite her recent orgasm, so was she. "You have somewhere else to be?"

"Fuck no, I do not." His hands slid down, tracing the shape of her body through her sundress until he reached her waist and his fingers dug in, clutching.

"Well, come on then." She pushed at him lightly and he fell away, happy to cede control to her. "Time for the dirty side of the hurricane."

"God, I love hurricanes." He followed her down the hallway, but when she stopped at her bedroom, the first door on the left, he almost barreled right past her until she grabbed his hand, tugging him to a stop at her door.

"This is your room?" He looked down the hallway, and Sophie understood his confusion. The layouts in their places were probably similar, with the master bedroom at the end of the hallway. The room that was still Aunt Alice's.

"Since I was five!" she said as cheerfully as she could, but her heart plummeted. She didn't like this. Next, he was going to ask her why she'd never moved into the master bedroom, even though she'd lived alone in this place for a while now. She'd try to explain that while sometimes the days were long, the years were short, and while she hadn't intended to keep her great-aunt's room as a shrine, she'd also never gotten around to moving in there.

They'd been kissing and touching, and until a few moments ago Tristan had practically been shaking with how much he wanted Sophie. But now, in the dark hallway, his blood seemed to have calmed, and Sophie wanted to cry. So much for romance. No wonder she was usually on her own when it came to orgasms.

"Hey." Derailed mood or not, Tristan seemed more than eager to get it back on track. He stepped closer, an arm sliding around her waist. His embrace was more comforting than sexy, but his warmth was everything she wanted. "Where'd you go?" His lips brushed her forehead, sending a thrill through her blood even as her throat closed up.

"I'm sorry." She could barely speak. "I think . . . I think I'm not very good at this."

"I'm sure that's not true." His voice was gentle while his hands were soothing, one rubbing a slow circle on her back while another slid through her hair. "But we can stop, you know. Go back into the living room if . . ."

That was a horrifying thought, so horrifying that she stretched on her toes, capturing his mouth with hers, and the rest of his sentence was lost in their kiss. "I want this," she said between kisses, barely allowing herself to come up for air. "I want you."

"You've got me." He turned them like they were dancing, walking backwards into her room and tugging her along after him. A few steps into the darkened bedroom, he paused. "I can't see shit in here."

A watery giggle burst out of Sophie. "Hold on. I have candles."

"Of course you do." He stood still while she made her way to her nightstand, and the lighter that she'd placed next to the three-wick pillar candle there. She'd anticipated a dark bedroom; she just hadn't anticipated bringing a guest in here. Once it was lit, she moved to the one on her bureau, and warm candlelight filled the room.

Now that he could see, Tristan moved in behind her, his front grazing her back as she put the lighter down on the bureau. He moved her hair over her left shoulder, and his lips brushed her neck—the smallest of touches that sent shivers all through her. "How about this . . ." The tip of his tongue grazed the shell of her ear, and the murmur of his voice was all she could hear. "You tell me what you want and I'll make it happen. Okay?"

She tried to answer, but he chose that moment to nibble on her ear, and she forgot how to speak. Her knees sagged and Tristan was there, one hand flat on her belly, holding her flush against him. She nodded instead, turning in his arms and reaching for him. She thought she'd ruined the mood, but when he bent to kiss her it all came roaring back—that shimmering in her blood, the desperate way he clutched at her. The mood was back, and it wasn't going away again. Not if she could help it.

"What do you want?" he asked again, his voice hoarse from their kiss. His arousal made her bold, and she reached for his shirt, tugging it free from his shorts.

"Off" was all she said, and he obeyed immediately, pulling the collared polo shirt over his head and tossing it aside. Sophie caught her breath, suddenly remembering the dirty dream she'd had about him so many weeks ago. Her subconscious hadn't been too far off. Tristan was lean but toned, a runner's body, his belly paler than his arms, his chest lightly furred with a sprinkling of blond hair. She'd seen that hair before, on nights when the ghost tours were over and he'd taken off his cravat and undone the top button of his shirt. It had been like getting a glimpse of ankle in Victorian times, so getting the full view now felt almost obscene.

Tristan didn't push; he stood still in the candlelight, watching Sophie watch him. "Do you just wanna look?" He cocked an eyebrow.

She shook her head and stepped closer, reaching out one hand as though she were in a dream. Maybe she was; it would be just like her to have another erotic dream about Tristan, about the two of them making love during a hurricane. She let her fingertips dance across his flat stomach. He sucked in a breath at her touch, muscles contracting, and he felt better than any dream ever could. But he still didn't move; he seemed determined to let her take the lead here.

So she did. Her throat had gone completely dry, and she licked her lips, swallowing hard as she let her hand glide down, meeting her other hand at his belt buckle. "I can't believe you dressed business casual for a hurricane," she said as she undid his belt. "Did you iron these khakis this morning?"

"Of course. The power was still on." A laugh gusted out of him. "Nothing wrong with being well-dressed," he said in a shaky voice as his belt met his shirt on the floor.

"There is right now," she said. "In fact, I don't think I want you to be dressed at all."

"Like I said. Whatever you want."

Sophie didn't know where she found the courage. She'd never been this bold in her life. But with Tristan it didn't feel like boldness. It felt normal to pop the button on his shorts. It was the most natural thing in the world to let her fingers trace the fine line of hair beneath his navel, sliding down to his waistband and then under it.

Tristan's breath shuddered out of him as she reached down, curling her hand around him. His flesh leapt at her touch, and when she stroked him once, twice, he broke his stillness to slide a hand around the back of her neck.

"God. Sophie." Her name was a plea, whispered on a sigh as his grip tightened on her nape. "Can I touch you?"

"Soon." She smiled at his frustrated groan. She almost felt bad for him, but it had been a long time since she'd been alone in the dark with a man sighing her name. Soon she would relinquish control, but right now she was having too much fun. She pushed on his shorts and they fell to the floor, his boxers following. His erection, now freed, bobbed between them, and God, he looked proud. He looked strong. There was something about him being completely naked while she was still fully dressed that sent a thrill through her. He should look vulnerable, but the way he met her eyes told her just how much he was holding back.

"How soon?" He stepped closer, kicking his discarded clothing to the side. He still made no move to undress her.

"Real soon," she promised. She let herself look at him, really look. She hadn't realized until this moment, right as her dry spell was coming to an end, just how long it had been. There was a nice little stockpile of toys in her nightstand, and they were great. But compared to warm skin and muscle and trembles and sighs . . .

Sophie wasn't one for wicked smiles, but this one felt good. "I need to taste you first." Everything about him looked delicious, and she couldn't wait another minute to get her mouth on him.

"Oh, *God.*" His head dropped back. "You may actually kill me."

She clucked her tongue. "Don't be a baby." Then she used her tongue for better things.

She started slow, settling her mouth at his throat, tasting the vulnerable skin there. He sighed, those sighs turning deeper and breathier as she worked her way down his chest, her hands wandering across his skin in the wake of the path her mouth was taking.

"No," he said as she sank to her knees. "Absolutely not." He tugged at her arm weakly while she looked up with innocent eyes.

"You said anything I want." He'd grown even harder while she'd touched him, and now his cock pulsed in her hand, almost impossibly hot.

"I know." His breath came faster, almost labored in his chest—a man who was holding on by a single, unraveling thread. "But you do that and it's over in five seconds, I swear to God."

"We have all night," Sophie said. "It's gonna be raining for a while." She took off her glasses, leaning up to set them on the edge of her bed. She wasn't going to need to see anything far away for a while; right now everything was happening up close. Very close.

"Okay . . ." The word trailed off into a moan as she stroked him, her palm gathering his wetness and spreading it. "Don't say I didn't warn you."

"Noted." Her heart pounded in her ears as she bent toward him. All bravado aside, she hadn't done this in a long time. She had no idea if she was even any good at it. She leaned forward, planting a tiny kiss on the very tip of him, and his body jerked in response. That was a good start.

She bent to him in earnest, working him with her mouth and gentle swirls of her tongue. He twitched and trembled in her mouth, and she gave a long, slow suck. He was large but not massive—less "oh God how is this even going to fit" and more "he's going to fit *just right*." Sophie had just established a gentle, rocking rhythm when Tristan gave a cry, and strong hands hauled her to her feet.

"Nope." His hands were iron bands around her upper arms, and his breath shuddered in his chest. He looked absolutely wrecked—

hair mussed, mouth open, eyes glazed. She'd done that. She'd finally made him snap. Something inside her glowed at that knowledge.

He turned them, holding her at arm's length, and walked her backwards until she was perched on the edge of her bed. He picked up her glasses and moved them to the relative safety of her nightstand, then bent once more to get something out of the pocket of his shorts, tossing it to the nightstand next to her glasses. Then he finally, *finally*, stepped into her personal space, and her knees fell apart to welcome him as he bunched the skirt of her sundress in his hands, hauling the fabric upward. She stood to help him pull it off over her head.

Sophie's sudden insecurity was like a dash of cold water. "Sorry," she said almost immediately. "I've been told I have the body of a twelve-year-old boy."

He was incredulous, his expression snapping from ravished to livid. "What idiot said that?" He regained focus fast, obviously getting rid of the thought with a shake of his head. When Tristan stepped closer, Sophie sank to sit on the bed again. Then he was closer still, his mouth on her neck as he settled onto her, his knee between her thighs, nudging them apart. She barely had time to enjoy the full force of his weight before he rolled them, draping her across his body.

"The thing is . . ." he said as he made quick work of her bra clasps, "I've been a twelve-year-old boy." He drew her bra down her arms and tossed it over his shoulder. "If I'd looked like this, I never would have left the house." Her underwear followed soon after, both undergarments thrown into the darkness. She wasn't going to need them.

A surprised giggle burst out of her, and his eyes practically disappeared as he grinned to match her. He lifted his head up to catch her mouth with his, their smiles mingling together.

Tristan anchored her to him, a hand flat on her back, as he tilted them both to one side, his other arm stretching out toward the nightstand. Sophie rested her chin on her folded hands and watched him get a condom out of his wallet.

"You want any help with that?"

"Absolutely not," he said for the second time that night. He didn't even look at her as he tossed his wallet to the side, concentrating all his attention on the foil packet in his hands, tearing it open. "I'm on a hair trigger as it is. You touch me right now, and it's all premature fireworks."

"I like fireworks . . ."

"That's good news for me." And they were moving again, Tristan rolling her under him, and Sophie realized this was really happening. That business-casual guy she'd met over oysters at The Haunt all those months ago, the guy she'd screamed at in the street all those weeks ago, was now in her bed. He was running his hands up the insides of her thighs, parting them, settling between them. He was tilting her hips, lining himself up, pushing inside. And she was reaching for him, sliding her hands over his warm skin, hooking her heels around his hips, pulling him in so close that she couldn't tell where he ended and she began. As he'd warned her, it didn't take long before his thrusts began to stutter, and he slid a hand between them, searching, finding, circling, stroking.

"Come on," he panted in her ear. "You can go again."

And she could.

Outside her boarded-up windows, the wind and rain continued to pummel Boneyard Key. But inside, Sophie was warm and safe, with the least likely man—the most perfect man—to make her feel that way.

Thirty-One

Broken glass.

Broken glass, and a shitload of water. Everywhere.

Tristan stood in the doorway of his condo, frozen to the spot. His brain couldn't comprehend what he was seeing.

It was a gorgeous day outside. Bright sunshine, a slight breeze off the water. You'd never know that just twelve hours ago a hurricane had plowed through Boneyard Key. Except, of course, for the smashed plate-glass window in Tristan's living room. That same breeze from off the water danced playfully through the space, ruffling the now-damp pile of mail on the table by the door that had somehow remained untouched by the storm.

His first thought was *My dad's gonna kill me*, like Hurricane Flynn had been some kind of rager that he'd thrown here in this condo. His dad had told him not to trash the place, and it was well and truly trashed.

He must have spoken the words out loud, because next to him, Sophie's hand slid into his. "Hey." She gave his hand a squeeze. "It's gonna be okay."

Sophie. She was the absolute best part of this hurricane. She was the best part of everything, as far as he was concerned. He still couldn't believe that he'd woken up with her curled in his arms. They'd fallen asleep long after the hurricane had slowed to a light rain, reaching for each other in the dark over and over all night. They'd woken up this morning sometime between two and ten in the morning; hard to tell when the windows were boarded up and the power was out. Tristan had lost count of the number of times he'd reflexively hit an unresponsive light switch.

From behind them in the breezeway came the sound of heavy footsteps on the stairs. "Hey, Sophie!" Nick called when he hit the landing. Sophie jumped and dropped Tristan's hand as she turned around. "You make it through the storm okay?" He revved the screw gun in his hand like he was firing a six-shooter in the air. "Ready for me to take off those shutters—oh, shit." He looked over Tristan's shoulder at the carnage that was his living room. "That doesn't look good."

"No," Tristan said. "It doesn't." It wasn't even his place, but he still mourned that hardwood flooring. And that living room set; the couch looked like it had soaked up rainwater like a sponge. The glass-and-steel coffee table had been upended but otherwise looked undamaged. Palm fronds lay scattered across the living room like favors from an especially violent party.

Nick stepped past him into the condo, and now that it had been breached, Tristan was able to go inside too. Nick headed straight for the broken window, his work boots crunching on the broken glass on the floor. "So no hurricane shutters, huh?"

Tristan shook his head. "Apparently Dad wanted to save a buck when he bought the place."

"Well, that was smart." Nick peered out onto the balcony, then let his gaze sweep the carnage in the living room. "And hey, the good news is that it's not your place, right? Not your problem."

"Woooo." Tristan made a feeble raise-the-roof gesture, and Nick snorted.

"How about the rest of the place?" Sophie stepped into the condo, and Nick immediately darted toward her.

"What the hell are you doing? There's broken glass everywhere, and you're in those little flip-flops? Go put real shoes on." He scolded her like an older brother, and Sophie reacted in kind, screwing up her face in a scowl before retreating to her own place.

Tristan looked down at his own flip-flopped feet. Nick hadn't been concerned at all for him.

The rest of the condo seemed intact. It was just the living room that had been hit, but it had been hit hard. That huge window would need replacing, of course. And probably the floor. All the furniture.

Like Nick said, though. At least it wasn't his place.

"So, you rode out your first hurricane." Nick crossed his arms and leaned against the kitchen counter. "Congrats. Did you lose your shit when that happened?" He nodded toward the broken window, and Tristan blinked at it. When had it shattered? Had it been when he'd had his hand down Sophie's underwear in the living room? Or later that night, when he'd dug his second emergency condom from the depths of his wallet?

"Um. Not really. I was . . ." He glanced uncertainly toward the front door. This morning, he and Sophie had shared a pot of cold brew coffee she'd prepped in her French press the day before, but they hadn't talked about . . . well, they hadn't talked about *them*. Tristan didn't want to spill the beans if she didn't want him to. This was her town, and he was more than happy to follow her lead. But she wasn't here to lead. She was back in her place, putting real shoes on.

Nick nodded, thankfully not following Tristan's thoughts. "You were in the bathroom, right? That's what you do. A room with no windows, so you don't get a face full of glass."

Tristan nodded dumbly while his cheeks burned. He was an actor; lying was practically a hobby of his. But in front of this guy, who was basically Sophie's big brother? Who could probably kill him with that screw gun if he wanted?

"He was with me last night." Sophie's voice in the doorway was a sigh of relief in Tristan's brain. She stood just inside the front door, hands on her hips and sneakers on her feet, daring Nick to say something.

He didn't take the dare. Sure, his eyebrows crawled up his forehead as he looked from Tristan to Sophie and back again, but he held up his hands in a placating gesture. "Hey, I'm just here to take down some shutters."

"You need help?" Tristan remembered how Sophie had struggled the other day.

Nick considered Tristan for longer than it really should have taken to determine his worthiness to carry heavy things. Finally, he nodded. "Put some damn shoes on first." He clomped in his work boots out of Tristan's condo and into the breezeway.

Tristan put some damn shoes on.

Between the three of them, they made quick work of both the exterior shutters and the sheets of plywood that had boarded up Sophie's interior windows. Afterward, Nick accepted a partially cold bottle of water from the cooler in Sophie's kitchen.

"How's the rest of the town?" Sophie bit on her bottom lip absently, and Tristan wished Nick would go away so he could take over that task. Instead he concentrated on his own bottle of water. *A gallon per person per day*, he thought absently. It seemed like a lot, but with the power still out in this late-July humidity, he'd probably sweat that much out before noon.

"Not that bad." Nick shrugged. "Some flooding here and there. Branches down all over, you know. The usual. A tree hit Cassie's house but just knocked a couple shingles loose. I can fix those myself this weekend. I think so far the worst I've seen is at your place." He nodded over to Tristan, including him in the conversation.

"Anything else I can do to help? I mean, I put shoes on and everything." Taking down the shutters had been hard work, but now that they were down and put away, he felt adrenalized. Something about having been cooped up all night—not that he was complaining about how he'd spent that time—made him want to be out in the world.

Nick considered him for a long moment, glanced over at Sophie—who was all wide-eyed innocence—then nodded. "Come on down. Join the cleanup effort. I have the generator up and running at the café, and Ramon has food going for folks."

"Breakfast burritos?" Sophie lit up in a way that would make Tristan jealous if she weren't talking about food.

"That's his tradition."

"Can I bring anything?"

Nick shook his head. "We should be good on water and sodas, and we already brought down the beer for the hurricane party we didn't have. But if you have some extra cords, I could use them for the charging station."

Their conversation sounded like one they had regularly, as though hurricanes and long-term power outages were a regular occurrence. But this was a coastal town, so they probably were. Nick and Sophie somehow made it sound more like party planning than storm recovery.

"We'll be along." Sophie nodded firmly, and Tristan liked the way the word *we* sounded in her mouth. He also liked the way she said it so matter-of-factly, as though not only was it a given that they'd be downtown to help clean up, but that it would be the both of them. Together. Yeah, he really liked the sound of that.

On their walk downtown, Tristan got his own cleanup efforts started. The first step was to start a group text with his father and the condo's property manager, attaching pictures of the broken window and the other damage to the front half of the condo, and offering to be available to meet with whatever insurance representatives and contractors necessary. After that, the conversation was mostly between his dad and the property manager. Tristan checked in every so often, but they were still deep in talks about water remediation and what would or wouldn't be covered under the homeowner's insurance. None of his business.

He was good at texting and walking at the same time, but when they got to The Haunt, he glanced up and his steps slowed.

"Damn." He clicked his phone off and stuck it in his back pocket. He and Sophie surveyed Beachside Drive.

Sophie nodded. "It looks worse than it is." Which was good, honestly, because on the surface it looked awful. A thin layer of receding water covered the street, and there was debris everywhere: sand, branches, palm fronds, and Spanish moss everywhere you looked. A live oak in front of the Chamber of Commerce leaned on its side, its roots exposed from where they came out of the ground, the top of the tree resting on the roof of the building. A few shingles had been knocked off and were scattered on the lawn, but otherwise the roof looked intact. Sophie was right; the streets were a mess, but the actual damage seemed minimal.

"You know how the town was destroyed? The original one?" Sophie nodded out toward the water, where Cemetery Island was way off in the distance. "There have been lots of hurricanes since then, but nothing that's hit has ever kept Boneyard Key down for long."

She hugged his arm as they started walking again. "My personal theory is that this town is protected. Like, the Great Storm was bad enough that the people of Boneyard Key don't need to go through it again."

The Tristan of a few months ago would laugh at the notion. But now . . . well, it was as good a theory as any.

Downtown, Hallowed Grounds was bustling. While the front door was propped open, all the action seemed to be happening on the sidewalk out front. A propane-powered flattop griddle was going, manned by Ramon, and as they got closer, the smell of scrambled eggs and bacon made Tristan's stomach growl.

"Me too." Sophie grinned up at him, placing a hand on her stomach. "I kinda forgot about breakfast."

"Well, we were busy." Tristan's mind flashed back to exactly what they were busy doing, early in the morning in Sophie's rumpled bedsheets. The way his fingers had slid so easily inside her, the way her moans turned breathy as he touched her just the right way. The way she kissed him right after she came, lazy and ope and unabashedly satisfied. He loved the way he could put that look on her face.

But he should stop thinking about that right now, because putting that look on her face right there in the middle of slightly flooded Beachside Drive wasn't on the agenda. He took another swig of water and told his body to calm the hell down.

"Ramon's breakfast burritos are a hurricane tradition, you'll see." She tugged on his arm, and what could Tristan do but follow?

"Hey!" Ramon called out in greeting as they approached the griddle. "I've got food here if you're hungry—" He stirred a massive batch of hash browns with a spatula and nodded toward a huge plastic platter filled with aluminum-foil-wrapped packages. "The ones wrapped in red don't have bacon, in case you're vegetarian."

Sophie held up the tangle of cords she'd brought from her place, and Ramon lit up. "Ah, perfect! Charging station is right there."

The charging station was a large power bank sitting on one of the outdoor café tables, hooked up to a small generator that buzzed away on the sidewalk. There were five cords plugged in, each with a phone already connected.

Sophie checked her phone. "I'm good for a bit, but I brought my cord if anyone needs it." She plugged in her cord, and Tristan followed suit with his cord, but he connected his phone. The battery had drained some during the post-hurricane group text, and he had a feeling he was going to need a full charge until all of this was dealt with.

Next they hit up the food. Sophie grabbed a burrito for each of them while Tristan got them each a fresh bottle of water from the cooler next to the griddle.

"Shouldn't we get to work first?" Tristan looked around uncertainly. "I feel like I should earn this."

But Ramon waved off his concern. "Nah. Gotta fuel up. Eat first, then work. If you're into power tools, they need help chainsawing some tree limbs over on Palmetto. Some other people are starting to get organized at the Chamber of Commerce. Cassie's up at her place; they had some limbs down too."

Sophie nodded, but it was obvious she was only half listening. Her attention was focused on the package she was unwrapping. She practically tore the foil away in her haste to take a bite. Her eyes closed in bliss as she chewed.

"Ramon," she said, her mouth still mostly full, "I swear these are the best part of hurricane season. Why doesn't Nick let you serve these at the café?"

He barked out a laugh. "Because I don't want to get up that early every day, you kidding me? Let Nick do his little pastries in the morning. These are for special occasions."

It was a breakfast burrito, Tristan thought as he unwrapped his. Why was Sophie treating it like a religious experience?

Then he took a bite.

Tristan was familiar with the saying "hunger is the best sauce." He knew now that the saying should really be "twenty-four hours of hurricane snacks is the best sauce." The eggs were fluffy and hot, with just the right amount of cheese melted into them to play off the crisp saltiness of the bacon. The shredded potatoes were perfectly seasoned and added amazing texture. But this being the first home-cooked meal he'd had since even before the power went out made it taste even better.

Sophie caught his eye, and he could tell that she knew what he was thinking. "Amazing, right?"

Tristan nodded, too overcome to even speak. All he could do was bite, chew, swallow, repeat. The best breakfast of his life, here on the sidewalk of a town with no electricity, looking out on the debris-strewn streets.

Then it was time to get to work. This kind of thing was new to him—a day filled with manual labor, getting a small town back in order after a disaster. His family was more the "hire someone to do that" type. But he threw himself into it, agreeing to anything and everything needed of him. The Florida sun grew higher in the sky and hotter on his skin as he worked, taking down the plywood that had boarded up windows, dragging tree limbs to the edge of the street to be picked up by debris crews later, raking stray palm fronds and Spanish moss and shingles into contractor bags.

The more he worked, the more he realized he wanted to work. This didn't feel like charity or obligation. It felt like community.

As he took a water break, late in the afternoon, Nick clapped him on the shoulder.

"Come on," he said. "Cold spot time."

"What?" Tristan dragged his wrist across his forehead and adjusted his borrowed work gloves. He noticed Vince, the aging rocker from steel-drum karaoke night, nodding in confirmation behind Nick. "You've got power at the bar?" Because damn, a cold beer really sounded good right now. A cold anything, really.

"Nah, man." Vince shook his head. "Just as dark there as everywhere else. We're not talking about that. We're talking about the cold spot."

"But that's . . ." The conversation was getting circular fast, so Tristan gave up, following them up the street, past Cassie's house, then past the fishing pier. He glanced over his shoulder, feeling almost guilty. He'd lost track of Sophie while they'd been working, and he should have grabbed her if they were going for a drink.

But, marching up the street and flanked by two locals, this also felt like some kind of initiation. Maybe he wasn't allowed a plus-one.

Tristan hadn't made it to The Cold Spot yet, despite Vince's invitation back when Tristan had sung show tunes at The Haunt. But he knew it was this squat, gray building whose silhouette indicated it had been a service station in another lifetime. There was no sign out front, just a red neon sign—dark for now, of course—that said Open. It looked the opposite of inviting. Maybe it was an elaborate tax shelter? He could imagine more than one washed-up rocker retiring to Florida under those kinds of pretenses.

There was a trickle of people heading in their direction. All had relieved smiles on their faces, nodding toward Vince. "Thanks, man," one of them said.

"Hey, anytime! You don't have to thank me," Vince answered. "I'm just the caretaker."

Tristan's steps faltered as they rounded the back of the building. Up until now he'd been too tired to question anything and had just been following along blindly. But now, as they came upon an open field with a rusted-out car and a welded-shut service bay door, he realized that they could be luring him back there to kill him. Damn. Oh well, he'd had a good run.

Nick strode ahead of the other two, finally stopping at what seemed to be a random spot, and his expression changed immediately. His eyes closed in bliss, his head falling back on his neck as he took some good, deep breaths.

Tristan couldn't even begin to fathom what he was seeing.

After a few moments Vince called out. "Okay, that's enough! It's the new guy's turn."

Nick nodded, rolling his shoulders as he stepped away, back toward Tristan and Vince. Vince nudged Tristan forward. "Your turn."

"My turn for what?" He fell forward a couple steps before turning to the two men. They motioned him back and Tristan complied, taking two steps backwards and

. . . suddenly he was freezing cold.

It felt like the sun had gone out, the ambient temperature plummeting around him. The sweat on his skin evaporated instantaneously, and he shivered. It was like walking into an overly air-conditioned movie theatre from the noonday sun. It was blissful relief, and almost too much at the same time. Tristan heaved a huge sigh of relief before it hit him.

This shouldn't be real. It was an honest-to-God cold spot. As in, a haunted place.

He shivered again, but this time not from the cold. Whose grave were they walking over here?

"I don't get it," he said, once Vince had had his turn cooling off and they were heading back downtown. "Sophie doesn't mention it on her tour. People would lose their minds if you took them there."

"That's why we don't take them there," Vince said. "Tourists would only ruin it."

"We like to keep it a locals-only secret," Nick said.

Tristan's heart leapt. "I'm a local?"

"You busted your ass today," Nick said. "I'd say you earned it."

Tristan had never felt so validated in his life.

Thirty-Two

W ater?" Libby offered a bottle, freshly dripping from the cooler, to Sophie.

"Yes, please." Sophie plugged her phone in at the charging station at Hallowed Grounds now that there was a free cord. Then she sank down to sit on the curb. Before opening her water, she rolled it around on her forehead, then rested it on the back of her neck. It had been a long day after not a lot of sleep the night before, and every muscle in her body was threatening to go on strike. Contractor bags lined the sidewalk in front of the Chamber of Commerce, filled with palm fronds and Spanish moss and other debris from the storm. She'd walked several blocks with friends and neighbors, helping drag tree limbs to the curb, and moving smaller branches once they'd been cut down to size.

Libby sat down beside her, cracking open her own bottle. "I like him," she said before taking a swig.

"Finally!" Ramon crowed from nearby. He'd long since cleaned off the flattop griddle and was now assembling sandwiches from the ingredients in the fridge at the café. He grinned down at Libby. "I've been waiting for years to hear you say that."

Libby scoffed. "Eavesdropping is rude, you know."

"Not when you're talking about how awesome I am. In that case, it's acceptable."

"I was talking to Sophie," she said primly. "About Tristan."

Ramon huffed and stuck his knife back in the mayo jar. "Eh, he's okay."

Libby rolled her eyes good-naturedly at Sophie, who gave her an eye roll right back. "You've said that before," Sophie reminded her.

"Well, it's worth repeating." Libby's blond ponytail almost brushed the sidewalk behind her as she leaned her head back, drinking most of the bottle in one go.

Sophie sighed and sipped her own water. She was hot, she was sweaty, and all she wanted was a long shower and her bed. The shower would be ice-cold, of course, since the power wasn't back on yet. It was going to be another long, dark, candlelit night. But at least they had running water. And tonight she could sleep with the windows open, so it wouldn't be as stuffy in her place.

And of course, there was Tristan. His place had sustained damage; there was no way he could sleep there. No, he was gonna have to stay at her place again. Darn.

"I like him too." It was a confession, but it was time to say it.

Libby wrapped an arm around Sophie in a sideways hug. "Thought you might." Then she dropped her arm, because they were both sweaty and gross. "Where is he, anyway? I saw him earlier over at I Scream Ice Cream, taking the shutters down."

"I don't know." Sophie leaned forward to look up and down the street. She'd lost track of him. "He'll turn up soon."

"He's with Nick." Ramon was still eavesdropping, but it wasn't like their conversation was that private anyway. "I think Nick and Vince took him to the cold spot to cool off."

"Really?" Libby gave a low whistle and raised her eyebrows at

Sophie. "I guess he's really one of us now. A full-fledged resident of Boneyard Key."

"I guess so." Sophie wasn't sure how to react. It was great that Tristan was accepted by the people she loved and was fitting in seamlessly. But just yesterday, he'd said he was calling off their little contest. If he'd ceded the contest to her, didn't that mean he'd be shutting his ghost tour down? Wouldn't he be leaving, sooner rather than later? She probably shouldn't get attached. And neither should Libby.

But then she saw him, coming down Beachside, chatting and laughing with Nick and Vince. Seeing him made her feel like everything in her life made sense. Like for the first time, her heart was sitting in her chest the way that it should.

His whole attitude lit up when he saw her. "Sophie!" He practically bounded over to where she sat on the curb, beaming down at her. "I was just at the cold spot. Like, the *real* cold spot! Have you been there? Of course you've been there. I mean, you've been there, right?"

"I've been there." She didn't want to sound amused but she couldn't help it. She'd seen him, that night at Poltergeist Pizza when the Parmesan cheese had appeared out of nowhere. And the night when he'd communicated with Sarah Hawkins via Cassie's refrigerator. This was no longer someone who was struggling to understand that ghosts existed and were a normal part of life around here. He was all the way there, understanding and accepting. Even excited about it. It was everything she could have hoped for.

Maybe she didn't need to think about him leaving town. Not yet.

"Anything else need doing today?" Tristan glanced around, but crowds were thinning as people began to make their way home in the waning sunlight.

"You can help by taking some of these sandwiches home," Ramon said. He wrapped up the bread and other nonperishables. The meat and cheese were already in the cooler; there was enough ice for everything to last another day or so.

"You made too many," Libby said as she got to her feet. "As usual." She brushed off the back of her denim cutoffs before stacking four of the wrapped sandwiches together. "Okay if I take some home to Nan?"

Ramon waved a hand. "That's what they're there for."

"Come on." Sophie reached up a hand and let Tristan haul her to her feet. "Let's get some food and then get home."

"Home," Tristan repeated. "I like the sound of that."

Sophie did too. More than she should.

Back at her place, Sophie hit the light switch in the bathroom and then swallowed a curse. Of course. No lights yet.

"I've done that so many times." Tristan appeared in the doorway with one of the LED lanterns from the kitchen. She set it in the corner of the bathroom counter. The light reflected off the mirror, sending a glow through the darkened room.

"I'd love to tell you that you get used to it, but I'd be lying. I think some of the guys even made a drinking game out of it last hurricane." She reached into the medicine cabinet for the ibuprofen bottle, shaking it in his direction. "Need some?"

Tristan's moan hit her right in the solar plexus. Well, maybe a little below it. "God, yes please. I'm going to be feeling this in the morning." His hand wrapped around hers, still holding on to the bottle. "You know what else I'd like to be feeling in the morning . . . ?"

"Your pickup lines are terrible." Sophie took the bottle back, shaking a couple tablets into her palm and passing them to him.

"I know. I'm exhausted. I promise I'll come up with something better after a shower." He swallowed the tablets dry—how were people able to do that? "You wanna help me brainstorm?"

"In the *shower*?" It was hard to sound scandalized through a giggle as he reached for her. "No, don't!" she protested as he stole a kiss. "I'm all sweaty and gross."

"So am I." He reached for the hem of her tank top, and she didn't protest as he pulled it up and over her head. "That's what the shower is for."

"It's going to be cold." She pulled off his T-shirt and ran a hand down his chest, lingering as she went.

"Hey, I was a horny teenager once. I took plenty of cold showers." He unbuttoned his shorts and bent past her to turn on the water. Sophie shucked her shorts, stepping back from the shower as the water came shooting out. Tristan didn't dodge in time, and he let out a yell that was mostly a gasp. "Shit. Okay, yeah. That's cold."

"Told you." But they helped each other finish undressing, letting the water run as though it was going to warm up without a working water heater.

The shower was freezing. Cold water hit warm skin, refreshing for a split second before turning punishing. They took turns hugging the shower wall, soaping and rinsing quickly while their bodies tried to adjust. Finally Tristan turned, guiding Sophie until her back was pressed against the wall, his body shielding hers from the cold water that beat against his back.

"You're gonna die of hypothermia." Sophie's protest was weak as his slick hands smoothed their way down her body.

"What a way to go." His mouth moved against her, hot against her increasingly cold skin, gliding down her body as though chasing the water that swirled down the drain. She pressed her back hard against the wall, fighting for the strength to remain upright when he sank to his knees, parting her thighs.

The water was cold. His shoulders, clutched under her hands, were cold. But Tristan's mouth remained hot, licking inside, exploring, savoring, as though he had all the time in the world. He didn't stop until she shuddered against him, her cries swallowed by the rush of water hitting cold tile. Once she could breathe again, she leaned forward over Tristan's body to turn off the shower.

"Oh, thank God." Tristan grinned up at her, but his teeth chattered just a little. "I really did think I might die there."

"Come on." Sophie reached for one of her fluffy pink towels, wrapping it around him and pulling him from the shower. "Won't take long to get warmed up." She had plans for that.

The power was still out the next morning. Another forced vacation day for Sophie, but there was still plenty to do. When Tristan's phone wasn't blowing up with texts from the condo's property manager, it was ringing with calls from water remediation specialists and insurance adjusters. Between phone calls, he and Sophie did what they could with his condo, sweeping up the broken glass and gathering damp towels to be washed once the power was back. After a while, Sophie began to notice a little crease appearing between Tristan's eyebrows every time he was on the phone, growing deeper and deeper with every call.

"This really shouldn't be my problem," he said later that afternoon. The two of them were back downtown outside of Hallowed Grounds, his long-suffering phone plugged into Nick's charging station.

Sophie nodded in agreement. "Seems like you're just the middleman."

"Should have known that free rent wouldn't be free." Sophie knew Tristan well enough by now to recognize a false smile. He checked his phone before leaning back again, an arm around

Sophie. Then he squinted off into the distance. "Is that smoke over there? Something on fire?"

"Where?" Sophie followed his gaze to the plume of smoke stretching up toward the sky. Her heart leapt, but in a good way. She knew what that smoke meant. "Oooh, come on." She was on her feet faster than her aching muscles would have liked. "Terry's got the wood-fired oven going over at the pizza place."

"Is that safe?" But he let her tug him to his feet, following her lead.

She nodded. "Come on," she said again. "You don't want to miss this." She could already taste the smoky char of the crust, its crispness shattering under her teeth. Like Ramon's breakfast burritos, this was a specific post-hurricane delicacy.

They were halfway through a sausage-and-pepperoni with extra sauce, sitting at one of the picnic tables by the beach, when the power came back. Behind them, the streetlight winked on, startling them with the sudden brightness. They instinctively cheered, while behind them came the sounds of everyone in town doing the same. It was a communal moment—a town-wide sigh of relief that the hurricane was truly over, and things could get back to normal.

But everything now was a new normal, one that Sophie preferred. Tristan's condo was a mess. The huge fans left by the water remediation people sounded like jet engines in the living room. Contractors would be coming in soon to rip out the living room floor. So the best part of this new normal was that Tristan came to stay with Sophie.

Waking up with Tristan quickly became the easiest, most natural part of her life. He was always up before her alarm went off. By the time she'd hit the snooze twice and yawned her way out into the kitchen, he was back from his run, showered and dressed, sipping on a second cup of coffee and checking his emails on his phone.

There was even a cup of coffee for her, still steaming on the counter, with just the right amount of cream and sugar.

Weeks went by this way. Most of his things remained next door, but bit by bit Tristan brought the necessities to her place in a backpack. They got ready for their respective ghost tours side by side now. It took Tristan forever to get into that getup, but Sophie had to admit the end result was worth it. There was something about a man in a suit, now that she let herself admit it.

Yeah, Sophie could really get used to this.

But should she?

They very carefully didn't talk about the future. Even when life settled down to a routine of day jobs and contractors and ghost tours on the weekend, there was no real good time to bring it up. *So, you know during the hurricane when you said you were conceding the contest? What does that mean, exactly? Are you leaving town soon, or . . . ?*

Sophie wasn't sure she wanted to know. The answer was likely to put an end date on all of this. And she wasn't ready to let anything go. Not yet.

Thirty-Three

Tristan had never been so happy in his life. He had also never been so sad.

The happy—that was almost all Sophie. She liked to sleep nestled in the hollow of his shoulder, and there had never been a better way to wake up.

Then there was the sad. October first was bearing down now. It had been circled on his mental calendar for so long that he couldn't believe the date was actually almost here.

"Labor Day weekend was great," Eric said on a Monday morning call. "In the black all the way across the board."

"But . . . ?" Tristan glanced over his shoulder at Sophie. She was in front of her laptop in her dining nook, headphones on, obviously in the zone. He slipped out the front door, easing it closed behind him. Once he was out in the breezeway, he relaxed. "Your voice says there should be a 'but' coming up."

"Yeah." Eric's sigh was a whoosh of breath over the phone. "We both know it won't be enough. We're turning a profit, which is great for any new business after just five years. But enough to pay back your dad?"

"The payment will ruin us." Tristan didn't need to be reminded.

"We still have the month of September. Let's table this for now and revisit at the end of the month, okay?" The news made him feel oddly lighter. Sure, his business was about to fail. But there was something in the knowing. The finality of it. He could stop worrying about the what-ifs.

"If it helps," Eric said, "your contest with Sophie really didn't have much to do with it."

"What do you mean?" Tristan turned, looking over his shoulder at Sophie's front door, as though she could hear them.

"I've been keeping an eye on the shared spreadsheet, of course. You're ahead, but you're both doing really well. In fact, you're mirroring each other. When your numbers are up, so are hers. When yours are down . . ."

"So I was never taking business away from her?" He was more relieved than he expected to be by that.

"Nope. She wasn't taking it away from you, either. Turns out, that little town really is big enough for two ghost tours. And who knows? Maybe she'll pick up the slack after you're gone."

After he was gone. That was the part he didn't want to think about. Besides, he still had a few weeks left in Boneyard Key. A few weeks left with Sophie. He was going to make the best of them.

Labor Day weekend had been a last hurrah when it came to tourist season, but the weekend after was still busy. Tristan had sold out both nights, and Sophie had too.

"It's September," he said on Friday night when she met him outside of Hallowed Grounds after their tours were over. "Shouldn't it be cooling off soon?" He'd shucked his coat while waiting for her, his cravat already off and stuck in a pocket.

Sophie just laughed. "Oh, honey, no. In Florida we get a couple weeks of fall, usually sometime in December. If we're lucky."

"Ugh." He plopped his top hat on her head. It was far too big for her, sliding down her forehead.

"Ugh," she echoed. "This is all sweaty." But she steadied the hat on her head and grinned up at him as they set off down the street.

Picking up a pizza after ghost tour nights was becoming a tradition with them. Tonight, they weren't the only ones at Poltergeist Pizza. Jo was there, leaning against the counter, talking to a young woman with purply maroon streaks in her dark brown hair. The maroon-haired woman's eyes lit up when she saw Tristan, as though he was an old friend.

"I'm so glad I ran into you." She leaned toward him, grasping his forearm. "I never got a chance to say thanks."

Tristan's mind went blank. "Thanks . . . ?"

"For clearing all those dead limbs off our property. After the hurricane. I have to say, I thought you were an annoying city boy when you first showed up in town, but I'm so glad I was wrong. Actually . . ." She pointed at him. "Hold that thought." And she was out the door, running off into the night.

"Who was that?" Tristan looked from Jo to Sophie. "What just happened?"

"Aura just happened." Jo's lips quirked up. "Don't worry, she's like that. She lives around the corner. I bet she'll be right back."

"Around the . . ." There was nothing around the corner. Unless she meant Spooky Brew or Mystic Crystals. *Oh.* Things started clicking together in his brain. There was a huge oak tree in front of Mystic Crystals that had lost a lot of limbs when Flynn came through. He'd pitched in with several other people to cut the limbs down to manageable sizes before piling them by the curb. He'd only glanced at that upstairs window two, maybe three times. It had been suspiciously glow-less when the town was out of power. But come to think of it, he hadn't spotted it since the hurricane. Maybe that ghost had moved on. Something to do with the hurricane? Tristan still wasn't clear on how all this ghost stuff worked.

She was back soon enough, and she was carrying . . . an arm?

"Here." She thrust the skeleton arm toward him, and Tristan shrank back in alarm. What the hell?

"It's a peace offering," Aura explained, and that did nothing to clear things up. "You're okay around here now. I feel bad for all the times I messed with you."

"Messed with . . ." More things clicked together in his brain. "That was *you*? In the window?"

She nodded enthusiastically. "That was me! Under a bedsheet."

"With the creepy green glow?"

"A light bulb. Left over from last Christmas."

"And the skeletal . . ." He looked again at the arm that Aura was brandishing in his direction. "Oh my god, this is plastic, isn't it?" In his defense, it looked incredibly realistic.

"I'll be the judge of that." Jo took the arm away from Aura, her hands encircling both the radius and ulna. Her eyes dropped closed for a few moments, then she snorted. "Oh, man, Tristan. You should see your face. She scared the crap out of you!" She offered the arm to Tristan, shoulder joint first. "But yeah. It's plastic."

As peace offerings went, it was . . . well, it was something. "Thanks," he said as he turned the plastic prop around in his hands. "I've always wanted an . . . arm."

The girls around him, Sophie included, burst into laughter, and he had to grin. God, he loved this town.

Sophie carried the pizza home, still wearing Tristan's hat, and he carried his lantern and his brand-new skeleton arm. He should talk to Sophie. He knew that. About October first. What he was about to lose, and what he would probably have to do.

But there just wasn't time. Not on their walk home, while he waved his plastic skeleton arm around like it was a sword. Not while they demolished their pizza, sitting cross-legged on the floor in front of her coffee table. Not when he slid between her bedsheets, with Sophie warm and waiting for him.

He still had a few weeks. It wasn't time to worry about the future yet.

Thirty-Four

On a Wednesday in late September, the last contractor left Tristan's condo for the last time. While Tristan took care of the final walk-through, making sure everything was done, Sophie closed her laptop for the day and made a stir fry for dinner. It was a weeknight, so no tours on the agenda for either of them. And finally, there were no contractors or insurance adjusters or property managers for Tristan to wrangle. It was just the two of them, plates of homemade beef and broccoli, and some stupid competition show involving food trucks.

Midway through the food truck judging, Tristan's phone buzzed on the coffee table. He groaned as he reached for it. "I really thought I was done for the day." Sophie muted the television as he checked the screen, then groaned again.

"It's my dad. I should take this." He levered to his feet. "Sorry." He bent to kiss her, his eyes pinched. Sophie didn't know much about Tristan's father, but she hated that he always put that look on Tristan's face.

"No worries."

But there were definitely worries. Sophie had learned by now that, when it came to a conversation with Tristan's father, it was

Oops, All Worries! She tried not to listen as Tristan breezed through an update on the condo.

"They finished the paint today, and they said it should take a day or two to be completely dry. Retractable hurricane shutters went in last week, and apparently that gets you a credit on the homeowner's insurance on the place, did you know that? The property manager should have all that info; she said she'll email it to you." Tristan paced the length of the living room, the crease between his eyebrows deepening the way it always did when he talked to his dad.

"Tours are going great. We had a little downturn there when the storm came through, obviously, so . . . well, yeah, Dad, tourists weren't exactly turning up in droves when the town didn't have power and was covered in hurricane debris. The second half of July was basically a wash, and of course August is pretty dead anyway, so . . . I dunno, Dad, factoring in a hurricane wasn't exactly on the spreadsheet." His lips pressed together hard as he listened, and more than once he cut his eyes in her direction. The pain in his expression made Sophie squirm on the sofa, and not in a good way.

"Well, there's still a couple weeks till October first. No, September isn't all that busy here, but we got a good foothold in Portland over the summer. That momentum might be enough to make it up . . ." His words broke off and he stopped pacing, looking like a puppet whose strings had been cut. "Yeah." It was a single word, but it seemed to sum up the entire conversation. Defeated.

While Tristan listened to his father on the other end—a deep, commanding voice that Sophie could hear through the phone but not understand—she was hung up on the date he'd just mentioned. October first. The end of their bet, which technically had been nullified back in July, but they'd been keeping their shared spreadsheet out of habit. Their antagonistic bet had become friendly competition.

But October first meant something else now. It hadn't been a date he'd pulled out of the air. He wasn't just a random dickhead businessman, come to town to put her out of business. He'd had something at stake here too. Something to prove to his father. Whatever it was, it had to be done by October first. And he'd been using their bet to do it. Alarm stirred in the back of Sophie's mind.

Tristan cleared his throat, and Sophie raised her eyebrows, waiting for whatever response Tristan was about to give. But he wasn't looking in her direction. His normal confidence was gone, and now he looked deflated. Like he no longer had anything to prove. "Yeah," he said again. He took the phone away from his ear and tossed it to the kitchen counter. "Fuck," he said softly.

She had to say something. "Is this about October first? The bet? The tours?"

"Not the bet." His voice was hoarse, his eyes still fixed on her Formica countertop.

"Because if it was still going on, you'd win. Not by much," she hastened to add, her old sense of competition taking over, "but you're ahead on the spreadsheet."

"That doesn't matter." He shook his head, still looking at nothing. "The bet was never about beating you. Not to me. It was about beating him. It's always been about beating him. So yeah, even if I win, I lose." His expression tightened as he seemed to digest his own words. "I'm going to lose everything."

Sophie tsked. "That's a little dramatic."

Tristan's laugh was a harsh bark, falling between them and echoing in the quiet room. "It's not. That's what this phone call was about. Come October first, he gets to look at the books for Ghouls Night Out. He's not going to like what he sees, and then he'll be pulling his seed money, the money he put in so I could get this business going. Without that money? It's over." He reached for his phone, flipping it over and over in his hands.

"It's all over?" Sophie didn't understand. "You mean Ghouls Night Out? Your whole business? In all the cities?"

He nodded glumly. "I'm over." He let his phone clatter to the kitchen counter.

Okay, that was bad. "What happens now?" She joined him at the counter, reaching for his hand.

He didn't take it. Tristan nudged his phone with a forefinger, idly watching it spin. "I'm sure Dad's got something great lined up for me." Bitterness dripped from every word. "I'll be back in New York, suit-and-tied, one of his underlings, like he's always wanted."

Back in New York. Sophie froze at those words, Tristan's voice fading over the roaring in her ears. "You're leaving?" Her words were a whisper.

"That was the agreement." His voice was a death knell. "I had five years to do my own thing, and when I failed—because he always knew I'd fail . . ." His mouth twisted in a grimace. ". . . I go work for him. Live out the future he's always planned for me."

He was leaving. Sophie shouldn't be surprised. *Of course* he was leaving. What had she expected?

"Well, maybe it won't be so bad," she said, even though it sounded like a million different kinds of bad. "Maybe—"

"Are you kidding me? It's going to be terrible." He broke off with an inarticulate sound, and Sophie's heart broke for him. He was just as upset to leave her as she was for him to leave. "Five years I've been doing this." His forefinger stabbed at the kitchen counter. "I put everything I had into this business, and now he's going to destroy it all."

Oh.

No. He wasn't upset about leaving Sophie. It was all about business to Tristan. Maybe he was more like his father than he realized. Sophie's broken heart hardened.

"Huh." Sophie crossed her arms, her eyebrows crawling up her forehead. "That sounds familiar. I know a little bit about someone trying to destroy something I've built for the past few years. In fact, he's right here in this room."

Tristan blew out a sigh, dismissing her words. "That's not the same thing. I didn't know you then."

"Oh, so when I was a stranger it was okay to destroy me?" Tristan's mouth fell open, and when he didn't have an immediate response, she kept going. A tear hit her cheek, angry and hot. "If we'd gone through with this bet, and you'd won? I'd have had to shut down my own business, that I built myself, in my own hometown." Sophie felt her voice getting louder, and she wasn't the type to have a screaming match in her own home, but screw it. "I don't have a daddy to offer me a fallback plan, you know. You were going to leave me with nothing."

"I wasn't . . ." But the look in his eyes said that she was right, and he didn't have a good argument. He visibly deflated. "Five years," he said again. "I worked so hard, and it'll all just be gone. I've lost everything."

Everything in this case being his business. Of course. It didn't seem to occur to him that when he went back to New York, he was losing Sophie too. It was probably for the best that they'd never made plans for the future. He obviously didn't consider her a real part of his.

"You haven't lost everything." Her voice sounded cold to her own ears, but she couldn't do it anymore. Any of this. Not with him. "You get to go back to your fancy New York apartment and live your fancy New York life. Your dad isn't leaving you high and dry with no options." She took a deep breath and did the hardest thing she'd ever had to do.

She broke her own heart.

"I think you should go."

Tristan blinked, as though seeing her for the first time since his phone had rung. "Sophie."

She shook her head hard, backed away. "Please. You're leaving soon anyway." She couldn't gesture toward the door because her arms were wrapped around her middle, holding herself together. She nodded in that direction instead. "You may as well just go now."

"No." So many emotions fluttered across his face. Surprise. Regret. "Sophie, we can . . ."

"Please," she said again.

Tristan's eyes looked shattered, but he didn't speak. Instead he calmly picked up his phone and stuck it in his pocket. He slid his feet into his flip-flops next to Sophie's umbrella stand. Her front door closed quietly behind him as he left.

Sophie got the remote and turned off the television. She no longer cared about food trucks.

She knew she shouldn't have let herself get used to Tristan. He wasn't going to stay.

No one ever stayed.

Thirty-Five

It was a fight.

It was just a stupid fight.

Tristan regretted walking out of Sophie's place the moment the door closed behind him. But he was still pissed off—talking to his dad always had that effect. And now he'd managed to piss off Sophie in the process. Taking the night to cool down was probably the best course of action.

His father's condo reeked of paint, and even though he slept with the windows open, he woke up with a headache. But he also awoke with new resolve. He would talk to Sophie. Apologize. They could make amends. They could . . .

He opened his front door to find his green backpack on the welcome mat. The one he used to bring things to and from Sophie's place. He picked it up with a sinking feeling and retreated to the kitchen. While the coffee brewed, he unzipped the backpack, almost certain what he would find. Yep. Toothbrush, the one that had lived on Sophie's sink for the past few weeks. Comb, razor, aftershave. All his toiletries on top of a handful of wadded-up T-shirts and shorts and, inexplicably, one lone sock. She'd done a sweep of her place and returned what was his.

Maybe it had been more than a stupid fight.

He needed fresh air. This place still smelled like paint, and he needed to think. After a shower he headed outside, lingering for a minute by Sophie's door. He raised a hand to knock, but slowly lowered it again. She'd sent a clear message with the backpack. She was done with him. He was on his own.

There was a smattering of tourists downtown, but Tristan avoided the usual places. The last thing he wanted was to confront Nick at Hallowed Grounds. News traveled fast in this town, so it was likely Tristan was persona non grata all over again.

The ice cream and coffee carts were open at the vacant lot near The Haunt, and as far as he knew, those guys didn't hate him yet. Ice cream was basically milk, and the cone was basically bread. That counted as breakfast.

He studied the coffee cart menu while he paid for his chocolate chocolate chip in a waffle cone. (Waffles were breakfast food; he was killing it here.) "You sell a lot of hot coffee? In this heat?"

The coffee cart guy laughed. He was older, maybe a little older than Tristan's dad, the white cast of his sunscreen doing little to hide the pink in his cheeks. "Oh, you'd be surprised." He lowered his voice as though imparting a secret. "Tourists, you know. Never can predict what they're gonna do."

"True." Tristan nodded gravely while raising his eyebrows—*tourists, amirite?*—and the two men laughed back. He felt like an insider, like a local. He loved that feeling. He hated that it was about to end.

He'd intended to take a walk downtown, but everywhere downtown reminded him of Sophie. Even the picnic area by the beach, where he found himself with his rapidly melting breakfast. He sat on one of the tables, his feet on the bench seat, finishing his ice cream while the waves slid in and out over the shoreline in a meditative rhythm. He'd always liked this spot, but had never figured out a way to feature it on the tour.

Sophie had. Like it was yesterday, he remembered the night they'd met, when he'd lurked in the dark, spying on her tour, absolutely dismayed that he'd met a cute girl and learned that she was his business rival, all in one night.

If you're out here at night—especially after a night out at The Haunt and you've had a drink or two—chances are you'll have company. Footsteps in the sand... Some people like to leave him a beer, opened on one of the picnic tables. That's how you win him over...

It was a simple story, all the more impactful for its lack of embellishment. Like the way she told all the stories on her tour. He could learn from her.

Then he remembered: he didn't need to. He had one foot out of the ghost tour business. Almost over now.

He hopped down from the picnic table, tossing his sticky napkin into the trash. How had everything become such a mess?

When he got back to the condo, he stopped short in the breezeway. Sophie was coming out of her place, locking her door. She turned and froze when she saw him.

"Hi." Hope surged through him as he took a step in her direction.

But hope died a little as she took a step away, her back practically pressed to her door. "Hi." She barely tossed the word between them, her lips pressed together, her expression pinched.

Tristan powered through. "Listen, I think we need to talk. I'm so sorry about—"

"No," she said quickly. "It's okay. We don't need to talk."

"We don't?" He didn't understand. Because of course they needed to talk. He was good at talking. He'd smoothed over worse fights in his life. If they could just—

But she shook her head, her face stony. "We don't," she repeated, and her tone would brook no argument. "You're leaving soon. You were always leaving soon. And your future doesn't involve me. You made that perfectly clear last night. Maybe we should just leave it at that."

All Tristan could do was stand there, poleaxed, as Sophie walked by him, down the breezeway, and down the stairs. They were done? Just like that? He didn't know what to say. And even if he did, he didn't have anyone to say it to. For all the inroads he'd made here over the last few months, it was clear that Boneyard Key was Sophie's town. His friends were her friends first. He was alone here.

Which was why he brought two beers with him to the picnic area that night.

He felt a little silly, opening both of them when he was only intending to drink one. He felt even sillier leaving one on the edge of the picnic table. He held his breath as he did so, but nothing happened. The longer he waited, the more nothing happened, until he blew out a sigh and took a swig from his own beer.

"I don't know what I expected." A flash of light? A ghostly hand to take the bottle? He shook his head and took another sip.

"I don't know what I'm doing." He was talking out loud to no one, but as he cast a glance at the bottle on the edge of the table, he thought maybe someone was listening. "I've been fighting for this business, fighting against my dad for so long, and I don't even know why. I'm not a businessman."

Still nothing. The waves continued to whisper their way to the shore; the streetlight above him blazed merrily, keeping the darkness at bay. The beer bottle hadn't moved from its place on the edge of the table.

This was stupid. Just sitting here, talking to nobody. He needed to move. He hopped off the picnic table and started walking parallel to the ocean, keeping well away from the water as it crept onshore, sipping at his beer.

"Eric's the businessman," he mused aloud. "He's the spreadsheet guy, the wizard behind the scenes who knows how to advertise, how to make the budget work. I've been drafting off him since college, and I've picked up some stuff. But it's in his blood, the way performing is in mine. That's why we've been such a good team all these years.

"I thought I had a good thing going, these tours. Even if the stories are a little silly, tourists love them. But Sophie's . . . Sophie's are better. Because they're not stories. She loves this town so much. And I love . . ."

He couldn't finish the sentence. He wanted to. It was written, there on his heart. *I love Sophie.* But what good would saying that out loud do? He'd already lost her.

Tristan drowned his emotion with another swig of beer. "Maybe that's it. She tells her stories, she runs her business, with love. Me, it's all about spite." Another sigh gusted out of him, joining the breeze sighing through the nearby palm trees.

That was when he heard it. Footsteps. Someone was following him.

Tristan glanced over his shoulder, but it was a dark night. The moon was a thin crescent in the sky, and even the sparkles off the water didn't give off much light. He couldn't see anyone behind him, but he could hear those footsteps, walking when he walked, stopping when he stopped.

Slowly, he looked at the almost-empty bottle in his hand. Awareness prickled the back of his neck, and there was that familiar swimmy feeling in his head, the one he'd gotten the night he'd been served by a poltergeist, and the night he'd apologized to Sarah Hawkins via a refrigerator.

The Beach Bum.

He'd shown up to take a walk with Tristan on the beach.

Well, that was what he'd wanted, wasn't it? He forced himself to keep walking. Keep talking.

"Spite," he repeated. "All this time, I've been doing this to spite my dad. But I can't build an entire career—hell, an entire life—on spite.

"What do I want?" He looked to his left as though the Beach Bum had spoken. "Good question. I mean, there's no denying that the tours are fun. My favorite part is putting on that costume and pretending to be someone different for a little while. Making people laugh, taking them on a little journey."

He chuckled. "I guess the hat was right. I do miss singing. Performing. I knew the minute I stepped out onstage for the first time that I was doing what I loved. Those lights hit you, and they're so bright. They burn your eyes. You can barely see the people in the audience, but you can hear them. When they laugh, when they applaud . . . there's nothing in the world like it."

Tristan had never walked this far up the beach. He'd passed Cassie's house a few minutes ago, and now he was coming up on the curve in the coastline that led to the fishing pier. Ahead he could barely make out the ragged stilts of the Starter Home, jutting out into the water. More of it had fallen away since the hurricane. He didn't want to think about it being gone.

"So that's what I want, I guess," he said. "Perform. Entertain. Make people smile." But that wasn't quite right. Right now, all he wanted was to make Sophie smile. He'd been good at that for a little while. He rubbed absently at the center of his chest. Was heartache a literal thing? Because right now, his heart ached for her, and all he could see in his mind's eye was her stony, pinched expression from earlier today. She had no more smiles for him.

"Anyway," he said to the Beach Bum. "I should probably head back. Thanks for the talk. You're a great listener."

The footsteps didn't follow him as he turned to head back to the picnic area. Tristan glanced over his shoulder, at the remains of the Starter Home. He had the unsettling feeling that he'd just walked the Beach Bum home.

He took his time heading back down the beach. All that waited for him was a stark white, vaguely paint-scented condo. Maybe he should stop at The Haunt first. Oysters and beer and steel-drum karaoke might help clear his head. As long as the coast was clear and Tony was still speaking to him.

As he got back to the picnic area, he picked up the beer bottle he'd set out earlier; littering was something that assholes did.

The bottle was empty.

Thirty-Six

Everything was going Sophie's way. Technically. Her ghost tour was safe, and she could keep doing what she loved. If she'd been able to go back in time and tell Sophie in March that Tristan had conceded and would soon be leaving town, Past Sophie would be thrilled. Past Sophie would throw a party and toss streamers off her second-floor balcony to accompany Tristan Martin getting the heck out of Boneyard Key.

But this was Present Sophie, and Present Sophie was miserable.

Cutting him out of her life had been the right thing to do. One of them had to be the adult; one of them had to recognize that what they had between them wasn't going to last, no matter how good it was.

But for a few weeks there it had been so good. So, so good.

It would be easier if she could hate him. If he'd been a liar from the jump, if he'd been as filled with corporate greed as he'd appeared the day he'd waltzed into Hallowed Grounds after their viral video and proposed that bet. But Tristan wasn't an evil mastermind, out to crush her under his heel. He was a kind, funny, sensitive soul, and watching him open up to Boneyard Key, and all its facets, had been the best part of her summer.

But summer was over. And this Thursday night in late September was already the worst part of her fall.

There was a pounding on her door, but she ignored it. She knew who it was. It was *Romance Resort* night, and she was here on her couch instead of at Cassie's house. She was letting everyone down. But she wanted to be alone. She was wallowing.

"Sophie!" Another series of loud knocks accompanied the shout. Libby.

"Sophie, you better be dead in there!" Cassie this time. "You better be dead on your kitchen floor and not just sitting there on the couch, feeling sorry for yourself and ignoring our texts!"

Sophie gave a guilty start from her spot on the couch, bundled up in one of Aunt Alice's quilts. It took a few good sniffs to clear away her tears before she hauled herself to her feet. Trailing the quilt after her like a patchwork cloak, she went to the front door and threw the bolt open before heading back to the couch.

The door burst open.

"Oh, good. You're alive." Libby threw her a sympathetic look before heading straight into the kitchen. "Look, I get you're going through it, but you need to answer your texts once in a while."

"Oh." Sophie raised her head from her flopped position, looking for her phone. It was face down on the coffee table, and when she picked it up, she gave a wince despite everything. The notification screen was covered; the photo she'd taken of the Starter Home at sunset a few years back was all but obscured. "Sorry." She ran her thumb over the screen, idly scrolling through the texts from Cassie and Libby—texts that grew more and more alarmed as Sophie wasn't answering. "Sorry," she said again.

Libby made a small, comforting sound, but Cassie wasn't as kind. "You better be." She closed the front door behind her and leaned against it. "I had to explain to Sarah that we couldn't watch

Romance Resort without you, so we'd have to put it off till next week. One of these days she's going to find out that it aired every night for two months, instead of me parceling it out to her once a week. And I'm going to be in huge trouble."

"I'm on Sarah's side here. Avoiding spoilers has been hell." Libby rummaged through Sophie's pantry, emerging with three boxes of macaroni and cheese and Sophie's largest pot. "Do you have milk?"

"I think so." Had Sophie even opened her fridge recently? She couldn't remember.

Libby busied herself in the kitchen while Cassie sat down next to Sophie. "Come on. Talk to us. What did he do? Do I need to sic Nick on his ass?"

That brought a watery smile. "No. He didn't do anything. He . . ." Wouldn't it be so much easier if he had? If he'd been a first-class jerk, and she could wash her hands of him? Say things to her friends like *Thank God that guy's gone.*

But she couldn't. So she just gave a weary shrug. "He's leaving." She barely got the words out when a fresh set of tears came. It felt like she'd always been crying. "And I knew he was leaving, but . . ." She didn't want to say it. She didn't want to sound like a whining child in front of her friends. But these were her *best* friends. If you couldn't be a whining child to them, who could you whine to?

"Everyone leaves." The words burst out of her before she could call them back. And once they were out, they just kept spilling out. "My mom. My dad. Aunt Alice. Now Tristan. Why can't anyone just *stay?*" The last word was a wail; Sophie tore her glasses off and tossed them to the coffee table, then buried her face in her hands for a good, hard cry.

No one spoke for a long moment, and in the back of her mind Sophie figured that Cassie was looking for a way to get the heck out of there. Libby had known her longer; Libby knew her baggage. But not Cassie. Cassie hadn't signed up for this.

But to her surprise, Cassie slid an arm around her. "Okay." She scooted over on the couch, pulling Sophie with her, until Sophie was lying with her head in Cassie's lap, still in her crazy quilt cocoon. "Okay," she said again, stroking Sophie's hair off her temples.

"I just . . . I feel like I'm losing everything." The tears kept coming, sobs wracking her body.

"You're not." Cassie's voice was soothing.

"Of course you're not," Libby chimed in from the kitchen. "You have us."

"And Nick," Cassie added. "He's told me more than once you're the little sister he wished he had instead of Courtney."

"There's nothing wrong with Courtney," Sophie said, defending her childhood friend through her tears.

"No, there isn't. I just think he likes you better. You get him. You love this town the way he does. And you have Sarah. She loves you, even though you made her miss *Romance Resort* tonight."

Sophie sniffed, a smile peeking through now. "I'll apologize to her."

"And Theo," Libby said. "And Terry always slips you free garlic knots. And Aura and Jo, and Tony . . . we've all known each other since we were kids. You have this whole town." Libby gestured widely with the wooden spoon she was using to stir the mac and cheese. "Boneyard Key loves you."

"Exactly." Cassie gave an emphatic nod. "Are you kidding? This town loves the shit out of you."

Something stirred in Sophie's chest. Hadn't Nan said something similar, back before Flynn? She was right, and tonight proved it. These people were her family. It was okay to lean on them.

But Cassie wasn't done. "And if Tristan doesn't love you—"

"He doesn't."

"What?"

"Love me." Oddly, this didn't bring a new set of tears. The sadness was too deep for that. It was the absolute rock bottom of her heart. "He doesn't love me. At least he never said it."

"Oh." She could all but see Cassie and Libby sharing a look over her head. "Well, fuck him, then," Cassie said decidedly. "I know it sucks and it hurts, but you deserve better."

Over a giant pot of macaroni and cheese and three spoons, along with most of a bottle of chardonnay Libby found in the back of the fridge, Sophie filled the others in on everything. The weeks of stolen kisses, bringing him over during Hurricane Flynn, the way he'd made her feel loved like no one ever had. Even though he'd never said the actual words, and neither had she. At the time it hadn't mattered.

Then she told them about that last phone call with his father, and the circumstances surrounding the ghost tour bet that she had never known.

"I have a wacky thought." Cassie licked at the backside of her spoon, getting off as much cheese sauce as she could. "Why don't you ask him to stay?"

"What?"

Cassie shrugged. "You said he doesn't want to stay. But does he know that you want him to stay? Because I bet that could change his mind."

"I can't ask him to stay." Sophie stared hard at the mac-and-cheese pot, scraping out the last spoonful. "He's going to work for his dad."

"Sounds like he hates his dad, though," Libby said, dividing the last of the wine between the three of them. "Job security or not, I bet he'd like being here with you better."

"I don't know about that," Sophie said.

"Did you ask?" Cassie finished off the wine in her glass.

"No, but . . ." Sophie didn't have a response. She hadn't asked. No, she'd made the decision for the both of them when she'd told him to leave.

"Just something to think about." Cassie tossed the words over her shoulder casually as she picked up the pot and spoons to take them into the kitchen.

Sophie thought about it. The way things were going, she'd be thinking about it all night. She hadn't slept much since he'd left; her room didn't feel like her room anymore. It felt like theirs, and she wanted him back in there more than almost anything.

Two things occurred to her at once. First: if her room didn't feel like her room anymore, she could do something about it. There was another bedroom in this place that she'd been loath to claim. But maybe it was time.

Second: the one thing she wanted more than to have Tristan back was for Tristan to be happy. Even if it wasn't with her. There was something she could do about that too.

Both things were urgent. She wanted to start them both at once.

Sophie blinked her tired, puffy eyes. She'd had enough of crying. She was ready for action.

"I want to move into Aunt Alice's room. Can you help me?"

If either of her friends were startled by the subject change, they didn't let it show. Libby even sighed in relief and sank back against the sofa cushions. "Yes. *Finally.*"

"What can we do?" Cassie didn't hesitate.

"I need to clear Aunt Alice's things out of there. I meant to, after she died, but . . ." She sighed. "I never got around to it." It was embarrassing, admitting out loud that she'd just closed off a room of her home and pretended it wasn't there for the past few years. That was no way to be an adult.

"Then let's do it." Cassie was always the one with a plan. "I'll come over Saturday with trash bags and gloves. We'll do keep/donate/trash piles."

She made it sound so easy that a glimmer of confidence peeked through the gloom in Sophie's soul. Moving into Aunt Alice's room was a twofold solution; her own room had too many memories of Tristan. But more than that, it was time for Sophie to be an adult in her own home.

That confidence carried on after the girls left, and it was time to focus on Project Number Two. Sophie washed her face, then she started a pot of coffee and opened her laptop.

"Let's spend some quality time with some spreadsheets."

Thirty-Seven

Tristan and Nick lingered at the door of The Cold Spot, in the way that men did when they had something emotional to say, but didn't want to say it.

Inside the bar, Vince had been effusive as he'd handed Tristan a *farewell to Boneyard Key* beer on the house. "Come back anytime," he'd said. "I need more people like you who know how to sing on karaoke nights. I can't do it all myself!"

Now, outside, Nick cleared his throat. "I have to say, I'm sorry to see you go. Got used to you being around."

This was practically gushing sentiment, coming from Nick. And Tristan could read between the lines. He wasn't just talking about himself. Tristan nodded slowly. "I'm sorry too," he said. "I really loved it here."

Nick gave a firm nod, then stuck out his hand. "Been good getting to know you, man. Have a safe trip back up north."

"Thanks." Nick's handshake was firm and sincere. "Would you . . . ah . . ." Tristan wasn't sure how to ask. He wasn't sure if he had the right to ask.

But Nick could read between the lines too. "I'll keep an eye on her, don't worry." His half smile was kind. "Been doing it for a long time now."

"Thanks," Tristan said again.

Another awkward moment of standing around, then Nick clapped him on the shoulder. "Safe travels." Then he was gone, walking down Beachside toward the fishing pier and downtown.

It was the only road into town, so Tristan followed. Golden hour was setting in, sunlight streaming through the Spanish moss that hung from the live oaks that lined this part of Beachside. He took his time, walking slow, saying goodbye to all the spots in Boneyard Key that had touched his heart. The fishing pier, with its view of Cemetery Island—he never had gotten around to checking it out. That little side path, where something that definitely wasn't a tree root had tripped him. He'd never gone down there again after that night. Best to let sleeping ghosts lie.

By the time he got to Cassie's house, Nick had already gone inside. Tristan lingered at the gate, smelling the cabbage roses that grew up around the picket fence. This had been the best setting he'd ever used for his pirate story, and he wasn't likely to ever find a better one.

He wouldn't need to, he remembered with a jolt. That part of his life was over now.

He mentally sent a farewell to Sarah Hawkins, who was somewhere inside Cassie's house, and kept going. Most of the souvenir shops were already closed, because of course they were. He let himself rant internally one more time about the ridiculous business ethics some of these places had before continuing on. His stomach growled, reminding him that The Cold Spot didn't have a menu, and he still needed to eat something. There was only one place he'd want to go for a last meal here in Boneyard Key.

Tony nodded at Tristan as he walked into The Haunt for what would be the last time. "Usual?"

"Please." Tristan took his usual barstool—he'd been here long enough to have a usual barstool—and fiddled with the coaster that Tony had placed in front of him. He'd just come from a farewell beer at The Cold Spot with Nick and Vince. Maybe they were only being kind because he was leaving town, but it was nice to know there was no animosity there, even though he and Sophie were no more.

The next test was Tony. Would his beer be half foam? Would the majority of the oysters on his plate have gone bad? Tristan was pleasantly surprised to find that his beer was crisp and cold, and the oysters couldn't have been fresher.

"Heard you're out of here." Tony wiped down the bar to Tristan's left and straightened the salt and pepper shakers.

Tristan squeezed a wedge of lemon over his oysters and picked up the Tabasco. "Good news travels fast, I guess."

"Nah." Tony tossed the rag under the counter. "You're one of the good ones. Sorry to see you go."

"Thanks." He took a sip of his beer to clear away the choked feeling in his throat. This was probably the biggest show of emotion that he'd ever seen from Tony. The guys in this town—at least the ones he'd met—were not particularly expressive.

The oysters were, as usual, excellent. Add that to the list of things he was really going to miss about this town. Tristan turned down a second beer—he'd already had two, and still needed his head clear this evening—and headed home.

Tristan's father's condo looked exactly as it had the moment he'd first walked in all those months ago: stark white walls, stainless-steel appliances, and white leather, steel, and glass furniture to match. There was a new seashell in the middle of the glass coffee table. The original one hadn't survived the storm.

The other difference was that retractable hurricane shutters had been installed. Tristan liked to think of that as his contribution to the place; Sophie couldn't be expected to rescue every single person who might stay here.

Sophie. It had been two weeks since he'd walked out her door, and one week and six days since she'd told him not to come back. He'd stuck it out through two more weekends of ghost tours, his trusty top hat helping him get into character when all his nerves were on edge, hoping he wouldn't run into Sophie and her tour, while also wanting nothing more than a glimpse of her.

Eric had programmed the site to stop taking reservations for the Boneyard Key location after the last weekend in September, so Tristan was done with all that now. The movers had come the day before to collect his boxes, and tomorrow morning he'd take the world's longest Uber ride to the nearest airport. He was about to leave Boneyard Key the way he'd arrived: with no one noticing.

There was one last stop he had to make, one last thing he needed to do before he left. He tapped the edge of the sealed manila envelope on the kitchen counter, and the sharp sound echoed off the bare white walls. It made him remember the warm, cozy nest that was Sophie's place, and there was that ache in his chest again.

Then his phone buzzed in his pocket, bringing him out of his gloomy thoughts. He gave the phone a wry smile as he looked at it. Thank God for Eric.

"How you holding up?" The fact that Eric could even ask that, could even be sympathetic, when Tristan's failure had cost them both their jobs, spoke volumes about what a good friend he was.

"I'm okay," he lied. He let the manila envelope drop back to the counter. "Did you send the final report to Dad yet?"

Eric shook his head. "It's not due till October first. Today's the twenty-ninth."

"But everything's accounted for. Shouldn't we just rip off the Band-Aid, send it in?"

"Nah. Screw him. October first is the deadline; he gets it at four fifty-nine on the first."

Petty till the end. Tristan huffed out a laugh. "At least we have the next month to wind down everything. I'll send the emails out to all the locations on the first, let them know that they have to operate independently after Halloween." Man, he'd really been looking forward to seeing what Boneyard Key did for Halloween. Bet it was epic. "We'll tell them all they can keep the scripts too. Fuck it."

"We can put something a little more formal in place than 'fuck it, keep the script.'" Eric sighed. "Listen. You did the best you could. Besides, you'll be okay. Your dad's got something lined up for you."

"Don't remind me. And don't worry; I'll have him bring you in somewhere too." While the possibility of working in the inner circle of a finance company sounded exciting to a spreadsheet-oriented guy like Eric, Tristan was less than enthused. He thought about the future that waited for him. The suits. The meetings. Long days spent indoors. Long nights spent working late, instead of walking around small towns, telling stories about pirates and their lovers. Not a lantern or frock coat in sight, much less a top hat.

God, it sounded depressing.

Eric changed the subject. "You give it to her yet?"

"Not yet." He picked up the envelope again. "I'm being a chickenshit." An easy thing to admit to his best friend.

"Well, knock that off. Put on the top hat. That always gives you confidence."

"Oh yeah. It'll look great with my shorts and flip-flops."

After hanging up, Tristan turned the envelope over and over in his hands as he watched the sun set over the water. He was really going to miss this. He was going to miss Boneyard Key. He was going to miss Sophie.

He let out a sigh. Talk about ripping off the Band-Aid.

Envelope in hand, he strode out the front door of the condo before he could change his mind. The walk from his door to Sophie's was about ten steps, but it felt like an eternity. One more deep breath to try and calm his racing heart, and he knocked on her door.

Thirty-Eight

Sophie sighed in relief at the knock on her door. God, *finally*. Terry had said that the deliveries were going to take a while tonight, but that hadn't been bad at all. She pushed back from her laptop and all but sprinted for the door. She was starving, and it wasn't until her place had gotten dark enough that she had to turn on a lamp that she remembered she'd forgotten to eat.

She opened the door and fell back a step. Tristan. She'd been thinking about him all day. Of course she had. Him being here now was like something out of a dream.

But when she opened her mouth, the stupidest thing came out. "You're not a pizza."

"I'm not." Tristan looked at her like she was a glass of water on a hot day. Like if she needed him to, he'd figure out a way to be a pizza. "Got one on the way, huh? Sausage and pepperoni? Extra sauce?" He glanced over his shoulder out into the breezeway.

"Of course." *Ask him to stay*, Cassie had said. Like it was that easy. And it probably was for Cassie. People stayed for people like her. Sophie's heart pounded at the thought of opening her mouth. At saying the words. At giving him the chance to break her heart a second time.

She couldn't do it. Instead, she swung the door a little wider. It wasn't an explicit invitation, but it was the best she could do right now.

"I won't take up much of your time." He sounded all professional as he stepped inside, and for the first time she noticed he held a manila envelope. It crinkled in his hands as he turned it around and around. His gaze roamed her walls, her bookcases, her sofa, as though he'd never seen her place. "I'm leaving tomorrow," he finally said.

"I figured." He'd probably intended for that to be the beginning of a longer sentence, but she didn't want to hear any more. Better to head him off. "I saw the movers yesterday. I thought maybe you'd already gone."

"What?" He looked at her like she'd suggested he take a baseball bat to a kitten. "You thought I'd leave without saying goodbye?"

She wouldn't have put it past him. "I didn't exactly leave the door open the last time we talked." She dropped her gaze, fixating on a swirl in the hardwood almost exactly halfway between them. "I'm sorry about that."

"No, I'm sorry." His words brought her eyes back up, and there was nothing but open honesty in his face. Okay, maybe a little regret too. A lot of regret. "I threw my privilege in your face, didn't I? That's not the kind of person I want to be. I wanted to give you this."

Sophie looked at the envelope that he'd all but pushed into her hands. Almost hopelessly crumpled now, it was sealed, with her name on the outside in his handwriting. She couldn't even begin to guess. "What is this?"

"Call it a parting gift," he said as she started to tear it open. "An apology. Call it whatever you want, if it means you'll take it. I just . . ." He paused, as though thinking better of something he wanted to say. "I wanted to say thank you, Sophie. For this summer. I didn't get to love you for very long, but they were the best few weeks of my life."

Love.

Sophie's heart stuttered at the word, and her brain skidded to a full stop. Screw the envelope; this was much more important. Her eyes darted up to his. There it was—that open honesty again. But she couldn't help but notice the tense he'd used. "You loved me?" It was better than nothing, she tried telling herself.

Tristan shook his head, and at first her heart sank, but then he said, "I love you." Present tense. He blinked hard, his blue eyes shining. "I'm pretty sure I always will. I'll never forget this town, and I'll never forget you."

That was great and all, but it was still a past tense thing, wasn't it? She took a shuddering breath and turned her attention back to the envelope in her hands. That seemed safer.

Inside were a few sheets of paper, stapled at the top corner. BONEYARD KEY GHOST TOUR BUSINESS PLAN, the cover page said. "What . . . Is this yours?"

"No," he said as she flipped through the pages. "It's yours. For your ghost tour. My own recent failure aside, I'm not the worst at putting together a business plan. I created a budget there, allocating for online advertising, even print if you're feeling spicy. And that last page there—" He stepped closer, turning the pages in her hands, and she couldn't breathe from how close he was. She would talk business plans all day if he would be this close to her. "That's your website. The account information is right there, and the hosting is paid for. All you have to do is log in and set it to go live."

"I've never had a website." She stared at the page as though it were in a foreign language.

"I know. It's been driving me nuts." His voice was wry, and Sophie's mouth kicked up in response. "You can sell tickets online this way, and you don't have to rely on Nick and his notepad."

"Hey, Nick likes that notepad." But she let out a small laugh, and so did he, because that was a lie. While Nick had never complained about their arrangement for the past six years, if she went in tomorrow and told him he didn't have to keep track of her reservations for her? That notepad would go merrily into the trash.

She flipped back to the beginning of the business plan. "You really think I could do this?" It seemed like a lot. It seemed . . . well, it seemed very adult. And she was getting good at being an adult lately.

"I think you can do anything," he said immediately. Had anyone ever believed in her as completely as he did?

It was that belief that gave her courage. She carefully put the envelope and the business plan onto her dining table, next to her open laptop. Her heart was pounding so hard she could feel it in her ears, her temples. *Ask him to stay.*

She took a breath, and she could barely get enough air in her lungs to speak, but it would have to do. "Then could I make you stay?"

Tristan looked at her as though she'd just turned his world upside down. Her heart pounded harder. Was there a way to unsay the words? Because surely he wasn't going to—

"Yes." The word landed between them with a solid thump of finality. "You want me to stay, I'll stay."

Sophie blinked. "Just like that?"

"Yeah. Of course. I told you before. You tell me what you want and I'll make it happen." But she could tell he was thinking hard. Trying to find a way out of it? No. No, he wasn't. "The movers already took my stuff, but I don't need my stuff. I can get new stuff. I have my laptop. I have my hat. Screw it. There's like a million souvenir T-shirts downtown. I can get a whole new wardrobe."

Adrenaline, combined with the idea of Tristan's entire wardrobe consisting of shirts like I got Beachside-faced on Shit Street made a giggle escape from Sophie's mouth. "We can get you some regular clothes."

"Or I can just have my stuff moved back. You really mean it?" He came closer, reaching out for her, and all she could do was nod dumbly. His palm, warm against her face, felt like home.

She closed her eyes and felt a tear hit her cheek. She'd missed him so much. When the tiniest of sobs escaped her, it was like a dam breaking. Tristan pulled her into his arms, and she kept nodding against his chest.

"Sophie." He whispered her name into her hair. It was a declaration. It was a prayer. "All I want is to stay here with you. I don't care about any of the rest of it. The worst part about that whole stupid bet, that stupid deal with my dad, was that it put an end date on us. I don't want an end date."

"Me neither." Her voice was muffled against him, and her glasses had gone a little askew, but she didn't care. She slid her arms around his back, holding him to her. She didn't want to pull away, now that she had him back.

"Of course, I don't have a place to live," he said. "Any chance I could crash here?"

Sophie's laugh was watery as she pulled back. "I think we could draw up a very reasonable rental agreement."

He ran his thumbs under her eyes, catching her tears. "Don't cry, Sophie. I never want you to cry." He straightened her glasses and kissed her nose. "Tell me more about this rental agreement," he said softly. "Do I get my own room?"

Sophie shook her head. "I'm in the primary bedroom now. Plenty of room for two. We can turn the other bedroom into an office."

"I like how that sounds. Especially that 'room for two' part." He was grinning now, and so was she, and when he bent to her, she tilted her head up to meet his mouth.

"Now," he said against her lips. "About those rental terms . . ."

"Good question." She punctuated the sentence with another kiss. "What's the going rate for half my bed?"

"I don't care. I'll pay it." He deepened their kiss, his hands sliding into her hair, holding her to him while their mouths got reacquainted with one another's skin.

Sophie hummed as they broke apart. "I like these terms already."

"I'm going to need to find a job too," he mused out loud, kissing the top of her head as he tucked her into him. "Do you know when that smoothie place is opening? Are they hiring?"

Now she had an image of him in a smoothie shop uniform, all neon-pastel T-shirt and matching visor. And while the image was funny as hell, awareness spiked within her. He didn't know. Of course he didn't know. Because she hadn't told him yet. Sophie choked out a laugh that sounded a lot like a sob as she pulled away from him. "I think I can help you out there."

She tugged on his hand, and he followed her to her laptop. "I thought you'd left," she said, waking her machine up. "I was going to email this to you later tonight. You know, after the pizza and the wine and the crying."

"I'm fine with the pizza and wine, but I object to the crying." He kissed her temple as she pulled up the shared spreadsheet that had been the bane of her existence all these months. The spreadsheet she'd spent the past couple of days revising.

"Have you sent your books to your dad yet?" She bit her lip. If she was too late . . .

Tristan rolled his eyes with a groan. "Don't remind me. No, not yet. Eric's going to send them at the very last minute on the first."

"Petty," Sophie said as relief swept through her. "I like that." She angled the laptop in Tristan's direction. "I made some adjustments."

"As much as I appreciate you cooking the books, I don't think that . . ." His voice trailed off. "What did you do, Sophie? This isn't cooking the books. This is broiling them."

She snorted. "It's a merger." Tristan didn't reply, his eyes roaming over her screen, so she continued. "We've been running two marginally successful ghost tours all spring and summer. So what if, together, we've actually been running one wildly successful ghost tour business? Would our combined profits be enough to make your dad happy?"

"I . . ." He sank into the chair next to her, pulling her laptop closer to scroll through the spreadsheet. "I don't understand."

"Will it get you out from under your dad's thumb?"

"I have to send this to Eric, but I think so." He turned incredulous eyes to her. "I can stay." The smile that broke out across his face looked like the most beautiful sunrise Sophie had ever seen. "Except I don't want to run one ghost tour."

"No?"

He shook his head. "I was wrong. So, so wrong that day at the coffee shop. Your stories matter. Not just to the tourists, but the town. So if I stay, I'm not taking you over. And you're not taking me over. Turns out, this town really is big enough for two ghost tours."

A surprised laugh bubbled up from Sophie's chest. "Are you kidding?"

Tristan shook his head. "Eric's got some hard data to back it up; I'll have him email it over." His gaze went back to the laptop, and he scrolled through the spreadsheet. "You were really going to do this for me? Let me present a faked merger to my dad, even when you thought I'd left?"

Sophie nodded. "I wanted you happy," she said. "Even if it

wasn't with me." She drew in the longest breath of her life. It was now or never, wasn't it? "Because I love you."

Tristan closed his eyes—a long, slow blink—and when he opened them again, they sparkled in the lamplight. He pushed the laptop aside and reached out a hand. She took it gladly and let him pull her into his lap, straddling his thighs.

"Is this real?" He looked at her in wonder, his eyes roaming her face.

"I sure hope so." She bent to kiss him, taking his small moan into her mouth. His hair slipped between her fingers like water. It didn't take long for their kiss to deepen, her glasses to be discarded to the table.

"God, I've missed you." His hands dropped to her hips, pulling her against him. She rocked in his lap, the ridge in his jeans telling her exactly how much he'd missed her. She couldn't judge; she'd missed him too.

Tristan's mouth moved to her jaw, behind her ear, down her throat. "I have so much to do."

His hands were busy, sliding up the back of her tank top, un-hooking her bra. "Yeah?" Sophie leaned back in his embrace, pull-ing her bra out through the armhole of her top.

Tristan's eyes sparked. "Nice trick. Come here." He pulled her close again. "As I was saying. I gotta email that spreadsheet to Eric. Cancel my car to the airport tomorrow. Hell, I gotta cancel my flight . . ."

"If you're working on your to-do list right now, I think we're do-ing this wrong." Sophie started unbuttoning his shirt—all these months in Boneyard Key and he still dressed like a businessman.

Tristan helped her take his shirt off, yanking at the garment im-patiently before tossing it to the floor. "Trust me," he said, "you're doing this exactly right."

The knock on the door startled them both, and they looked at each other in alarm before Sophie burst out laughing.

"Pizza's here." She straightened her clothes as she clambered off his lap, reaching for her glasses. "You hungry?"

"I really am." He caught her hand to pull her down for another slow, lingering kiss. "And after that, I'd love some pizza."

Much, much later, they had pizza. It was cold.

Epilogue

The moon was huge tonight, hanging low in the sky. Cemetery Island practically glowed in its light as Sophie detailed its tragic history.

"You can really kayak out there?" one of the tourists asked as Sophie led the tour group off the fishing pier and back to the street.

"Oh, absolutely! The bait shack opens pretty early in the morning, and you can rent a kayak and check it out for yourself." She gestured toward Jimmy's, the ramshackle building dark and locked up tight.

While Sophie led the tour south on Beachside, she deliberately kept her pace slow, and not just because she had a few senior citizens on tonight's tour. Tristan was out there too, his tour a few minutes and about a half block ahead of hers, and she didn't want to run into him.

Not until it was time.

"This is one of our most famous landmarks." Sophie slowed her steps and gestured to the Starter Home. "I admit that I have no idea if . . . it's . . . haunted . . ." Her voice trailed off as she realized that she had heard something unexpected.

Tristan.

She turned around and there he was. In full ghost tour guide gear, with his frock coat and cravat, his top hat and lantern, his tour group trailing behind him. She frowned. He was supposed to be further down the street, and she was supposed to catch up to him in front of Cassie's house. That was how they'd rehearsed it. That was how they'd been doing it for months now.

Why was he switching it up?

Then she caught his words, carried on the cool breeze coming off the Gulf of Mexico. "Now, I'll tell you more about the Beach Bum later in the tour, but sources say that this was actually his house at one point. In fact—"

"*What?*" The word burst from her mouth before she could check it. "What are you talking about? That's not true and you know it."

Some of the people in Tristan's tour turned to look at her, mouths sagging open. Tristan, standing directly under a streetlight, coughed once to hide his smile.

"Of course," he said, tipping his hat in her direction, "there are some who have differing opinions. Now, if you'll follow me," he continued, stepping out of his spotlight and back onto the sidewalk, gathering his tour group like chickens, "we're coming up to one of my favorite spots. Legend says there was a pirate that . . ."

Sophie rolled her eyes, pasted a smile on her face, and turned back to her group. "Ignore him," she said. "I know I do. Now, as I was saying, there's no real proof that the Starter Home is haunted. It's just a reminder of Boneyard Key's past."

"So who's the Beach Bum?"

Sophie bit back a sigh at the question. She was going to kill Tristan later. "The Beach Bum is a story for a little later in the tour, and I promise it's worth it. Now if you'll follow me . . ."

Tristan's detour, here at the Starter Home, had thrown Sophie off her rhythm. She walked faster, because she was already late. The point was to get to Cassie's house in time to catch the end of Tristan's pirate story. The point was to confront him *there*, not back at the Starter Home. Why hadn't he told her he was changing things up?

But no, she was right on time. It didn't take long for her and her charges to catch up to Tristan, who was winding up his pirate/lover tale. This was more like it. She knew her part, and she was ready.

"Her name was Arabella, and she lived in this very house. Reed the Ruthless and Arabella would meet in secret, under the light of the full moon, and they would—"

"Oh, they would *not!*" Sophie folded her arms on her chest and glared at Tristan. It was so hard to glare at him; life with Tristan was more smiles these days. She bit hard on the inside of her cheek to keep from laughing at his faux innocent expression.

"You have a real problem with me tonight, do you?" Tristan gave an exaggerated *tsk*, then turned back to his group as though she wasn't even there.

"I have a problem with you every night!" she called out, and some of her group laughed. Some of Tristan's did too.

"Mock if you must," he said. "But my stories are better."

"No, they're not," she shot back. "Mine are better. Because they're *true*."

He waved a bored hand. "Details, details."

"It's not details! It's people's lives we're talking about! The spirits of Boneyard Key are people's ancestors, loved ones. We owe it to them to tell the truth."

Tristan nodded as he broke character. "And that's what makes the tours here at Ghouls Night Out so special," he said, turning to address both tour groups now. "Here in Boneyard Key we offer a unique experience. Different stories from different tour guides. So if you've had a good time here tonight, and want to know more about Boneyard Key, consider taking the tour all over again tomorrow night, with the other guide. We guarantee a different experience each time." He tipped his hat at Sophie and her group, then turned back to his. "Anyway, as I was saying before I was so rudely interrupted. Arabella and her pirate . . ."

His voice trailed off as he led the group down the street, and Sophie heaved a great sigh. Thank goodness that was over. She was a terrible actress, but somehow playing opposite Tristan made it easy. Made it fun.

She turned back to her group, her normal, friendly smile back on her face. "So! We are standing in front of the Sarah Hawkins house, and I'd love to tell you a little bit about her. I promise it has nothing to do with pirates."

After the tour, she found Tristan at the coffee cart.

"That kicked ass!" His kiss tasted like the mocha latte in his hand.

Sophie nodded. "I think people come as much for our fight as they do for our ghost stories." That was the thing about viral moments; people wanted them recreated. Now that they knew Boneyard Key was big enough for two ghost tours, it hadn't taken long for Sophie and Tristan to figure out how to capitalize on their video from last spring, which was still making the rounds. They gave their separate tours, with an added moment of "accidentally" running into each other. It was great cross-advertising for both tours; let the audience hear just enough of the other tour guide's story to be intrigued enough to go on the tour a second time.

Her tour being under the Ghouls Night Out umbrella wasn't a big deal in the end. She still had her stories, told the way she wanted to tell them, honoring the residents of Boneyard Key, past and present. She also had a strong minority ownership in the company. And she was sleeping with the owner. No, Sophie didn't have a single thing to complain about these days.

It was a warm spring night, and the moon was high in the sky. No reason to hurry home. By unspoken agreement, their steps turned toward the beach, Tristan's arm slung around her shoulders.

"What was that you were saying about the Beach Bum and the Starter Home? Theo and I have almost locked down the text of the book, and we haven't found anything that says they're linked. Was that a new story you made up?"

Tristan shrugged, the movement of his shoulder nudging against her glasses.

"The Beach Bum and I hang out sometimes," he said. "He lets me know things." He glanced down at her, straightening her glasses. "Maybe I can help you figure it out. Your stories about our home should be as accurate as possible."

Our home. Sophie loved the way that sounded. And from the look on his face, so did he.

They paused at the picnic tables, watching the moonlight glint off the water. Sounds of the steel drum band at The Haunt echoed in the distance, but at this moment, they had the beach all to themselves. Something about it made Sophie bold. Or maybe it was just Tristan—nothing seemed risky when she was with him.

"Did I ever tell you about a dream I had?"

"Well, there was that one last week, where a fish was playing the piano. That one?"

"No, this one was a while back, before you and I were . . . you and I." Her heart pounded in her throat, but she forged ahead before her nerve left her completely. "We were here, on the beach."

"I like the way this is heading." He dropped his top hat and frock coat to the picnic table before sitting on the bench. "Tell me more." He tugged on her hands, pulling her between his knees.

"Well, you're in the water . . ." He nodded eagerly, and Sophie's cheeks were on fire. Was she really telling him this? "You're not wearing so many clothes."

Tristan's eyebrows shot up as a wicked grin took over his face. "Oooh. Is this a naked dream?" His hands slid around her waist, hooking his fingers in the belt loops of her jeans. "Because I approve."

Sophie nodded. "You were . . ."

"Wait a second." He squinted up at her. "You're telling me you had a naked dream about me before we were together?"

Oh, he was going to love this. "You remember the first time we kissed?"

"You mean when you kissed me?" He loved to remind her of that anytime he could.

"Yeah, yeah." Sophie tried to be annoyed, but he was too close, and she loved him too much. "Well, this was the night before that."

He sucked in a scandalized breath. "Sophie Horvath," he said with mock outrage. "You had a naked dream about me when we weren't even together? How accurate was it?"

"What?"

"How accurate was it?" he repeated. "I mean, you've seen me naked since then." Sophie made a pleased noise in agreement. "How did subconscious Sophie do at peeling back all my layers?" He waggled his eyebrows, and she huffed out a laugh.

"I don't know," she said, her voice teasing. "You're not naked in the water, are you?"

She was teasing, but Tristan nodded. "Good point." In one quick movement, he set her aside and surged to his feet, working on the buttons of his vest. He had it off in a flash, and before Sophie knew what was happening, he'd started unbuttoning his shirt.

"What are you doing?" Her voice was high and well on its way to shrill.

"Getting naked in the water," he said, as though it should be obvious. "For the sake of comparison." His dress shirt landed on top of his frock coat and vest, his undershirt following almost immediately. He toed off his shoes, hopping on each foot as he took off his socks.

"Okay, you weren't completely naked." Sophie hated being a stickler, but Tristan had already unbuttoned his pants; she was running out of time.

He cocked his head, holding his loosened pants around his hips. "Now you tell me?"

Sophie could feel laughter build in her chest, as involuntary as a hiccup. "You were wearing these board shorts. With pink flamingos on them."

Tristan considered that. "Hmmm. Well. I don't have board shorts with pink flamingos, but I can get some."

"You can get some?" she repeated with an incredulous laugh.

"I told you," he said. "You tell me what you want, and I will make it happen. But until then . . ." His pants fell to the sand, leaving him in his boxers. "Little blue puppy dogs will have to do."

Laughter burst from Sophie's chest, but died quickly as Tristan stepped toward her, reaching for her waistband. "What are you doing?"

"You think I'm the only one going in that water?" His nimble fingers made quick work of the button on her jeans and tugged the zipper down just as fast.

"Are you kidding me?" Sophie squealed and tried—not very hard—to get away.

"Were you in the water with me in the dream?" His hands, warm and strong, slid inside of her jeans, working them down around her hips.

"Well, yes, but . . ." While she protested, she also kicked off her sneakers while helping him shimmy her out of her jeans, and they joined his pants in the sand.

"Accuracy," he reminded her. "Come on." He tugged on her hand, leading her toward the water. "You can leave your hoodie on."

But she pulled it off too—in for a penny and all that—and started to follow him into the surf when she realized a crucial part was missing.

"Wait!" She pulled her hand free and darted toward the picnic tables. Tristan's shout of protest was cut off when she scooped up the top hat and rejoined him at the edge of the water. The tide came in, foam sizzling around their ankles.

"Hey, be careful with that. It's an antique." Tristan caught her hands when she perched the top hat on his head. Together, they settled the hat securely, and she tugged the brim down a little lower over his eyes before letting go.

"There," she said. "Accuracy."

"So you're telling me . . ." He tugged her close. "In this dream you had, I was wearing board shorts and a top hat, and nothing else?"

"Oh, I'm sorry," Sophie said. "Do your dreams make a whole lot of sense?"

"What else were we doing in this dream?" His palms were warm as they slid across the already cold skin of her waist. When standing ankle-deep in the Gulf wearing only her underwear, suddenly the warm spring night had become a lot cooler. Skinny-dipping in the ocean would be a lot more fun in July. Something to remember.

"Pretty much this." She skimmed her hands down his chest, enjoying the way his muscles tightened beneath her touch. "Maybe a little of this." Her fingertips flirted with the elastic of his waistband, dipping lower until he let out a gasp.

"God, your hands are cold." But he made no move to get away. Instead his hands began their own exploration, sliding down the back of her underwear to cup her rear. "So was it like this?"

"Pretty much." But that was a lie. In the dream his eyes kept shifting from blue to green. Now, she couldn't tell what color his eyes were; despite the moonlight, it was too dark, plus the brim of his hat threw shadows across his face. The water was freezing around their calves, and even though he was doing this for her, she couldn't wait to warm up back at home.

But then he bent to kiss her. Deeply, in a kiss that went on and on, like the water of the Gulf stretching out toward the horizon. And Sophie knew that real life was better than any dream could possibly be.

Acknowledgments

Writing a book is wild. It's my name on the cover, but so many people helped make this book happen.

First thanks always goes to my agent, Taylor Haggerty, and the whole Root Lit team, especially Jasmine Brown and Gabrielle Greenstein. Thanks for always being in my corner, answering my unhinged questions, and believing in my beach ghosts.

I remain, as always, eternally grateful for Kerry Donovan, my long-suffering editor, who always finds kind, constructive ways to say, "But what if you put an actual romance arc into this romance novel?" You somehow have a direct link to my brain and know what I'm trying to do with these characters, and you know how to bring out the best in them. Thank you for sticking with me.

Speaking of sticking with me, many thanks as well to the entire Berkley team: Genni Eccles for keeping me on track; Jessica Mangicaro and Kaila Mundell-Hill, who are so great at making sure people know my books exist; Colleen Reinhart and Sarah Maxwell, who make my covers look incredible; the tireless folks in the art department, who whip up graphics for me that my untalented ass could never; and the eagle-eyed copy editors, who try in vain to educate me on how commas work.

I couldn't write anything without my critique partners: Gwynne Jackson, Vivien Jackson, and Lindsay Landgraf Hess, who always drag me through my first draft kicking and screaming and are willing to listen and brainstorm when I have no idea what I'm doing (which is most of the time). Your encouragement and insight make my work so much better.

Writing can be such a lonely job—just you in front of your screen of choice. But that screen also contains friends who are also writing, and they make it all a little less lonely. Eva Leigh and Denise Williams, I appreciate you always. The folks in the WSBW and GSD Discords are indispensable and have kept me as sane as it's possible to be as a romance writer. I'd especially like to thank Rosiee Thor, M. K. England, Amy Ratcliffe, Linsey Miller, Beth Revis, and Leanne Schwartz, who kept me sprinting when I'd much rather be playing *Dragon Age: The Veilguard*.

My very specific thanks to *Gilmore Girls*. One day I will stop mining you for inspiration, but not yet! "What if Logan Huntzberger was a bisexual theatre kid who ran ghost tours?" was just too much fun to pass up.

With a job that is so intensely work-from-home, home becomes the most important place of all. Morgan, home is where you are. And the cats. And the dog. And the hummingbirds. And the neighbor's chickens, who occasionally show up in the yard. And the wind whistling through the bamboo. I love us and I love our home, wherever that may be.

Finally, I want to thank you, the reader. Whether this is your first time picking up one of my books, if you've hung out with me in Boneyard Key before, or if you're here with me after four books at the Willow Creek Renaissance Faire, I hope my words help provide a welcome escape. We all need that now, more than ever. Thanks for spending time with me.

While I was drafting this book, in which a hurricane hits Boneyard Key (with very little damage, because this is a rom-com), the very real Hurricane Helene devastated the city of Cedar Key, Florida. They have been rebuilding, and are open again for visitors. So if you're local (or even if you're not), I encourage you to take a trip there. Maybe go out to Atsena Otie Key and visit the cemetery. Hang out at a bar on Dock Street, and see if you can tell where the seeds of Boneyard Key were planted in my brain. Cedar Key needs our support (and our tourist dollars). Visit cityofcedarkey.org to find out more about this unique, resilient city.

Keep reading for a special look at
another paranormal romance
from Jen DeLuca

Haunted Ever After

~

That meeting could've been an email.

Cassie Rutherford clicked "LEAVE MEETING" and took out her earbuds. Once she'd confirmed that her camera was off, the bright smile slipped from her face and she let her forehead thunk to the table with a moan.

What a week. And it was only Monday. She'd made a lot of mistakes in her thirty-one years of life, and of them all, this one was . . . well, it wasn't the worst one. But it sure as hell was the most recent.

Her life was chaos. Cassie didn't like chaos. She liked checklists. She liked the satisfaction of a job well done. She didn't like moving boxes filling every room of her new house, turning her morning routine into an obstacle course. She didn't like having no idea where her saucepans were, since they weren't in the box labeled **KITCHEN**. And she really, really didn't like waking up a half hour before an all-hands meeting with a dead laptop.

Most small Florida tourist trap towns had a schtick, and her new town had apparently been dubbed the Most Haunted Small Town in Florida. At least that's what the sign outside of the Boneyard Key Chamber of Commerce said. How many towns had been competing for that title? That was Cassie's question.

They certainly leaned in to it hard around here. Flagpoles lined the historic downtown sidewalks, each one featuring a banner with a classic-looking Halloween ghost: white, vaguely blob shaped, big black eyes. They fluttered in the early-morning breeze in the world's laziest attempt to be spooky. T-shirts hung in the window of the I Scream Ice Cream Shop that she'd passed this morning. I had a spooky good time in Boneyard Key, Florida! proclaimed one of them. Boneyard Key, where the chills aren't just from the ice cream! said another one. Both were illustrated with cartoonishly ghoulish graphics: a skeletal hand poking out of a grave, ice-cream cone in hand.

And this was all in April. This place probably went apeshit for Halloween.

Cassie's newly purchased historic cottage had gingerbread trim, little balconies off the upstairs bedrooms, a backyard that ended in a seawall bordering the Gulf of Mexico, and unreliable electricity. She'd left her laptop plugged in on the kitchen table last night, but this morning it was drained of all juice, like an electricity vampire had stolen it during the night. Thank God for Hallowed Grounds (man, this town really leaned in to the ghost puns); she'd found this coffee shop down the street just in time.

Cassie's ears were sore from her earbuds, and she rubbed at one while she reviewed her notes from the meeting. Doodles, mostly. She'd spoken all of two times. Once to chime in on the Farnsworth account, confirming that she was aware of the deadline and that she was on track to reach it. The second time toward the end of the meeting when her work bestie, Mandy, had asked about her move. Yes, the move had gone great. Yes, her house was right on the water, and she could hear the waves when she went to sleep at night. But then she'd seen Roz's expression pucker, even through the laptop screen, and Cassie had cut the nonwork-related conversation short. She'd update everyone in the group chat later.

And say what, though? Everyone wanted to hear good things.

No one wanted to know what was really on her mind: that maybe she'd made the most expensive mistake of her life. One that was practically impossible to unwind.

God, she needed coffee.

Cassie closed her laptop and leveled a glare at what appeared to be the coffee shop's lone employee. Still on his goddamn phone, just like he had been when she'd walked in. He was tall and lean, slim hipped in faded jeans and a gray pocket tee. His hair was on the long side, falling in russet waves around his face and over his forehead, matching his close-trimmed beard. She couldn't see his eyes, as his head was bent over the phone in his hands, thumbs flying across the screen.

He looked too old to be a Gen Z, TikTok-addicted kid, but his attention had been on his phone when she'd come in. He hadn't even looked up as she'd come barreling through the door. Hadn't said a word as she beelined to a table in the back with a blessed outlet nearby. As much as she'd wanted to fuel up before the meeting, she had just enough time to hook up, access the Wi-Fi listed on the card on the table, and get logged in. Caffeine had to wait.

A glance down at her laptop showed that it was charged up, so she should really get home. Get some work done. Find her saucepans. Figure out what was wrong with her house. Probably something wrong with the wiring that the inspector had missed, which was way beyond her scope.

Too bad houses weren't like other retail purchases. No returning it for a refund, even though she had the receipt. She was locked into a mortgage now.

At this point, she could just go home and make coffee, but dammit, that was boring, and she'd promised herself a little treat after the shitty start to the day. She could get a coffee to go; she deserved it.

Coffee shop guy looked up with disdain as she approached the counter. "Oh. Are you actually gonna order something?" His voice was deeper than she'd expected, with an undertone of gravel. But all Cassie could see was blue. That clear crystal blue that made you think of Caribbean water. Of lab-created sapphires, because a blue that blue couldn't exist in nature. Damn, but this slacker barista had pretty eyes.

Then his words registered and she frowned, pretty eyes forgotten. "What do you mean?"

"I mean . . ." He jerked his head in a nod toward the table she'd just vacated. "You've been sitting there for almost an hour, using my Wi-Fi, without even so much as ordering a cup of coffee. This isn't a coworking space, you know. It's a business."

"Really? Damn." Cassie looked pointedly around the place. Empty. "Sorry to occupy your fanciest table."

His lips twitched, sending a thrill through her. She didn't like this guy; why did she care if he thought she was funny? "You want to order something or what?" Despite the almost-smile, his voice didn't sound much friendlier. Great.

"Iced latte, please. Hazelnut, if you have it."

"We have it." He sounded insulted that she implied otherwise. "Anything else?"

Her eyes strayed to the pastry case. It looked pretty picked over; this must be a popular breakfast spot. "Is that banana bread?"

"Yep." His voice was clipped as he moved to the espresso machine.

"And I was going to order when I got here, you know." She raised her voice over the hiss of the machine as he steamed the milk. "You had your face shoved in your phone. Maybe a little less time on Tinder and a little more time doing your job." The machine cut off, and she was suddenly yelling in the very empty café. The slacker barista didn't respond; he just shook his head, his back to her as he worked.

If Cassie didn't like chaos, she really didn't like being ignored. "I mean, what would your boss think . . ." There was a stack of business cards in a little plastic holder by the register, and she snatched one, reading from it. "What would Nick Royer think about your lack of service?"

"I dunno." He plonked the finished drink onto the counter in front of her, ice sloshing against the lid. "Why don't you ask him?"

His mouth did that almost-twitch thing again, and there was something in his eyes—those stunning blue eyes—that set off a warning bell in the back of Cassie's brain. But screw that—she was too annoyed to listen.

"Maybe I will!" she said to his back as he bagged a slice of banana bread from the pastry case. She grabbed a pen from the cup in front of her and flipped the business card over. "What's your name?"

"Nick." He tossed the banana bread onto the counter next to her iced latte. "Nick Royer."

Well. Shit.

Cassie looked down at her order. The iced latte was in a plastic cup, lid firmly on and a wrapped straw on top. The banana bread was in a little paper bag. He'd prepared her order to go without asking. He didn't want her there any more than she wanted to be there.

She looked back up at Nick. His arms were folded across his chest, biceps straining against the sleeves of his gray T-shirt. His mouth was set in a thin line, and his warm blue eyes now looked stone-cold. "That'll be seven fifty."

Her new life in her new town was off to a fantastic start.

Cassie reached for her drink while he ran her card, punching the straw in and taking a sip. She closed her eyes with a grateful sigh as caffeine sped through her bloodstream and her shoulders relaxed. The drink was perfect: just the right amount of hazelnut syrup, not too sweet, with enough bitter espresso to wake up her senses. This dickhead made a fantastic iced latte, which was unfortunate. She was going to have to keep coming back here, wasn't she?

She blinked her eyes open to see said dickhead holding her card out toward her. "Anything else?" The question was automatic; she was supposed to shake her head, take her stuff, and get the hell out.

But inspiration struck. "You don't happen to know a good electrician, do you?"

Nick stopped short, blinked at what had to be an unexpected question. "A what?"

"Electrician. Handyman. Someone who can tell me why half the outlets in the house don't seem to work."

He shook his head, baffled. "Can't you just message the owner?"

"The what?" Now it was Cassie's turn to be baffled.

"The owner," he repeated with exaggerated patience. This guy really didn't like her. "Through the app or whatever. You don't fix stuff yourself in a vacation rental. That's the owner's responsibility."

"I am the owner. It's my house. Wait." A horrible thought occurred to Cassie. "You think I'm a tourist?"

"Well, yeah." He rubbed at the back of his neck as his brow furrowed. "You have the look."

"The *look*?" She glanced down at herself. She'd been in such a hurry this morning that she'd thrown on the first thing she could find: denim cutoffs and the Give me the Oxford comma or give me death T-shirt she'd gotten from her Secret Santa at work last year. Her hair was up in a bun because styling it had been out of the question. At least she was wearing her nicer flip-flops.

"Sure," Nick said. "Lots of tourists come in here with their laptops, get some work done while they're on vacation." He waved a hand toward her laptop bag. "So I just figured . . ."

Cassie crossed her arms over her chest; she couldn't believe this.

This was worse than not getting carded at the liquor store. Worse than being called *ma'am*. "I haven't lived in Florida for my entire life to be called a tourist."

A laugh came out of Nick's chest like a bark, an involuntary reaction that seemed to startle even himself. "Point taken. Sorry about that." That almost-twitch thing his mouth had been doing gave way to an actual smile, crooked and even a little bit apologetic. Something in the air shifted between them, the animosity from the past few minutes dissolving like sugar in the rain.

That shift made her take a risk. "Any chance we can start over? I was caffeine deprived before, and this is the best coffee I've had in a long time." She stuck her hand across the counter. "I'm Cassie."

"Nick." His hand was warm around hers, his handshake a solid grip. "And I think I can help you out with that handyman thing. Here . . ."

Nick came out from behind the counter, walking—no, sauntering— toward the front door. Clearly this café was his domain, and he was at home here. What must that be like? To be at home somewhere? Cassie had a home, technically, but she didn't feel at home there. Not yet.

He stopped at the bulletin board to the left of the door that she must have rushed right by when she'd come in. It was covered in so many business cards and flyers that the cork of the board had practically disappeared. Some of the cards were yellowed with age, while others looked like they'd just been pinned there yesterday. Nick scanned the board, his hands resting on his slim hips, before finally selecting one of the older cards.

"Here you go." He stuck the pushpin back in the board and handed her the card. "Give Buster a call. If he can't fix it, it can't be fixed."

"Is that his slogan?" And was that his real name? She examined the card, and sure enough: BUSTER BRADSHAW, with a little graphic of a hammer and a phone number. Minimalist, this guy. She was honestly surprised not to see a little ghost peeking out from behind the hammer.

Nick chuckled. "It should be. So which house is yours, anyway?"

Cassie turned and peered out the window, pointing down the street. "Down that way a little. Yellow house, where the street bends to the right toward the pier?"

"Wait." Nick's eyebrows crawled up his forehead. "You're in the Hawkins House?"

"The what?" That name meant nothing to her. The seller had been a nebulous LLC, probably a flipper, and hadn't been named Hawkins. "No. It's the Rutherford house now." She tapped her own chest. "As of nine days ago anyway."

"No shit." He leaned in conspiratorially. "What's it like in there?"

"Um. Well, right now it's filled with boxes since I haven't unpacked yet. But otherwise it's fine."

"I mean, everything okay there? Since you've moved in?"

"Yes?" Her answer was more of a question. What was he getting at? "Is there a reason it wouldn't be?"

"No weird noises? Anything like that?"

"Nothing except the wonky electric. What else would there . . . oh." She bit back a sigh. "Is this because of the ghost thing that this town is all about? I told you, I'm not a tourist. You don't have to do . . ." She waved a hand. "All that."

He watched her for a second before nodding slowly. "Right. Anyway, give Buster a call." He gestured at the card. "He'll set you up right. And make sure you tell him you're at the Hawkins House. I bet he'll come running."

"Okaaay." She drew the word out slowly. There was something

Nick wasn't telling her about her house, but she wasn't going to look a gift horse in the mouth. Anything that would make her life easier at this point was welcome. "Thanks," she said instead.

"Anytime." There was that crooked smile again. "Welcome to Boneyard Key."

As Cassie pushed the heavy glass door open, she noticed three little neon ghosts escaping as steam from the neon coffee cup in the window. Yeah. He'd definitely been talking about the ghost thing.

But what did her house have to do with it?

Author photo by Morgan H. Lee

Jen DeLuca is the *USA Today* bestselling author of the Well Met and the Boneyard Key series. She lives in the Arizona desert with her husband, their rescue dog, and almost too many cats.

Ready to find
your next great read?

Let us help.

Visit prh.com/nextread

Penguin
Random
House